398.2
Fea

Fearless girls, wise
women, and beloved
sisters.

DATE			

Fearless Girls,
Wise Women,
AND
Beloved Sisters

Fearless Girls, Wise Women, AND Beloved Sisters

Heroines in Folktales from Around the World

EDITED BY
Kathleen Ragan

W. W. NORTON & COMPANY
New York London

The text of this book is set in Centaur
with the display set in New Rix Fancy
Desktop composition by Gina Webster
Manufacturing by Quebecor Printing, Fairfield Inc.
Book design by Charlotte Staub

Library of Congress Cataloging-in-Publication Data

Fearless girls, wise women, and beloved sisters : heroines in
folktales from around the world / edited by Kathleen Ragan.
p.   cm.
Includes bibliographical references and index.
ISBN 0-393-04598-6
I. Women heroes—Folklore. I. Ragan, Kathleen.
GR515.S39   1998
398.2'082—DC21   97-30438
                    CIP

W. W. Norton & Company, Inc., 500 Fifth Avenue,
New York, N.Y. 10110
http://www.wwnorton.com

W. W. Norton & Company Ltd., 10 Coptic Street,
London WC1A 1PU

2 3 4 5 6 7 8 9 0

*For
Charley,
Colleen, &
Deirdre*

CONTENTS

Tales from North and South America

NATIVE AMERICANS

NEW WORLD NEWCOMERS

Tales from Asia

Tales from the Pacific

Tales from Sub-Saharan Africa

Tales from North Africa and the Middle East

ACKNOWLEDGMENTS

I would like to thank everyone who has helped make this book possible. Thank you for the discussions, the babysitting, the comments on drafts, follow-ups in libraries that I left behind, and most of all, thank you for being my friends.

Specifically and very specially I would like to thank: Charley Lineweaver, my husband, for his love and staunch support during all the time we've known each other, and also for all the xeroxing, book-lugging, reading, re-reading, and discussions of this book; Colleen and Deirdre, my daughters, for helping edit the stories; Irene Ragan, my mother, who encouraged me and did lots of library leg-work; Maureen Ragan who read the whole manuscript, twice; Reference Librarian Silvestra Praino, Assistant to the Reference Librarian Joan Pappalardo, their coworkers at the Mahwah Public Library and all the libraries and librarians who participate in the country-wide Inter-Library Loan System for their processing of many, many books and gathering of information; Cornelia and Iain Bamforth for their intellectual and childcare contributions; Sally Lineweaver, Ann Messina, Maret Hensick, William A. Ragan, Bridget Ragan, John David Ragan, Charlie Morrison, Cherissa Yarkin; my agent, Robin Straus; my editor, Jill Bialosky; Eve Grubin and Lucy Anderson. Thanks also to all people responsible for the libraries I used with open stacks and "unweeded" collections. I have a great intellectual debt to such scholars as Bonnie S. Anderson, Carol Gilligan, Sarah Blaffer Hrdy, Judith P. Zinsser, and Jack Zipes. My very grateful thanks also to the women of the women's movement for their courage and determination to effect change.

Ahmed Al-Shahi and F. C. T. Moore. "The Sultan's Daughter" and "Yousif Al-Saffani." Copyright © Ahmed Al-Shahi and F. C. T. Moore, 1978. Reprinted from *Wisdom of the Nile: A Collection of Folk-Stories from Northern and Central Sudan*, translated by Ahmed Al-Shahi and F. C. T. Moore, (1978). Reprinted by permission of Oxford University Press.

Genevieve Barlow. "The Magic Eagle" from *Latin American Tales* by Genevieve Barlow. Copyright © 1966. Reprinted by permission of The National Textbook Company.

Ronald M. Berndt and Catherine H. Berndt. "The *Mogwoi's* Baby" and "Biriwilg (Told by Women)" from *The Speaking Land* by Ronald M. Berndt and Catherine H. Berndt. Published by Inner Traditions International, Rochester, VT 05767. Copyright © 1994 R. M. Berndt and C. H. Berndt. Published by Penguin Books Australia Ltd. Copyright © 1989. Reprinted by permission of Inner Traditions International and Penguin Books Australia, Ltd.

Joseph Bruchac. "The Vampire Skeleton" from *Iroquois Stories: Heroes and Heroines, Monsters and Magic* by Joseph Bruchac. Copyright © 1985. Reprinted by permission of The Crossing Press: Freedom, CA, USA.

Inea Bushnaq. "Women's Wiles" from *Arab Folktales* by Inea Bushnaq, copyright © 1986 by Inea Bushnaq. Reprinted by permission of Pantheon Books, a division of Random House, Inc.

Muriel Paskin Carrison. "The Story of Princess Amaradevi" from *Cambodian Folk Stories from the Gatiloke* by Muriel Paskin, copyright © 1987. Reprinted by permission of Charles E. Tuttle Co.

P. C. Roy Chaudhury. "A Rani's Revenge," "How Parvatibai Outwitted the Dacoits," and "The Importance of Lighting" from *Best Loved Folk-Tales of India* by P. C. Roy Chaudhury. Copyright © 1986. Reprinted by permission of Sterling Publishers Pvt. Ltd.

Ella E. Clark. "Chief Joseph's Story of Wallowa Lake" and "The Origin of the Potlatch" from *Indian Legends of the Pacific Northwest* by Ella E. Clark, copyright © 1953. Reprinted by permission of University of California Press.

Harold Courlander. "Moremi and the Egunguns" from *Tales of Yoruba Gods and Heroes* by Harold Courlander. Copyright © 1973 by Harold Courlander. Reprinted by permission of The Emma Courlander Trust.

C. Fillingham Coxwell. "Altyn-Aryg" and "The Story of the Wife Who Stole a Heart" from *Siberian and Other Folktales* by C. Fillingham Coxwell. Copyright © 1925. Reprinted by permission of The C. W. Daniel Company Ltd.

Asha Dhar. "The 'Pink Pearl' Prince" from *Folktales of Iran* by Asha Dhar. Copyright © 1978. Reprinted by permission of Sterling Publishers Pvt. Ltd.

Wolfram Eberhard. "The Festival of Pouring Water" from *Folktales of China* by Wolfram Eberhard. Trans. Desmond Parsons. From Folktales of the World series, General Editor, Richard M. Dorson. Copyright © 1965 by Wolfram Eberhard. Reprinted by permission of University of Chicago Press.

Frank Edgar. "The Woman, Her Husband, Their Children and the Dodo" and "Ku-Chin-Da-Gayya and Her Elder Sister and the Dodos" from *Hausa Tales and Traditions: An English Translation of "Tatsuniyoyi Na Hausa,"* Volume II translated and edited by Neil Skinner, copyright © 1977. (Madison: The University of Wisconsin Press.) Reprinted by permission of The University of Wisconsin Press.

Richard Erdoes and Alfonso Ortiz. "The Flying Head" and "Where the Girl Saved Her Brother" from *American Indian Myths and Legends* by Richard Erdoes and Alfonso Ortiz, editors, copyright © 1984 by Richard Erdoes and Alfonso Ortiz. Reprinted by permission of Pantheon Books, a division of Random House, Inc.

Ruth Finnegan. "The Spider, Kayi, and the Bush Fowl," "The Story of Two Women," and "The Man Killed for a Spinach Leaf." Copyright © Oxford University Press 1967. Reprinted from *Limba Stories and Story-Telling* by Ruth Finnegan (1967) by permission of Oxford University Press.

Suzanne Crowder Han. "The Tiger and the Coal Peddler's Wife" from *Korean Folk and Fairy Tales* by Suzanne Crowder Han. Copyright © 1991. Reprinted by permission of Hollym International Corp.

Christie Harris. "The Princess and Mountain Dweller" from *The Trouble with Princesses*. Copyright © 1980. "The Princess and the Magic Hat" from *Mouse Woman and the Vanished Princesses*. Copyright © 1976. Reprinted by permission of the author.

Laurens Hillhouse and Marie Mohr-Grandstaff. "The Creation of Lake Asbold" from *Man in Essence* by Laurens Hillhouse and Marie Mohr-Grandstaff. Copyright © 1990. Reprinted by permission of Hillhouse Publications, 1422 Meek Ave., Napa, CA.

Naomi Kipury. "Elephant and Hare" from *Oral Literature of the Maasai* by Naomi Kipury. Copyright © 1983. Reprinted by permission of Heinemann Educational Books, Ltd, Nairobi.

Louise Kuo and Yuan Hsi. "Maiden Liu, the Songster" excerpted from *Chinese Folktales,* copyright © 1976 by Louise Kuo and Yuan Hsi. Reprinted by permission of Celestial Arts, P. O. Box 7123, Berkeley, CA, 94707.

Margaret Lawrie. "Uzu, the White Dogai" from *Myths and Legends of Torres Straits* by Margaret Lawrie. Copyright © 1971. Reprinted by permission of the author.

Sorche Nic Leodhas. "The Stolen Bairn and the Sìdh" from the book *Thistle*

and Thyme, Tales and Legends from Scotland by Sorche Nic Leodhas. Copyright ©
1962, Sorche Nic Leodhas. Reprinted by permission of McIntosh and Otis,
Inc. Published by Holt, Rinehart and Winston.

John LeRoy. "Revival and Revenge." This excerpt is reprinted with permission of the publisher from *Kewa Tales* by John LeRoy (Vancouver: UBC
Press, 1985). All rights reserved by the Publisher.

Charlotte Leslau and Wolf Leslau. "The Midwife of Dakar" and "How the
Milky Way Came to Be" from *African Folk Tales* by Charlotte Leslau and Wolf
Leslau. Copyright © 1963. Reprinted by permission of The Peter Pauper
Press.

William A. Lessa. "How Pulap Acquired the Art of Navigation" and "Rola
and the Two Sisters" from *More Tales from Ulithi Atoll, A Content Analysis* by
William A. Lessa, copyright © 1980. Reprinted by permission of University of California Press.

Shujiang Li and Karl W. Luckert. "Sailimai's Four Precious Things" and
"The Phoenix and Her City." Reprinted from *Mythology and Folklore of the Hui,
a Muslim Chinese People* by Shujiang Li and Karl W. Luckert by permission of
the State University of New York Press, copyright © 1994, State University
of New York.

He Liyi. "A Woman's Love" from *The Spring of Butterflies and Other Chinese
Folktales* by He Liyi. Copyright © 1985. Reprinted by permission of Harper
Collins Publishers, London.

D. L. R. Lorimer and E. O. Lorimer. "The Story of the City of Nothing-
in-the-World" from *Persian Tales* by D. L. R. Lorimer and E. O. Lorimer.
Copyright © 1919. Reprinted by permission of MacMillan and Company,
Ltd, London.

Ursula McConnel. "The Black Snake Man and His Wife, the Dove" from
Myths of the Muŋkan by Ursula McConnel, copyright © 1957. Reprinted by
permission of Helen H. Cook.

Georgios A. Megas. "The Child Who was Poor and Good" from *Folktales of
Greece* by Georgios A. Megas. Trans. Helen Colaclides. From Folktales of the
World series, General Editor, Richard M. Dorson. Copyright © 1970 by
the University of Chicago. Reprinted by permission of University of
Chicago Press.

Exaltacion Mercado-Cinco. "The Magic Coin" from *A Compilation and a
Study of Selected Fairy Tales of Eastern Leyte* by Exaltacion Mercado-Cinco.
Copyright © 1969. Reprinted by permission of Divine Word University of
Tacloban.

Maurice Metayer. "The Legend of the Coppermine River" and "The Huntress" from *Tales from the Igloo* by Maurice Metayer. Copyright © 1977.
Reprinted by permission of St. Martin's Press and A. G. Nanogak.

Norah and William Montgomerie. "Whuppity Stoorie" from *The Well at the World's End, Folk Tales of Scotland* by Norah and William Montgomerie. Copyright © 1975. Reprinted by permission of Canongate Press, Scotland. Vusamazulu Credo Mutwa. "Nonikwe and the Great One, Marimba" from *Indaba, My Children* by Vusamazulu Credo Mutwa. Copyright © 1966. Reprinted by permission of Kahn & Averill.

Ngumbu Njururi. "Wacu and the Eagle" from *Agikuyu Folk Tales* by Ngumbu Njururi. Copyright © 1966. Reprinted by permission of Oxford University Press, Nairobi.

Howard Norman. "Story of a Female Shaman" from *Northern Tales: Traditional Stories of Eskimo and Indian Peoples* by Howard Norman, copyright © 1990 by Howard Norman. Reprinted by permission of Pantheon Books, a division of Random House, Inc.

Dov Noy. "Who Is Blessed with the Realm, Riches, and Honor?" from *Folktales of Israel* by Dov Noy with assistance of Dan Ben-Amos. Trans. Gene Baharav. From Folktales of the World series, General Editor, Richard M. Dorson. Copyright © 1963 by the University of Chicago. Reprinted by permission of University of Chicago Press.

George Papshvily and Helen Papshvily. "Davit" from *Yes and No Stories, A Book of Georgian Folktales* by George Papshvily and Helen Papshvily. Copyright © 1946. Reprinted by permission of HarperCollins Publishers, New York.

Minnie Postma. "Nanabolele, Who Shines in the Night" and "Jackal and Hen" from *Tales from the Basotho* by Minnie Postma. Copyright © 1974. Reprinted by permission of the Postma Family.

Paul Radin. "A Woman for a Hundred Cattle" from *African Folktales* by Paul Radin. Copyright © 1964. Reprinted by permission of Princeton University Press.

A. W. Reed. "Rau-Whato" from *Treasury of Maori Folklore* by A. W. Reed. Copyright © 1963. Reprinted by permission of Reed Publishing (NZ) Ltd.

A. W. Reed and Inez Hames. "Kumaku and the Giant" from *Myths and Legends of Fiji and Rotuma* by A. W. Reed and Inez Hames. Copyright © 1967. Reprinted by permission of Reed Publishing (NZ) Ltd.

James Riordan. "Marichka" from *Russian Gypsy Tales* by James Riordan. Copyright © 1992. Reprinted by permission of Canongate Press, Scotland and Interlink Books, USA.

Peninnah Schram. "The Innkeeper's Wise Daughter" from *Jewish Stories One Generation Tells Another* by Peninnah Schram. Copyright © 1987. Reprinted by permission of the publisher, Jason Aronson, Inc., Northvale, N.J., © 1987.

Keigo Seki. "The Monkey Bridegroom" from *Folktales of Japan* by Keigo Seki. Trans. Robert J. Adams. From Folktales of the World series, General Editor,

Richard M. Dorson. Copyright © 1963 by the University of Chicago. Reprinted by permission of University of Chicago Press.

Jacqueline Simpson. "The Night Troll" and "'My Jon's Soul'" from *Icelandic Folktales and Legends* by Jacqueline Simpson. Copyright © 1979. Reprinted by permission of B. T. Batsford. Reprinted by permission of University of California Press.

Ruth Q. Sun. "The Child of Death" from *Land of Seagull and Fox* by Ruth Q. Sun. Copyright © 1966. Reprinted by permission of John Weatherhill.

Warren S. Walker and Ahmet E. Uysal. "The Feslihancı Girl" from *More Tales Alive in Turkey* by Warren S. Walker and Ahmet E. Uysal. Copyright © 1992. Reprinted by permission of the author.

Diane Wolkstein. "I'm Tipingee, She's Tipingee, We're Tipingee, Too" from *The Magic Orange Tree and Other Haitian Folktales* by Diane Wolkstein. Copyright © 1978. Reprinted by permission of the author.

FOREWORD

The Female Hero and the Women Who Wait
JANE YOLEN

Hero is a masculine noun. It means an illustrious warrior, a man admired for his achievements and qualities, the central male figure in a great epic or drama.

A *heroine*, on the other hand, is the female equivalent. Or is she really his equal in the epic? We might as well have called her a hero-ess or a hero-ette, some kind of diminutive subset of real heroes. The heroine is the one who carries spears but does not hurl them. The one who dresses well but does not dirty her nails in the fight. The one who lies down in a glass casket, until revived by an awakening kiss.

Or so the Victorian folk tale anthologists would have had us believe. They regularly subverted and subsumed the stories that starred strong and illustrious female heroes, promoting instead those stories that showed women as weak or witless or, at the very best, waiting prettily and with infinite patience to be rescued. And the bowdlerizers did it for all the very best of reasons—for the edification and moral education of their presumed audiences.

A hundred years later, the same thing happened. Walt Disney, with his groundbreaking fairy tale films, re-emphasized the helpless, hapless heroine, who, he posited, has to be rescued by mice, birds, rabbits, deer, and other assorted cute fauna, or by a bunch of half-men, or dwarfs. As Jack Zipes wrote in *Fairy Tale As Myth, Myth As Fairy Tale*: "The young women are like helpless ornaments in need of protection, and when it comes to the action of the (Disney) film, they are omitted." So powerful are the Disney retellings that the diminution of the folk tale heroine was complete.

We, the reading and viewing public, then accepted whole cloth that in folklore, as in life, everyone but the heroine is a capable being.

Was this life reflecting art or art reflecting life? As story lovers we conveniently forgot the ancient tales of Diana of the hunt, or Atalanta the strongest runner in the kingdom, or the inordinate wrath of the mother goddess Ceres, or the powerful female warriors known as Amazons, or the thousand and one other stories with a heroic female at the core. We accepted the revisionist Cinderella, patient and pathetic, forgetting how, in over five hundred European variants alone, she had made her way through a morass of petty politics or run away from an abusive father to win a share of a kingdom on her own. We let the woodsman save Little Red Riding Hood when earlier versions had already shown her—and her grandmother—the truly capable actors in the drama.

In book after book, film after film, we edited, revised, redacted, and destroyed the strength of our female heroes, substituting instead a kind of perfect pink-and-white passivity.

Why? I do not know. I grew up in the forties and fifties, and that kind of cheery, behind-the-active-scenes and sleeping beauty was the acceptable female mode then. Women strived for a dimity divinity. The fairy tale books reflected it, encouraged it, set it out as the norm.

However, in the past twenty-five years there has been a re-evaluation of the female hero in folklore. Perceptive anthologists have begun to resurrect the female hero, showing us some of the riches that are still in the storehouses of folklore, unremarked but quite remarkable. They have uncovered stories of the most admirable women heroes, young and old, who have been strong actors in their own epic narratives. Marina Warner calls such rescue work "snatching (the stories) out of the jaws of misogyny itself." And we are all—women and men—inheritors of this wealth, so long hidden from us.

Anthologist Kathleen Ragan, has, with the publication of this book, become an important figure in the restoration of the feminine aspect of the hero. She gives us here the broadest selection of female hero stories than has been published before. Her finds come from all corners of the globe; her female heroes are all ages and in all stages of life. These women save villages, ride into battle, figure out riddles and rituals, rescue themselves from ogres, make predictions, call down storms. They rule wisely and well.

The stories were always there.

Only we were not.

Look, for example, at the bare-boned Salishan story about the two girls stolen by giants, a tale recounted in a back issue of the *American Folklore Society* but not otherwise generally known outside of the tribe. It has all the elements of a great runaway story, in which a brave and wily hero escapes a captor. But in this instance, the hero is not one but two young girls who bide their time bravely and then make their escape back to their own people. Without Ms. Ragan's own wily rescue effort, the story would be lost to the greater readership.

Or the tale she offers from the Philippines, "The Magic Coin," about a poor storekeeper and three beautiful fairy women who buy clay pipes with a strange ten-centavo piece. Tales about magical exchanges, where the fey folk make an unspoken bargain with a human, are popular around the world. But this particular story is hardly known outside its own culture. It was found by Ms. Ragan in a thesis about fairy tales in Eastern Leyte.

In her own way, Ms. Ragan is a hero, too, battling the demons of publishing, going into the depths of old libraries, and bringing back to her people—as Joseph Campbell's traditional hero is supposed to do—a boon. Or in Ms. Ragan's case, a book. It is only a single letter's difference after all, and I think an acceptable and magical transfiguration.

INTRODUCTION

My daughter and I have been reading books together since she was about a year old. When she began to appreciate stories, I rifled my parents' basement bookshelves for my childhood favorites, books by Dr. Seuss. I supplemented the Seuss I found in the basement with the Seuss stash at our public library. We read *One Fish Two Fish, Red Fish Blue Fish, Green Eggs and Ham,* and of course *The Cat in the Hat.*[1] My daughter loved the rhythm and rhymes, just as I did when I was a little girl. She memorized whole pages and sat on the couch pretending to read. "I am Sam. / Sam I am."

The more I read, the more uncomfortable I became. I couldn't find any female characters in these books. I found myself changing the pronouns from male to female when I read stories to her. It was hard to do. The pronouns had to be consistent throughout the book. I also had to remember which ones I'd changed because if I slipped up the next time we read the book, my daughter would catch it immediately.

One night we read *If I Ran the Zoo* as a bedtime story. A part of the story described hens roosting in each others' topknots. When it said, "Another one roosts in the topknot of *his.* / And another in *his,* and another in *HIS* . . . ," I got angry.[2] Since when is a hen masculine? As soon as my daughter went to sleep for the night, I picked up *And to Think That I Saw It on Mulberry Street.* I looked for female characters. There were none. In fact the only mention of a woman occurred in the lines, "Why Jack or Fred or Nat / Say even Jane could think of that." I picked up *The 500 Hats of Bartholomew Cubbins.* I looked for women. Even the crowd scenes were exclusively male. On the last page a silhouette of Bartholomew's parents included the only woman in the book. (I thought that possibly I'd chanced upon the worst.) I tried one more, *Horton Hatches the Egg.* Finally I found a female character. Mayzie, a lazy mother bird convinces Horton, the male elephant, to sit on her egg while she vacations. Horton endures many hardships nurturing the egg; Mayzie never comes back.

I did a more thorough survey, hoping to find Seuss books with positive, exciting female characters.[3] I found that over 90 percent of the characters were male, and when major characters *were* female, they were negative: Lazy Mayzie who wouldn't sit on her egg, vain and silly Gertrude McFuzz, stuck up Lolla Lee Lou, and the nasty kangaroo mother who tries to kill all those sweet little Who's in *Horton Hears a Who*. Those books weren't only teaching my daughter the beauty of whimsical rhymes, they were also teaching her that she was a nobody (over 90 percent of the world was male), that she should be a nobody (Sally in *The Cat in the Hat*), and that if by chance she did do something, like lay an egg, she wouldn't have the strength of character to hatch it.

I continued to count. I counted books in my local library, which prides itself on being very gender conscious, yet there were at least twice as many male protagonists as female protagonists in the children's fiction section.[4] In the scarcity and poor quality of heroines my daughter was constantly told "you don't exist, you're not important." I love my girl too much to let her listen to that. In talking with other mothers it became obvious that many felt the same way. "I change the pronouns, too." "I know what you mean, but there's nothing we can do." "I know, we've read *Madeline*[5] about a thousand times already."

My search for heroines migrated to the fairy tale section. Although there were five to ten editions of "Sleeping Beauty," "Snow White," and "Cinderella," each illustrated by a different person, there was a very limited depth to the stock of heroines in the library picture book collection. No matter how many beautifully illustrated Cinderella stories one reads, these do not explore other qualities, such as Joan of Arc's courage, a mother's love, or Marie Curie's intelligent determination. The current selection of fairy tales presented to children makes a sharp differentiation in the treatment of girls and boys. The female role models are beautiful, passive, and helpless victims: Cinderella, Sleeping Beauty, Snow White, Little Red Riding Hood. Male role models include a range of active characteristics: adventurous Jack the Giant Killer, resourceful Puss in Boots, the underestimated third son who makes the princess laugh, and the gallant knight who rides up the glass mountain.

My first impulse to correct this prejudice was to choose fairy tales that had active heroines and retell the tales for young picture book readers. One librarian told me, "You won't find quality heroines in fairy tales because those tales were written down in a time when the social mores insisted on silent, passive women." An examination of readily available folktales and folktale anthologies upholds this point of view. Most published anthologies of world folktales, and collections of regional folktales have a very low percentage of female characters—for example, 4 percent female protagonists (not necessarily heroines) in a book of 220 folktales and 2 percent female protagonists in a book of 107 folktales.* Examination of the female protagonists represented in these anthologies showed that many of the women were negative characters: a nagging mother-in-law who makes life intolerable even for the devil, a woman who personifies the misery in the world, or women who allow themselves to be mutilated by loved ones. Secondary characters like the wicked witch and the wicked stepmother abound. This convinced me of the need for an anthology of folktales with positive women as the main characters.

My studies of folklore had indicated that in most oral traditions folk and fairy tales naturally contain heroines as well as heroes. However the tales we read in anthologies are not simply literal transcriptions of every tale in a culture's oral tradition. First someone collects tales, selecting and transliterating the ones perceived as the best. Then an editor selects from among the collected tales, translates and possibly edits these tales to make an anthology. It seems that male editors have simply—and understandably—picked their favorite stories. As one man said to me, "Who wants to read 'Cinderella'?"

Instead of searching through several books, I began to search whole libraries for folktales with positive female protagonists. In reviewing over 30,000 stories, I unearthed inspiring heroines in folktales from all over the world. These forgotten heroines are courageous mothers, clever young girls, and warrior women; they rescue their villages from monsters, rule wisely over kingdoms, and outwit judges, thieves, and tigers. Mother's love overcomes even the silence imposed by death, and a female Prometheus brings navigation to Micronesia. Seven Thai women, after severing the head of a monster, carry it for seven years to free their country of the monster's curse. A Cheyenne woman gallops into the thick of battle to rescue her brother. To save her people, a Yoruba woman faces messengers from the land of the dead. In the original German edition of Grimms' fairy tales (*Kinder und Hausmärchen*, 1812), I found that Little Red Riding Hood walks through the woods a second time, meets another big, bad wolf and vanquishes this wolf herself.

In other words, the low percentages in most current folk and fairy tale collections belie the fact that remarkable heroines can be found in folktales from all over the world. The subtle and pervasive power of editing has been severely underestimated.

Despite the unbalanced ratio, some people think heroines aren't needed.[6] One rationale is that the gender is irrelevant because children iden-

---

* For exceptions see For Further Reading, Young Adult section, pp. 436–37.

tify with the main character regardless of the gender of that character. Another rationale is that the fairy tale represents the journey of discovery of a single individual who has an active and a passive part and children identify with the protagonists regardless of gender. If this were the case, if gender were a toss-up, irrelevant because everyone identifies with the protagonist regardless of gender, then one would expect a fifty-fifty split between heroines and heroes. However, the percentage is approximately 10 percent female protagonists to 90 percent male protagonists.[7] The one-to-nine heroine-to-hero ratio is no accident. It does matter to editors, readers, storytellers, and listeners whether the active protagonist is female or male.

Especially when one goes closer to the storyteller, one finds more and more active heroines. For example, in the first edition of Grimms' *Fairy Tales* there are about 40 tales with female protagonists out of a total of 210 stories—even the Grimms, notorious for encouraging the silence of females have 19 percent female protagonists, a far cry from the 5 percent found in many modern anthologies of folktales.

In addition to these rational explanations, my own observations support the idea that the sex of the characters matters to children. When girls play house, they often fight over who gets to be the mother. In fact, many times they end up playing house with multiple mothers, sisters, and babies and no father at all. If a boy is present, he's usually the father. When asked why he didn't want to go to Disney's *Pocahontas* a little boy responded, "That's a girls' movie." My daughter is Nala from *The Lion King* and she is the little girl who fetches water in the last three minutes of *The Jungle Book*. She consistently identifies with female characters unless she has no choice.

What ultimately catapulted me into action was a little girl at my daughter's preschool. On one parent-participation day that I attended, the teacher had just finished reading a book to a semi-circle of three-year-olds. "Who were you?" the teacher asked the group. The boys and several girls had identified with the hero of the story. One little girl, however, inched forward, opened the book, and began turning the pages. Finally she found the page for which she had been searching. "There I am!" she cried triumphantly and pointed to a picture of a little girl in a crowd, the only little girl pictured in the book. My heart went out to her. I finally appreciated the powerful means of suppression that the absence of heroines in picture books represents. This gave me the confidence to start compiling this anthology of folktales with women protagonists to aid parents, teachers, writers, storytellers, and illustrators in their search for heroines.

As the research and editing of this book progressed it also came to be a journey of discovery for me. I had been a Cinderella enthusiast for years and have read hundreds of variants from Grimms' "Aschenputtel" to Jane Austen's *Pride and Prejudice.* After reading folktales in childhood and then the variants on folktale themes in literature, I returned to folktales as an adult. I returned because I felt that somehow they were meant to answer questions and fulfill a need. When I began editing this book, I looked for flawless women characters to serve as perfect role models. The more I read, the more I began to suspect a reason for my somehow unsatisfied yet undying consumption of fairy tales. When only a few stories in a volume have female protagonists, it is impossible to acquire a range of characters. The one or two heroines must be perfect in every possible way: kind, intelligent, patient, and more, all wrapped in a flawless beauty. After reading thousands of fairy tales and finding inspiring heroines of all types—young, old, persevering, patient, loving, courageous, clever, stubborn, adventurous—it seemed to me that the heroines I chose no longer had to be perfect. I found I could smile at a cantankerous character and admire her perseverance. I could sympathize with a woman who turned over a hard-won kingdom to her much-loved husband. I could even forgive myself for not becoming as patient or as beautiful as Cinderella.

Choosing the Folktales

In choosing folktales for this collection there were certain defining factors. The source books are in English or have been translated into English. Thus the largest selection was available from countries that had once been or still are under British or American influence. The libraries used were American, which automatically gave a certain American rather than British flavor. A good example of the constraints these conditions imposed on this anthology is the dearth of South American Indian stories as compared to North American Indian stories. My respect for the diverse cultures of the world counteracted this constraint somewhat. Considerable effort was made to unearth tales from every part of the world and to make this a truly multicultural anthology.

Sources used were as close to the oral literature as possible. Recently collectors have stressed the importance of writing down the storytellers' actual words. In translating and writing down tales, however, most collectors have retold and edited the stories to some extent. Collectors and storytellers differ, and I have not tried to make the stories uniform, but have left the flavor and idiosyncracies of the tellers and the cultures intact.

One of the greatest dilemmas was the definition of a heroine. The following criteria served as a guideline: The main characters are female and they are worthy of emulation. They do not serve as the foil to the "good" character in the story, and they are not wicked queens, Mother Miserys, or nagging mothers-in-law. A second criteria was that the tale must center in and around the heroine. For example the tale "Gawain and the Lady Ragnell"[8] was not included in this anthology because although the "lesson" of the tale is that a woman should control her own life, the action centers on the man, Gawain. Thirdly, my daughters acted as the touchstone for many of the tales. My older daughter pleaded eloquently for the exclusion of female protagonists who died at the end of the story.

A fourth criteria was the narrative style. In *The Speaking Land* [9] the editors included the same tale told once by a man and once by a woman. It is a tale of an Australian Aboriginal woman, Biriwilg, who walks around in search of a place to live. The tale told by the man is concise but flat and Biriwilg's thoughts are reactions to men in the story. In the tale told by the woman, Biriwilg has her own voice. She meets another woman and they talk about which direction to go. She names places. When she finds her place, she tells us directly, "Here I'll put myself, where the place is good and the cave-house is good. . . ." She turns herself into a painting on the wall. "Here I put myself. I am Biriwilg. . . . I came this way, and here I'll stay for ever: I put myself. I stand outside, like a drawing I stand. But I am a woman . . . I stand like a person, and I keep on standing here for ever."

Webster's dictionary[10] defines a heroine as "a mythological or legendary woman having the qualities of a hero . . . a woman admired for her achievements and noble qualities and considered a model or ideal." Webster's heroes' qualities include: "great strength, courage or ability . . . an illustrious warrior." I anticipated finding tales of women warriors, intelligent women, and courageous women. I also anticipated a category of "feminine heroic" qualities: women who use lateral thinking, kind women, persevering women, and protective women. However, as tales with female protagonists were found, a whole new class of heroines emerged. Some "heroines" did things that resonated with my innermost feelings but that refused to be classified as heroic: a woman who sensed the importance of an insignificant looking coin, a girl who loved to dance, or a woman who told a story. A simple conversation between two women when taken at face value could elicit a shrug of the shoulders. Yet underneath this ordinary conversation, the effort that women make to keep relationships alive in a family or a community swells like the incoming tide.

We no longer have the opportunity to sit in a group around the fire in the evenings and listen to the tales told by the village storyteller. In exchange we now have a world community that tells its stories by proxy. Through tales collected and written down in books, the world can share in Biriwilg's trek in the outback as well as a parlor conversation in China. We can compare and learn about what all humans share, what holds us all together, and we can pass on this knowledge as we have done for centuries.

> When you were still a little child your father went up to the capital and brought me back as a present this treasure; it is called a mirror. This I give you before I die. If, after I have ceased to be in this life, you are lonely and long to see me sometimes, then take out this mirror and in the clear and shining surface you will always see me—so will you be able to meet with me often and tell me all your heart; and though I shall not be able to speak, I shall understand and sympathise with you, whatever may happen to you in the future.[11]

This book too is a mirror, a mirror of different civilizations and centuries, a mirror that can talk. It came about because I am convinced that we women must discover, understand, accept, respect, and love who we are.

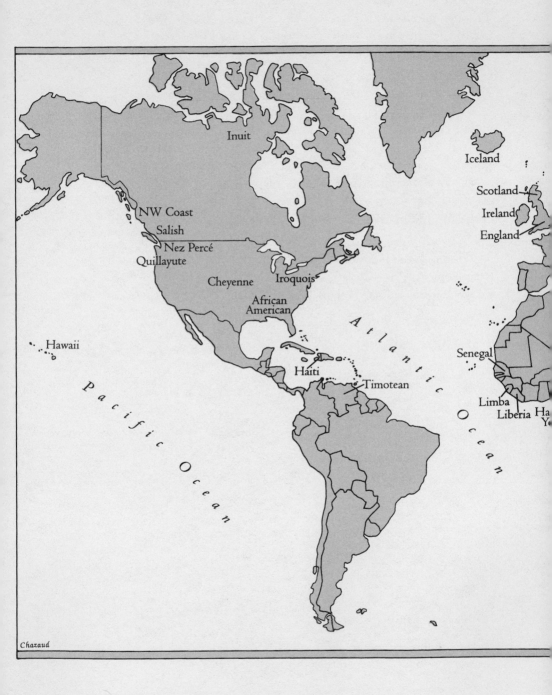

Inuit

Iceland

Scotland

Ireland

England

NW Coast

Salish

Nez Percé

Quillayute

Cheyenne

Iroquois

African
American

Atlantic

Senegal

Hawaii

Háiti

Timotean

Ocean

Limba

Liberia Ha

Y

Pacific

Ocean

Chazaud

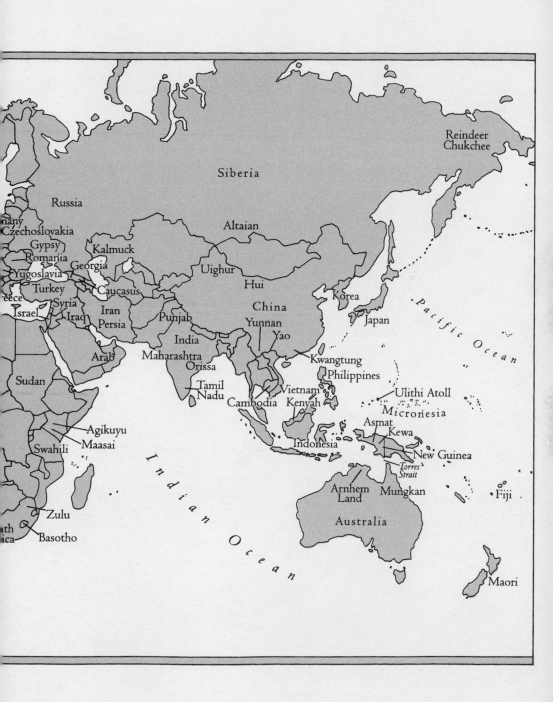

Tales
from
Europe

Iceland

Sweden

Scotland

Ireland

Russia

England

Germany

Czechoslovakia

Gypsy

Kalmuck

Romania

Georgia

Yugoslavia

Caucasus

Turkey

Greece

Syria

Iran

Israel

Iraq

Persia

The Stolen Bairn and the Sìdh

Scotland[12]*

[shē] There was a path that ran along near the edge of a cliff above the sea, and along this path in the gloaming of a misty day, came two fairy women of the Sìdh.° All of a sudden both of them stopped and fixed their eyes on the path before them. There in the middle of the path lay a bundle. Though naught could be seen of what was in it, whatever it was moved feebly and made sounds of an odd, mewling sort.

The two women of the Sìdh leaned over and pushed away the wrappings of the bundle to see what they had found. When they laid their eyes upon it, they both stood up and looked at each other.

"'Tis a bairn,"[†] said the first of them.

"'Tis a mortal bairn," said the other.

Then they looked behind them and there was nothing there but the empty moor with the empty path running through it. They turned about and looked before them and saw no more than they had seen behind them. They looked to the left and there was the rising moor again with nothing there but the heather and gorse running up to the rim of the sky. And on their right was the edge of the cliff with the sea roaring below.

[shē] Then the first woman of the Sìdh spoke and she said, "What no one comes to be claiming is our own." And the second woman picked up the bairn and happed[‡] it close under her shawl. Then the two of them made off along the path faster than they had come and were soon out of sight.

About the same time, two fishermen came sailing in from the sea with their boat skirling along easy and safe away from the rocks. One of them looked up at the face of the black steep cliff and let out a shout.

"What's amiss?" asked the other.

"I'm thinking someone's gone over the cliff!" said the first man. "Do you not see?"

---

* This number and those that follow each story title refer to notes that give pertinent information on less well-known cultures and bibliographical information on each story. These notes can be found at the back of the book. Footnotes marked with a symbol in the text itself will be found at the bottom of each page. The world map on pp. xxviii–xxix indicates the region where each story was collected. There is also a regional map at the beginning of each section.

° *Sìdh*, the fairy folk of Ireland in Gaelic folklore, pronounced "she."

[†] *Bairn*, child.

[‡] *Hap*, to wrap up for warmth.

The other one peered through the gloaming. "I see a bit of somewhat," said he. "Happen 'tis a bird."

"No bird is so big," said the first fisherman, and he laid his hand on the tiller of the boat.

"You'll not be going in! The boat'll break up on the rocks!" cried his companion.

"Och, we'll not break up. Could I go home and eat my supper in peace thinking that some poor body might be lying out here and him hurt or dying?" And he took the boat in.

It came in safe, and they drew it above the waves. Up the cliff the two of them climbed and there they found a young lass lying on a shelf of rock. They got her down and laid her in the boat, and off they sailed for home.

When they got there, they gave her over to the women to nurse and tend. They found that she was not so much hurt as dazed and daft. But after two days she found her wits and looked up at them.

"Where is my babe?" she cried then. "Fetch my bairn to me!"

At that, the women drew back and looked at one another, not knowing what to say. For they surely had no bairn to give her!

At last one old cailleach* went over to her and said, "Poor lass. Call upon your Creator for strength! There was no bairn with you upon the cliff. Happen he fell from your arms to the sea."

"That he did not!" she cried impatiently. "I wrapped him warm and laid him safe on the path while I went to search for water for him to drink. I did not have him with me when I fell. I must go find him!"

But they would not let her go, for she was still too weak from her fall o'er the cliff. They told her the men would go by the path and fetch the bairn to her. So the men went, and they walked the path from one end to the other, but never a trace of the bairn did they find. They searched the whole of the livelong day, and at night they came back and told her. They tried to comfort her as well as they could. He'd surely been found, they said, by a passer-by, and he'd be safe and sound in some good soul's house. They'd ask around. And so they did. But nobody had seen the child at all.

She bided her time till her strength came back. Then she thanked them kindly for all they'd done and said she'd be going now to find her bairn. He was all she had in the world, for his father was dead.

The fisherfolk would have had her remain with them. They'd long given the child up for dead, and they'd learned to love her well.

* *Cailleach*, an old woman.

"I'll come back and bide with you when I have my bairn again," said she. "But until then, farewell."

She wandered about from croft* to croft and from village to village, but no one had seen him nor even so much as heard of anyone finding such a bairn. At last in her wandering she came to a place where some gypsies had made their camp. "Have you seen my bairn?" she asked. For she knew they traveled far and wide and she hoped that they might know where he was. But they could tell her nothing except that all the bairns they had were their own. She was so forlorn and weary that they felt pity for her. They took her in and bathed her tired feet and fed her from their own pot.

When they had heard her story, they said she must bide with them. At the end of the week they'd be journeying north to meet others of their clan. They had an ancient grandmother there who had all the wisdom in the world. Perhaps she'd be able to help.

So she stayed with the gypsies and traveled northward with them. When they got there, they took her to the ancient grandmother and asked her to help the lass.

"Sit thee down beside me," the old crone said, "and let me take thy hand." So the grieving lass sat down beside her and there the two of them stayed, side by side and hand in hand.

The hours went by and night came on and when it was midnight the ancient grandmother took her hand from the lass's hand. She took herbs from the basket which stood at her side and threw them on the fire. The fire leaped up, and the smoke that rose from the burning herbs swirled round the old gypsy's head. She looked and listened as the fire burned hot. When it had died down, she took the lass's hand again and fondled it, weeping sorrowfully the while.

"Give up thy search, poor lass," said she, "for thy bairn has been stolen away by the Sìdh. They have taken him into the Sìdhean,° and what they take there seldom comes out again."

The lass had heard tell of the Sìdh. She knew that there were no other fairies so powerful as they.

"Can you not give me a spell against them," she begged, "to win my bairn back to me?"

The ancient grandmother shook her head sadly. "My wisdom is only as old as man," she said. "But the wisdom of the Sìdh is older than the beginning of the world. No spell of mine could help you against them."

---

* *Croft,* a small farmhold that is worked by a tenant.
° *Sìdhean,* the realm of the Sìdh.

"Ah, then," said the lass, "if I cannot have my bairn back again, I must just lie down and die."

"Nay," said the old gypsy. "A way may yet be found. Wait yet a while. Bide here with my people till the day we part. By that time I may find a way to help you."

When the day came for the gypsies to part and go their separate ways, the old gypsy grandmother sent for the lass again.

"The time has come for the people of the Sìdh to gather together at the Sìdhean," said she. "Soon they will be coming from all their corners of the land to meet together. There they will choose one among them to rule over them for the next hundred years. If you can get into the Sìdhean with them, there is a way that you may win back your bairn for yourself."

"Tell me what I must do!" said the lass eagerly.

"For all their wisdom, the Sìdh have no art to make anything for themselves," said the old gypsy woman. "All that they get they must either beg or steal. They have great vanity and desire always to possess a thing which has no equal. If you can find something that has not its like in all the world you may be able to buy your bairn back with it."

"But how can I find such a thing?" asked the lass. "And how can I get into the Sìdhean?"

"As for the first," the old grandmother said, "I am not able to tell you. As for the second, perhaps you might buy your way into the Sìdhean." Then the old gypsy woman laid her hand on the lass's head and blessed her and laid a spell upon her that she might be safe from earth and air, fire and water, as she went on her way. And having done for her all that she could, she sent her away.

The gypsies departed and scattered on their ways, but the lass stayed behind, poring over in her mind the things that she had been told.

'Twould be not one but two things she must have. One would buy her into the Sìdhean, and the other would buy her bairn out of it. And they must be rich and rare and beyond compare, with no equal in the world, or the Sìdh would set no value upon them. Where could a poor lass like herself find the likes of that?

She couldn't think at all at first because her mind was in such a maze. But after a while she set herself to remember all the things she'd ever been told of that folks spoke of with wonder. And out of them all, the rarest things that came to her mind were the white cloak of Nechtan and the golden stringed harp of Wrad. And suddenly her mind was clear and she knew what she must do.

Up she got and made her way to the sea. There she went up and down, clambering over the sharp rocks, gathering the soft white down, shed from the breasts of the eider ducks that nested there.

The rocks neither cut nor bruised her hands and feet, nor did the waves beat upon her with the rising tide. The heat of the sun did her no harm, and the gales and tempests held away from her and let her work in peace. True it was, the spell of the ancient gypsy grandmother protected her from earth and water, fire and air.

When she had gathered all the down she needed, she sat herself down and wove a cloak of it so soft and white that one would have thought it a cloud she had caught from the sky.

When the cloak was finished, she cut off her long golden hair. She put a strand of it aside and with the rest she wove a border of golden flowers and fruits and leaves all around the edges of the cloak. Then she laid the cloak under a bit of gorse.

Off she went, hunting up and down the shore, seeking for something to make the frame of her harp. And she found the bones of some animal of the sea, cast up by the waves. They were bleached by the sun and smoothed by the tides till they looked like fine ivory. She bent them and bound them till she had a frame for the harp. Then she strung it with strings made from the strand of hair she had laid aside. She stretched the strings tight and set them in tune and then she played upon it. And the music of the harp was of such sweetness that the birds lay motionless on the air to listen to it.

She laid the cloak on her shoulders and took the harp on her arm and set off for the Sìdhean. She traveled by high road and byroad, by open way and by secret way, by daylight and by moonlight, until at last she came to the end of her journey.

She hid herself in a thicket at the foot of the Sìdhean. Soon she could see the Sìdh people coming. The lass watched from behind the bushes as they walked by. They were a tall dark people with little in size or feature to show that they belonged to the fairy folk, except that their ears were long and narrow and pointed at the top and their eyes and brows were set slantwise in their faces.

As the lass had hoped, one of the Sìdh came late, after all the rest had passed by into the Sìdhean. The lass spread out the cloak to show it off at its best. She stepped out from the thicket and stood in the way of the fairy. The woman of the Sìdh stepped back and looked into her face. "You are not one of us!" she said angrily. "What has a mortal to do at a gathering of the Sìdh?"

And then she saw the cloak. It flowed and rippled from the collar to the hem, and the gold of the border shone as the sea waves shine with the sun upon them. The Sìdh woman fell silent, but her slanting eyes swept greedily over the cloak and grew bright at sight of it.

"What will you take for the cloak, mortal?" she cried. "Give it to me!"

"The cloak is not for sale," said the lass. Cunningly she swirled its folds so the light shimmered and shone upon it, and the golden fruits and flowers glowed as if they had life of their own.

"Lay the cloak on the ground and I'll cover it over with shining gold, and you may have it all if you'll leave me the cloak," the fairy said.

"All the gold of the Sìdh cannot buy the cloak," said the lass. "But it has its price . . . "

"Tell me then!" cried the Sìdh woman, dancing with impatience. "Whate'er its price you shall have it!"

"Take me with you into the Sìdhean and you shall have the cloak," the lass said.

"Give me the cloak!" said the fairy, stretching her hand out eagerly. "I'll take you in."

But the lass wouldn't give the cloak up yet. She knew the Sìdh were a thieving race that will cheat you if ever they can.

"Och, nay!" she said. "First you must take me into the Sìdhean. Then you may take the cloak and welcome."

So the fairy caught her hand and hurried her up the path. As soon as they were well within the Sìdhean the lass gave up the cloak.

When the people of the Sìdh saw that a mortal had come among them, they rushed at her to thrust her out. But the lass stepped quickly behind the fairy who had brought her in. When the fairy people saw the cloak they forgot the lass completely. They all crowded about the one who had it, reaching to touch it and begging to be let try it on.

The lass looked about her and there on a throne at the end of the hall she saw the new king of the Sìdh. The lass walked through the Sìdh unheeded and came up to him boldly, holding the harp up for him to see.

"What have you there, mortal?" asked the king.

"'Tis a harp," said the lass.

"I have many a harp," said the king, showing but little interest.

"But never a one such as this!" the lass said. And she took the harp upon her arm and plucked the golden strings with her fingers. From the harp there rose upon the air one note filled with such wild love and long-ing that all the Sìdh turned from the cloak to wonder at it. The king of the Sìdh stretched out both hands. "Give me the harp!" he cried.

"Nay!" said the lass. "'Tis mine!"

A crafty look came into the king's eyes. But he only said idly, "Och, well, keep it then. But let me try it once to see if the notes are true."

"Och, they're true enough," the lass answered. "I set it in tune with my own hands. It needs no trying." She knew well that if he ever laid his hands upon it, she'd never get it back into her own.

"Och, well," said the king. "'Tis only a harp after all. Still, I've taken a fancy to it. Name your price and mayhap we'll strike a bargain."

"That I'd not say," said the lass. "I made the harp with my own hands and I strung it with my own golden hair. There's not another its like in the world. I'm not liking to part with it at all."

The king could contain himself no longer. "Ask what you will!" he cried. "Whatever you ask I'll give. But let me have the harp!"

And now she had him!

"Then give me my bairn your women stole from the path along the black cliff by the sea," said the lass.

The king of the Sìdh sat back in his throne. This was a price he did not want to pay. He had a mind to keep the bairn amongst them.

So he had them bring gold and pour it in a great heap at her feet.

"There is a fortune your king himself might envy," he said. "Take all of it and give me the harp."

But she only said, "Give me my bairn."

Then he had them add jewels to the heap till she stood waist-deep in them. "All this shall be yours," he tempted her. "'Tis a royal price for the harp."

But she stood steadfast and never looked down at the jewels.

"Give me my bairn!" said she.

When he saw that she would not be moved, he had to tell them to fetch the child for her. They brought the bairn and he knew his mother at once and held out his arms to her. But the king held him away from her and would not let her take him.

"The harp first!" said the king.

"The bairn first!" said the lass. And she would not let him lay hand on the harp till she had what she wanted. So the king had to give in. And once she had the child safe in her arms, she gave up the harp.

The king struck a chord upon the harp and then he began to play. The music rose from the golden strings and filled all the Sìdhean with music so wonderful that all the people of the Sìdh stood spellbound in their tracks to listen. So rapt were they that when the lass walked out of the Sìdhean with her bairn in her arms, they never saw her go. So, she left them there with the king on his throne playing his harp, and all of the people of the Sìdh standing still to listen—maybe for the next hundred years for all anyone knows.

The lass took her bairn back to the fisherfolk who had been kind to her, as she'd promised to do. And she and her bairn dwelt happily there all the rest of their days.

Magic enters the feathers and the bleached bones when the heroine gathers them with her own hands. It permeates the cape when she uses her own hair to weave the cape's borders. When she strings the harp with her own golden hair, the heroine gives voice to the powerful magic of her love and determination. "From the harp there rose upon the air one note filled with such wild love and longing that all the Sìdh turned from the cloak to wonder at it."

Through the centuries, folktales have carried the hopes and dreams of all the people who listen to them and who tell them. In the face of famine, a ruthless feudal lord, or an overwhelming industrial society, folktales encourage people to hope and to act. They affirm that the power to create a better world, the power to right a wrong, the power to live joyfully, exists in each of us if only we can believe in ourselves and give voice to our magic.

The Three Sisters and Their Husbands, Three Brothers

Ireland[13]

In the county Cork, a mile and a half from Fermoy, there lived three brothers. The three lived in one house for some years and never thought of marrying. On a certain day they went to a fair in the town of Fermoy. There was a platform on the fair ground for dancing and a fiddler on the platform to give music to the dancers. Three sisters from the neighbourhood, handsome girls lively and full of jokes, made over to the three brothers and asked would they dance. The youngest and middle brother wouldn't think of dancing, but the eldest said, "We mustn't refuse; it wouldn't be good manners."

The three brothers danced with the girls, and after the dance took them to a public-house for refreshments.

After a while the second brother spoke up and said, "Here are three sisters, good wives for three brothers; why shouldn't we marry? Let the eldest brother of us take the eldest sister; I will take the second; the youngest brother can have the youngest sister."

It was settled then and there that the three couples were satisfied if the girls' parents were. Next day the brothers went to the girls' parents and got their consent. In a week's time they were married.

Each of the three brothers had a good farm, and each went now to live on his own place. They lived well and happily for about ten years, when one market-day the eldest sister came to the second and asked her to go to Fermoy with her.

In those days women used to carry baskets made of willow twigs, in which they took eggs and butter to market. The second sister said she hadn't thought of going, but she would go, and they would ask the youngest sister for her company.

All three started off, each with a basket of eggs. After they had their eggs sold in the market they lingered about for some time looking at people, as is usual with farmers' wives. In the evening, when thinking of home, they dropped into a public-house to have a drop of drink before going. The public-house was full of people, chatting, talking, and drinking. The three sisters did not like to be seen at the bar, so they went to a room upstairs, and the eldest called for three pints of porter, which was brought without delay.

It is common for a farmer or his wife who has a ten-shilling piece or a pound, and does not wish to break it, to say, "I will pay the next time I come to town"; so the eldest sister said now. The second sister called for three pints, and then the third followed her example.

'Tis said that women are very noisy when they've taken a glass or two, but whether that is true or not, these three were noisy, and their talk was so loud that Lord Fermoy, who was above in a room finishing some business with the keeper of the public-house, could not hear a thing for their chat, so he sent the landlord to tell the women to leave the room. The landlord went, and finding that they had not paid their reckoning yet, told them it was time they were paying their reckoning and moving towards home.

One of the sisters looked up and said, "The man above [God] will pay all. He is good for the reckoning."

The man of the house, thinking that it was Lord Fermoy she was speaking of, was satisfied, and went upstairs.

"Have they gone?" asked Lord Fermoy.

"They have not, and they say that you will pay the reckoning."

"Why should I pay when I don't know them? We'll go down and see who they are and what they mean."

The two went down, and Lord Fermoy saw that they were tenants of his; he knew them quite well, for they lived near his own castle. He liked the sisters, they were so sharp-witted.

"I'll pay the reckoning, and do you bring each of these women a glass of punch," said he to the man of the house.

The punch was brought without delay.

"Here is a half sovereign for each of you," said Lord Fermoy. "Now go home, and meet me in this place a week from today. Whichever one of you during that time makes the biggest fool of her husband will get ten pounds in gold and ten years' rent free."

"We'll do our best," said the sisters.

Each woman of them was anxious, of course, to do the best she could. They parted at the door of the public-house, each going her own way, and each thinking of what could be done to win the ten pounds and ten years' rent.

It had happened that the eldest sister's husband became very phthisicky* and sickly a couple of years after his marriage and fell into a decline. On the way home the wife made up her mind what to do. She bought pipes, tobacco, candles, and other articles needed at a wake. She

---

*Phthisicky, asthmatic, wheezy, or tuberculous.

was in no hurry home, so 'twas late enough when she came to the house. When she looked in at the window she saw her husband sitting by the fire with his hand on his chin and the children asleep around him. A pot of potatoes, boiled and strained, was waiting for her.

She opened the door. The husband looked at her and asked, "Why are you so late?"

"Why are you off the table, and where are the sheets that were over you?" asked she as if in a fright; "or the shirt that I put on you? I left you laid out on the table."

"Sure I am not dead at all. I know very well when you started to go to the market, I wasn't dead then, and I didn't die since you left the house."

Then she began to abuse him, and said that all his friends were coming to the wake, and he had no right to be off the table tormenting and abusing herself and the children, and went on in such a way that at last he believed himself dead and asked her in God's name to give him a smoke and he would go up again on the table and never come down till he was carried from it.

She gave him the pipe, but didn't let him smoke long. Then she made him ready, put him on the table, and spread a sheet over him. Now two poles were stretched overhead above the body and sheets hung over and down on the sides, as is customary. She put beads between his two thumbs and a Prayer-book in his hands. "You are not to open your eyes," said she, "no matter what comes or happens." She unlocked the door then and raised a terrible wailing over the corpse. A woman living opposite heard the wailing, and said to her husband:

"Oh, it is Jack that is dead, and it is a shame for you not to go to him."

"I was with him this evening," said the husband, "and what could kill him since?"

The wife hurried over to Jack's house, found the corpse in it, and began to cry. Soon there was a crowd gathered, and all crying.

The second sister going past to her own home by a short cut, heard the keening* and lamenting. "This is my sister's trick to get the ten pounds and ten years' rent," thought she, and began to wail also. When inside she pinched the dead man, and pulled at him to know would he stir; but it was no use, he never stirred.

The second sister went home then, and she was very late. Her husband was a strong, able-bodied man, and when she wasn't there to milk the cows he walked up and down the path watching for her, and he very angry. At last he milked the cows himself, drove them out, and then sat

---

Keening, wailing, loud lamenting, mourning.

down in the house. When the wife came he jumped up and asked, "What kept you out 'til this hour? 'Twas fitter for you to be at home long ago than to be strolling about, and the Lord knows where you were."

"How could I be here, when I stopped at the wake where you ought to be?"

"What wake?"

"Your brother's wake. Jack is dead, poor man."

"What the devil was to kill Jack? Sure I saw him this evening, and he's not dead."

He wouldn't believe, and to convince him she said, "Come to the field and you'll see the lights, and maybe you'll hear the keening."

She took him over the ditch into the field, and seeing the lights he said, "Sure my poor brother is dead!" and began to cry.

"Didn't I tell you, you stump of a fool, that your brother was dead, and why don't you go to his wake and go in mourning? A respectable person goes in mourning for a relative and gets credit for it ever after."

"What is mourning?" asked the husband.

"'Tis well I know," said she, "what mourning is, for didn't my mother teach me, and I will show you."

She brought him to the house and told him to throw off all his clothes and put on a pair of tight-fitting black knee breeches. He did so; she took a wet brush then, and reaching it up in the chimney, got plenty of soot and blacked him all over from head to foot, and he naked except the black breeches. When she had him well blackened she put a black stick in his hand. "Now," said she, "go to the wake, and what you are doing will be a credit to the family for seven generations."

He started off wailing and crying. Whenever a wake house is full, benches and seats are put outside, men and women sit on these benches till some of those inside go home, then those outside go in. It is common also for boys to go to wakes and get pipes and tobacco, for every one gets a pipe, from a child of three to old men and women. Some of the boys at Jack's wake, after getting their pipes and tobacco, ran off to the field to smoke, where their parents couldn't see them. Seeing the black man coming, the boys dropped their pipes and ran back to the wake house, screaming to the people who were sitting outside that the devil was coming to carry the corpse with him. One of the men who stood near was sharper-sighted than others, and looking in the direction pointed out, said:

"Sure the devil is coming! And people thought that Jack was a fine, decent man, but now it turns out that he was different. I'll not be waiting here!" He took himself off as fast as his legs could carry him, and others after him.

Soon the report went into the wake house, and the corpse heard that the devil was coming to take him, but for all that he hadn't courage to stir. A man put his head out of the house, and, seeing the black man, screamed, "I declare to God that the devil is coming!" With that he ran off, and his wife hurried after him.

That moment everybody crowded so much to get out of the house that they fell one over another, screeching and screaming. The woman of the house ran away with the others. The dead man was left alone. He opened one eye right away, and seeing the last woman hurrying off he said:

"I declare to the Lord I'll not stay here and wait for the devil to take me!" With that he sprang from the table, and wrapped the sheet round his body, and away with him then as fast as ever his legs could carry him.

His brother, the black man, saw him springing through the door, and, thinking it was Death that had lifted his brother and was running away with him to deprive the corpse of wake and Christian burial, he ran after him to save him. When the corpse screamed the black man screamed, and so they ran, and the people in terror fell into holes and ditches, trying to escape from Death and the devil.

The third sister was later than the other two in coming home from Fermoy. She knew her husband was a great sleeper, and she could do anything with him when he was drowsy. She looked into the house through a window that opened on hinges. She saw him sitting by the fire asleep; the children were sleeping near him. A pot of potatoes was standing by the fire. She knew that she could get in at the window if she took off some of her clothes. She did so and crawled in. The husband had long hair. She cut the hair close off to his head, threw it in the fire and burned it. Then she went out through the window, and, taking a large stone, pounded on the door and roused her husband at last. He opened the door, began to scold her for being out so late, and blamed her greatly.

"'Tis a shame for you," said he. "The children are sleeping on the floor, and the potatoes boiled for the last five hours."

"Bad luck to you, you fool!" said the woman. "Who are you to be ordering me? Isn't it enough for my own husband to be doing that?"

"Are you out of your mind or drunk that you don't know me?" said the man. "Sure, I am your husband."

"Indeed you are not," said she.

"And why not?"

"Because you are not; you don't look like him. My husband has fine long, curly hair. Not so with you; you look like a shorn wether."*

* *Wether*, male sheep, ram.

He put his hands to his head, and, finding no hair on it, cried out, "I declare to the Lord that I am your husband, but I must have lost my hair while shearing the sheep this evening. I'm your husband."

"Be off out of this!" screamed the woman. "When my husband comes he'll not leave you long in the house, if you are here before him."

In those days the people used bog pine for torches and lighting fires. The man having a bundle of bog pine cut in pieces, took some fire and went towards the field, where he'd been shearing sheep. He went out to know could he find his hair and convince the wife. When he reached the right place he set fire to a couple of pine sticks, and they made a fine blaze. He went on his knees and was searching for the hair. He searched the four corners of the field, crawling hither and over, but if he did, not a lock of hair could he find. He went next to the middle of the field, dropped on his knees, and began to crawl around to know could he find his hair. While doing this he heard a terrible noise of men, and they running towards him, puffing and panting. Who were they but the dead man and the devil? The dead man was losing his breath and was making for the first light before him. He was in such terror that he didn't see how near he was to the light, and tumbled over the man who was searching for his hair.

"Oh, God help me!" cried the corpse. "I'm done for now!"

Hearing his brother's voice, the black man, who was there, recognised him. The man looking for the hair rose up, and seeing his brothers, knew them; then each told the others everything, and they saw right away that the whole affair was planned by their wives.

The husbands went home well fooled, shame-faced, and angry. On the following day the women went to get the prize. When the whole story was told it was a great question who was to have the money. Lord Fermoy could not settle it himself, and called a council of the gentry to decide, but they could not decide who was the cleverest woman. What the council agreed on was this: To make up a purse of sixty pounds, and give twenty pounds and twenty years' rent to each of the three, if they all solved the problem that would be put to them. If two solved it they would get thirty pounds apiece and thirty years' rent; if only one, she would get the whole purse of sixty pounds and rent free for sixty years.

"This is the riddle," said the council to the sisters: "There are four rooms in a row here; this is the first one. We will put a pile of apples in the fourth room; there will be a man of us in the third, second, and first room. You are to go to the fourth room, take as many apples as you like, and when you come to the third room you are to give the man in it half of what apples you'll bring, and half an apple without cutting it. When you come to the second room you are to do the same with what apples you will have left. In the first room you will do the same as in the third and second. Now we will go to put the apples in the fourth room, and we'll give each of you one hour to work out the problem."

"It's the devil to give half an apple without cutting it," said the elder sister.

When the men had gone the youngest sister said, "I can do it and I can get the sixty pounds, but as we are three sisters I'll be liberal and divide with you. I'll go first, and let each come an hour after the other. Each will take fifteen apples, and when she comes to the man in the third room she will ask him how much is one-half of fifteen; he will say seven and a half. She will give him eight apples then and say, 'This is half of what I have and half an apple uncut for you.' With the seven apples she will go to the second room and ask the man there what is one-half of seven; he will say three and a half. She will give him four apples and say, 'Here are three apples and a half and the half of an uncut apple for you.' With three apples left she will go to the man in the first room and ask what is the half of three. He will answer, 'One and a half.' 'Here are two apples for you,' she will say then; 'one apple and a half and the half of an uncut apple.'"

The eldest and second sister did as the youngest told them. Each received twenty pounds and twenty years' rent.

Our image of women who succeed has been dominated by the intense repetition of a limited number of role models, Cinderella, Snow White, Sleeping Beauty, all characterized primarily by their beauty. Yet, physical appearance is only one of many characteristics that people possess. The Empress Theodora, (c. 497–548), celebrated not for her beauty but for her wit, was a true-life Cinderella who rose from poverty in her youth to become Empress of the Eastern Roman Empire. History sparkles with witty women: Liu San Mei in China (see p. 240), Cleopatra in Alexandria, Dorothy Parker in New York. In this story the three sisters, who are full of jokes and laughter, achieve a secure livelihood for their families not through their looks, but through their wit.

The Corpse Watchers

Ireland[14]

There was once a poor woman that had three daughters, and one day the eldest said, "Mother, bake my cake and kill my cock, till I go seek my fortune." So she did, and when all was ready, says her mother to her, "Which will you have—half of these with my blessing, or the whole with my curse?" "Curse or no curse," says she, "the whole is little enough." So away she set, and if the mother didn't give her her curse, she didn't give her her blessing.

She walked and she walked till she was tired and hungry, and then she sat down to take her dinner. While she was eating it, a poor woman came up, and asked for a bit. "The dickens a bit you'll get from me," says she; "it's all too little for myself"; and the poor woman walked away very sorrowful. At nightfall she got lodging at a farmer's, and the woman of the house told her that she'd give her a spade-full of gold and a shovel-full of silver if she'd only sit up and watch her son's corpse that was waking in the next room. She said she'll do that; and so, when the family were in their bed, she sat by the fire, and cast an eye from time to time on the corpse that was lying under the table.

All at once the dead man got up in his shroud, and stood before her, and said, "All alone, fair maid!" She gave him no answer, and when he said it the third time, he struck her with a switch, and she became a grey flag.*

About a week after, the second daughter went to seek her fortune, and she didn't care for her mother's blessing no more *nor* her sister, and the very same thing happened to her. She was left a grey flag by the side of the other.

At last the youngest went off in search of the other two, and she took care to carry her mother's blessing with her. She shared her dinner with the poor woman on the road, and she told her that she would watch over her.

Well, she got lodging in the same place as the others, and agreed to mind the corpse. She sat up by the fire with the dog and cat, and amused herself with some apples and nuts the mistress gave her. She thought it a pity that the man under the table was a corpse, he was so handsome.

* *Flag*, probably a flagstone.

But at last he got up, and says he, "All alone, fair maid!" and she was-
n't long about an answer:

> "All alone I am not,
> I've little dog Douse and Pussy, my cat;
> I've apples to roast, and nuts to crack,
> And all alone I am not."

"Ho, ho!" says he, "you're a girl of courage, though you wouldn't have
enough to follow me. I am now going to cross the quaking bog, and go
through the burning forest. I must then enter the cave of terror, and climb
the hill of glass, and drop from the top of it into the Dead Sea." "I'll follow you," says she, "for I engaged to mind you." He thought to prevent
her, but she was as stiff as he was stout.

Out he sprang through the window, and she followed him till they
came to the "Green Hills," and then says he:

> "Open, open, Green Hills, and let the Light of the Green Hills
> through";
> "Aye," says the girl, "and let the fair maid, too."

They opened, and the man and woman passed through, and there they
were, on the edge of a bog.

He trod lightly over the shaky bits of moss and sod; and while she was
thinking of how she'd get across, the old beggar appeared to her, but
much nicer dressed, touched her shoes with her stick, and the soles spread
a foot on each side. So she easily got over the shaky marsh. The burning
wood was at the edge of the bog, and there the good fairy flung a damp,
thick cloak over her, and through the flames she went, and a hair of her
head was not singed. Then they passed through the dark cavern of hor-
rors, where she'd have heard the most horrible yells, only that the fairy
stopped her ears with wax. She saw frightful things, with blue vapours
round them, and felt the sharp rocks, and the slimy backs of frogs and
snakes.

When they got out of the cavern, they were at the mountain of glass;
and then the fairy made her slippers so sticky with a tap of her rod, that
she followed the young corpse easily to the top. There was the deep sea
a quarter of a mile under them, and so the corpse said to her, "Go home
to my mother, and tell her how far you came to do her bidding: farewell."
He sprung head foremost down into the sea, and after him she plunged,
without stopping a moment to think about it.

She was stupefied at first, but when they reached the waters she recovered her thoughts. After piercing down a great depth, they saw a green
light towards the bottom. At last they were below the sea, that seemed a

green sky above them; and sitting in a beautiful meadow, she half asleep, and her head resting against his side. She couldn't keep her eyes open, and she couldn't tell how long she slept: but when she woke, she was in bed at his house, and he and his mother sitting by her bedside, and watching her.

It was a witch that had a spite to the young man, because he wouldn't marry her, and so she got power to keep him in a state between life and death till a young woman would rescue him by doing what she had just done. So at her request, her sisters got their own shape again, and were sent back to their mother, with their spades of gold and shovels of silver. Maybe they were better after that, but I doubt it much. The youngest got the young gentleman for her husband. I'm sure she deserved him, and, if they didn't live happy, THAT WE MAY!

An adventurous youngster leaves home to seek fortune in life. The youngster's kindness is rewarded with the aid of a supernatural being. A task is set. The protagonist successfully overcomes all obstacles, rescues a future marriage partner, and wins a fortune. In the most well-known folktales with this plot, the adventurous youngster is male and the future marriage partner is often a passive, rather somnolent princess. The stories with adventurous men have been repeated so often, some people consider it the only pattern.

The Crookened Back

Ireland[15]

Peggy Barrett was once tall, well-shaped, and comely. She was in her youth remarkable for two qualities, not often found together—of being the most thrifty housewife and the best dancer in her native village of Ballyhooley. But she is now upwards of sixty years old, and during the last ten years of her life she has never been able to stand upright. Her back is bent nearly to a level, yet she has the freest use of all her limbs that can be enjoyed in such a posture; her health is good, and her mind vigorous, and in the family of her eldest son, with whom she has lived since the death of her husband, she performs all the domestic services which her age and the infirmity just mentioned allow. She washes the potatoes, makes the fire, sweeps the house (labours in which she good-humouredly says "she finds her crooked back mighty convenient"), plays with the children, and tells stories to the family and their neighbouring friends, who often collect round her son's fireside to hear them during the long winter evenings. Her powers of conversation are highly extolled, both for humour and in narration, and anecdotes of droll or awkward incidents connected with the posture in which she has been so long fixed, as well as the history of the occurrence to which she owes that misfortune, are favourite topics of her discourse. Among other matters, she is fond of relating how, on a certain day, at the close of a bad harvest, when several tenants of the estate on which she lived concerted in a field a petition for an abatement of rent, they placed the paper on which they wrote upon her back, which was found no very inconvenient substitute for a table.

Peggy, like all experienced story-tellers, suited her tales, both in length and subject, to the audience and the occasion. She knew that, in broad daylight, when the sun shines brightly, and the trees are budding, and the birds singing around us—when men and women, like ourselves, are moving and speaking, employed variously in business or amusement—she knew, in short (though certainly without knowing or much caring wherefore), that when we are engaged about the realities of life and Nature, we want that spirit of credulity, without which tales of the deepest interest will lose their power. At such times Peggy was brief, very particular as to facts, and never dealt in the marvellous. But round the blazing hearth of a Christmas evening, when infidelity is banished from all companies, at

least, in low and simple life, as a quality, to say the least of it, out of season—when the winds of "dark December" whistled bleakly round the
walls, and almost through the doors of the little mansion, reminding its
inmates that as the world is vexed by elements superior to human power,
so it may be visited by beings of a superior nature—at such times would
Peggy Barrett give full scope to her memory, or her imagination, or both,
and upon one of these occasions she gave the following circumstantial
account of the "crookening of her back."

   "It was, of all days in the year, the day before May Day that I went out
to the garden to weed the potatoes. I would not have gone out that day,
but I was dull in myself and sorrowful, and wanted to be alone; all the
boys and girls were laughing and joking in the house, making goaling-
balls, and dressing out ribands for the mummers* next day. I couldn't bear
it. 'Twas only at the Easter that was then past (and that's ten years last
Easter; I won't forget the time) that I buried my poor man, and I thought
how gay and joyful I was, many a long year before that, at the May Eve
before our wedding, when, with Robin by my side, I sat cutting and
sewing the ribands for the goaling-ball I was to give the boys on the next
day, proud to be preferred above all the other girls of the banks of the
Blackwater by the handsomest boy and the best hurler° in the village; so
I left the house and went to the garden.

   "I stayed there all the day, and didn't come home to dinner. I don't
know how it was, but somehow I continued on, weeding, and thinking
sorrowfully enough, and singing over some of the old songs that I sung
many and many a time in the days that are gone, and for them that never
will come back to me to hear them. The truth is, I hated to go and sit
silent and mournful among the people in the house, that were merry and
young, and had the best of their days before them. 'Twas late before I
thought of returning home, and I did not leave the garden till some time
after sunset. The moon was up; but though there wasn't a cloud to be
seen, and though a star was winking here and there in the sky, the day
wasn't long enough gone to have it clear moonlight. Still, it shone enough
to make everything on one side of the heavens look pale and silvery-like,
and the thin white mist was just beginning to creep along the fields. On
the other side, near where the sun was set, there was more of daylight, and
the sky looked angry, red, and fiery through the trees, like as if it was
lighted up by a great town burning below.

   "Everything was as silent as a churchyard; only now and then one

---

* *Mummers*, those who go merrymaking in disguise, especially during festivals.
° *Hurler*, one that takes part in a game of hurling, an Irish game resembling field hockey.

could hear far off a dog barking, or a cow lowing after being milked. There wasn't a creature to be seen on the road or in the fields. I wondered at this first, but then I remembered it was May Eve, and that many a thing, both good and bad, would be wandering about that night, and that I ought to shun danger well as others. So I walked on as quick as I could, and soon came to the end of the demesne* wall, where the trees rise high and thick at each side of the road, and almost meet at the top. My heart misgave me when I got under the shade. There was so much light let down from the opening above that I could see about a stone-throw before me. All of a sudden I heard a rustling among the branches on the right side of the road, and saw something like a small black goat, only with long wide horns turned out instead of being bent backwards, standing upon its hind-legs upon the top of the wall, and looking down on me.

"My breath was stopped, and I couldn't move for near a minute. I couldn't help, somehow, keeping my eyes fixed on it; and it never stirred, but kept looking in the same fixed way down at me. At last I made a rush, and went on; but I didn't go ten steps when I saw the very same sight, on the wall to the left of me standing in exactly the same manner, but three or four times as high, and almost as tall as the tallest man. The horns looked frightful; it gazed upon me as before; my legs shook, and my teeth chattered, and I thought I would drop down dead every moment. At last I felt as if I was obliged to go on; and on I went; but it was without feeling how I moved, or whether my legs carried me. Just as I passed the spot where this frightful thing was standing, I heard a noise as if something sprung from the wall, and felt like as if a heavy animal plumped down upon me, and held with the fore-feet clinging to my shoulder, and the hind ones fixed in my gown, that was folded and pinned up behind me.

"'Tis the wonder of my life ever since how I bore the shock; but so it was, I neither fell, nor even staggered with the weight, but walked on as if I had the strength of ten men, though I felt as if I couldn't help moving, and couldn't stand still if I wished it. Though I gasped with fear, I knew as well as I do now what I was doing. I tried to cry out, but couldn't; I tried to run, but wasn't able; I tried to look back, but my head and neck were as if they were screwed in a vice. I could barely roll my eyes on each side, and then I could see, as clearly and plainly as if it was in the broad light of the blessed sun, a black and cloven foot planted upon each of my shoulders. I heard a low breathing in my ear; I felt, at every step I

* *Demesne*, domain, estate, landed property, and/or the land attached to a mansion or country house.

took, my leg strike back against the feet of the creature that was on my back. Still I could do nothing but walk straight on. At last I came within sight of the house, and a welcome sight it was to me, for I thought I would be released when I reached it.

"I soon came close to the door, but it was shut; I looked at the little window, but it was shut too, for they were more cautious about May Eve than I was; I saw the light inside, through the chinks of the door; I heard 'em talking and laughing within; I felt myself at three yards' distance from them that would die to save me—and may the Lord save me from ever again feeling what I did that night, when I found myself held by what couldn't be good nor friendly, but without the power to help myself, or to call my friends, or to put out my hand to knock, or even to lift my leg to strike the door, and let them know that I was outside it! 'Twas as if my hands grew to my sides, and my feet were glued to the ground, or had the weight of a rock fixed to them. At last I thought of blessing myself; and my right hand, that would do nothing else, did that for me. Still the weight remained on my back, and all was as before. I blessed myself again: 'twas still all the same. I then gave myself up for lost: but I blessed myself a third time, and my hand no sooner finished the sign than all at once I felt the burthen spring off my back; the door flew open as if a clap of thunder burst it, and I was pitched forward on my forehead, in upon the middle of the floor. When I got up my back was crookened, and I never stood straight from that night to this blessed hour."

There was a pause when Peggy Barrett finished. Those who had heard the story before had listened with a look of half satisfied interest, blended, however, with an expression of that serious and solemn feeling which always attends a tale of supernatural wonders, how often soever told. They moved upon their seats out of the posture in which they had remained fixed during the narrative, and sat in an attitude which denoted that their curiosity as to the cause of this strange occurrence had been long since allayed. Those to whom it was before unknown still retained their look and posture of strained attention, and anxious but solemn expectation. A grandson of Peggy's, about nine years old (not the child of the son with whom she lived), had never before heard the story. As it grew in interest, he was observed to cling closer and closer to the old woman's side; and at the close he was gazing steadfastly at her, with his body bent back across her knees, and his face turned up to hers, with a look through which a disposition to weep seemed contending with curiosity. After a moment's pause, he could no longer restrain his impatience; and catching her grey locks in one hand, while the tear of dread and wonder was just dropping from his eyelash, he cried: "Granny, what was it?"

The old woman smiled, first at the elder part of her audience, and then at her grandson, and patting him on the forehead, she said: "It was the Phooka."*

This is a story about a storyteller telling a story. In a cozy room, protected from the winds of dark December, grandmother Peggy Barrett creates Irish folklore's wonder, fear, and mystery through her personality and talent. The reader is privileged to experience a great storyteller in the warm and personal surrounding of family and friends. This intimate environment is a milieu that women cherish and nurture. It is the environment in which many women tell their tales.

Women are storytellers, whether mothers recounting their own childhood to their children, librarians telling folktales at story hour, grandmothers passing on the lore of the olden days, or neighbors socializing. Before traditional South African society became overpowered by modern industrial society, tales were told in the homestead predominantly by older women. Yet when tales came to be put into books, women disappeared from the literary scene.[16] This seems to be a pattern. The classic volumes of folktales carry the names of men: Grimm (Germany), Eberhard (China), Asbjornson and Moe (Scandanavia), although in many cases women provided the tales. Collectors chose tales told by men over the same ones told by women. Men's tales became "legitimate" folklore while women's tales were degraded and classified as exaggeration or gossip.[17]

* *Phooka*, a mischievous hobgoblin or malignant goblin, can also mean the Devil.

The Horned Women

Ireland[18]

A rich woman sat up late one night carding and preparing wool, while all the family and servants were asleep. Suddenly a knock was given at the door, and a voice called—"Open! open!"

"Who is there?" said the woman of the house.

"I am the Witch of the One Horn," was answered.

The mistress, supposing that one of her neighbours had called and required assistance, opened the door, and a woman entered, having in her hand a pair of wool carders, and bearing a horn on her forehead, as if growing there. She sat down by the fire in silence, and began to card the wool with violent haste. Suddenly she paused and said aloud: "Where are the women? They delay too long."

When a second knock came to the door, and a voice called as before— "Open! open!"

The mistress felt herself constrained to rise and open to the call, and immediately a second witch entered, having two horns on her forehead, and in her hand a wheel for spinning the wool.

"Give me place," she said; "I am the Witch of the Two Horns," and she began to spin as quick as lightning.

And so the knocks went on, and the call was heard, and the witches entered, until at last twelve women sat round the fire—the first with one horn, the last with twelve horns. And they carded the thread, and turned their spinning wheels, and wound and wove, all singing together an ancient rhyme, but no word did they speak to the mistress of the house. Strange to hear, and frightful to look upon were these twelve women, with their horns and their wheels; and the mistress felt near to death, and she tried to rise that she might call for help, but she could not move, nor could she utter a word or a cry, for the spell of the witches was upon her.

Then one of them called to her in Irish and said—

"Rise, woman, and make us a cake."

Then the mistress searched for a vessel to bring water from the well that she might mix the meal and make the cake, but she could find none. And they said to her—

"Take a sieve and bring water in it."

And she took the sieve and went to the well; but the water poured from it, and she could fetch none for the cake, and she sat down by the well and wept. Then a voice came by her and said—

"Take yellow clay and moss and bind them together and plaster the sieve so that it will hold."

This she did, and the sieve held the water for the cake, And the voice said again—

"Return, and when thou comest to the north angle of the house, cry aloud three times and say, 'The mountain of the Fenian* women and the sky over it is all on fire.'"

And she did so.

When the witches inside heard the call, a great and terrible cry broke from their lips, and they rushed forth with wild lamentations and shrieks, and fled away to Slieve-namon, where was their chief abode. But the Spirit of the Well bade the mistress of the house to enter and prepare her home against the enchantments of the witches if they returned again.

And first, to break their spells, she sprinkled the water in which she had washed her child's feet (the feet-water) outside the door on the threshold; secondly, she took the cake which the witches had made in her absence, of meal mixed with the blood drawn from the sleeping family. And she broke the cake in bits, and placed a bit in the mouth of each sleeper, and they were restored; and she took the cloth they had woven and placed it half in and half out of the chest with the padlock; and lastly, she secured the door with a great cross-beam fastened in the jambs, so that they could not enter. And having done these things she waited.

Not long were the witches in coming back, and they raged and called for vengeance.

"Open! Open!" they screamed. "Open, feet-water!"

"I cannot," said the feet-water, "I am scattered on the ground and my path is down to the Lough."°

"Open, open, wood and tree and beam!" they cried to the door.

"I cannot," said the door, "for the beam is fixed in the jambs and I have no power to move."

"Open, open, cake that we have made and mingled with blood," they cried again.

"I cannot," said the cake, "for I am broken and bruised, and my blood is on the lips of the sleeping children."

Then the witches rushed through the air with great cries, and fled back to Slieve-namon, uttering strange curses on the Spirit of the Well, who

---

* *Fenian*, Irish.
° *Lough*, lake or a bay or inlet of the sea.

had wished their ruin; but the woman and the house were left in peace, and a mantle dropped by one of the witches in her flight was kept hung up by the mistress as a sign of the night's awful contest; and this mantle was in possession of the same family from generation to generation for five hundred years after.

In most folktale collections, evil queens, nasty stepsisters, and wicked witches abound. Too often there are two daughters, one good, one bad, and they are pitted against each other. In this story, the mother fights against female witches. I had wanted to avoid this picture of competition between women because it is so prevalent in available folktales. After all, women are remarkable models of cooperation. The first step toward developing social life in mammals was probably taken when female mammals learned to tolerate each other and cooperate with each other even though they were competing for the same resources.[19] Yet, women do compete. In analyzing the most recent evidence in primatology, Sara Blaffer Hrdy built a picture of the female primate in all her complexity. "By and large, these females are highly competitive, socially involved, and sexually assertive individuals."[20] Competition as well as cooperation are necessary parts of the female character as it has and continues to evolve.

Whuppity Stoorie

Scotland[21]

The Goodman* of Kittlerumpit was a bit of a vagabond. He went to the fair one day and was never heard of again.

When the Goodman had gone, the Goodwife° was left with little to live on. Few belongings she had, and a wee son. Everybody was sorry for her, but nobody helped her. However she had a sow, that was her consolation, for the sow was soon to farrow, and she hoped for a fine litter of piglets.

But one day, when the Wife went to the sty to fill the sow's trough, what did she find but the sow lying on her back, grunting and groaning, and ready to die.

This was a blow to the Goodwife, so she sat down on the flat knocking stone, with her bairn on her knee, and wept more sorely than she did for the loss of her Goodman.

Now, the cottage of Kittlerumpit was built on a brae,† with a fir-wood behind it. So, as the Goodwife was wiping her eyes, what did she see but a strange little old woman coming up the brae. She was dressed in green, all but a white apron, a black velvet hood, and a steeple-crowned hat on her head. She had a walking-stick as long as herself in her hand. As the Green Lady drew near, the Goodwife rose and made a curtsey.

"Madam," said she, "I'm the most unlucky woman alive."

"I don't want to hear piper's news and fiddler's tales," said the Green Lady. "I know you've lost your Goodman, and your sow is sick. Now, what will you give me if I cure her?"

"Anything you like," said the stupid Goodwife, not guessing who she had to deal with.

"Let's wet thumbs on that bargain," said the Green Lady.

So thumbs were wet, and into the sty she marched.

The Green Lady looked at the sow with a frown, and then began to mutter to herself words the Goodwife couldn't understand. They sounded like:

"Pitter patter,
Haly watter."

---

* *Goodman*, Mister.
° *Goodwife*, Mrs., Madam.
† *Brae*, hill, hillside, or the brow of a hill.

Then she took out of her pocket a wee bottle with some kind of oil in it, and rubbed the sow with it above the snout, behind the ears, and on top of the tail.

"Get up, beast," said the Green Lady. Up got the sow with a grunt, and away to her trough for her dinner.

The Goodwife of Kittlerumpit was overjoyed when she saw that.

"Now that I've cured your sick beast, let us carry out our bargain," said the Green Lady. "You'll not find me unreasonable. I always like to do a turn for small reward. All I ask, and *will* have, is that wee son in your arms."

The Goodwife gave a shriek like a stuck pig, for she now knew that the Green Lady was a fairy. So she wept, and she begged, but it was no use.

"You can spare your row," said the fairy, "shrieking as if I was as deaf as a door nail; but I can't, by the law we live by, take your bairn till the third day after this; and not then, if you can tell me my name."

With that the fairy went away down the brae and out of sight.

The Goodwife of Kittlerumpit could not sleep that night for weeping, holding her bairn so tight that she nearly squeezed the breath out of him.

The next day she went for a walk in the wood behind her cottage. Her bairn in her arms, she went far among the trees till she came to an old quarry overgrown with grass, and a bonny spring well in the middle of it. As she drew near, she heard the whirring of a spinning-wheel, and a voice singing a song. So the Wife crept quietly among the bushes, and peeped over the side of the quarry. And what did she see but the Green Lady at her spinning wheel singing:

> "Little kens our goodwife at home
> That WHUPPITY STOORIE is my name!"

"Ah, ah!" thought the Goodwife, "I've got the secret word at last!"

So she went home with a lighter heart than when she came out, and she laughed at the thought of tricking the fairy.

Now, this Goodwife was a merry woman, so she decided to have some sport with the fairy. At the appointed time she put her bairn behind the knocking stone, and sat down on it herself. She pulled her bonnet over her left ear, twisted her mouth on the other side as if she were weeping. She looked the picture of misery. Well, she hadn't long to wait, for up the brae came the fairy, neither lame nor lazy, and long before she reached the knocking stone, she skirled out:

"Goodwife of Kittlerumpit! You well know what I have come for!"

The Goodwife pretended to weep more bitterly than before, wringing her hands and falling on her knees.

"Och, dear mistress," said she, "spare my only bairn and take my sow!"

"The deil* take the sow for my share," said the fairy. "I didn't come here for swine's flesh. Don't be contrary, Goodwife, but give me your child instantly!"

"Ochon, dear lady," said the weeping Goodwife, "leave my bairn and take me!"

"The deil's in the daft° woman," said the fairy, looking like the far end of a fiddle. "I'm sure she's clean demented. Who in all the earthly world, with half an eye in their head would be bothered with the likes of you?"

This made the Goodwife of Kittlerumpit bristle, for though she had two bleary eyes, and a long red nose besides, she thought herself as bonny as the best of them. She soon got up off her knees, set her bonnet straight, and with her hands folded before her, made a curtsey to the ground.

"I might have known," said she, "that the likes of me isn't fit to tie the shoe-strings of the high and mighty fairy WHUPPITY STOORIE!"

The name made the fairy leap high. Down she came again, dump on her heels, and whirling round, she ran down the hill like an owlet chased by witches.

The Goodwife of Kittlerumpit laughed till she nearly burst. Then she took up her bairn and went into her house, singing to him all the way:

> "Coo and gurgle, my bonny wee tyke,
> You'll now have your four-houries†
> Since we've gien‡ Nick a bone to pick,
> With his wheels and his WHUPPITY STOORIES."

✾ *This story resembles "Rumplestiltskin," where the female protagonist gets bumped around from one obnoxious man to another: a bragging father, who lies that she can spin straw into gold; a greedy king, who threatens her life if she doesn't spin straw into gold; and an unscrupulous rascal, Rumplestiltskin, who spins for her only if she will give him her first-born child. Her child is only saved by happenstance when a royal messenger discovers Rumplestiltskin's name. Why didn't she do something to change the situation, like tell the king the truth? Why would she want to marry the greedy king anyway? Why on earth did she agree to give away her child?*

---

* *Deil*, devil.
° *Daft*, silly, foolish, and mad; insane.
† *Four-houries*, nap.
‡ *Gien*, given.

Why didn't she grab Rumplestiltskin by the scruff of his neck and turn him over to the king?

"Whuppity Stoorie" presents a similar problem with more plausible motivations. Poverty-stricken, abandoned by her husband, the Goodwife of Kittlerumpit must feed her child and herself. She gets no support from the community, "Everybody was sorry for her, but nobody helped her." Desperately preoccupied, she is tricked into a bad bargain without knowing what's at stake. Ultimately, the Goodwife herself, not some royal messenger, discovers the fairy's name, thus saving her child and herself.

Folktales, for all their fairies and magic, must remain true on an emotional level. They must deal with real motivations and real feelings. "Whuppity Stoorie" resonates strongly with a woman's truth when it represents the Goodwife's isolated and vulnerable position. "Whuppity Stoorie" offers encouragement when, despite the lack of support from husband or community, the Goodwife prevails.

Molly Whuppie

England[22]

Once upon a time there was a man and a wife had too many children, and they could not get meat for them, so they took the three youngest and left them in a wood. They travelled and travelled and could see never a house. It began to be dark, and they were hungry. At last they saw a light and made for it; it turned out to be a house. They knocked at the door, and a woman came to it, who said: "What do you want?" They said: "Please let us in and give us something to eat." The woman said: "I can't do that, as my man is a giant, and he would kill you if he comes home." They begged hard. "Let us stop for a little while," said they, "and we will go away before he comes." So she took them in, and set them down before the fire, and gave them milk and bread; but just as they had begun to eat a great knock came to the door, and a dreadful voice said:

> "Fee, fie, fo, fum,
> I smell the blood of some earthly one.

"Who have you there wife?" "Eh," said the wife, "it's three poor lassies cold and hungry, and they will go away. Ye won't touch 'em, man." He said nothing, but ate up a big supper, and ordered them to stay all night. Now he had three lassies of his own, and they were to sleep in the same bed with the three strangers. The youngest of the three strange lassies was called Molly Whuppie, and she was very clever. She noticed that before they went to bed the giant put straw ropes round her neck and her sisters', and round his own lassies' necks he put gold chains. So Molly took care and did not fall asleep, but waited till she was sure every one was sleeping sound. Then she slipped out of the bed, and took the straw ropes off her own and her sisters' necks, and took the gold chains off the giant's lassies. She then put the straw ropes on the giant's lassies and the gold on herself and her sisters, and lay down. And in the middle of the night up rose the giant, armed with a great club, and felt for the necks with the straw. It was dark. He took his own lassies out of bed on to the floor, and battered them until they were dead, and then lay down again, thinking he had managed fine. Molly thought it time she and her sisters were out of that, so she wakened them and told them to be quiet, and they slipped out of the house. They all got out safe, and they ran and ran, and never stopped until morning, when they saw a grand house before them. It turned out to be a king's house: so Molly went in, and told her story to the king. He said: "Well, Molly, you are a clever girl, and you have managed well; but, if you would manage better, and go back, and steal the giant's sword that hangs on the back of his bed, I would give your eldest sister my eldest son to marry." Molly said she would try. So she went back, and managed to slip into the giant's house, and crept in below the bed. The giant came home, and ate up a great supper, and went to bed. Molly waited until he was snoring, and she crept out, and reached over the giant and got down the sword; but just as she got it out over the bed it gave a rattle, and up jumped the giant, and Molly ran out at the door and the sword with her; and she ran, and he ran, till they came to the "Bridge of one hair"; and she got over, but he couldn't, and he says, "Woe worth ye, Molly Whuppie! never ye come again." And she says: "Twice yet, carle,"* quoth she, "I'll come to Spain." So Molly took the sword to the king, and her sister was married to his son.

Well, the king he says: "Ye've managed well, Molly; but if ye would manage better, and steal the purse that lies below the giant's pillow, I would marry your second sister to my second son." And Molly said she would try. So she set out for the giant's house, and slipped in, and hid again below the bed, and waited till the giant had eaten his supper, and was snoring sound asleep. She slipped out, and slipped her hand below the pillow, and got out the purse; but just as she was going out the giant wakened, and ran after her; and she ran, and he ran, till they came to the "Bridge of one hair," and she got over, but he couldn't, and he said, "Woe worth ye, Molly Whuppie! never you come again." "Once yet, carle," quoth she, "I'll come to Spain." So Molly took the purse to the king, and her second sister was married to the king's second son.

After that the king says to Molly: "Molly, you are a clever girl, but if you would do better yet, and steal the giant's ring that he wears on his finger, I will give you my youngest son for yourself." Molly said she would try. So back she goes to the giant's house, and hides herself below the bed. The giant wasn't long ere he came home and, after he had eaten a great big supper, he went to his bed, and shortly was snoring loud. Molly crept out and reached over the bed, and got hold of the giant's hand, and she pulled and she pulled until she got off the ring; but just as she got it off the giant got up, and gripped her by the hand, and he says: "Now I have catcht you, Molly Whuppie, and, if I had done as much ill to you as ye have done to me, what would ye do to me?"

---

* *Carle*, churl, boor, a base or lowbred fellow, used as a term of contempt.

Molly says: "I would put you into a sack, and I'd put the cat inside wi' you, and the dog aside you, and a needle and thread and a shears, and I'd hang you up upon the wall, and I'd go to the wood, and choose the thickest stick I could get, and I would come home, and take you down, and bang you till you were dead."

"Well, Molly," says the giant, "I'll just do that to you."

So he gets a sack, and puts Molly into it, and the cat and the dog beside her, and a needle and thread and shears, and hangs her up upon the wall, and goes to the wood to choose a stick.

Molly she sings out: "Oh, if ye saw what I see."

"Oh," says the giant's wife, "what do ye see, Molly?"

But Molly never said a word but, "Oh, if ye saw what I see!"

The giant's wife begged that Molly would take her up into the sack till she would see what Molly saw. So Molly took the shears and cut a hole in the sack, and took out the needle and thread with her, and jumpt down and helped the giant's wife up into the sack, and sewed up the hole.

The giant's wife saw nothing, and began to ask to get down again; but Molly never minded, but hid herself at the back of the door. Home came the giant, and a great big tree in his hand, and he took down the sack, and began to batter it. His wife cried, "It's me, man"; but the dog barked and the cat mewed, and he did not know his wife's voice. But Molly came out from the back of the door, and the giant saw her, and he ran after her; and he ran and she ran, till they came to the "Bridge of one hair," and she got over but he couldn't; and he said, "Woe worth you, Molly Whuppie! never you come again." "Never more, carle," quoth she, "will I come again to Spain."

So Molly took the ring to the king and she was married to his youngest son, and she never saw the giant again.

This spunky heroine captures the hearts and dreams of little girls the way her more famous male counterpart, Jack (of beanstalk fame), attracts little boys. Molly Whuppie takes charge. She rescues herself and her sisters from the dangers of the woods and the giant. To win a secure, rich home Molly returns to outwit, outdare, and outhustle the biggest, baddest giant around. And she can run like the wind!

The Treasure of Downhouse

England[23]

About half a mile to the west of the market town of Tavistock, in Devon, there stands a large farmstead called Downhouse. Although the house was rebuilt about the year 1822, the original building was considered to have been an extremely ancient place, and to have possessed a reputation for being haunted by the ghost of a very tall man.

The family who resided at Downhouse before the building was rebuilt knew by long experience the exact hour of the night at which the ghost made its appearance, and they always took great care to be in bed before the dreaded hour arrived.

Now it happened that one of the children living in the house fell desperately ill, and while the worried mother was watching anxiously by the bedside, the child asked for water. The woman quickly fetched a jug of water which was standing on a table near the bed, but the child refused to drink any of the contents of the jug, and demanded fresh water straight from the pump in the yard.

The little boy's request caused the poor woman great distress, as it was just about the time of night the ghost was in the habit of walking.

While the distracted mother was considering what course to take, the sick child again asked fretfully for fresh water from the pump, and, bravely suppressing her fear for the sake of her darling son, the woman exclaimed, "In the name of God, I will go down," and she walked swiftly from the room.

As she went down the stairs she fancied she saw a shadow following her, and then she clearly heard footsteps, and just as she reached the pump, she felt a hand on her shoulder. With a start of terror she turned round, and saw the shadowy figure of a tall man standing close behind her. Summoning up all her courage, she said to the spectre, "In the name of God, why troublest thou me?" The ghost replied, "It is well for thee that thou hast spoken to me in the name of God, this being the last time allotted to me to trouble this world, or else I should have injured thee. Now do as I tell thee, and be not afraid. Come with me and I shall direct thee to a something which shall remove this pump: under it is concealed treasure."

Whatever the "something" happened to be, when used it enabled the pump to be removed without any great difficulty, and in a cavity thus revealed a great heap of gold and silver coins!

The spectre instructed the woman to take the treasure and use it to improve the farm, and if anyone were foolish enough to molest her, or steal the money, the person concerned would suffer great misfortune.

The ghost then ordered the woman to take fresh water to her sick child, who, as a reward for the mother's great courage and firm trust in God, would soon recover from his serious illness.

Suddenly a cock crowed loudly in the farmyard, and, as though the sound were a signal that the time had come for departure, the apparition became less distinct, rose slowly into the air, and, after assuming the shape of a small bright cloud, gradually disappeared.

When I had my children, I left my career and became a stay-at-home mom. I felt a great sense of achievement and pleasure as I learned to care for my babies. At the same time, from the world outside my home, I experienced a violent drop in prestige. People who previously might have listened attentively, turned on their heels and left me in mid-sentence once they found out that I was "just" a mother. This heroic mother is the first of several in this anthology. The setting is commonplace—a home. The situation is commonplace—a mother up at night with her sick child. This story epitomizes the quotidian courage at the root of every mother's life.

The Hand of Glory

England[24]

One evening, between the years 1790 and 1800, a traveller dressed in woman's clothing arrived at the Old Spital Inn, the place where the mail coach changed horses in High Spital, on Bowes Moor. The traveller begged to stay all night, but had to go away so early in the morning, that if a mouthful of food were set ready for breakfast, there was no need the family should be disturbed by her departure. The people of the house, however, arranged that a servant-maid should sit up till the stranger was out of the premises, and then went to bed themselves.

The girl lay down for a nap on the long settle by the fire, but before she shut her eyes, she took a good look at the traveller, who was sitting on the opposite side of the hearth, and espied a pair of men's trousers peeping out from under the gown. All inclination for sleep was now gone; however, with great self-command, she feigned it, closed her eyes, and even began to snore.

On this, the traveller got up, pulled out of his pocket a dead man's hand, fitted a candle to it, lighted the candle, and passed hand and candle several times before the servant-girl's face, saying as he did so, "Let those who are asleep be asleep, and let those who are awake be awake." This done, he placed the light on the table, opened the outer door, went down two or three steps which led from the house to the road, and began to whistle for his companions.

The girl (who had hitherto had presence of mind to remain perfectly quiet) now jumped up, rushed behind the ruffian, and pushed him down the steps. Then she shut the door, locked it, and ran upstairs to try to wake the family, but without success; calling, shouting, and shaking were alike in vain. The poor girl was in despair, for she heard the traveller and his comrades outside the house. So she ran down and seized a bowl of blue [i.e., skimmed milk] and threw it over the hand and candle; after which she went upstairs again, and awoke the sleepers without any difficulty. The landlord's son went to the window, and asked the men outside what they wanted. They answered that if the dead man's hand were but given to them, they would go away quietly, and do no harm to anyone.

This he refused, and fired among them, and the shot must have taken effect, for in the morning stains of blood were traced to a considerable distance.

This story does not revolve around the reward of marriage for the heroine. The repetition of a limited number of heroine's tales has left us with the feeling that all stories must end with a beautiful girl's marriage to her Prince Charming. With a wider range of female characters, each story can focus on the special part of the heroine's life that best exemplifies her particular strength. One evening this servant-maid exercises her keen observation, great self-command, and her ability to think under pressure. She saves herself, the household, and all the other people whom the robbers would have harmed using the dead man's hand.

Tamlane

England[25]

Young Tamlane was son of Earl Murray, and Burd Janet* was daughter of Dunbar, Earl of March. And when they were young they loved one another and plighted their troth. But when the time came near for their marrying, Tamlane disappeared, and none knew what had become of him.

Many, many days after he had disappeared, Burd Janet was wandering in Carterhaugh Wood, though she had been warned not to go there. And as she wandered she plucked the flowers from the bushes. She came at last to a bush of broom and began plucking it. She had not taken more than three flowerets when by her side up started young Tamlane.

"Where come ye from, Tamlane, Tamlane?" Burd Janet said; "and why have you been away so long?"

"From Elfland I come," said young Tamlane. "The Queen of Elfland has made me her knight."

"But how did you get there, Tamlane?" said Burd Janet.

"I was a-hunting one day, and as I rode widershins° round yon hill, a deep drowsiness fell upon, and when I awoke, behold! I was in Elfland. Fair is that land and gay, and fain would I stop but for thee and one other thing. Every seven years the Elves pay their tithe to the Nether world, and for all the Queen makes much of me, I fear it is myself that will be the tithe."

"Oh can you not be saved? Tell me if aught I can do will save you, Tamlane?"

"One only thing is there for my safety. Tomorrow night is Hallowe'en, and the fairy court will then ride through England and Scotland, and if you would borrow me from Elfland you must take your stand by Miles Cross between twelve and one o' the night, and with holy water in your hand you must cast a compass all around you."

"But how shall I know you, Tamlane," quoth Burd Janet, "amid so many knights I've ne'er seen before?"

"The first court of Elves that come by let pass, let pass. The next court you shall pay reverence to, but do naught nor say aught. But the third

---

* *Burd*, a (now obsolete) poetic word for woman, lady, and later, maiden.

° *Widershins*, (usually withershins) in a direction opposite to the usual, or in a direction contrary to the course of the sun, considered as unlucky.

40

court that comes by is the chief court of them, and at the head rides the Queen of all Elfland. And by her side I shall ride upon a milk white steed with a star in my crown; they give me this honour as being a christened knight. Watch my hands, Janet, the right one will be gloved but the left one will be bare, and by that token you will know me."

"But how to save you, Tamlane?" quoth Burd Janet.

"You must spring upon me suddenly, and I will fall to the ground. Then seize me quick, and whatever change befall me, for they will exercise all their magic on me, cling hold to me till they turn me into red-hot iron. Then cast me into this pool and I will be turned back into a mother-naked man. Cast then your green mantle over me, and I shall be yours, and be of the world again."

So Burd Janet promised to do all for Tamlane, and next night at midnight she took her stand by Miles Cross and cast a compass round her with holy water.

Soon there came riding by the Elfin court, first over the mound went a troop on black steeds, and then another troop on brown. But in the third court, all on milk white steeds, she saw the Queen of Elfland and by her side a knight with a star in his crown with right hand gloved and the left bare. Then she knew this was her own Tamlane, and springing forward she seized the bridle of the milk-white steed and pulled its rider down. And as soon as he had touched the ground she let go the bridle and seized him in her arms.

"He's won, he's won amongst us all," shrieked out the eldritch* crew, and all came around her and tried their spells on young Tamlane.

First they turned him in Janet's arms like frozen ice, then into a huge flame of roaring fire. Then, again, the fire vanished and an adder was skipping through her arms, but still she held on; and then they turned him into a snake that reared up as if to bite her, and yet she held on. Then suddenly a dove was struggling in her arms, and almost flew away. Then they turned him into a swan, but all was in vain, till at last he was changed into a redhot glaive,° and this she cast into a well of water and then he turned back into a mother-naked man. She quickly cast her green mantle over him, and young Tamlane was Burd Janet's for ever.

Then sang the Queen of Elfland as the court turned away and began to resume its march.

> "She that has borrowed young Tamlane
> Has gotten a stately groom,

* *Eldritch*, weird, eerie, uncanny.
° *Glaive*, halberd or sword.

She's taken away my bonniest knight
Left nothing in his room.

"But had I known, Tamlane, Tamlane,
A lady would borrow thee,
I'd hae ta'en out thy two grey eyne,*
Put in two eyne of tree.

"Had I but known, Tamlane, Tamlane,
Before five came from home,
I'd hae ta'en out thy heart o' flesh,
Put in a heart of stone.

"Had I but had the wit yestreen°
That I have got to-day,
I'd paid the Fiend seven times his teind†
Ere you'd been won away."

And then the Elfin court rode away, and Burd Janet and young
Tamlane went their way homewards and were soon after married after
young Tamlane had again been sained‡ by the holy water and made
Christian once more.

*"Tamlane" is a good example of how the telling of a tale can strengthen or
weaken the heroine. In this story, the male character's instruction about how he
can be rescued takes precedence over the heroine's actually doing the rescuing. One is
even hard-pressed to remember the heroine's name because the title "Tamlane" focuses
the reader's attention on her lover and not on the brave young woman, Burd Janet. Yet
Janet performs a hair-raising rescue. She braves the spirits that wander the world on
Halloween. She sums up the strongest sort of determination when she believes her heart
and not her eyes. Janet clasps her lover to her though he's turned to ice that freezes, roaring fire that burns, and a snake that rears up as if to bite her. Janet holds on tenaciously until she breaks the fairies' power and rescues her beloved.*

---

* *Eyne*, eyes.
° *Yestreen*, yesterday.
† *Teind*, tithe, a tenth of earnings paid in support of the church.
‡ *Sained*, blessed.

The Night Troll

Iceland[26]

On a certain farm, whoever stayed at home to mind the house on Christmas Eve while the others were at Evensong* used to be found next morning either dead or out of his mind. The servants there thought this very bad, and few wanted to be the one to stay at home on Christmas Eve. On one occasion a young girl offered to mind the farm; the others were delighted, and went off. The girl sat in the main room, and sang to a child which she held in her arms.

During the course of the night someone comes to the window, and says:

> Fair seems your hand to me,
> Hard and rough mine must be,
> Dilly-dilly-do.

Then says she:

> Dirt did it never sweep,
> Sleep, little Kari, sleep,
> Lully-lully-lo.

Then the voice at the window says:

> Fair seem your eyes to me,
> Hard and rough mine must be,
> Dilly-dilly-do.

Then says she:

> Evil they never saw,
> Sleep, Kari, sleep once more,
> Lully-lully-lo.

Then the voice at the window says:

> Fair seem your feet to me,
> Hard and rough mine must be,
> Dilly-dilly-do.

Then says she:

* *Evensong*, vespers, evening prayer.

Dirt did they never crush,
Hush, little Kari, hush,
Lully-lully-lo.

Then the voice at the window says:

Day in the east I see,
Hard and rough mine must be,
Dilly-dilly-do.

Then says she:

Stand there and turn to stone,
So you'll do harm to none,
Lully-lully-lo.

Then the uncanny creature vanished from the window. But in the morning when the people came home, a huge stone had appeared in the path between the farm buildings, and it has stood there ever since. Then the girl spoke of what she had heard—but she had seen nothing, for she never once looked round—and it must have been a Night-Troll which had come to the window.

This self-possessed young girl has the courage to mind the farm on Christmas Eve knowing that the possible consequence is death. Without the slightest sign of fear she creates an invincible haven in the room. The fire crackles as a log slips, the child turns a warm cheek to nestle against the girl's arm, the lilt of the lullaby pauses in the air. The heroine turns her back on, excludes, never even looks at her adversary. She has the steely sang-froid to parry each of the troll's deadly challenges with an impromptu rhyming verse of her own. Equally as important, she gets in the last word. "Stand there and turn to stone / So you'll do harm to none."

Especially in northern Europe, this ability to speak in rhyme was a highly effective weapon for confronting supernatural creatures like night-trolls, trolls which turn to stone when exposed to daylight.

The Grateful Elfwoman

Iceland[27]

A peasant's wife once dreamed that a woman came to her bedside, whom she knew to be a Huldukona (elfwoman) and who begged her to give her milk for her child, two quarts a day, for the space of a month, placing it always in a part of the house which she pointed out. The good-wife promised to do so, and remembered her promise when she awoke. So she put a milkbowl every morning in the place which the other had chosen, and left it there, always on her return finding it empty. This went on for a month; and at the end of the month she dreamed that the same woman came to her, thanked her for her kindness, and begged her to accept the belt which she should find in the bed when she awoke, and then vanished. In the morning the goodwife found beneath her pillow, a silver belt, beautifully and rarely wrought, the promised gift of the grateful elfwoman.

An unassuming peasant woman responds to a call for help and sets out a bowl of milk every day. She is no illustrious, muscular warrior. Her act requires charity of spirit and regularity. Is this heroic?

In my search for folktales with heroines, I found women with heroic qualities like strength, courage, intelligence. There were other women whom I instinctively knew to be heroines, but they refused to be classified as heroic in the traditional sense of the word. They performed simple acts, like the steadfast regularity with which this peasant woman put out the milk. They operated on a subtle, not a grandiose scale—this peasant woman saved the life of a child not by killing a dragon, but by her willingness to respond to a mother in need. These women represent a new class of heroines, heroines of an intimate world, like this woman who kept her promise to a dream.

"My Jon's Soul"

Iceland[28]

There were once an old cottager and his wife who lived together. The old man was rather quarrelsome and disagreeable, and, what's more, he was lazy and useless about the house; his old woman was not at all pleased about it, and she would often grumble at him and say the only thing he was any good at was squandering what she had scraped together—for she herself was constantly at work and tried by hook or by crook to earn what they needed, and was always good at getting her own way with anybody she had to deal with. But even if they did not agree about some things, the old woman loved her husband dearly and never let him go short.

Now things went on the same way for a long time, but one day the old man fell sick and it was obvious that he was in a bad way. The old woman was sitting up with him, and when he grew weaker, it occurred to her that he could hardly be very well prepared for death, and that this meant there was some doubt as to whether he would be allowed to enter Heaven. So she thinks to herself that the best plan will be for her to try and put her husband's soul on the right road herself. Then she took a small bag and held it over her husband's nose and mouth, so that when the breath of life leaves him it passes into this bag, and she ties it up at once. Then off she goes towards Heaven, carrying the bag in her apron, comes to the borders of the Kingdom of Heaven and knocks on the door.

Out comes Saint Peter, and asks what her business may be.

"A very good morning to you, sir," says the old woman. "I've come here with the soul of that Jon of mine you'll have heard tell of him, most likely—and now I'm wanting to ask you to let him in."

"Yes, yes, yes," says Peter, "but unfortunately I can't. I have indeed heard tell of that Jon of yours, but I never heard good of him yet."

Then the old woman said: "Well, really, Saint Peter, I'd never have believed it, that you could be so hard-hearted. You must be forgetting what happened to you in the old days, when you denied your Master."

At that, Peter went back in and shut the door, and the old woman remained outside, sighing bitterly. But when a little time has passed, she knocks on the door again, and out comes Saint Paul. She greets him and asks him his name, and he tells her who he is. Then she pleads with him for the soul of her Jon—but he said he didn't want to hear another word from her about that, and said that her Jon deserved no mercy.

Then the old woman got angry, and said: "It's all very well for you, Paul! I suppose you deserved mercy in the old days, when you were persecuting God and men! I reckon I'd better stop asking any favours from you."

So now Paul shuts the door as fast as he can. But when the old woman knocks for the third time, out comes the Blessed Virgin Mary.

"Hail, most blessed Lady," says the old woman. "I do hope you'll allow that Jon of mine in, even though that Peter and Paul won't allow it."

"It's a great pity, my dear," says Mary, "but I daren't, because he really was such a brute, that Jon of yours."

"Well, I can't blame you for that," says the old woman. "But all the same, I did think you would know that other people can have their little weaknesses as well as you—or have you forgotten by now that you once had a baby, and no father for it?"

Mary would hear no more, but shut the door as fast as she could.

For the fourth time, the old woman knocks on the door. Then out comes Christ himself, and asks what she's doing there.

Then she spoke very humbly: "I wanted to beg you, my dear Saviour, to let this poor wretch's soul warm itself near the door."

"It's that Jon," answered Christ. "No, woman; he had no faith in Me."

Just as He said this He was about to shut the door, but the old woman was not slow, far from it—she flung the bag with the soul in it right past Him, so that it hurtled far into the halls of Heaven, but then the door was slammed and bolted.

Then a great weight was lifted from the old woman's heart when Jon got into the Kingdom of Heaven in spite of everything, and she went home happy; and we know nothing more about her, nor about what became of Jon's soul after that.

What a tough and quick-witted old woman this is! She has the courage to speak up even if she is talking to Peter, Paul, and Mary. And when she speaks up, she doesn't beat about the bush. Instead of rationalizing and making excuses for Jon's bad behavior, she reminds the saints of their own human failings. She ties them to Jon in a way they'd rather forget. When her appeal to a common humanity fails, she determinedly knocks once more and outmaneuvers Christ by whipping that soul-in-the-bag past the pearly gates.

The Ghost at Fjelkinge

Sweden[29]

During the early half of the seventeenth century many of the best estates in Skåne* belonged to the family of Barkenow, or more correctly, to the principal representative of the family, Madame Margaretta Barkenow, daughter of the renowned general and governor-general, Count Rutger Von Ascheberg, and wife of Colonel Kjell Kristofer Barkenow.

A widow at twenty-nine, she took upon herself the management of her many estates, in the conduct of which she ever manifested an indomitable, indefatigable energy, and a never-ceasing care for her numerous dependents.

On a journey over her estates, Madame Margaretta came, one evening, to Fjelkinge's inn, and persisted in sleeping in a room which was called the "ghost's room." A traveler had, a few years before, slept in this room, and as it was supposed had been murdered, at least the man and his effects had disappeared, leaving no trace of what had become of them. After this his ghost appeared in the room nightly, and those who were acquainted with the circumstance, traveled to the next post, in the dark, rather than choose such quarters for the night. Margaretta was, however, not among this number. She possessed greater courage, and without fear chose the chamber for her sleeping room.

After her evening prayers she retired to bed and sleep, leaving the lamp burning. At twelve o'clock she was awakened by the lifting up of two boards in the floor, and from the opening a bloody form appeared, with a cloven head hanging upon its shoulders.

"Noble lady," whispered the apparition, "I beg you prepare, for a murdered man, a resting place in consecrated ground, and speed the murderer to his just punishment."

Pure in heart, therefore not alarmed, Lady Margaretta beckoned the apparition to come nearer, which it did, informing her that it had entreated others, who after the murder had slept in the room, but that none had the courage to comply. Then Lady Margaretta took from her finger a gold ring, laid it in the gaping wound, and bound the apparition's head up with her pocket handkerchief. With a glance of unspeakable thank-

---

* *Skåne*, region at the southernmost tip of Sweden.

fulness the ghost revealed the name of the murderer and disappeared noiselessly beneath the floor.

The following morning Lady Margaretta instructed the bailiff of the estate to assemble the people at the post house, where she informed them what had happened during the night, and commanded that the planks of the floor be taken up. Here, under the ground, was discovered a half decomposed corpse, with the countess's ring in the hole in its skull, and her handkerchief bound around its head.

At sight of this, one of those present grew pale and fainted to the ground. Upon being revived he confessed that he had murdered the traveler and robbed him of his goods. He was condemned to death for his crime, and the murdered man received burial in the parish churchyard.

The ring, which is peculiarly formed and set with a large grayish chased stone, remains even now in the keeping of the Barkenow family, and is believed to possess miraculous powers in sickness, against evil spirits and other misfortunes. When one of the family dies it is said that a red, bloodlike spot appears upon the stone.

Madame Margaretta Barkenow is the competent and respected manager of many estates. She manages effectively and energetically but still tenderly. Margaretta has courage and gives orders, but she also binds up the ghost's head wound with her pocket handkerchief. Would a rich lord or male corporate executive do that?

Little Red Cap

Germany[30]

Once upon a time there was a sweet little girl. Everyone who saw her loved her, especially her grandmother who just couldn't give the child enough. Her grandmother once gave her a little cap of red velvet. It suited her so well and she wore it so often, she was called Little Red Cap.

One day her mother said to her, "Come, Little Red Cap, here is a piece of cake and a bottle of wine. Take them over to Grandmother. She is sick and weak and they will make her feel better. Be good, be polite, and say hello from me. Go the way you're supposed to and don't leave the path, or you'll fall and break the bottle and Grandmother will have nothing." Little Red Cap promised to be good.

The grandmother lived in the forest, half an hour from the village. In the woods a wolf came up to Little Red Cap. She didn't know what an evil animal he was and she wasn't afraid of him.

"Good day, Little Red Cap."

"Thank you and you too, Wolf."

"Where are you going so early, Little Red Cap?"

"To grandmother's house."

"What are you carrying under your apron?"

"My grandmother is sick and weak. To help her get stronger I'm taking her some wine and some cake we baked yesterday."

"Little Red Cap, where does your grandmother live?"

"Further into the forest another fifteen minutes or so. Her house is next to some hazelnut bushes under the three large oak trees. Surely you know the place," said Little Red Cap.

The wolf thought to himself, This is my lucky day! But how can I manage this so that I trap her. He said, "Little Red Cap, haven't you seen how lovely the flowers are here in the woods? Why aren't you looking around? Why, I don't think you even hear how sweetly the little birds are singing. You're marching straight ahead as if you were going to school in the village, but it's so beautiful out here in the forest."

Little Red Cap opened up her eyes and saw how the sunbeams broke through between the trees and beautiful flowers blossomed everywhere. She thought, If I brought Grandmother a bouquet of fresh flowers, she'd like that. It's so early in the day, I'll still arrive in plenty of time. She ran into the forest and searched for flowers. As she picked one flower, it seemed that another prettier one was growing further off and she ran to pick that one, going deeper, always deeper into the forest. The wolf, however, went straight to the grandmother's house and knocked on the door.

"Who is there?"

"It's Little Red Cap. I'm bringing you cake and wine, let me in."

"Just push the handle down," called the grandmother, "I am too weak and can't get up."

The wolf pushed the handle down. The door swung open. He entered, went straight to the grandmother's bed and swallowed her up. He then put on her clothes, put on her cap, lay in her bed and pulled the curtains closed.

Little Red Cap skipped here and there picking flowers. She picked flowers until she had so many she couldn't hold any more. Only after that did she set off toward grandmother's house. Little Red Cap found it odd that the door stood open. As she stepped into the room, it seemed so eerie she thought, Oh, my goodness, how frightened I feel and usually I love to be with Grandmother! Little Red Cap went to the bed and pulled back the curtains. There lay the grandmother with her cap pulled low over her face. She looked so strange. "Oh, Grandmother, what big ears you have!"

"The better to hear you with."

"Oh, Grandmother, what big eyes you have!"

"The better to see you with."

"Oh, Grandmother, what big hands you have!"

"The better to grab you with!"

"But, Grandmother, what a horribly big mouth you have!"

"The better to eat you with!" At that the wolf leaped out of the bed and swallowed poor Little Red Cap.

Satisfied, the wolf lay back down in bed, fell asleep and began to snore very loudly. A hunter walked past the house and thought, How the old woman is snoring! I'd better see if she's okay. He stepped into the room and walked over to the bed. There he saw the wolf he'd long been searching for. The hunter thought, The wolf's definitely eaten the grandmother, but maybe she can still be saved, I won't shoot. Then, he took some scissors and cut open the wolf's stomach. After he had made a couple of snips, he saw a little red cap shining, a few more snips and the girl sprang out and shouted, "Oh, how frightened I was. How dark it was inside the wolf's body!" Then the old grandmother also came out alive.

Little Red Cap fetched large, heavy stones to put into the wolf's stomach. When the wolf awoke, he tried to leap up and run away but the stones were so heavy that he fell right back down dead. Then all three were happy. The hunter took the wolf's skin. The grandmother ate the cake and drank the wine which Little Red Cap had brought. Little Red Cap thought, Never again will I go off the path and run into the forest all alone when Mother has forbidden it.

It is also said that Little Red Cap took cake to her old grandmother again. When another wolf spoke to her and wanted to lure her off the path, Little Red Cap was on her guard. She walked straight ahead. She told her grandmother that she had seen a wolf. He had wished her good day, but his eyes had stared so wickedly that, "If I hadn't been out in the open on the road, he would have gobbled me up."

"Come," said the grandmother, "We'll lock the door, so he can't get in."

Shortly thereafter the wolf knocked on the door and called out, "Open up Grandmother, it's Little Red Cap. I'm bringing you some cake."

The grandmother and Little Red Cap kept still and didn't open the door. Then the wicked wolf prowled around the house a few times and finally leaped up onto the roof. He planned to wait until Little Red Cap went home in the evening. Then he would sneak after her and, in the darkness, devour her. However, the grandmother knew what the wolf had in mind.

Now, in front of the house stood a large stone trough. "Get the bucket, Little Red Cap. Yesterday I cooked sausages. Carry the water in which they were cooked and pour it into the trough." Little Red Cap carried water until the big, big trough was completely full. The aroma of sausages wafted up into the wolf's nose. He sniffed and peered down. Finally he stretched so far out that he could no longer hold on and he began to slip. He slid down off the roof into the large trough and he drowned. Then Little Red Cap went home safely and merrily.

This version of "Little Red Riding Hood" keeps the ending from the first edition of Grimms' Kinder und Hausmärchen *(1812) where Little Red Cap goes through the woods a second time. This time, she recognizes the danger and doesn't speak to the wolf. She asks her grandmother's advice. She carries water until the big, big trough is completely full. These paragraphs change Little Red Riding Hood from a victim into a heroine. This Little Red Riding Hood is different from the others who just get eaten and rescued and admonished not to talk to strangers. In the complete Grimms' folktale, Little Red Cap goes home "safely and merrily" not because the hunter rescues her, but because she has learned to recognize and deal with danger.*

One of the strengths of oral literature is that over centuries the stories are worked out between the storytellers and the audiences. Once folktales are written down, an editor can change details, story lines, and even story endings, to conform to the editor's ideas without reference to the audience. In the case of Grimms' "Little Red Cap," editor after editor of children's books has chosen not to include the Grimms' ending. In the twenty different picture book editions in seventy libraries in my local area, not one included the key ending paragraphs. To a male editor, this ending might seem like an anti-climax since he's already eaten the grandmother and Little Red Riding Hood and then rescued them as the hunter. Maybe female editors were too used to the story as they had heard it in their own childhood. When I told my three-year-old daughter the complete Grimms' story, she was so excited she acted out many times the way Little Red Riding Hood confidently walked past the second wolf without speaking to him. This is precisely the part that has been edited out! To a live, vocal, female, three-year-old audience, this ending made all the difference.[31]

The Wood Maiden

Czechoslovakia[32]

Betushka was a little girl. Her mother was a poor widow with nothing but a tumble-down cottage and two little nanny-goats. But poor as they were Betushka was always cheerful. From spring till autumn she pastured the goats in the birch wood. Every morning when she left home her mother gave her a little basket with a slice of bread and a spindle.

"See that you bring home a full spindle," her mother always said.

Betushka had no distaff, so she wound the flax around her head. Then she took the little basket and went romping and singing behind the goats to the birch wood. When they got there she sat down under a tree and pulled the fibers of the flax from her head with her left hand, and with her right hand let down the spindle so that it went humming along the ground. All the while she sang until the woods echoed and the little goats nibbled away at the leaves and grass.

When the sun showed midday, she put the spindle aside, called the goats and gave them a mouthful of bread so that they wouldn't stray, and ran off into the woods to hunt berries or any other wild fruit that was in season. Then when she had finished her bread and fruit, she jumped up, folded her arms, and danced and sang.

The sun smiled at her through the green of the trees and the little goats, resting on the grass, thought: "What a merry little shepherdess we have!"

After her dance she went back to her spinning and worked industriously. In the evening when she got home her mother never had to scold her because the spindle was empty.

One day at noon just after she had eaten and, as usual, was going to dance, there suddenly stood before her a most beautiful maiden. She was dressed in white gauze that was fine as a spider's web. Long golden hair fell down to her waist and on her head she wore a wreath of woodland flowers.

Betushka was speechless with surprise and alarm.

The maiden smiled at her and said in a sweet voice:

"Betushka, do you like to dance?"

Her manner was so gracious that Betushka no longer felt afraid, and answered:

"Oh, I could dance all day long!"

"Come, then, let us dance together," said the maiden. "I'll teach you."

With that she tucked up her skirt, put her arm about Betushka's waist, and they began to dance. At once such enchanting music sounded over their heads that Betushka's heart went one-two with the dancing. The musicians sat on the branches of the birch trees. They were clad in little frock coats, black and gray and many-colored. It was a carefully chosen orchestra that had gathered at the bidding of the beautiful maiden: larks, nightingales, finches, linnets, thrushes, blackbirds, and showy mocking-birds.

Betushka's cheeks burned, her eyes shone. She forgot her spinning, she forgot her goats. All she could do was gaze at her partner who was moving with such grace and lightness that the grass didn't seem to bend under her slender feet.

They danced from noon till sundown and yet Betushka wasn't the least bit tired. Then they stopped dancing, the music ceased, and the maiden disappeared as suddenly as she had come.

Betushka looked around. The sun was sinking behind the wood. She put her hands to the unspun flax on her head and remembered the spindle that was lying unfilled on the grass. She took down the flax and laid it with the spindle in the little basket. Then she called the goats and started home.

She reproached herself bitterly that she had allowed the beautiful maiden to beguile her and she told herself that another time she would not listen to her. She was so quiet that the little goats, missing her merry song, looked around to see whether it was really their own little shepherdess who was following them. Her mother, too, wondered why she didn't sing and questioned her.

"Are you sick, Betushka?"

"No, dear mother, I'm not sick, but I've been singing too much and my throat is dry."

She knew that her mother did not reel the yarn at once, so she hid the spindle and the unspun flax, hoping to make up tomorrow what she had not done today. She did not tell her mother one word about the beautiful maiden.

The next day she felt cheerful again and as she drove the goats to pasture she sang merrily. At the birch wood she sat down to her spinning, singing all the while, for with a song on the lips work falls from the hands more easily.

Noonday came. Betushka gave a bit of bread to each of the goats and ran off to the woods for her berries. Then she ate her luncheon.

"Ah, my little goats," she sighed, as she brushed up the crumbs for the birds, "I mustn't dance today."

"Why mustn't you dance today?" a sweet voice asked, and there stood the beautiful maiden as though she had fallen from the clouds.

Betushka was worse frightened than before and she closed her eyes tight. When the maiden repeated her question, Betushka answered timidly:

"Forgive me, beautiful lady, for not dancing with you. If I dance with you I cannot spin my stint and then my mother will scold me. Today before the sun sets I must make up for what I lost yesterday."

"Come, child, and dance," the maiden said. "Before the sun sets we'll find some way of getting that spinning done!"

She tucked up her skirt, put her arm about Betushka, the musicians in the treetops struck up, and off they whirled. The maiden danced more beautifully than ever. Betushka couldn't take her eyes from her. She forgot her goats, she forgot her spinning. All she wanted to do was to dance on forever.

At sundown the maiden paused and the music stopped. Then Betushka, clasping her hands to her head, where the unspun flax was twined, burst into tears. The beautiful maiden took the flax from her head, wound it round the stem of a slender birch, grasped the spindle, and began to spin. The spindle hummed along the ground and filled in no time. Before the sun sank behind the woods all the flax was spun, even that which was left over from the day before. The maiden handed Betushka the full spindle and said:

"Remember my words:

> Reel and grumble not!
> Reel and grumble not!"

When she said this, she vanished as if the earth had swallowed her.

Betushka was very happy now and she thought to herself on her way home: "Since she is so good and kind, I'll dance with her again if she asks me. Oh, how I hope she does!"

She sang her merry little song as usual and the goats trotted cheerfully along.

She found her mother vexed with her, for she had wanted to reel yesterday's yarn and had discovered that the spindle was not full.

"What were you doing yesterday," she scolded, "that you didn't spin your stint?"

Betushka hung her head. "Forgive me, mother. I danced too long." Then she showed her mother today's spindle and said: "See, today I more than made up for yesterday."

Her mother said no more but went to milk the goats and Betushka put away the spindle. She wanted to tell her mother her adventure, but she thought to herself: "No, I'll wait. If the beautiful lady comes again, I'll ask her who she is and then I'll tell mother." So she said nothing.

On the third morning she drove the goats as usual to the birch wood. The goats went to pasture and Betushka, sitting down under a tree, began to spin and sing. When the sun pointed to noon, she laid her spindle on the grass, gave the goats a mouthful of bread, gathered some strawberries, ate her luncheon, and then, giving the crumbs to the birds, she said cheerily:

"Today, my little goats, I will dance for you!"

She jumped up, folded her arms, and was about to see whether she could move as gracefully as the beautiful maiden, when the maiden herself stood before her.

"Let us dance together," she said. She smiled at Betushka, put her arm about her, and as the music above their heads began to play, they whirled round and round with flying feet. Again Betushka forgot the spindle and the goats. Again she saw nothing but the beautiful maiden whose body was lithe as a willow shoot. Again she heard nothing but the enchanting music to which her feet danced of themselves.

They danced from noon till sundown. Then the maiden paused and the music ceased. Betushka looked around. The sun was already set behind the woods. She clasped her hands to her head and looking down at the unfilled spindle she burst into tears.

"Oh, what will my mother say?" she cried.

"Give me your little basket," the maiden said, and I will put something in it that will more than make up for today's stint."

Betushka handed her the basket and the maiden took it and vanished. In a moment she was back. She returned the basket and said:

"Look not inside until you're home!
Look not inside until you're home!"

As she said these words she was gone as if a wind had blown her away.

Betushka wanted awfully to peep inside but she was afraid to. The basket was so light that she wondered whether there was anything at all in it. Was the lovely lady only fooling her? Halfway home she peeped in to see.

Imagine her feelings when she found the basket was full of birch leaves! Then indeed did Betushka burst into tears and reproach herself for being so simple. In her vexation she threw out a handful of leaves and was going to empty the basket when she thought to herself:

"No, I'll keep what's left as litter for the goats."

She was almost afraid to go home. She was so quiet that again the little goats wondered what ailed their shepherdess.

Her mother was waiting for her in great excitement.

"For heaven's sake, Betushka, what kind of a spool did you bring home yesterday?"

"Why?" Betushka faltered.

"When you went away this morning I started to reel that yarn. I reeled and reeled and the spool remained full. One skein, two skeins, three skeins, and still the spool was full. 'What evil spirit has spun that?' I cried out impatiently, and instantly the yarn disappeared from the spindle as if blown away. Tell me, what does it mean?"

So Betushka confessed and told her mother all she knew about the beautiful maiden.

"Oh," cried her mother in amazement, "that was a wood maiden! At noon and midnight the wood maidens dance. It is well you are not a little boy or she might have danced you to death! But they are often kind to little girls and sometimes make them rich presents. Why didn't you tell me? If I hadn't grumbled, I could have had yarn enough to fill the house!"

Betushka thought of the little basket and wondered if there might be something under the leaves. She took out the spindle and unspun flax and looked in once more.

"Mother!" she cried. "Come here and see!"

Her mother looked and clapped her hands. The birch leaves were all turned to gold!

Betushka reproached herself bitterly: "She told me not to look inside until I got home, but I didn't obey."

"It's lucky you didn't empty the whole basket," her mother said.

The next morning she herself went to look for the handful of leaves that Betushka had thrown away. She found them still lying in the road but they were only birch leaves.

But the riches which Betushka brought home were enough. Her mother bought a farm with fields and cattle. Betushka had pretty clothes and no longer had to pasture goats.

But no matter what she did, no matter how cheerful and happy she was, still nothing ever again gave her quite so much pleasure as the dance with the wood maiden. She often went to the birch wood in the hope of seeing the maiden again. But she never did.

I watch my little girls dance. They skip and march. They tumble. One spins as fast as she can, arms outstretched then falls with a plop and a laugh to the floor. When I give them scarves, they twirl them, make them float in the air, wrap them around waists, arms, ankles; one tucks the pink sequined scarf into her pants and crawls on all fours like a cat. They know how to have fun. As they grow older, we teach children what we have learned from history, novels, and the evening news—to view life as one obstacle after another. Little Red Riding Hood goes off the path to pick the lovely flowers and she is eaten by a wolf.

However, in "The Wood Maiden," the heroine is rewarded for going off the path. Her spinning, her duty, and her work forgotten, Betushka is rewarded for her joyful impluse to dance. Dance in the rain, dance in the sunlight, dare to expect joy in your life.

The Child Who Was Poor and Good

Greece[33]

Once upon a time there was a poor woman who had four girl-children. To raise them, the unhappy creature went out to work. A harder worker you could not have wished to find, but even so, her daily wage all went on food. She was barely able to earn enough to purchase their daily bread. She had to let them go about unclad and unshod, for there was not a mite left over to buy them clothes. If ever some good Christian dame were to give her some old, worn garment, she would make it over for the eldest, and then would cut it down to fit the second and the third. For the fourth and littlest girl nothing remained. Winter and summer she went about in only a ragged little shirt, barefoot and barechested.

One year, the winter was severe with rain, cold, and snow! The unhappy fourth child shivered and could not get warm. At last, she said to her mother: "Mother, I must leave this place and go and find another mother who can make me a little garment now and then. I shall die if I stay here longer. I cannot go on with only this little shirt to wear."

So the child left her home and walked and walked. On the road she found a little bird under a tree. The bird was young and featherless, and it had fallen from the nest. Little squawks came from its beak for it had not the strength to fly back up the tree and would die down on the ground. The child was sorry for it. She took it in her little hands and warmed it between her palms. She looked about her, and when she saw a man coming along the road, she asked him to put the bird back in the nest. And so it was she who saved it.

The child again went along her way and passed amid some branches. She saw a spider spinning its web, up and down, back and forth, the web growing and growing the while, you might have thought there was some great haste about it.

The child halted, and said, "I will not break the web, but go round the other way, so as not to grieve the spider."

The spider said, "Thank you, my good child. What would you have me do for you in return for your kindness to me? Where are you going, all unclad and barefoot?"

"I am going to find some cloth and take it to my mother to make me a little garment, for I am cold."

"Go, then," said the spider to the child, "and on your return, come this way again and tell me what I can give you in my fashion."

So the child went on, and farther away she came across a bramble. As she tried to go past it, her little shirt caught on its thorns and was torn to shreds, so that she was mother-naked. The poor child fell to crying—it would have broken your heart to see and hear her.

Her sobs were heard by a lamb that was grazing in the meadow a little way off.

The lamb said to the child, "What ails you, child? Why do you weep? Have you had a whipping?"

"Oh," wailed the child. "I was going to find a little garment to keep me warm, and as I was going past the bramble it tore my little shirt to shreds and left me mother-naked."

So the lamb asked the bramble, "Wherefore did you this harm? What is to become of the child now?"

"Give her some of your wool and I will card it. Let her give it to her mother to make her something to wear, for wool will keep her warm," said the bramble.

The lamb began to walk all round and around the bramble, the wool came off on the thorns, and the child plucked it off already carded. When she had gathered a fair quantity, she said, "Thank you, little lamb! Now I will run back to my mother, so she can set about spinning the yarn, weaving it, cutting the cloth, and sewing it, so that I can wear it when I go to Communion at Christmas."

She was running on her way, full of joy, when it crossed her mind that her mother would not have time, going out to her work every day as she did, to do all this by Christmas, and she at once grew sad. When she reached the foot of the tree where the bird's nest was, what do you think! There, before her, was the bird's mother.

"You dear child!" said the bird's mother. "How can I thank you? How can I repay your goodness in saving my little one's life? What is that you have in your arms?"

The child told her that it was the wool the lamb had given her, and that she was hurrying to take it to her mother to spin, weave, cut, and sew to make her a little garment to wear at Christmas when she would go to Communion.

"Let me spin it for you," said the bird.

She took it in her beak, and flew up very high, so as to pull it into a long thread. And by the time she flew down again (if you could only have seen!), she had spun the thread and rolled it into a ball. The child took it and went on her way. When she got to the spider's web, the spider was waiting for her.

"Well, how did you fare? Did you find anything at all?"

When the spider saw the balls of thread in the child's arms, it took the thread and began to weave it, quick as lightning, and as fine as any weaver.

The child took the cloth to her mother, who cut it into a little dress, sewed it, put it on the child, and made her pretty. She went to the church, and all the folk kissed and hugged her for being so fine and warmly clad.

"Mother, I must leave this place and go and find another mother who can make me a little garment now and then. I shall die if I stay here longer." This desperate little girl takes her destiny into her own hands with quiet strength. With the help of friends won through her kindness, she saves her life and "all the folk kissed and hugged her for being so fine and warmly clad." The dependable happy ending in fairy tales gives the audience confidence that no matter what demanding tasks are set, or danger confronted, everything will turn out right.

Oral tales represent a cooperative effort between storyteller and audience over many years. Compare this folktale of oral tradition with the literary folk tale, "The Little Match Girl," written by Hans Christian Andersen. Although Andersen was inspired by folk traditions, he wrote his own stories with his own distinct message, unhampered and unaided by an actively participating audience. The poor match girl must sell matches but no one buys. She is freezing so she lights match after match and in the flames visualizes what she needs, a warm fire or food. She is found dead, surrounded by burnt matches. In literary fairy tales, the author can make the heroine die without having to discuss it with anybody. Andersen's heroines, the Little Match Girl and the Little Mermaid both die to their worlds and Perrault's Little Red Riding Hood dies inside the wolf. My daughters gave their opinions on many stories considered for this anthology, "Mom, it's not so good when she dies at the end."

The Pigeon's Bride

Yugoslavia[34]

There was once a King who had an only daughter. She was as love-ly as a princess ought to be and by the time she reached a mar-riageable age the fame of her beauty had spread far and wide over all the world. Neighboring kings and even distant ones were already send-ing envoys to her father's court begging permission to offer their sons as suitors to the Princess's hand. As he had no son of his own the Princess's father was delighted that the day was fast approaching when he might have a son-in-law, and long before even the name of any par-ticular prince was discussed the Princess's mother had planned the wedding down to its last detail.

The Princess alone was uninterested.

"I'm not ready to get married yet," she'd say to her parents every day when they'd begin telling her about the various princes who were anx-ious to gain her favor. "Why such haste? I'm young and there's plenty of time. Besides, just now I'm too busy with my embroidery to be bothered with a crowd of young men."

With that, before the King could reprove her, the Princess would throw her arms about his neck, kiss him under the corner of his mus-tache, and go flying off to the tower-room where she had her embroi-dery frame.

Her mother, the Queen, was much upset by the Princess's attitude.

"In my youth," she said, "girls were not like this. We were brought up to think that courtship and marriage were the most important events in our lives. I don't know what's getting into the heads of the young girls nowadays!"

But the King, who was still smiling from the tickling little kiss which the Princess had planted under the corner of his mustache, always answered:

"Tut! Tut! We needn't worry yet! Take my word for it when some particular young man comes along she'll be interested fast enough!"

At this the Queen, ending the discussion every day with the same words, would shake her head and declare:

"I tell you it isn't natural for a girl to be more interested in embroi-dery than in a long line of handsome young suitors!"

The Princess was interested in her embroidery—there's no doubt about that. She spent every moment she could in the tower-room, working and singing. The tower was high up among the treetops. It was reached by winding stairs so narrow and so many that no one any older than the Princess would care to climb them. The Princess flew up them like a bird, scarcely pausing for breath. At the top of the stairs was a trap-door which was the only means of entrance into the tower-room. Once in the tower-room with the bolt of the trap-door securely fastened, the Princess was safe from interruption and could work away at her embroidery to her heart's content. The tower had windows on all sides, so the Princess as she sat at her embroidery frame could look out north, east, south, and west.

The clouds sailed by in the sky, the wind blew and at once the leaves in the treetops began murmuring and whispering among themselves, and the birds that went flying all over the world would often alight on some branch near the tower and sing to the Princess as she worked or chatter some exciting story that she could almost understand.

"What!" the Princess would think to herself as she looked out north, east, south, and west. "Leave my tower and my beautiful embroidery to become the wife of some conceited young man! Never!"

From this remark you can understand perfectly well that the particular young man of whom her father spoke had not yet come along. And I'm sure you'll also know that shutting herself up in the tower-room and bolting the trap-door was not going to keep him away when it was time for him to come. Yet I don't believe that you'd have recognized him when he did come any more than the Princess did. This is how it happened:

One afternoon when as usual she was working at her embroidery and singing as she worked, suddenly there was a flutter of wings at the eastern window and a lovely Pigeon came flying into the room. It circled three times about the Princess's head and then alighted on the embroidery frame. The Princess reached out her hand and the bird, instead of taking fright, allowed her to stroke its gleaming neck. Then she took it gently in her hands and fondled it to her bosom, kissing its bill and smoothing its plumage with her lips.

"You beautiful thing!" she cried. "How I love you!"

"If you really love me," the Pigeon said, "have a bowl of milk here at this same hour to-morrow and then we'll see what we'll see."

With that the bird spread its wings and flew out the western window.

The Princess was so excited that for the rest of the afternoon she forgot her embroidery.

"Did the Pigeon really speak?" she asked herself as she stood staring out the western window, "or have I been dreaming?"

The next day when she climbed the winding stairs she went slowly for she carried in her hands a brimming bowl of milk.

"Of course it won't come again!" she said, and she made herself sit down quietly before the embroidery frame and work just as though she expected nothing.

But exactly at the same hour as the day before, there was a flutter of wings at the eastern window, the sound of a gentle *coo! coo!* and there was the Pigeon ready to be loved and caressed.

"You beautiful creature!" the Princess cried, kissing its coral beak and smoothing its neck with her lips, "how I love you! And see, I have brought you the bowl of milk that you asked for!"

The bird flew over to the bowl, poised for a moment on its brim, then splashed into the milk as though to take a bath.

The Princess laughed and clapped her hands and then, as she looked, she saw a strange thing happen. The bird's feathers opened like a shirt and out of the feather shirt stepped a handsome youth.

(You remember I told you how surprised the Princess was going to be. And you're surprised, too, aren't you?)

He was so handsome that all the Princess could say was, "Oh!"

He came slowly towards her and knelt before her.

"Dear Princess," he said, "do not be frightened. If it had not been for your sweet words yesterday when you said you loved me I should never have been able to leave this feather shirt. Do not turn from me now because I am a man and not a pigeon. Love me still if you can, for I love you. It was because I fell in love with you yesterday when I saw you working at your embroidery that I flew in by the open window and let you caress me."

For a long time the Princess could only stare at the kneeling youth, too amazed to speak. He was so handsome that she forgot all about the pigeon he used to be, she forgot her embroidery, she forgot everything. She hadn't supposed that any young man in the whole world could be so handsome! Why, just looking at him, she could be happy forever and ever and ever!

"Would you rather I were still a pigeon?" the young man asked.

"No! No! No!" the Princess cried. "I like you ever so much better this way!"

The young man gravely bowed his head and kissed her hand and the Princess blushed and trembled and wished he would do it again. She had never imagined that any kiss could be so wonderful.

They passed the afternoon together and it seemed to the Princess it was the happiest afternoon of all her life. As the sun was sinking the youth said:

"Now I must leave you and become a pigeon again."

"But you'll come back, won't you?" the Princess begged.

"Yes, I'll come back to-morrow but on one condition: that you don't tell any one about me. I'll come back every day at the same hour but if ever you tell about me then I won't be able to come back any more."

"I'll never tell!" the Princess promised.

Then the youth kissed her tenderly, dipped himself in the milk, went back into his feather shirt, and flew off as a pigeon.

The next day he came again and the next and the next and the Princess fell so madly in love with him that all day long and all night long, too, she thought of nothing else. She no longer touched her embroidery but day after day sat idle in the tower-room just awaiting the hour of his arrival. And every day it seemed to the King and the Queen and all the people about the Court that the Princess was becoming more and more beautiful. Her cheeks kept growing pinker, her eyes brighter, her lovely hair more golden.

"I must say sitting at that foolish embroidery agrees with her," the King said.

"No, it isn't that," the Queen told him. "It's the big bowl of milk she drinks every afternoon. You know milk is very good for the complexion."

"Milk indeed!" murmured the Princess to herself, and she blushed rosier than ever at the thought of her wonderful secret.

But a princess can't keep growing more and more beautiful without everybody in the world hearing about it. The neighboring kings soon began to feel angry and suspicious.

"What ails this Princess?" they asked among themselves. "Isn't one of our sons good enough for her? Is she waiting for the King of Persia to come as a suitor or what? Let us stand together on our rights and demand to know why she won't consider one of our sons!"

So they sent envoys to the Princess's father and he saw at once that the matter had become serious.

"My dear," he said to the Princess, "your mother and I have humored you long enough. It is high time that you had a husband and I insist that you allow the sons of neighboring kings to be presented to you next week."

"I won't do it!" the Princess declared. "I'm not interested in the sons of the neighboring kings and that's all there is about it!"

Her father looked at her severely.

"Is that the way for a princess to talk? Persist in this foolishness and you may embroil your country in war!"

"I don't care!" the Princess cried, bursting into tears. "I can't marry any of them, so why let them be presented?"

"Why can't you marry any of them?"

"I just can't!" the Princess insisted.

At first, in spite of the pleadings of both parents, she would tell them no more, but her mother kept questioning her until at last in self-defense the Princess confessed that she had a true love who came to her in the tower every afternoon in the form of a pigeon.

"He's a prince," she told them, "the son of a distant king. At present he is under an enchantment that turns him into a pigeon. When the enchantment is broken he is coming as a prince to marry me."

"My poor child!" the Queen cried. "Think no more about this Pigeon Prince! The enchantment may last a hundred years and then where will you be!"

"But he is my love!" the Princess declared, "and if I can't have him I won't have any one!"

When the King found that nothing they could say would move her from this resolution, he sighed and murmured:

"Very well, my dear. If it must be so, it must be. This afternoon when your lover comes, bring him down to me that I may talk to him."

But that afternoon the Pigeon did not come. Nor the next afternoon either, nor the next, and then too late the Princess remembered his warning that if she told about him he could never come back.

So now she sat in the tower-room idle and heartbroken, reproaching herself that she had betrayed her lover and praying God to forgive her and send him back to her. And the roses faded from her cheeks and her eyes grew dull and the people about the Court began wondering why they had ever thought her the most beautiful princess in the world.

At last she went to the King, her father, and said:

"As my love can no longer come back to me because I forgot my promise and betrayed him, I must go out into the world and hunt him. Unless I find him life will not be worth the living. So do not oppose me, father, but help me. Have three pairs of iron shoes made for me and three iron staffs. I will wander over the wide world until these are worn out and then, if by that time I have not found him, I will come home to you."

So the King had three pairs of iron shoes made for the Princess and three iron staffs and she set forth on her quest. She traveled through towns and cities and many kingdoms, over rough mountains and desert places, looking everywhere for her enchanted love. But nowhere could she find any trace of him.

At the end of the first year she had worn out the first pair of iron shoes and the first iron staff. At the end of the second year she had worn out the second pair of iron shoes and the second iron staff. At the end of the third year, when she had worn out the third pair of iron shoes and the third staff, she returned to her father's palace looking thin and worn and sad.

"My poor child," the King said, "I hope now you realize that the Pigeon Prince is gone forever. Think no more about him. Go back to your embroidery and when the roses begin blooming in your cheeks again we'll find some young prince for you who isn't enchanted."

But the Princess shook her head.

"Let me try one thing more, father," she begged, "and then if I don't find my love I'll do as you say."

The King agreed to this.

"Well, then," the Princess said, "build a public bath-house and have the heralds proclaim that the King's daughter will sit at the entrance and will allow any one to bathe free of charge who will tell her the story of the strangest thing he has ever heard or seen."

So the King built the bath-house and sent out his heralds far and wide. Men and women from all over the world came and bathed and told the Princess stories of this marvel and that, but never, alas, a word of an enchanted pigeon.

The days went by and the Princess grew more and more discouraged.

"Isn't it sad," the courtiers began whispering, "how the Princess has lost her looks! Do you suppose she ever was really beautiful or did we just imagine it?"

And the neighboring kings when they heard this remarked softly among themselves:

"It's just as well we didn't hurry one of our sons into a marriage with this young woman!"

Now there was a poor widow who lived near the bath-house. She had a daughter, a pretty young girl, who used to sit at the window and watch the Princess as people came and told her their stories.

"Mother," the girl said one day, "every one in the world goes to the bath-house and I want to go, too!"

"Nonsense!" the mother said. "What story could you tell the Princess?"

"But everybody else goes and I don't see why I can't!"

"Well, my dear," the mother promised, "you may just as soon as you see or hear something strange. Talk no more about it now but go, fetch me a pitcher of water from the town well."

The girl obediently took an empty pitcher and went to the town well. Just as she had filled the pitcher she heard some one say:

"Mercy me, I fear I'll be late!"

She turned around and what do you think she saw? A rooster in wooden shoes with a basket under his wing!

"I fear I'll be late! I fear I'll be late!" the rooster kept repeating as he hurried off making a funny little clatter with his wooden shoes.

"How strange!" the girl thought to herself. "A rooster with wooden shoes! I'm sure the Princess would love to hear about him! I'll follow him and see what he does."

He went to a garden where he filled his basket with fresh vegetables—with onions and beans and garlic. Then he hurried home to a little house. The girl slipped in after him and hid behind the door.

"Thank goodness, I'm on time!" the rooster murmured.

He put a big bowl on the table and filled it with milk.

"There!" he said. "Now I'm ready for them!"

Presently twelve beautiful pigeons came flying in by the open door. Eleven of them dipped in the bowl of milk, their feather shirts opened, and out they stepped, eleven handsome youths. But the Twelfth Pigeon perched disconsolately on the windowsill and remained a pigeon. The eleven laughed at him and said:

"Poor fellow, your bride betrayed you, didn't she? So you have to remain shut up in your feather shirt while we go off and have a jolly time!"

"Yes," the Twelfth Pigeon said, "she broke her promise and now she goes wandering up and down the world hunting for me. If she doesn't find me I shall nevermore escape the feather shirt but shall have to fly about forever as a pigeon. But I know she will find me for she will never stop until she does. And when she finds me, then the enchantment will be broken forever and I can marry her!"

The eleven youths went laughing arm in arm out of the house and in a few moments the solitary Pigeon flew after them. Instantly the girl slipped out from behind the door and hurried home with her pitcher of water. Then she ran quickly across to the bath-house and all out of breath she cried to the Princess:

"O Princess, I have such a wonderful story to tell you all about a rooster with wooden shoes and twelve pigeons only eleven of them are not pigeons but handsome young men and the twelfth one has to stay in his feather shirt because—"

At mention of the enchanted pigeons, the Princess turned pale. She held up her hand and made the girl pause until she had her breath, then she questioned her until she knew the whole story.

"It must be my love!" the Princess thought to herself. "Thank God I have found him at last!"

The next day at the same hour she went with the girl to the town well and when the rooster clattered by in his wooden shoes they followed him home and slipping into the house, they hid behind the door and waited. Presently twelve pigeons flew in. Eleven of them dipped in the milk and came out handsome young men. The Twelfth sat disconsolately on the window sill and remained a pigeon. The eleven laughed at him and twitted him with having had a bride that had betrayed him. Then the eleven went away laughing arm in arm. Before the Twelfth could fly after them, the Princess ran out from behind the door and cried:

"My dear one, I have found you at last!"

The Pigeon flew into her hands and she took him and kissed his coral beak and smoothed his gleaming plumage with her lips. Then she put him in the milk and the feather shirt opened and her own true love stepped out.

She led him at once to her father and when the King found him well trained in all the arts a prince should know he accepted him as his future son-in-law and presented him to the people.

So after all the Princess's mother was able to give her daughter the gorgeous wedding she had planned for years and years. Preparations were begun at once but the Queen insisted on making such vast quantities of little round cakes and candied fruits and sweetmeats of all kinds that it was three whole months before the wedding actually took place. By that time the roses were again blooming in the Princess's cheeks, her eyes were brighter than before, and her long shining hair was more golden than ever.

All the neighboring kings were invited to the wedding and when they saw the bride they shook their heads sadly and said among themselves:

"Lost her looks indeed! What did people mean by saying such a thing? Why, she's the most beautiful princess in the world! What a pity she didn't marry one of our sons!"

But when they met the Prince of her choice, they saw at once why the Princess had fallen in love with him.

"Any girl would!" they said.

It was a big wedding, as I told you before, and the only guest present who was not a king or a queen or a royal personage of some sort was the poor girl who saw the rooster with wooden shoes in the first place. The Queen, of course, had wanted only royalty but the Princess declared that the poor girl was her dear friend and would have to be invited. So the Queen, when she saw that the Princess was set on having her own way, had the poor girl come to the palace before the wedding and decked her out in rich clothes until people were sure that she was some strange princess whom the bride had met on her travels.

"My dear," whispered the Princess as they sat down beside each other at the wedding feast, "how beautiful you look!"

"But I'm not as beautiful as you!" the girl said.

The Princess laughed.

"Of course not! No one can be as beautiful as I am because I have the secret of beauty!"

"Dear Princess," the poor girl begged, "won't you tell me the secret of beauty?"

The Princess leaned over and whispered something in the poor girl's ear.

It was only one word:

"Happiness!"

The princess's lover lays down a rule: don't communicate. "... if ever you tell about me then I won't be able to come back any more."

Obeying this rule cuts the princess off from her large network of relationships; it begins to alienate her from the parents she loves and threatens to bring war to the country for which she feels responsible. She tries to stop the harm being done to her world and tells her parents the truth. As a result she is separated from her lover and her family and she gets the cold shoulder from the rest of her world.

Often the heroine in this type of tale must prove through self-denial that she is worthy. She does penance for her "sin." Until she humbles herself she is an outcast. After she has worn out the shoes or completed the tasks, she regains her lover.[35]

The ending of "The Pigeon's Bride" is different. This princess does not succeed with self-denial. Wearing out the iron shoes does not earn her her lover. She wanders the world alone and when she returns looking thin and worn and sad, none of the neighboring princes want to marry her. Now the heroine rises to the challenge, she gets the unusual idea to listen to stories. "Men and women from all over the world came and bathed and told the Princess stories of this marvel and that . . . " The story has returned to the crux of the problem, the rule don't communicate. At the beginning, the princess chose to talk to her parents. Now, for the second time, the princess chooses to communicate rather than to obey the rule. Chatting and listening to people from all over the world prove to be the definitive solution. The Princess regains her beloved by being true to herself.

How the King Chose a Daughter-in-Law

Romania[36]

Once upon a time there was a king who was so rich and powerful that all his neighbours were afraid of him. This king had a son who was so handsome and brave, with such long, curly hair, that people talked of him even in foreign countries and beyond the sea.

When the king felt that he was growing weak he called his son and told him he thought it was time he got married—for everybody likes to see his family settled at some time or another.

The king also said he wanted a good, hard-working daughter-in-law and not some silly featherbrain. He decided to build a very great palace with a thousand rooms and then to invite all the kings and princes in the neighbourhood, with their daughters. Whichever daughter could find her way through all the rooms without getting lost should be chosen for his daughter-in-law.

They sent for skilled workmen from all over the world, each one cleverer than the next, and they built a palace so big that you could never see all of it at once. When they had finished, the king sent letters to all his neighbours and invited them all to bring their daughters to call on him.

As the news of this wonderful palace spread abroad, people began to stream in from the four corners of the world so that there seemed to be no end to the visitors. When everybody had arrived, the king told them his plan and invited the girls to try their luck.

All the girls tried but not one of them was able to find the way right round all the rooms, there were so many of them and it was all so complicated. When the king saw this he began to lose hope.

Now, among the great crowd of people there had come a poor old woman and her daughter, anxious not to miss the splendid sight. After all the kings' daughters and the boyars'* daughters had gone away, feeling very much ashamed of their failure, the old woman's daughter thought she would have a try. The old woman pulled at her sleeve and began to scold her and tell her she ought not to make so bold. But when the king's son saw the girl looking as lovely as a peony he went up to her and asked her to have a try as well.

The old woman's daughter went into that very wonderful palace and

* *Boyar*, a member of a privileged landholding class in Romania.

began to go from room to room. In one of them she found an engagement ring; she picked it up and put it on her finger. In another room she found a wedding dress. She put that on too and when she finally came out, she had brought something with her as a token from every one of the rooms.

The king had to keep his word and they held a really grand wedding. At the wedding the king asked her what it was she had done so as not to get lost. She said that she had brought her distaff with her when she left home and that she had worked hard and spun a whole distaff full of thread on the way there. When she went into the palace, she had left her distaff at the door and had held the other end of the thread as she wandered all the way round the palace. On her way back she had wound the thread up again on her spindle and in that way she had managed not to get lost.

And from that time on there has been a saying that clever folk can be found in mud huts too, not only in palaces.

The heroine who solves the labyrinth in this tale is poor and nameless. The old woman's daughter leaves her distaff at the entrance and uses the thread, which she has spun herself, to track the maze. She uses her own intelligence to figure out the method and her own handiwork as the means. A prince of Greek mythology, Theseus, also finds his way through a labyrinth, but he is given a ball of magic thread by Princess Ariadne who had been given the ball plus instructions by Daedalus, the architect of the maze. Prince Theseus was noble and strong enough to kill the Minotaur in the maze but he wasn't as independently resourceful as this young peasant girl.

Marichka

Gypsy[37]

This happened in olden times. A gypsy band was wandering about the land led by an old *ataman* who was wise and strong. And great was his hold over the gypsies. All had to obey; swift retribution awaited any waverer.

Now this *ataman* had a beautiful wife and a daughter whose name was Marichka. How the gypsy men envied the chief his strength, wisdom and power, how they envied him his lovely wife—though no one dared to show it.

But there was one gypsy in the band who not only envied him, he had fallen wildly in love with his wife. And so enflamed with passion was he that he vowed nothing would stand in his way. No one knew of this love, he concealed it well; only the *ataman*'s wife noticed his ardent glance, though she kept silent, not wishing to hurt her husband, and perhaps fearing he would punish the reckless gypsy should he know. Why spill blood needlessly?

For a long time the young gypsy kept his feelings to himself, but finally they boiled over and he lay in wait to kill the chief. One morning early, before the sun was up, he hid behind a tree at the edge of the woods, leapt out and plunged a long knife into the leader's heart.

No one would have known of the murder had not Marichka, the dead man's daughter, gone for water at that early hour; she had glanced towards the leafy oak beneath which the deed was done. She told nobody of what she had seen that morning.

From then on the murderer became leader of the clan; he wielded power over people and, of course, forced the dead chief's widow to become   his wife.

As Marichka grew up she became more and more beautiful, as graceful as her mother had once been; and though her heart harbored thoughts of revenge, she always appeared kind and gentle to the new *ataman*—she did not wish him to guess her secret.

She was biding her time.

Yet when she began to feel his glance upon her, she realized the time for revenge was nigh.

One day the *ataman* told Marichka to meet him at dawn within the forest, and she agreed. They met beneath that selfsame leafy oak, on the very spot where her father had been struck down. And now, as the gypsy stretched out his arms to embrace her, a terrible scream rent the still air . . . and steel glinted in his breast.

Marichka is no Hamlet. She never wavers. She conceals her knowledge, bides her time, and at the proper moment she avenges her father's death.

Davit

Georgia[38]

There was, there was, and yet there was not, there was once a man who had two children, a daughter named Svetlana and a son, Davit.

This son loved to hunt, and he started every morning at dawn and hunted the whole day through until the sunset. But, one morning, when the usual time came for him to go out, he could not rise, and he lay as dead. All day he was that way. Only when the sun went down in the evening did life return to him.

From then on, that was his Fate.

His father called doctors and wise men and magicians and old women. Nothing helped. When all else failed, his sister, Svetlana, decided to go and ask the sun, himself, what would cure her brother.

On her feet, she put a pair of shoes made of stone. "Until these wear out," she swore, "I will not give up my journey to the sun."

She walked and walked. Who knows how far she walked?

She came, one evening, in the first year of her travels, to a little village.

"Have you a room for me?" she asked an old lady standing in the doorway of the first house she passed.

"All guests come from God," the woman answered. "Enter and be welcome."

But, that night, Svetlana could not sleep for she heard a woman screaming. She called the old lady and asked her the reason.

"It is my son's wife," she answered. "For three months, she has been in labor but her child will not be born."

Svetlana thought a minute. Then she told the story of her journey. "And," she concluded, "if I find the sun, I will ask him what will help your daughter-in-law."

"Do," urged the old lady, and, next day, she prepared a bag of food for Svetlana to carry on her way.

She walked and walked. I cannot tell you how far she walked.

One day, as she passed through a barren field, she saw a thin sheep staring with hungry eyes at the fresh grass in the meadow beyond. Yet, all that kept him from it was a thicket hedge.

"Why do you not go over and eat grass, sheep?" Svetlana asked him. (I must tell you that this all happened in the days when men and animals still lived like friends and could speak, one to the other, in the same language.)

The sheep only answered, "Where are you going?"

"I am trying to find my way to the sun." She told again the story of her brother.

When the sheep heard this, he said, "Perhaps the sun could help me, too. For three years, I have stood here hungry, and I dare not go into the next field lest the thicket hedge catch my wool and hold me fast."

"If I see the sun," Svetlana promised, "I shall surely ask him to help you, too."

She walked and walked. Only God can tell you how far she walked.

At last, in a clearing in the middle of a forest, she came to a stag whose antlers grew so tall they were lost in the sky.

"Where are you going, my dear?" the stag inquired.

Once more Svetlana told her story.

"Please," said the stag, "I dare not go into the forest for my horns are so long they catch in everything. When you reach the sun, ask him what I should do."

"Gladly," Svetlana answered. "But one thing worries me. I am beginning to wonder how I shall ever find the sun."

"Climb up my antlers," offered the stag. "I have no idea how far they go, but, at the rate they have been growing, I think they must reach beyond everything. I will wait here and, when you are ready, you may come down the same way."

She went up and up and up, past the treetops, past the flying birds, past the clouds, past the moon who looked at her coldly, past the stars and, at last, she reached the floor of heaven. There, she found a neat, small house and, sitting on the doorstep, was a little, old woman with gray hair.

"My goodness," the old lady said. "You frightened me. You are the first person from the earth who has ever found her way up here. What brought you?"

"I want to see the sun," Svetlana answered, and she told her why.

"I am the sun's mother. I will try my best to help you. Stay here tonight, but I must change you into a broom. The sun does not like human beings around."

At dusk, she changed her over and stood her in the corner with the dustpan to keep her company.

As soon as the sun came in the door, he sniffed the air. "Some human being has been here."

"No, my child," his mother told him. "Perhaps the wind is blowing from the earth today. Sit down and eat your supper."

She had cooked everything he liked and, as he ate, she talked to him.

"You know, my life is sometimes very dull here. I am alone from dark to dark. Of course, for you it's quite a different thing. You have a chance to see the world. Tell me of your experiences. Tell me of the human beings you shine upon."

"Human beings," the sun said, with his mouth full of carrots. "Why do you want to hear about them? They never do anything but make me trouble so I have to get rid of them."

"What do you mean?"

"Well, not long ago a nice hazy day came—a good chance for me to throw my rays at my sweetheart, the moon. But a young man kept shooting his gun at me until, to get some peace, I had to strike him."

The sun's mother got up, took the broom, brushed a few crumbs away and set the broom down by her chair. "Will the young man never be cured?" she asked.

"Yes," the sun said, "if he stays for seventeen days in a curtained room where I can find no chink to crawl through."

"Think of that!" cried his mother in astonishment. "Lamp, broom, and walls! Do you hear how clever my son is? Tell me some more, my dear. I suppose you see people in all kinds of trouble you might help?"

"In a window I shine through quite regularly, I see a woman three months in labor."

"What would help her?"

"If she moves from the soft mattress where she lies to a bed of hard boards covered with straw, her child will be born."

"Bag, broom, and basket! Hear that!" said the old lady. "The world is certainly an interesting place. Tell me more."

"Under a tree where I throw dappled shadows every day, stands a sheep who is afraid to cross the thicket lest the thorns catch his wool and hold him."

"I don't suppose there is any help for him."

"Yes, if he would go straight to the thorn thicket and walk along brushing first his one side and then his other against it. That would pull out all his old wool and he could go through without fear."

"Plate, broom, and spoon! Was there ever anybody like my son! I had no idea life down on the earth was like that. Does every animal get into some kind of trouble? Oxen? Cows? Deer, too?"

"There is even a stag whose horns have grown so long he cannot go into the forest."

"Then he must die?"

"No, not if he finds a spring and stamps his hoof in the mud until water collects in the print, and then drinks it and shakes his head."

"Stove, broom, and pot! Listen to my son! There is nobody like him."

"Now, Mother, I must rest, for my day starts early."

He went to bed.

Next morning, as soon as he left for work, his mother changed Svetlana back. "Do you remember everything he said?" she asked.

"Yes, but how can I be sure it will work?"

"Try it on the stag."

Svetlana thanked her, walked to the edge of heaven, stepped out on to the stag's antlers and descended.

"Any news?" the stag said, as soon as she jumped off his back. "Did you find out anything?"

She told him what to do, and by luck there was a spring near by. He stamped his front paw. Water collected. He put his soft nose in and drank, shook his head and, with a great crack, his antlers snapped off.

He ran round and round the clearing; he rolled on the grass; he rubbed his sides against the tree bark, and then he came back.

"I don't know how to thank you." He licked her cheek with his rough, red tongue. "Would you care to have my antlers to hang in your house? Human beings seem to be proud of doing that."

But Svetlana refused and went on. In the same way, she saved the sheep and the woman in labor, and came home to her brother.

There she darkened the room and, in great anxiety, waited through sixteen days. On the seventeenth, her brother rose in the morning, a whole man again.

Only then did she take off her stone shoes. The toe of one was almost chipped away; the sole of the other was polished so thin that light shone through it.

In this world, next to a good mother, what can a man have better than a good sister?

Doctors, wise men, magicians, and old women have failed, so Svetlana embarks upon a fabulous quest to save her brother. With dauntless persistence, she travels where no one has gone before. "I want to see the sun," Svetlana says. She returns with the cure for her brother as well as solutions for the needy she met on her travels. She is a heroine par excellence. However, details in this story indicate that it was told from a man's point of view. Svetlana's name is not used in the title. She is given the stone/iron shoes of self-denial like the princess in "The Pigeon's Bride" (p. 63). At the end, Svetlana receives the back-handed compliment of the male point of view: "Next to a good mother, what can a man have better than a good sister?" The way in which a tale is told can strengthen or weaken the heroine. In this case, Svetlana's adventurous spirit and determination shine through despite a male filter.

Anait

Caucasus[39]

Once upon a time young Vachagan, the only son of King Vacha, was standing on his balcony. It was a spring morning. Many different birds were singing in the garden. But best of all sang the Nightingale. As soon as he began to sing all the other birds would fall silent and listen, seeking to master the secrets of his art: one would imitate his twittering, another—his trills, a third—his whistling and then, all together, they would repeat the melodies they had just learnt. But Vachagan was not listening. His heart was troubled by quite other matters.

His mother, Queen Ashkhen, came up to him and said:

"Vacha, my little son, I see you have some sorrow. Do not hide it from us, tell us the cause of your sadness."

"Mother, I have no taste for the pleasures of life. I want to go away to some secluded retreat, to the village of Atsik, for instance."

"I suppose the only reason why you want to go to Atsik is to be near that cunning Anait of yours?"

"How do you know her name, Mama?"

"The nightingales in our garden told me about her. Vacha, dearest boy, do not forget that you are the son of the King of Afghanistan. A King's son must select a Princess for his bride, or a woman of rank, but not a simple peasant girl. The King of Georgia has three daughters, you may choose any of them. The Prince of Gugar has a beautiful daughter, the only heir to his rich estates. And the daughter of the Prince of Syunik is beautiful, too. Or even Varsenik, the daughter of our chief warlord whom we have brought up and who has grown to maidenhood under our eyes—what fault do you find in her?"

"Mother, I want no one but Anait . . . "

And Vachagan ran out into the garden.

Vachagan had just turned twenty. He had been very delicate, pale and weak.

"Vachagan, my son," his father had said, "all my hope is in you. You will have to marry, for that is the way of the world."

But Vachagan would not listen. Early in the morning he would go off into the mountains to hunt and he would come home late in the evening. Many princes desired his friendship, but he avoided them. He would take with him only his brave and devoted servant Vaginak and his faithful sheep-dog Zangi. Folk they met out hunting could not tell which was the Prince, which the servant; they were both dressed in the same plain hunts-man's garb: a bow slung over their shoulders and a broad-bladed dagger at their belts.

This outdoor life did Vachagan good: he grew more manly, stronger and healthier. Once it happened that Vachagan and Vaginak came to the village of Atsik and sat down by the spring to rest. At that time the vil-lage maidens came to draw water at the spring. Vachagan was thirsty and asked for some water. One of the maidens filled a jug and offered it to Vachagan; suddenly, another snatched away the jug and poured out the water. Then she again filled the jug and again poured out the water. Vachagan's throat was parched with thirst and it seemed as though the maiden were teasing him—now holding the jug under the trickle of water, now emptying it again. Only after she had done this six times did she offer the jug to Vachagan.

Vachagan drank and asked the girl:

"Why did you not give me water straight away? Were you teasing me or joking?"

"It is not our custom here to joke with strangers," answered the girl. "But you were tired and hot and the cold water might have done you harm. That's why I was slow."

The maiden's answer impressed Vachagan and her beauty enchanted him.

He asked:

"What is your name?"

"Anait," answered the girl.

"Who is your father?"

"My father is the shepherd of this village—Aran. But why do you ask our names?"

"Is it a sin to ask someone's name?"

"If it is not, then you say who you are and from whence you come."

"Should I tell you the truth or a lie?"

"Whichever you think better matches your own dignity."

"My dignity were better matched by the truth, and the truth is that I may not yet say who I am. But I give you my word that I shall soon tell you."

"Very well. And now give me back my jug."

Bidding farewell to the Prince, Anait took her jug and walked away. The hunters returned home. The devoted Vaginak told the Queen all that had happened. That was how Vachagan's mother had come to know her son's secret.

Vachagan would not hear of any other bride. At last the King and Queen agreed to his choice. They sent Vaginak and two important noblemen to Atsik to ask for the hand of Anait.

The shepherd Aran gave them a courteous welcome. The guests sat down on the carpet which Aran laid out for them.

"What a wonderful carpet!" said Vaginak. "I suppose it was woven by the mistress of the house?"

"I have no wife," answered Aran. "She died ten years ago. The carpet was woven by my daughter Anait."

"Even in the great rooms of our King there is no carpet as beautiful as this. We are glad that your daughter is so skilled," said the noblemen. "Her fame has spread to the palace itself. The King has sent us to speak with you. He wants you to give your daughter's hand in marriage to his only son, the heir to the throne."

The noblemen expected Aran not to believe his ears or to leap from his place with joy. But the shepherd did neither. He sank his head and began to trace the patterns of the carpet with his forefinger.

Vaginak said:

"Why are you sad, Brother Aran? It is joy we have brought you, not sorrow. We do not wish to take your daughter by force. If you wish— you will give her away, if you do not—you will not."

"Dear guests," replied Aran, "the thing is that I will not constrain my daughter. If she consents, then I have nothing to say against it."

At that moment Anait came in carrying a basket of ripe fruits. She bowed to the guests, set the fruit out on a dish and, having served them with it, sat down to work at her lace-frame. The noblemen gazed at her and were all astonished at the swiftness of her fingers.

"Anait, why do you work alone?" asked Vaginak. "You have many pupils, or so I have heard."

"Yes," said Anait. "But I have let them all go to help with the grape-harvest."

"I hear you teach your pupils to read and write?"

"Yes," answered Anait. "Now even our shepherds read and teach one another while grazing their sheep. All the tree trunks in our forests have words carved upon them. The fortress walls, the stones and rocks are written upon with coal. One writes one word, the next continues. . . . And so our ravines and mountains have become full of written words."

"There is no such respect for learning where we come from," replied Vaginak. "Town-dwellers are lazy. But if you would come to live with us you would teach them all application. Anait, leave off your work for a moment, I have business with you. See what gifts the King has sent you."

Vaginak produced silk dresses and precious jewelry. Anait glanced at them briefly and asked:

"How have I deserved such favour from the King?"

"The son of our King, Vachagan, saw you at the spring. You gave him water to drink and pleased him. And the King sent us to ask your hand in marriage for the Prince. This ring, these necklaces, these bangles—they are all for you!"

"So the huntsman was the King's son?"

"Yes."

"He is a youth of great beauty. But does he know any trade?"

"Anait, he is the son of the King. All his subjects are there to serve him. He does not need a trade."

"That's all very well, but a ruler may become a servant. Everyone should know a trade whether he be king, servant or prince!"

Anait's words astonished the noblemen. But the shepherd Aran approved his daughter's words.

"You mean to say you are refusing the Prince simply because he does not know a trade?" asked the noblemen.

"Yes. And take back all these things you have brought with you. And tell the Prince that he pleases me well but that—and may he forgive me for it!—I have taken an oath never to marry a man who knows no trade."

The ambassadors saw that Anait was firmly resolved and did not insist. They returned to the palace and told the King all that had happened.

When they heard Anait's decision, the King and Queen were very glad. Now Vachagan would surely relinquish his intention.

But Vachagan said: "Anait is right. I should be master of some trade like everybody else."

The King called a council of noblemen and they all agreed that the most suitable trade for a Prince was the weaving of brocade. A skilled master of this craft was brought from Persia. In the course of one year Vachagan had learnt to weave brocade and had woven a length for Anait from fine golden threads which he sent to her through Vaginak.

When she received it, Anait said:

"In the words of the proverb: 'The trials of fate will find him unafraid: need's must, and he will ply the weaver's trade!' Tell the Prince that I consent, and take him this carpet as a gift from me."

So the preparations for the wedding were begun and it was celebrated for seven days and seven nights.

However, soon after the wedding Vachagan's devoted friend and servant Vaginak disappeared. He was searched for far and wide until at long last all hope of finding him had to be abandoned. In the meantime the King and Queen, having lived to a ripe old age, died, and Vachagan became King in his father's stead.

Once Anait said to her husband:

"Oh King, I see that you lack sound knowledge of your realm. People do not tell you the whole truth. They speak as though all were well. But perhaps this is not quite so? It would be a good thing for you to go walking through your kingdom from time to time dressed either as a beggar or as a tradesman or as a workman."

"You are right, Anait," replied the King. "Before, when I used to go hunting, I knew the people better. But how can I go away now? Who will rule the kingdom in my absence?"

"I will," answered Anait and added: "No one will even know that you are away!"

"All right, I shall set out on my journey tomorrow. If I do not return within twenty days then you will know I am either dead or have met with some misfortune!"

King Vachagan began to wander through his realm dressed as a simple peasant. He saw much and heard much, and at last he came to the town of Perozh.

In the centre of the town was a wide square. There was a market there and all round the market stood the workshops of the tradesmen and the stalls of the merchants.

Once Vachagan was sitting on this square. Suddenly he saw a crowd of people following an old man. The old man walked very slowly. The people cleared the road before him and set down bricks for him to step on. Vachagan asked the first comer who the old man might be. He was answered:

"Don't you know? That is our high priest. He is so holy that he will not even put foot to the ground in case he might inadvertently crush some insect."

Then the people spread out a carpet on the square and the high priest sank down upon it on his knees and rested. Vachagan pushed his way through to the front to get a closer look at the old man and to hear what he had to say. The great priest had sharp eyes. He looked at Vachagan and saw at once that this was someone from far away and asked:

"Who are you and what are you doing here?"

"I am a workman from another land," answered Vachagan. "I have come to this town seeking employment."

"Good. Come with me. I will give you work and pay you well."

Vachagan nodded his head in sign of agreement. The great priest whis-

pered a few words to his attendants and they all went off in different
directions. Some time later they returned with porters carrying every
conceivable kind of stores. Then the high priest rose and set off for his
own house. Vachagan followed him in silence. So they came to the city
gates.

Here the high priest blessed the people and they all went their separate ways. There remained only the priests, the porters and Vachagan.
Leaving the town behind them they came to a great wall. The high priest
got out a key and opened the gates. Behind the wall was a spacious square
in the middle of which rose a temple surrounded by cells. The porters
put down their loads on the ground. The high priest led the porters and
Vachagan round to the other side of the temple, opened an iron door and
said:

"Go in, you will be given employment here."

Amazed they filed silently in and found themselves in a dark underground passage. The high priest locked the door behind them. Knowing
that their retreat was cut off, the workmen went on and forward.

They walked on for a long time. Suddenly, far ahead, they caught sight
of a pale gleam of light and they emerged into a cave from whence came
the sound of groans and cries. The prisoners looked around the rocky
walls with amazement, listening to the groans and cries. At that moment
a kind of shadow loomed towards them through the half-light. Gradually
getting nearer and growing denser, it took on a human form. Vachagan
went up to the shadow and asked loudly:

"Who are you, man or devil? If you are a man, tell me where we are."

The shadow came closer and stopped, trembling, before them. It was
a man, but such a man! With the face of a corpse, sunken eyes and sharp
cheek-bones: in a word, a skeleton, each of whose bones could be counted. Gibbering and weeping, he said:

"Follow me. I will show you everything."

After a narrow passage they all came out to a second cave. Here many
people were lying writhing in their death agonies. In the third cave were
huge cauldrons in which, apparently, dinner was cooking. Vachagan bent
over one of the cauldrons and recoiled in horror, saying nothing to his
comrades. Then they found themselves in yet another corridor. Here in
the semi-darkness several hundred deathly pale people were at work:
some embroidering, some knitting, others sewing. The corpse-like man
said:

"The Devil-Priest who enticed you all here by deceit brought us, also,
into this underground place. I do not know how many years I have been
here, for here there is neither day nor night but only eternal, unending

gloom. I only know that all who came here together with me are dead. They bring people here, those who know some trade and those who do not. The first are made to work until they die, the second are taken away to the slaughter-house and come at last to those terrible cauldrons which you have just seen. The old Devil-Priest is not alone: all the priests help him."

Vachagan, having taken a good look, recognised the speaker as his own devoted Vaginak. But he said nothing in case the joy of reunion should snap the slender thread of Vaginak's life.

When Vaginak went away, Vachagan asked his companions who they were and what they could do. One said he was a tailor, another a weaver, and Vachagan decided to declare the rest his assistants. Soon footsteps were heard and a fierce priest appeared before them accompanied by an armed rabble.

"Are you the new arrivals?" asked the priest.

"Yes, at your Grace's service," replied Vachagan.

"Which of you knows any trade?"

"We all do!" said Vachagan. "We can weave precious brocades worth a hundred times more than gold."

"Does your cloth really cost so dear?"

"I do not lie. And you can always put me to the test."

"I'll put you to the test all right. Now tell me what instruments and materials you need and you will go to work in the general workshop."

"Our work will not go well there," Vachagan objected. "It would be better for us to work here. And as far as food is concerned, you must know that we are none of us meat-eaters: we will die if we eat meat."

"All right," said the priest. "I will send you bread and vegetables, but if your work is less precious than you boast I shall send you to the slaughter-houses and give orders that you all have a nice little dose of torture before you are killed."

The priest sent them fruit and bread. They shared the bread with Vaginak and the others, and Vachagan got down to work. He swiftly wove a length of splendid brocade and covered it with patterns which told of all the torments of this underground hell. But not every eye would know how to decipher the patterns. The priest was delighted with the brocade.

Vachagan said:

"I told you that our cloth is worth a hundred times more than gold. But know that its real value is double this again, because of the talismans we weave into it. It is a pity that ordinary people set no store by them. The only person who knows their true worth is the wise Queen Anait."

When he heard the true worth of the brocade the greedy priest's eyes nearly popped out of his head. He decided not to share the profits with anyone. He said nothing to the high priest and did not even show him the brocade but set out with it then and there.

Anait had been ruling the country well and all were content. No one even knew that the King had gone away. But the Queen herself was very anxious. Ten days had already passed since the covenanted time, and Vachagan had not returned. At night she had horrible dreams. During the day she was troubled by various hallucinations. The dog Zangi kept howling and whining. Vachagan's stallion would take no fodder and whinnied pitifully, like a foal left behind by its mother. The hens crowed like cocks and the cocks cried in the evening with the voices of pheasants. The ripples of the river flowed silently without lap or gurgle. Anait the courageous was full of fear. She even started at her own shadow.

One morning she was informed of the arrival of a foreign merchant offering some precious merchandise.

Anait ordered the stranger to be brought into her presence.

A man with a terrible face bowed low before her and held out a length of golden brocade on a silver tray. She looked at the cloth, not noticing the patterns and asked:

"What is the price of your brocade?"

"Gracious Sovereign, it is three hundred times as dear as gold, if we consider only the work and the material, as for my own labour and industry, it is for Your Grace yourself to judge their worth."

"Is it really so very dear?"

"Most gracious Queen, there is a priceless virtue upon it. You see these patterns? They are not simple patterns, but talismans. Whoever wears this cloth will be safeguarded all their days from all sorrow and misfortune."

"Really?" asked Anait and opened out the brocade on which there were no talismans but patterns of letters. Silently, Anait read them:

My incomparable Anait, I have fallen into a terrible hell. He who brings you this brocade is one of the demon-jailers of this hell. Vaginak is with me. Seek us East of Perozh, beneath a walled temple. Without your help we shall all perish.

Vachagan.

Shattered, Anait read the letter a second and then third time. She pretended to be admiring the pattern and then said:

"You are right, the patterns of your brocade have a power for mirth and comfort: only this morning I was sad and now I am merry and light of heart. This brocade is priceless. I would not hesitate to give half my kingdom for it. But you probably know yourself that no created thing is worth more than the creator?"

"Long life attend Your Majesty, you speak the truth!"

"Bring me the man who made this brocade. He must be rewarded equally with you."

"Gracious Queen," the greedy priest replied. "I do not know who made it. I bought it from a Jew in India, and he bought it from an Arab, and as for the Arab—who knows where he came by it?"

"But you have only just said yourself that the materials and the work cost you much money. Therefore you did not buy the brocade, you yourself had it woven."

"Gracious Queen, that's what they told me in India, and I . . . "

"Silence!" Anait grew angry. "I know who you are. Hey, men, to me! Take this man and throw him into prison!"

After this order had been carried out, Anait ordered the trumpeter to sound the alarm. The townsfolk, whispering anxiously among themselves, foregathered outside the palace. No one knew what it was all about.

Anait appeared on the balcony, armed from head to foot.

"Citizens," she said. "The life of your King is in danger. Let all those who love him and to whom his life is dear follow me. By midday we should be in the town of Perozh."

In an hour's time the whole town was in arms. Anait mounted her fiery steed and ordered: "Forward! Follow me!" and set off at a gallop for Perozh. On the square at Perozh she pulled her excited stallion back onto his haunches. The inhabitants took her for a divinity come down from the skies, fell on their knees and bowed to the ground before her.

"Where is your leader?" asked Anait proudly.

"I, your servant, I am the leader here," said one of the folk of Perozh.

"You careless steward! You do not even know what goes on in the temple of your Gods!"

"Your humble servant knows nothing," the leader of the townsfolk answered, bowing.

"Perhaps you don't even know where your temple is?"

"Indeed I do, indeed—of course!"

"Then show me the way."

The leader set out with Anait. Behind them walked the crowd. The priests thought that the people were coming to pray and opened the first iron door. Anait rode into the square and ordered them to open the temple. Only then did the priests realise what was afoot. The high priest flung himself on the valiant rider, but Anait's clever horse trampled him with his hoofs.

Then the troops came up and quickly put an end to the rest of the priests. The people watched in terror and amazement.

"Come closer," cried Anait. "See what is hidden in the sanctuary of your Gods!"

Quickly they broke down the doors of the temple. A terrible sight met the people's eyes. From out of the hellish dungeons came crawling people like spectres from beyond the grave. Many were dying and could scarcely keep upright on their shaky legs. Others, blinded by the light, were tottering on their feet. Last of all came Vachagan and Vaginak. They walked with closed eyes so that the brilliant light of day should not blind them. The men-at-arms ran down into the hell below and began to carry out the bodies of the dead, the instruments of torture and the tools of the craftsmen.

The citizens helped them, deeply ashamed.

Then Anait entered the hastily rigged up tent where Vachagan and Vaginak were awaiting her. The lovers sat down side by side and could not take their eyes off one another. Vaginak kissed his lady's hand and burst into tears:

"Incomparable Queen, you saved our lives today!"

"You're wrong there, Vaginak," Vachagan contradicted him. "The Queen saved us long ago, on the day she asked: 'And does the son of your King know a trade?' Do you remember how you laughed in answer to that question?"

The story of the adventures of good King Vachagan spread through all the towns and villages. Even in other countries they spoke of it and all praised Vachagan and Anait. The wandering minstrels—*Ashugs*—made songs about them. It is a pity that these songs are no longer remembered. But to make up for it, the story of Vachagan and Anait is still told to this day.

"What is your name?"
"Anait," answered the girl . . . "But why do you ask our names?"
"Is it a sin to ask someone's name?"
"If it is not, then you say who you are . . . "
"Should I tell you the truth or a lie?"
"Whichever you think better matches your own dignity."
This conversation epitomizes a common double standard in folktales. The man knows about the woman but she does not know about him or is forbidden to tell others what she knows about him. For example, in the myth "Cupid and Psyche," Cupid has seen the beautiful Psyche but he comes to her at night after all the lights are out and

forbids her to try to see him.[40] *Bluebeard forbids his wife to enter the room that holds his past. In "The Pigeon's Bride" (p. 63), the pigeon abandons the Princess when she talks about him.*

Anait has given her name. Then she says, " . . . say who you are." The prince does not give his name. Instead he gives Anait a choice based on the double standard. "Should I tell you the truth or a lie?" Anait's wisdom comes to the fore. She bypasses his choice and refuses to take responsibility for whether he lies or tells the truth. His own character must decide that. He himself must take responsibility for his choice.

Anait insisted on honesty, equality, and mutual respect at the outset. The prince understood and valued this. That is what made him love her. Anait insists on honesty throughout the story. She has vowed not to marry a man without a trade. She explains, "a ruler may become a servant." Prince Vachagan listens, understands, values her advice, and follows it. She knows that he will be a good partner in life because he is a man who knows how to listen to a woman.

The Fortune-Teller

Russia[41]

In a certain village there lived an old woman, and she had a son, neither too big nor too small, but not old enough to work in the fields. Things came to such a pass that they had nothing in the larder. So the old woman put on her thinking cap and racked her brains to find a way to make ends meet and have a loaf of bread to eat. She thought and thought, until she had an idea. So she said to the boy: "Go lead away somebody's horses, tether 'em to that there bush and give 'em some hay, then untether 'em again, lead 'em to that there hollow and leave 'em there." Now her son was a smart lad, and no mistake. No sooner did he hear this, than off he went, led away some horses and did what his mother had told him. For it was said of her that she knew more than ordinary folk and could read the cards now and then when asked.

When the owners saw their horses had gone, they went in search of them, hunting high and low, poor devils, but there was not a sign of them. "What are we to do?" they cried. "We must get a fortune-teller to find 'em for us, even though it means paying through the nose." Then they remembered the old woman and said: "Let's go to her and ask her to read the cards; like as not she'll tell us summit about 'em." No sooner said than done. They went to the old woman and said: "Granny, dear. We have heard say that you know more than ordinary folk. That you can read the cards and tell all from 'em like an open book. Then read 'em for us, dear mistress, for our horses are gone." Then the old woman said to them: "My strength is failing, dear masters! I am forever a-wheezing and a-gasping, sirs." But they replied: "Do as we ask, dear mistress! It is not for naught. We shall reward you for your pains."

Shuffling and coughing, she laid out the cards, peered hard at them and although they told her nothing—what of it; hunger is no brother, it teaches you a thing or two—said: "Well, I never! Look here, sirs! It seems your horses are in that there place, tethered to a bush." The owners were overjoyed, rewarded the old woman for her pains and went to look for their beasts. They came to the bush, but there was no sign of the horses, though you could see where they had been tethered 'cause part of a bridle was hanging on the bush and there was lots of hay around. They had been there, but now they were gone. The men were grieved, poor devils, and didn't know what to do. They thought it over and went back to the old woman. If she had found out once, she would tell them again.

So they came to the old woman, who was lying on the stove-bed, a-wheezing and a-gasping like goodness knows what was ailing her. They begged her earnestly to read the cards for them again. She pretended to refuse as before, saying: "My strength is failing, I am plagued by old age!"—so that they would give her a bit more for her pains. They promised to begrudge her nothing if the horses were found and give her more than before. So the old woman climbed down from the stove-bed, shuffling and coughing, laid out the cards again, peered hard at them and said: "Go look for them in that there hollow. That's where they are for sure!" The owners rewarded her handsomely for her pains and set off again to look. They reached the hollow and found their horses safe and sound; so they took them and led them home.

After that the stories spread far and wide about the old woman with second sight who could read the cards and tell you surely what would come to pass. These rumours reached a certain rich gentleman who had lost a chest full of money. When he heard about the old fortune-teller, he sent his carriage to bring her to him without delay, no matter how poorly she felt. He also sent his two manservants, Nikolasha and Yemelya (it was they who had pinched their master's money). So they came for the old woman, all but dragged her into the carriage by force and set off home. On the way the old woman began to moan and groan, sighing and muttering to herself: "Oh, dear. If it weren't for no cash and an empty belly I would never be a fortune-teller, riding in a carriage for a fine gentleman to lock me up where the ravens would not take my bones. Alas, alack! No good will come of this!"

Nikolasha overheard her and said: "Hear that, Yemelya! The old girl's talking about us. Looks as if we're for it!"* "Steady now, lad," said Yemelya. "Perhaps you just imagined it." But Nikolasha told him: "Listen for yourself there she goes again." The old woman was scared out of her wits. She sat quiet for a while, then began moaning again: "Oh, dear! If it weren't for no cash and an empty belly this would never have happened!" The lads strained their ears to catch what she was saying. After a bit she went on again about "no cash and an empty belly," blathering all sorts of nonsense. When the lads heard this, they got a real fright. What were they to do? They agreed to ask the old woman not to give them away to their master, because she kept saying: "If it weren't for Nikolasha and Yemelya, this would never have happened." In their excite-

---

* "No cash" and Nikolasha, "empty belly" and Yemelya are similar enough for the thieves to mistake the old lady's words for their own names.

ment the two rascals thought the old woman was talking about Nikolasha and Yemelya, not no cash and an empty belly!

No sooner said than done. They begged the old woman: "Have pity on us, Granny dear, and we'll say prayers for you forever more. Why ruin us and tell the master all? Just don't mention us, keep quiet about it; we'll make it worth your while." Now the old woman was no fool. She put two and two together, and her fear vanished in a trice. "Where did you hide it, my children?" she asked. "It was the Devil himself tempted us to commit such a sin," they wailed. "But where is it?" repeated the old woman. "Where else could we hide it but under the bridge by the mill until the good weather comes." So they reached an agreement and then arrived at the rich gentleman's house. When he saw they had brought the old woman, their master was beside himself with joy. He led her into the house and plied her with all manner of food and drink, whatever she fancied, and when she had eaten and drunk her fill, he asked her to read the cards and find out where his money was. But the old woman had her wits about her and kept saying that her strength was failing and she could hardly stand. "Come now, Granny," said the gentleman. "Make yourself at home, sit down, if you like, or lie down if you don't feel well enough to sit, only read the cards and find out what I asked. And if you can tell me who took my money and I find it again, I'll not only wine and dine you, but reward you handsomely with anything that you fancy."

And so, a-wheezing and a-gasping as if afflicted by some terrible malady, the old woman took the cards, laid them out and peered hard at them, muttering to herself all the time. "Your lost chest is under the bridge by the mill," she said finally. No sooner had he heard the old woman's word, than the gentleman sent Nikolasha and Yemelya to find the money and bring it to him. He did not know it was they who had taken it. So they found it and brought it to their master; and their master was so overjoyed to see his money, that he did not count it, and gave the old woman a hundred rubles straightaway and a nice little present besides, promising not to forget her service to him in the future as well. Then having entertained her lavishly, he sent her home in his carriage and gave her something for the road as well. On the way Nikolasha and Yemelya thanked the old woman for not betraying them to their master and gave her some money too.

After that the old woman was more famous than ever and settled down to a life of ease with all the bread she wanted, and other fare in abundance, and plenty of livestock too. And she and her son lived and prospered and drank beer and mead. For I was there and drank mead-wine, it touched my lips but not my tongue.

In a certain village there was an old and single mother. Her son was too young to work. Her larder was empty. She comes up with a crazy idea, a desperate scam, but this is a folktale and it works.

In the face of famine, a ruthless feudal lord, or an overwhelming industrial society, fairy tales give people, the unprivileged masses, hope and inspiration. First the tale presents a real problem, the empty larder, and reinforces the people's dissatisfaction with their lot. However, the tale happens "Once upon a time" or "In a certain village." This frees up the imagination. An improbable solution that might otherwise be rejected out of hand is thought of and made to work, like this old woman's scam. A different tale could start with the same problem and come up with a totally different solution, like "Whuppity Stoorie" (p. 29), where guessing the fairy's name is the solution, or "The Child Who Was Poor and Good" (p. 60), where the little girl makes friends who help her. In folktales ideas flow without morose reality being on hand to veto every improbable suggestion. With consistently happy endings, fairy tales guarantee success. The audience returns to their daily struggles. However the utopian message of the fairy tale remains despite the reality: Believe that you can better your situation, use your head, you can do it! [42]

The Tsarítsa Harpist

Russia[43]

In a certain kingdom in a certain land once there lived a Tsar and a Tsarítsa. He lived with her for some time, then he thought he would go to that far distant country, the Holy Land. So he issued orders to his ministers, bade farewell to his wife, and set out on his road.

It may-be far, it may-be short, he at last reached that distant land, the Holy Land. And in that country then the Accursed King was the ruler. This King saw the Tsar, and he bade him be seized and lodged in the dungeon. There were many tortures in that dungeon for him. At night he must sit in chains, and in the morning the Accursed King used to put a horse-collar on him and make him drive the plough until the evening. This was the torment in which the Tsar lived for three whole years, and he had no idea how he should tear himself away or send any news of himself to his Tsarítsa. And he sought for some occasion. And he wrote her this little line: "Sell," he said, "all my possessions and come to redeem me from my misfortune."

When the Tsarítsa received the letter she read it through and said to herself, "How can I redeem the Tsar? If I go myself, the Accursed King will receive me and will take me to himself as a wife. If I send one of the ministers, I can place no reliance on *him*." So what did she advise? She cut off her red hair, went and disguised herself as a wandering musician, took her *gusli*,* and never told anybody, and so set out on her road and way.

She arrived at the Accursed King's courtyard and began to play the *gusli* so finely as had never been heard or listened to for ages. When the King heard such wonderful music he summoned the harpist into the palace. "Hail, *guslyár!*° From what land have you come? From what kingdom?" asked the King.

"I do not journey far in the wide white world: I rejoice men's hearts and I feed myself."

"Stay with me one day and another day, and a third, and I will reward you generously."

So the *guslyár* stayed on, and played for an entire day in front of the

* *Gusli*, a three-cornered, triangle-like harp with many strings carried by troubadours. There were various sizes, but it was always portable.
° *Guslyár*, one who plays the *gusli*.

King, and he could never hear enough of her. "What wonderful music! why, it drove away all weariness and grief as though at a breath."

So the *guslyár* stayed with the King three days, and was going to say farewell.

"What reward can I offer you for your labour?" asked the King.

"Oh, your Majesty, give me one prisoner who has sat long in the prison; I must have a companion on the road! I wish to go to foreign kingdoms, and I have no one with whom I can exchange a word."

"Certainly! Select whom you will," said the King, and he led the *guslyár* into the prison.

The *guslyár* looked at the prisoners, selected the Tsar, and they went out to roam together.

As they were journeying on to their own kingdom the Tsar said, "Let me go, good man, for I am no simple prisoner, I am the Tsar himself. I will pay you ransom for as much as you will; I will grudge you neither money nor service."

"Go with God," said the *guslyár*: "I do not need you at all."

"Well, come to me as my guest."

"When the time shall come, I will be there."

So they parted, and each set out on his own way. The Tsarítsa went by a circuitous route, reached home before her husband, took off her *guslyár*'s dress and arrayed herself like an empress.

In about one hour cries rang out and the attendants came up to the palace, for the Tsar had arrived. The Tsarítsa ran out to meet him, and he greeted them all, but he did not look at her. He greeted the ministers and said, "Look, gentlemen, what a wife mine is! Now she flings herself on my neck, but when I sat in prison and sent her a letter to sell all my goods and to redeem me she did nothing. Of what was she thinking if she so forgot her liege husband?"

And the ministers answered the Tsar, "Your Majesty, on the very day the Tsarítsa received your letter she vanished no one knows where, and has been away all this time, and she has only just appeared in the palace."

Then the Tsar was very angry and commanded, "My ministers, do ye judge my unfaithful wife according to justice and to truth. Where has she been roaming in the white world? Why did she not try to redeem me? You would never have seen your Tsar again for ages of eternity, if a young *guslyár* had not arrived, for whom I am going to pray God, and I do not grudge giving him half my kingdom."

In the meantime the Tsarítsa got off her throne and arrayed herself as the harpist, went into the courtyard and began to play the *gusli*. The Tsar heard, ran to meet her, seized the musician by the hand, led her into the palace and said to his Court, "This is the *guslyár* who rescued me from my confinement." The *guslyár* then flung off his outer garment, and they then all recognised the Tsarítsa. Then the Tsar was overjoyed and for his joy he celebrated a feast which lasted seven whole days.

"What wonderful music! why it drove away all weariness and grief as though at a breath." The Tsarítsa uses her musical talent to save her husband, but she can only do it in the guise of a man. History is full of women whose works of art were published under a man's name because it was improper or impossible to publish as a woman. The author, George Eliot, was a woman. Fanny Mendelssohn's music compositions were published under her famous brother's name. True to fairy tale form, this tale has a happy ending and the Tsarítsa receives full credit for her brave and resourceful rescue of her husband. However, the names of many women cannot be given a place in history next to their contributions. Their own names have been lost because they worked using men's names.

Tales
from
North and
South America

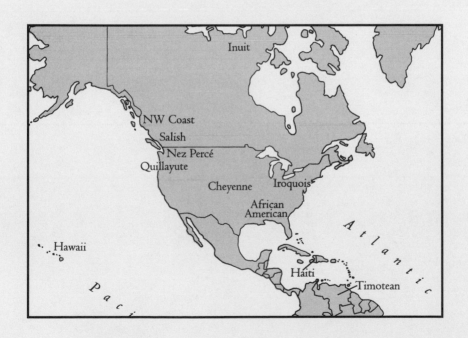

The Vampire Skeleton

Iroquois[44]

Many years ago there was a man who was said to be an evil wizard. Though no one could prove it, it was said that in the dark of the night he would turn into an owl and go about doing bad things. When he died, no one was unhappy. He had no family and his body was placed—as was the custom in those days—in a box made of cedar wood which was left inside his lodge deep in the woods.

Many moons passed. It was the time of long nights. A woman, her husband and their small child came travelling through the woods. As they walked, the man complained. "Why is it that we must go visit your relatives? Why is it we must bring them food? We hardly have food enough for ourselves. Now we must walk through this deep snow and it is late at night."

The woman said nothing. She was embarrassed that he complained so about helping others. She trudged on ahead, breaking a trail through the snow. Their little boy rode in the cradleboard on her back. Most of the food was in the pack she carried in her arms. Then they came to a clearing. There, in front of them, was an old lodge.

"Ah," her husband said, "this is a place we can spend the night. It is a long walk to the nearest village."

The woman did not like the look of the place. "I am not tired," she said. "Let us keep walking."

But the husband would not listen. "It is decided," he said. "We shall stay here."

As they came closer to the place, the little boy woke up in his cradleboard and began to cry. It was very hard for the woman to soothe him. "If your child is not quiet," said the husband as he looked around the lodge, "I will not get much sleep." He walked over to one corner of the room where a bed had been made of spruce boughs. Near the bed was a large cedar box. "There is only one bed," said the man. "I shall sleep in it since it is closer to the door. Then if any trouble comes I can protect you and the child." He climbed onto the bed, wrapped his blankets about him and was soon asleep.

The woman made herself as comfortable as she could on the floor in the middle of the lodge. It was cold and she only had one small blanket which she wrapped around her child. Grandmother Moon's bright face was just beginning to appear from behind a cloud when she finally fell asleep.

How long she slept she did not know, but a strange sound wakened her. It was like the sound of an owl crushing the bones of a mouse. She opened her eyes slowly and looked around. Grandmother Moon's light was shining in through the open door. Her husband still lay wrapped in his blankets on the bed, but the woman sensed that something was wrong. She crept closer to look at him and saw a terrible thing. Her husband was dead. His throat had been torn out. Near his bed the cedar box was bathed in moonlight and its lid was open. She looked into it and saw an even more frightening thing! Within the box was the skeleton of a large man. The teeth of the skeleton were red with blood.

Ah, she thought, That is the body of one who was evil when he was alive. Even death has not stopped him from thirsting for human blood. He is satisfied now, but soon he will come after me and my child. I must not let him know he has been discovered.

Crawling silently back to the place on the floor where her baby lay wrapped in the blanket and cradleboard, she pretended to go to sleep. Then, slowly as a heron moves when it is stalking a fish, she began to move toward the open door, dragging her baby with her. When she was finally close to the doorway, swiftly as a leaping deer she sprang to her feet and rushed through the door, the cradleboard in her arms. Her feet sank in the deep snow as she ran. Now she was out of the clearing and on the trail to the village. She heard a terrible cry. "HOOO-WEHHH-HH! HOOO-WEHHHH!" It was the scream of the vampire skeleton. It had discovered she was gone and was on her trail.

On she ran, on and on. Then the cry sounded again. "HOOO-WEHHHH! HOOO-WEHHH! HOOO-WEHHHH!" It was closer than before, but she kept running. She could see that the night was ending. The light which comes before dawn was beginning to paint the eastern sky. If only she could run just a little further!

"HOOO-WEHHH! HOOO-WEHHH! HOOO-WEHHH! HOOO-WEHHH!" Again that awful cry came, right behind her. Her blood froze and she stumbled with fear but she kept on running. Her husband had said the village was far away, but she knew his words were only an excuse to hide his laziness. Ahead she saw a tree marked with a circle and a cross. It was the sign of a village's boundaries. She could hear feet crunching in the snow behind her as she ran but she did not look back. A clearing opened and she saw many lodges. Light flickered through the door of the closest lodge and she stumbled inside. Men and women looked up in surprise at the wild-eyed woman who stood before them holding a baby.

"A monster," she said, "outside. It chases me!" Several of the men stepped out, clutching their war clubs. There, at the edge of the village, the creature stood, its jaws covered with blood, its eyes glowing like red flames. It came no closer and as the dawn light grew stronger it turned, went back into the trees and was gone.

When the woman had finished her story, a wise old woman spoke. "I was afraid this would happen. That lodge was the home of one whose name we do not speak. He was said to be a lover of evil. Now we must go to that place and dig out the root before it grows more wicked fruits."

Before the sun was two hands high, a group of warriors came with the wise old woman and the woman who had lost her husband to the lodge deep in the woods. Inside they found the body of the woman's husband still on the bed. All of the flesh had been eaten from his body. Within the cedar box, covered with blood, the skeleton of the wizard lay. The wise old woman placed herbs inside the cedar box and in front of the doorway.

"Now," she said, "pile dry wood all around." The men did as she told them. Then she set fire to the wood. "Stand in a circle all around the lodge," she said. "Watch and see if anything comes out of the flames."

Soon the whole lodge was burning. A noise like the screaming of a man began to come from the middle of the flames. Something was running back and forth within the lodge, trying to get out. Then, just as the walls of the lodge collapsed, a huge screech owl flew out. The circle of men struck at it, but it flew into the forest.

So it was that the skeleton was destroyed. The woman who lost her husband found friends in the village. Eventually she married a man who helped her and listened to her advice. And it is said that from that time on people who died were no longer placed in cedar boxes above the ground. Instead they were buried in the earth. This way a wandering spirit would not find it so easy to escape and roam the night.

Traditionally the Iroquois lived in longhouses, which averaged 50 to 100 feet in length and 16 to 18 feet wide. Each longhouse was headed by a clan mother. Women owned the family's property and arranged the marriages. Children inherited clan membership (Bear, Wolf, Deer, etc.) through their mothers. When a man married, he went to live with his wife's clan but he never became a part of her clan. The Iroquois were a democratic society and although men were the chiefs, the women controlled the nomination process.

The Iroquois were by tradition a matrilineal society, maybe that is why this story presents so many details reflecting a woman's perspective. The woman trudges on ahead, breaking a path through deep snow, the child in a cradleboard on her back, she also car-

ries most of the food. The man walks along complaining. "Why is it that we must go visit your relatives? Why is it we must bring them food?" The woman says nothing but is "embarrassed that he complained so about helping others." She senses the evil of the vampire lodge. He does not. He refuses her advice, "It is decided. . . . We shall stay here." As the woman comforts the crying child, the man remarks, "If your child is not quiet . . . I will not get much sleep." He hogs the bed and the blankets and is finally killed by the vampire. The woman's emotional intelligence and fast legs help her escape to the haven of a village.

At the end of the story "Davit" (p. 77), the heroine is praised from a man's point of view, " . . . next to a good mother, what can a man have better than a good sister?" The end of "The Vampire Skeleton" focuses on the woman's point of view. "The woman . . . found friends in the village. Eventually she married a man who helped her and listened to her advice."

The Flying Head

Iroquois[45]

In days long past, evil monsters and spirits preyed upon humans. As long as the sun was shining, the monsters hid unseen in deep caves, but on stormy nights they came out of their dens and prowled the earth. The most terrible of all was the great Flying Head. Though only a scowling, snarling head without a body, it was four times as tall as the tallest man. Its skin was so thick and matted with hair that no weapon could penetrate it. Two huge bird wings grew from either side of its cheeks, and with them it could soar into the sky or dive down, floating, like a buzzard. Instead of teeth, the Flying Head had a mouth full of huge, piercing fangs with which it seized and devoured its prey. And everything was prey to this monster, every living being, including people.

One dark night a young woman alone with her baby was sitting in a longhouse. Everybody had fled and hidden, because someone had seen the great Flying Head darting among the treetops of the forest. The young mother had not run away because, as she said to herself, "Someone must make a stand against this monster. It might as well be me." So she sat by the hearth, building a big fire, heating in the flames a number of large, red-hot, glowing stones.

She sat waiting and watching, until suddenly the Flying Head appeared in the door. Grinning horribly, it looked into the longhouse, but she pretended not to see it and acted as if she were cooking a meal. She made believe that she was eating some of the red-hot rocks, picking them up with a forked stick and seeming to put them into her mouth. (In reality she passed them behind her face and dropped them on the ground.) All the while she was smacking her lips, exclaiming: "Ah, how good this is! What wonderful food! Never has anyone feasted on meat like this!"

Hearing her, the monster could not restrain itself. It thrust its head deep inside the lodge, opened its jaws wide, and seized and swallowed in one mighty gulp the whole heap of glowing, hissing rocks. As soon as it had swallowed, the monster uttered a terrible cry which echoed throughout the land. With wings flapping the great Flying Head fled, screaming, screaming, screaming over mountains, streams and forest, screaming so that the biggest trees were shaking, screaming until the earth trembled, screaming until the leaves fell from the branches. At last the screams were fading away in the distance, fading, fading, until at last they could no longer be heard. Then the people everywhere could take their hands from their ears and breathe safely. After that the Flying Head was never seen again, and nobody knows what became of it.

"Someone must make a stand against this monster. It might as well be me."
    This young mother realizes that she and her child might die. However, to save her village and all the other villages threatened by the Flying Head she chooses to confront the monster. This choice demands more than spontaneous bravery. It requires courage.

Where the Girl Saved Her Brother

Cheyenne[46]

In the summer of 1876, the two greatest battles between soldiers and Indians were fought on the plains of Montana. The first fight was called the Battle of the Rosebud. The second, which was fought a week later, was called the Battle of the Little Bighorn, where General Custer was defeated and killed. The Cheyennes call the Battle of the Rosebud the Fight Where the Girl Saved Her Brother. Let me tell you why.

Well, a hundred years ago, the white men wanted the Indians to go into prisons called "reservations," to give up their freedom to roam and hunt buffalo, to give up being Indians. Some tamely submitted and settled down behind the barbed wire of the agencies, but others did not.

Those who went to the reservations to live like white men were called "friendlies." Those who would not go were called "hostiles." They were not hostile, really. They didn't want to fight; all they wanted was to be left alone to live the Indian way, which was a good way. But the soldiers would not leave them alone. They decided to have a great roundup and catch all "hostiles," kill those who resisted, and bring the others back to the agencies as prisoners.

Three columns of soldiers entered the last stretch of land left to the red man. They were led by Generals Crook, Terry, and Custer. Crook had the most men with him, about two thousand. He also had cannon and Indian scouts to guide him. At the Rosebud he met the united Sioux and Cheyenne warriors.

The Indians had danced the sacred sun dance. The great Sioux chief and holy man, Sitting Bull, had been granted a vision telling him that the soldiers would be defeated. The warriors were in high spirits. Some men belonging to famous warrior societies had vowed to fight until they were killed, singing their death songs, throwing their lives away, as it was called. They painted their faces for war. They put on their finest outfits so that, if they were killed, their enemies would say, "This must have been a great chief. See how nobly he lies there."

The old chiefs instructed the young men how to act. The medicine men prepared protective charms for the fighters, putting gopher dust on their hair, or painting their horses with hailstone designs. This was to render them invisible to their foes, or to make them bulletproof. Brave Wolf had the most admired medicine—a mounted hawk that he fastened to the back of his head. He always rode into battle blowing his eagle-bone whistle—and once the fight started, the hawk came alive and whistled too.

Many proud tribes were there besides the Cheyenne—the Hunkpapa, the Minniconjou, the Oglala, the Burned Thighs, the Two Kettles. Many brave chiefs and warriors came, including Two Moons, White Bull, Dirty Moccasins, Little Hawk, Yellow Eagle, and Lame White Man. Among the Sioux was the great Crazy Horse, and Sitting Bull—their holy man, still weak from his flesh offerings made at the sun dance—and the fierce Rain-in-the-Face. Who can count them all, and what a fine sight they were!

Those who had earned the right to wear warbonnets were singing, lifting them up. Three times they stopped in their singing, and the fourth time they put the bonnets on their heads, letting the streamers fly and trail behind them. How good it must have been to see this!

Crazy Horse of the Oglala shouted his famous war cry: "A good day to die, and a good day to fight! Cowards to the rear, brave hearts—follow me!"

The fight started. Many brave deeds were done, many coups counted. The battle swayed to and fro. More than anybody else's, this was the Cheyenne's fight. This was their day. Among them was a brave young girl, Buffalo-Calf-Road-Woman, who rode proudly beside her husband, Black Coyote. Her brother, Chief Comes-in-Sight, was in the battle too. She looked for him and at last saw him surrounded, his horse killed from under him. Soldiers were aiming their rifles at him, while their Crow scouts circled around him and waited for an opportunity to count coups. But he fought them off with courage and skill.

Buffalo-Calf-Road-Woman uttered a shrill, high-pitched war cry. She raced her pony into the midst of the battle, into the midst of the enemy. She made the spine-chilling, trilling, trembling sound of the Indian woman encouraging her man during a fight. Chief Comes-in-Sight jumped up on her horse behind her. Buffalo-Calf-Road-Woman laughed with joy and the excitement of battle and all the while she sang. The soldiers were firing at her, and their Crow scouts were shooting arrows at her horse, but it moved too fast for her and her brother to be hit. Then she turned her horse and raced up the hill from which the old chiefs and the medicine men were watching the battle.

The Sioux and Cheyenne saw what she was doing, and then the white soldiers saw it too. They all stopped fighting and watched the brave girl saving her brother's life. The warriors raised their arms and set up a mighty shout—a long, undulating war cry that made one's hairs stand on

end. And even some of the soldiers threw their caps in the air and shouted "Hurrah!" in honor of Buffalo-Calf-Road-Woman.

The battle was still young. Not many men had been killed on either
side, but the white general was thinking, "If their women fight like this,
what will their warriors be like? Even if I win, I will lose half my men."
And so General Crook retreated a hundred miles or so. He was to have
joined up with Custer, Old Yellow Hair, but when Custer had to fight
the same Cheyenne and Sioux again a week later, Crook was far away
and Custer's regiment was wiped out. So in a way, Buffalo-Calf-Road-
Woman contributed to that battle too.

Many who saw what she had done thought that she had counted the
biggest coup—not taking life but giving it. That is why the Indians call
the Battle of the Rosebud the Fight Where the Girl Saved Her Brother.

The spot where Buffalo-Calf-Road-Woman counted coup has long
since been plowed under. A ranch now covers it. But the memory of her
deed will last as long as there are Indians. This is not a fairy tale, but it
is a legend.

*Many of us share an image of the Cheyenne and Sioux living in tepees, their
braves on horseback hunting buffalo or in feathered warbonnets galloping into
battle. Rarely does one picture women riding into battle and even less often "counting
coup." Counting coup gained a warrior much more honor than just shooting someone
from a distance. To count coup one had to approach a live, unharmed enemy and hit
him on the head with the coup stick or touch the enemy with a hand or rescue someone
from the midst of the enemy, as the heroine in this story does. "Many who saw what
she had done thought that she had counted the biggest coup—not taking life but giving
it."*

Chief Joseph's Story of Wallowa Lake

Nez Percé[47]

Many years ago, probably as long ago as two men can live, our tribe was strong and had many warriors. Every summer they went over into the buffalo country to hunt buffalo. So did the Blackfeet, who lived east of the Big Shining Mountains.

One summer when Red Wolf, chief of the Nez Percé, and a few of his warriors were hunting buffalo, they were attacked by a large band of Blackfeet. Most of Red Wolf's men were killed.

All the next winter our people made bows and arrows for an attack of revenge. When summer came, Red Wolf and his warriors went to the buffalo country. There the two tribes met and fought again. This time the Nez Percé were strong. Not one was killed, and the band returned home with many horses and many scalps taken from the Blackfeet. Summer after summer the two tribes met in the buffalo country east of the great mountains, and summer after summer they fought. Every boy went to the buffalo country as soon as he was big enough to fight. Old Chief Red Wolf died, and young Chief Red Wolf led the warriors in his place.

One summer, when a large number of our people were in the buffalo country, the Blackfeet attacked them in the night. All our people were asleep. Many Nez Percé warriors were killed. The rest, pursued by the Blackfeet, had to fight again and again as they fled toward home.

The night Red Wolf reached his village, he was worn and weak, and he had only a few warriors left. But the Blackfeet were still powerful. Unable to follow the Nez Percé to their village in the darkness, they camped across the lake. They planned to kill the old men and take the women and children prisoners in the morning.

All night the Blackfeet kept big fires burning, and all night they shouted and danced. But our people built no fires. There was no dancing among them. Instead, there was wailing for the dead. There was sorrow in Red Wolf's tepee.

Chief Red Wolf had only one child, a beautiful daughter named Wahluna. Everyone loved Wahluna, and she loved her people and her father dearly. She knew that he was too weak to fight again, and she knew that not enough warriors were left to fight against the Blackfeet.

Unseen by her family and friends, Wahluna slipped away from the village to her canoe among the willows. Without a sound she paddled across the lake to the camp of the Blackfeet, beached her canoe, and walked toward the biggest fire.

There a huge warrior, with six Nez Percé scalps hanging from his belt, was speaking to the other men. When he had finished, Wahluna came out into the firelight and said, "I am Wahluna, daughter of Red Wolf. I have come to speak to the great chief of the Blackfeet."

"I am Bloody Chief, war chief of the Blackfeet," the big man replied. "What has the daughter of Red Wolf to say to me?"

"I come to plead for my people. They do not know I have come. Our young warriors have been killed. Our women are now wailing for the dead, and we have no fires in our village. My father says that tomorrow you will kill us all. But I know you do not want the scalps of old men and of women and children. I beg you to return to your country without more fighting. We can never fight Bloody Chief again, for our warriors are dead."

Then Wahluna lay down upon the sand and buried her face. Tlesca, the son of Bloody Chief, spread his robe over her shoulders and said to her, "You are brave, and you love your people. My heart grieves with yours. I shall not fight your people again."

These words from the young warrior made his father angry. "Her people are dogs. Pick up your robe, Tlesca. The girl must die."

Tlesca did not move. "Red Wolf is not a dog," he said. "He has fought bravely. For days we have followed him over rough mountain trails. We have seen him stagger from hunger, but when he turned to fight, his heart was brave. I am the only one of our warriors strong enough to fight him singlehanded, and yet my shoulder was broken by his war club. The daughter of Red Wolf is not a dog. I will leave my robe on her shoulders."

Bloody Chief's heart was softened, for he loved the young warrior. "My son's words are good," he said. "I will lay my robe on his."

Wahluna then arose and started toward her canoe. She knew that her people would live. As she reached for her paddle, she found Tlesca standing beside her.

"The daughter of Red Wolf is brave," he said, "and she is beautiful. When twelve moons have passed, listen in the middle of the night. You will hear a great owl hooting down by the lake. Come then, and Tlesca will speak."

Wahluna returned to her village. Her people were not attacked. They could build their fires again.

She counted the moons until twelve had passed. One night when all in the village were asleep, she heard the great owl down by the lake. Leaving her tepee, she slipped through the village and down to the edge of the water. There she found Tlesca waiting.

He said to her, "Some of the Blackfeet daughters look upon Tlesca with favor, because he is a great warrior. But Tlesca's heart is with Wahluna. He wants her to be his wife."

"It cannot be," said Wahluna. "My people would kill Tlesca and give his bones to the wolves, even as the Blackfeet warriors have given our warriors' bones to the wolves."

"When six more moons have passed," Tlesca answered, "Wahluna will hear the howl of a gray wolf. If she will cross the lake, Tlesca will speak again."

Again Wahluna counted the moons. When the sixth one was passing, she heard a gray wolf howl in the middle of the night. She slipped away to her canoe and paddled noiselessly across the lake. Tlesca was waiting.

"I have talked with my father," he said. "His heart has softened. Tomorrow morning, I will bring him and all our chiefs and many of our warriors to the village of Red Wolf. We will smoke the peace pipe with your father and his warriors. We will catch fish in your lake, and you can come to the buffalo country without harm from us."

Next morning Wahluna reported to her father what Tlesca had said. Red Wolf told his men. Together they waited. Bloody Chief and Tlesca and many warriors of the Blackfeet came to the Nez Percé village. They seated themselves around the campfire with Red Wolf and his men. They smoked the peace pipe together and were brothers.

Then the great chief of the Blackfeet said to Red Wolf, "My son's heart is with your daughter. He wants her for his wife. He is a great warrior."

Red Wolf answered, "My daughter has told me. Her heart is with Tlesca. She may go to his lodge."

Then Red Wolf sent runners to the Nez Percé people along the Kookooskia and to his friends among the Yakima and Cayuse. He invited them to a wedding feast.

At sunset on the first day of the feast, Wahluna and Tlesca went out on the lake in a canoe. The people on shore stood watching them paddle toward the mountains. Suddenly, the waters became troubled. Tlesca and Wahluna began to pull toward the shore. Ripples and then waves came over the lake. The waves became larger. Some demon seemed to be rising from the depths of the lake.

Soon a serpent's head appeared. Then a giant serpent rose out of the water, swam round the canoe, jumped high, and gave the boat a sharp blow with its tail.

Wahluna and Tlesca were never seen again. For days people of both tribes looked for their bodies, but they were never found. With sad hearts the Blackfeet went back to their country. They were sure that the Great Spirit was angry with them and so had taken away the young chief whom they loved.

The Nez Percé also thought that the Great Spirit was angry because they had made peace with their ancient enemy. Fearing that they might be punished a second time, they never again went out on the lake at the foot of the Wallowa Mountains.

Wahluna walks unarmed into the enemy village. By negotiating an honorable surrender, she saves the lives of her people. Made possible by Wahluna's initiative, a Juliet and Romeo relationship develops between her and Tlesca, the son of the enemy chief. This relationship might have brought about a more successful rapprochement between the tribes.

This story was told in about 1870 to three white men hunting in the Wallowa Mountains of northeastern Oregon. They had been invited to join a group of Nez Percé hunters also in pursuit of elk. While the men were drying their elk meat, Eagle Wing, the Nez Percé leader, entertained them with this story of the Nez Percé and Blackfeet Indians. Eagle Wing came to be known as Chief Joseph and it was he who in 1877 tried to negotiate a settlement with the whites to save his people. Fear of retaliation forced him to lead his people on a desperate march toward freedom in Canada, but they were stopped just short of the border.[48]

The Origin of the Potlatch

Quillayute [49]

A strange bird once appeared in the ocean in front of the village. All the young men of the Quillayute went out and tried to shoot it, but no one could hit it. Every day Blue Jay, a slave of Golden Eagle, watched the hunters try to shoot the strange bird.

One day Golden Eagle said to Blue Jay, "Eh, my children can catch that queer-looking bird."

"Oh, no," replied Blue Jay quickly. "They are girls."

Golden Eagle's daughters overheard the two men, but they said nothing. Next day the two younger sisters went into the woods and stayed all day. Many days they spent in the woods, telling no one what they were doing. Although they were girls, just imagine—they were making arrows!

One morning, before daylight, they went to the forest and brought in the arrows they had made. When they returned to the village, all the hunters had gone out in their canoes to try again to shoot the strange-looking bird. The two sisters disguised themselves by tying their hair in front so as to hide their faces. No one could recognize them. Then they paddled their canoe in a zigzag line until they were near the bird. The older of the sisters killed it with her third arrow.

That evening the girls said to their father, "We caught the bird and then we hid it in the woods. We want to use its feathers as presents, for the feathers are of many colors. Will you tell Blue Jay to invite all the birds to come to our lodge tomorrow?"

Next morning Blue Jay went out with the invitation. Soon all kinds of birds were gathered in the lodge of Golden Eagle. "My daughters caught the strange bird," the host explained, "the bird of many colors. They want to give each of you a present."

The girls gave certain colors to different birds—yellow and brown feathers to Meadowlark, red and brown to Robin, brown only to Wren, yellow and black to the little Finch. They gave to each bird the colors it was to have. They kept giving until they had no more feathers left.

Ever since then, certain birds have had certain colors. And since then, there have been potlatches. This was the first potlatch, the first giving of gifts from the people who invite to the people who are invited.

In this story, two girls founded the potlatch. The potlatch was a ceremonial gift-giving feast among the Native Americans along the coast from Oregon to Alaska. The potlatch was given to celebrate a marriage or to assert formal claims to fishing rights and was a time for community matters like children's ear-piercing and the official announcement of names. The host gave each guest gifts. The more the host gave, the more respect was gained. The key factor was the quantity of goods given away or destroyed. In some tribes a slave might be clubbed to death to show how little value the owner placed on property. Although the giver might temporarily be impoverished, wealth would be regained during future potlatches. In the potlatch there was an interesting departure from repaying insult with insult. If any guest felt slighted by the quality or quantity of gifts received, dissatisfaction was expressed by giving the host a gift, which the host then was expected to top.

The Princess and Mountain Dweller

People of the Northwest Coast [50]

It happened in the time of long ago, when things were different along the mountainous Northwest Coast. Then, wealth and social position were cherished. And the proper behavior of a marriageable princess was all important.

Now, as it happened, one proud and spirited princess—Maada—was none too happy with her sudden change from carefree girl to marriageable princess. She was like a deer deprived of its freedom. Now, instead of running joyfully along the beach and the trails, she was expected to move as a dignified young lady should, surrounded by a flutter of high-ranking attendants. Only her grandmother seemed to see her still as a child.

Her grandmother was keeper of a special box that held special food for special visitors. But she could never resist slipping bits of the special food to her two granddaughters, Maada and her little sister. And when she was challenged about the missing tidbits, she could never resist saying, "The old shaggy dog took it away from me." Though everyone knew where it had really gone.

One day she gave the two girls the very last bits of precious mountain sheep tallow. And that might not have mattered so much if a canoeload of important visitors had not arrived unexpectedly from somewhere along the river. And even that might not have mattered so much if the girls' father had not been head chief of the village, the natural host for such important visitors.

He was a man of great pride. His house was the biggest of the big, handsomely decorated cedar houses on the Street of Chiefs. His hospitality was famous. His small son was heir to a mighty chieftainship in another village. And his elder daughter was so beautiful that she was being sought in marriage by the noblest families along the coast. Indeed, the unexpected canoe carried one of the most desirable of these suitors.

When the big totem-crested canoe arrived, the chief sent his young men down to carry up the travellers' belongings. He put on a fine robe and ordered the Dance of Welcome. And he asked his wife to provide some special tallow tidbits so that the honored guests might chew the fat around the fire until a proper feast was prepared for them.

His wife went quickly to the grandmother, only to be told that the last bit of precious tallow was gone. "The old shaggy dog took it away from me," the grandmother told her son's wife.

"Indeed?" the chief woman said, turning suspicious eyes on her two daughters. "Did you take the tallow?" she asked them in quiet anger.

Maada raised her head defiantly, while the little princess blinked back tears. They couldn't answer, for they had just snatched up the hard pieces of tallow from their wooden food dishes and popped them into their mouths to hide them, for their grandmother's sake, of course. They had also dropped mats over the telltale dishes.

Their mother glared at the uncomfortable girls. Then, after glancing furiously around, she snatched the mats off their food dishes. "There are hairs on these dishes," she said as she streaked an angry finger along the polished wood.

"The old shaggy dog's hairs," the grandmother suggested; and her eyes twinkled.

"Indeed?" the chief woman snapped. Then she grabbed Maada by the nose to make her open her mouth. She yanked out a piece of hard fat so fiercely that it scratched the inside of the girl's mouth.

"Glutton!" she stormed at her daughter. "A girl of your rank a glutton!" For gluttony was a terrible thing, especially for a princess. "You had better go off to the hills and marry Mountain Dweller, whose house is crammed with fine foods!" she raged. Then, turning away to share her husband's shame before the noble visitors, she looked for sweet hemlock sap cakes, which were much inferior to tallow as a special tidbit.

The princess was deeply shamed by the nose-grabbing and cheek-scratching, and by the taunt of "Glutton!" Yet she held her head high, as a princess must, and sat with the noble visitors until she could slip away to her sleeping place behind a screen at the rear of the great cedar house. As she slipped away, her eyes were flashing. And no sooner were she and her little sister safely behind the screen than she said, "I shall indeed go off to the hills and marry Mountain Dweller."

The little princess opened her eyes wide in dismay. For who knew what he would be like, this famous hunter whose house was crammed with fine foods. And people said there were terrible beings guarding the approach to his house. "But if you go, I'll go," she said. For the little princess adored her sister.

She helped dig a hole so that they could escape from under the rear wall. She helped place the long wooden food dishes in their sleeping places and cover them with fur robes. And then she crept with her angry sister into the dark woods. But who knew if the Wild Woman of the Woods and other fearsome narnauks* might be watching? she thought, as she hugged her rich marten skin robe about her. For princesses, even escaping princesses, must wear rich marten skin robes.

Next morning, when the two girls did not appear, their mother went behind the screen to rouse them. "Get up and greet our guests!" she whispered fiercely to the two fur-covered mounds. She snatched off Maada's sleeping robe, only to be confronted with the long, handsomely decorated food dish. She snatched off the other robe. And there was the other dish. Then she saw the hole under the rear wall.

"The princesses have run away," she whispered to the relatives.

At once a group of hunters went off in search of them. And by skillful tracking, they finally reached a spot near where the two girls were carefully hidden.

"Why don't we make a noise?" the little princess whispered. For she was most willing to be caught and taken back to her grandmother. "But . . . maybe not," she added as she caught the angry glint in her sister's eyes. Then they both almost held their breath until the searchers had gone off in another direction.

"Why don't we get caught?" Maada challenged as soon as she dared to raise her voice. "My nose is still bruised and my cheek is still hurting. I know what she said to me. And I know what she was thinking. That I'm a glutton, fit only to marry a chief whose house is crammed with fine foods." Giving her poor little sister no choice but to follow, she scrambled on up the mountain.

"I'm hungry," the little princess whimpered, as soon as she could catch her breath long enough to whimper.

"There'll be plenty to eat there," Maada grimly reminded her. Indeed, she too was hungry, having been too angry to eat with the noble visitors the night before. But she was not a glutton. She could go on forever without food, if need be.

They had gone a long, steep, hungry, weary way before they came upon a little mouse trying to get over a big log.

"Poor little mouse!" the little princess said, though she was much too weary to do anything but flop down where she was.

"Poor little mouse!" Maada agreed. And she lifted it gently over the big log.

In a minute they both heard a small, squeaky, but commanding voice call out, "Come in, my dears!" And when they glanced toward the voice,

* *Narnauks*, supernatural beings.

they were astonished to see a house there in the wilderness. A house decorated with Mouse totems.

"Mouse Woman?" the little princess gasped; and now her eyes were shining. For it was well known that the awesome little narnauk, who could appear to people as a mouse or as the tiniest of grandmothers, was a friend to young people who had fallen into trouble. "Mouse Woman!"

Indeed, when they entered the house, there was the tiniest grandmother they had ever seen, looking up at them with her big, busy mouse eyes.

"Why did you come here?" she asked them. But after one answering flash from Maada's eyes, she dismissed the question with a wave of a tiny hand. "You have helped me, my dear," she said, "so I shall help you." She placed some salmon by the fire to roast, and gave them a bowl of cranberries to be going on with. Then she waited until they had eaten well before she asked, "Why did you come here, Granddaughters?"

"Because, Grandmother," Maada answered, "because my mother said I should marry Mountain Dweller." There were tears to blink back, but not too many tears for her to notice that Mouse Woman's ravelly little fingers were itching to touch the long woolen tassels both princesses wore as ear ornaments. Being much too proud to expect something for nothing, she threw one of her ear ornaments into the fire—a proper way to offer a gift to a Spirit Being.

But the mouse in this Spirit Being was so strong that before the tassel was more than scorched, Mouse Woman spirited it out of the fire and her ravelly little fingers began tearing at it. Then, having received her favorite gift, she properly proceeded to give, in return, her favorite giving—advice to young people in trouble.

"I will direct you to Mountain Dweller's house," she told them. "But I warn you of the dangers you will face. Guarding the approach to the house are terrible beings disguised as everyday things."

"Terrible beings?" the little princess whispered, pulling her now-slightly-tattered marten skin robe tightly about her.

"Dangers, Grandmother?" Maada challenged. Clearly she was ready and willing to face even the Ogre. She had said that she would marry Mountain Dweller, and she would marry Mountain Dweller. "Tell me of the dangers, Grandmother!"

"I will tell you of three of the dangers," the tiny narnauk agreed. "And I will give you magical weapons to overcome them. But I cannot tell you of the fourth danger. That you must discover and deal with on your own."

"We will deal with it, Grandmother, when the time comes. But first, what of the other three dangers?"

Mouse Woman was gazing at Maada with interest. "Perhaps you are the one," she said, mysteriously. And while the little princess huddled fearfully into her marten skin robe, the big princess listened carefully to the tiny narnauk's advice about dealing with the fighting dogs, the floating kelp and Crushing-Mountain, which guarded the approach to Mountain Dweller's house. Then she thankfully placed Mouse Woman's gifts of a magical fish, a magical knife and a magical whetstone in the pouch at her waist, ready to be used against the three dangers.

"I don't really like fighting dogs and . . . and floating kelp and . . . crushing-mountains," the little princess protested. Then, catching the flash in her sister's eyes, she added, "But maybe I'll like seeing them shrink back." Her voice was a small, frightened whisper.

In the morning, Maada took a purposeful breath and went boldly on her way, with her little sister following none-too-boldly behind her.

It all happened as Mouse Woman had said it would happen.

They had not gone far along the trail when two gigantic fighting dogs rushed at them, snarling and growling. Their long fangs were terrifying as the dogs crouched, ready to spring at the girls' throats; the growls in their fierce throats made the little princess cling fearfully to her trembling sister.

But even as she recoiled from the dogs in horror, Maada managed to throw the magical fish to them.

The fighting dogs pounced on it. And when they had devoured it, they began to gambol as playfully as mountain lambs, as Mouse Woman had said they would.

Nevertheless, she almost held her breath as she slipped past them, holding her little sister's hand tightly. Then, with a grateful prayer to the tiny narnauk, the two went on their way.

Soon they reached the water, as Mouse Woman had said they would. And there was the floating kelp, glittering in two separate rafts of writhing brown tubes and bobbing kelp heads. There was the canoe waiting for them. And there, at the foot of a tree near the canoe, was the moss.

With trembling fingers, Maada cut out a large clump of the moss with the magical knife, as Mouse Woman had instructed.

"Kelp in a lake?" the little princess whispered, swallowing.

"No doubt it's a bottomless lake with an underground channel going out to the sea," Maada said. A thought that did little to cheer her sister.

As they moved fearfully out onto the water, the two glittering rafts of writhing brown tubes and bobbing kelp heads began to move toward one another, from each side of the canoe. And as the girls paddled closer, great tubes rose from the water, flailing like the giant tentacles of Monster Octopus, threatening to encircle and crush the canoe.

Swallowing her alarm, Maada tossed the clump of moss between them. At once the floating kelp stopped writhing and flailing, and the two rafts moved back to let the canoe pass.

The canoe shot ahead, with the girls frantically paddling.

"I . . . don't like floating kelp," the little princess confessed as they beached the canoe on the far side of the mountain lake.

Right ahead of them rose Crushing-Mountain, with a great cut in its solid rock—the cut they must pass through to reach the house of Mountain Dweller. And even as they watched, the rock on each side of the cut began to close in, ready to crush them as soon as they had entered.

Even as she recoiled in horror, Maada hurled the magical whetstone into the cut.

At once the mountain shrank back on both sides of the cut, and the girls raced through without harm. But now there was no way to get back.

"I wonder what the fourth danger is," the little princess whispered, glancing fearfully about on all sides of the valley they had come into.

It was a beautiful alpine valley, dotted with small trees and brilliant with mountain flowers. And across the valley stood a big, handsome cedar house.

"At least there'll be lots of food there," the little princess said.

Then they saw the young man. Appearing from behind a clump of alpine fir trees, he was walking toward them.

"Maybe . . . he's the fourth danger," the little princess whispered. "Even a handsome young chief could be a danger." For sometimes dreadful beings appeared as young men to deceive you.

He was indeed a handsome young chief, with a hunting bow held close to his strongly muscled body. His headband, skin apron, and quiver were beautifully decorated with mountain symbols; and caribou ear ornaments swung as he walked.

"Welcome, Princesses!" he greeted them, after one glance of appraisal at their marten skin robes and their ornaments. "Why have you come here?"

"I have come to marry Mountain Dweller," Maada told him. And though her cheeks flushed, she held her head high.

The handsome young chief regarded her with interest. "Perhaps you are the one," he said, as mysteriously as Mouse Woman had said it. "I am Mountain Dweller. And I have been waiting for a proud and spirited princess." Without another word, he led them to his house across the valley.

They had known that Mountain Dweller was a famous hunter. Now they saw that he was also a wealthy one. For his house was even larger and finer than their father's. Its posts were magnificently carved; its screens were beautifully painted with mountain symbols. And on all sides great coppers glinted in the firelight. But they could see little of these treasures. For everywhere in the big windowless house were piles of handsomely decorated food boxes and bowls, and elegant wealth chests that were no doubt filled with precious fur robes and crested horn spoons and finely woven mats and carved food dishes.

Maada's eyes brightened over this crowded display of wealth as they had brightened over the handsome face and form of the man she had said she would marry. Yet . . . She shivered in her fine marten skin robe as she pulled it more closely about her.

Mountain Dweller caught the slight movement. Pointing to a large screen that cut off one corner of the great house, he said, "Do not go behind that screen, Princess! Do not even peep behind it! For there is danger."

"The fourth danger," the little princess mumbled, clinging to her sister's hand as she gazed at the screen with frightened eyes.

Maada swallowed as she nodded in agreement. This was indeed the fourth danger. And Mouse Woman had given her no magical weapon to hurl at it. Now, they were on their own.

They were indeed on their own. For after his visitors had eaten and slept and eaten again, Mountain Dweller picked up his bow and quiver. "Do not go behind that screen, Princess!" he warned. Then, with an anxious-yet-strangely-pleading look at the proud and spirited young lady, he went off hunting.

Sounds had begun to come from behind the screen.

"I think the fourth danger is an evil woman," the big princess whispered, picking up one of the sticks near the fire.

"But . . . we won't even peep, will we?" the little princess whispered back. She, too, picked up one of the sticks.

Her sister was sniffing the air. "An evil woman cooking," she went on. Whiffs of roasting meat and rendering fat had begun to waft over and around the screen. And with them came a terrifying odor of evil.

"We won't even peep, will we?" the little princess insisted, huddling behind one of the crowding chests.

"If we never know what the fourth danger is," her sister challenged, "how can we deal with it?"

"We could go home," the little girl suggested.

"How could we get back through Crushing-Mountain?" her sister challenged. "How could we stop the fighting dogs from attacking us?" She grasped her stick fiercely, but she knew it would be useless against terrible beings disguised as everyday things.

"Well . . ." the little girl said. But if she had any further suggestions, they were lost in quiet whimpers.

"I came here to marry Mountain Dweller," her sister reminded her. "So I shall marry Mountain Dweller." Yet there was fear as well as purpose in the dark eyes that kept glancing at the mysterious screen.

It was a long, lonely, terrifying day. Firmly clutching the stoutest sticks they could find, the girls walked in the lovely alpine meadow. But at last they had to go back into the crowded house, where sounds still came from behind the screen, and whiffs of roasting meat and rendering fat. And the terrifying odor of evil!

If only Mountain Dweller would not leave them on their own with the fourth danger! Yet it was late that evening before he came back from his hunting, and it was early the next morning when he went off. Again with the same warning, again with the same anxious-yet-strangely-pleading look at the proud and spirited young lady.

And so it went until the fourth day.

"Unless we want to stay cowering here forever," Maada said that morning, as soon as Mountain Dweller had gone off, "we must deal with the fourth danger." Fiercely grasping her stout stick, she moved stealthily through the piles of handsomely decorated food boxes and bowls and the elegant wealth chests, while her terrified little sister clung to her robe. Then, taking a deep breath and grasping her stout stick even more fiercely, she rounded the screen.

And there—almost touching her!—was the evil woman. Red-rimmed eyes leered at her from a wizened face and a straggle of dirty gray hair. One scrawny, claw-tipped hand clutched a side of mountain sheep standing on its end by the fire; the other held a dipper of flaming oil. And quick as the girl's gasp, the evil woman flung the burning oil over the side of meat and pushed the heavy flaming mass at the princess, to kill her.

But, also quick as a gasp, the princess bashed back with her stout stick, knocking the meat and the witch into the fire—where she went up in one quick, choking cloud of black smoke. And that was the end of the evil woman. Unless, as people later said, the choking cloud of black smoke turned into the choking clouds of black gnats that plagued hunters in the hills.

Maada sank to the floor, trembling with relief, while her little sister clung to her, howling.

Then Mountain Dweller was lifting her to her feet. "I knew you were the one," he said, embracing her with joy. "And you said you would marry Mountain Dweller."

First, though, he took them back to their father's house, with a gift of fine foods. And now Crushing-Mountain did not try to crush them; the floating kelp did not try to encircle and crush their canoe; the fighting dogs stayed as quiet as mountain lambs. For the evil was gone from the hills. Unless, as people later said, the gnats that pestered them were the evil woman. But that was a danger that even the little princess could deal with.

When they neared the village, they heard sounds of mourning. And when they met the young brother, who was heir to a mighty chieftainship in another village, they saw that his face was blackened in mourning for them.

He stared at them in alarm, then turned to race, shrieking, back to the village.

"He thinks we're ghosts," Maada told Mountain Dweller.

"My sisters! My sisters!" the small prince shrieked as he rushed into the village.

"You're sure it's your sisters?" his mother demanded, grasping his heaving shoulders in desperate hope. Her tear-stained face, too, was blackened in mourning for her daughters.

In answer, the boy raced back to his sisters. Fearfully snatching a tatter from his younger sister's robe, he turned to race off again.

"It is the princesses!" everyone cried out, looking at the tatter. For only princesses wore fine marten skin robes. And they all rushed out to welcome the lost girls and the handsome young chief who came with them.

The proud and spirited princess married Mountain Dweller, as she had said she would. Then, with slaves to serve her, she went back to the magnificent-but-crowded house by the alpine meadow. And it was much less crowded when her husband had sent many well-filled food boxes and bowls to her family as a marriage gift.

Indeed, Mountain Dweller continued to send so many gifts of fine foods, and there was always so much precious mountain sheep tallow in the special box, that the grandmother never again had to say, "The old shaggy dog took it away from me."

In "The Princess and Mountain Dweller" and the next story, "The Princess and the Magical Hat," the writer, Christie Harris, combined material from several culturally-related tribes of the Pacific Northwest. One of these tribes, the Haida, lived on Queen Charlotte Island off the coast of British Columbia. In huge wooden canoes they hunted whales and sea otters. They are famous for their beautifully carved cedar houses, totem poles, and wooden masks. Like the Iroquois, the Haida were a matrilineal society, in which clans and property were inherited through the female line.

Maada is told, "Do not go behind that screen, Princess! Do not even peep behind it! For there is danger." For three days she obeys. But on the fourth day, she refuses to be intimidated. Maada confronts the fourth danger. "Taking a deep breath and grasping her stout stick . . . she rounded the screen." Maada determines to face the danger head-on, even though it means disobeying Mountain Dweller's orders. She claims her right to be independent, her right to knowledge, her right to live without fear, and she wins the handsome young chief as a husband. Her decision is not viewed as unwarranted curiosity or recalcitrance but as a positive decision reflecting her own independent and courageous character.

How different Maada's action seems from that of Bluebeard's wife, who also disobeys her husband when she enters a forbidden chamber. The European tale "Bluebeard" has been used as a cautionary tale to warn women against the "sins" of curiosity and disobedience. "Bluebeard" focuses so strongly on Bluebeard's wife's "sins," one is apt to forget that her husband is a serial murderer who is concealing the bodies of his former wives.[51]

The Princess and the Magical Hat

People of the Northwest Coast[52]

It was in the days of very long ago, when things were different. Then, supernatural beings roamed the vast green wildernesses of the Northwest Coast. And one of those most feared by the seagoing people was Great-Whirlpool-Maker, who lived on a remote island and haunted the waters. His terrifying power was in his hat.

Now this magical hat was woven of spruce roots, like ordinary hats. It had an ordinary design of killer whales. But instead of being topped by several plain woven rings, like the hats of great chiefs, it was woven into a towering spiral. And instead of being rounded off at the top like ordinary hats, it was woven into a deep well and topped by a living surf bird. When the bird spun itself about, it started a whirling of the magical water in the well. And then, when the bird flew off, it released a terrible, whirling power that could suck down even the greatest of the great northern canoes as if it were nothing but a bit of driftwood.

The seagoing people of the north moved in awe of Great-Whirlpool-Maker. They were careful never to spit into the sea or to do anything else that might offend the spirits of the ocean. For who knew when Great-Whirlpool-Maker might wreak vengeance on them?

Now, as well as his terrifying hat, Great-Whirlpool-Maker had bad eyes, a keen nose, a taste for human beings, and a very stupid son.

Son-of-Great-Whirlpool-Maker was so muddleheaded that he wanted to marry a human princess, when obviously such a marriage would keep his father licking his lips in agony every time he glanced at his daughter-in-law. For, of course, not even Great-Whirlpool-Maker could eat his own daughter-in-law.

"Stupid son," his father said almost daily, "you must not marry a human princess."

"Why not?" his son answered almost daily, proving his muddleheadedness, if such proof had been needed. And he kept his big ears alert for word of a suitably beautiful princess.

Now you know that, in the days of very long ago, totem pole villages edged many of the lonely beaches of the Northwest Coast. Standing with their backs to big, snow-capped mountains, the villages were bright with the carved and painted emblems of the clans. Their crested canoes dared the wild western rivers; they threaded the wild maze of off-shore islands; they ranged the wild coast.

In one such village, in the biggest of the big cedar houses, lived a princess called Slender-One. And in the way of the northern people, this princess was expected to marry her father's nephew and heir. (For, of course, her father and his relatives belong to a different clan from her mother and her brothers, for marriage arrangements.) But so beautiful was Slender-One that high ranking young men from many villages came to her village with much ceremony to ask if she would marry them.

One day such a suitor arrived with ten canoes full of relatives. And the relatives came in their most magnificent regalia, dancing on cedar planks that had been laid across the canoes. Yet Slender-One's mother and two brothers and three uncles shook their heads and said, "No."

Later, another such suitor arrived with ten canoes full of relatives. Again the relatives came in their most magnificent regalia, dancing on cedar planks that had been laid across the canoes. And again Slender-One's mother and two brothers and three uncles shook their heads and said, "No."

Later, yet another such suitor arrived with ten canoes full of relatives. Again the relatives came in their most magnificent regalia, dancing on cedar planks that had been laid across the canoes. And yet again Slender-One's mother and two brothers and three uncles shook their heads and said, "No."

Then another suitor arrived. But this one came alone in a sealskin canoe. And this time Slender-One's mother and two brothers and three uncles and everyone else in the village gasped in terror. For a sealskin canoe meant a supernatural suitor. And this one was wearing a towering hat with a living surf bird on top.

"It's Son-of-Great-Whirlpool-Maker," people muttered. And they trembled with terror. They didn't want the princess to marry into that family. But how could a seagoing people dare to offend a family with a hat that could release a power that could suck down even the greatest of the great northern canoes as if it were no more than a bit of driftwood?

There was one wild hope.

Son-of-Great-Whirlpool-Maker was stupid.

"Perhaps we can substitute a slave girl for Slender-One," her mother dared to hope. "He'd never know the difference."

Slender-One had ten slave girls. Her relatives dressed one of them in fine clothes. And, with much ceremony, they escorted her down to the beach.

Son-of-Great-Whirlpool-Maker was indeed stupid. In fact, on this occasion, he had been muddleheaded enough to take a hat he couldn't handle—his father's magical hat. It rose above his big ears in a towering swirl. On top of it sat the living surf bird, who was very annoyed with the whole proceeding. The bird was so annoyed that it kept flying off the hat in a way that terrified its wearer even more than it terrified the people of the village. For, of course, Son-of-Great-Whirlpool-Maker had certainly not intended to do anything with the hat, except impress people.

Son-of-Great-Whirlpool-Maker was indeed stupid. But the surf bird was not. So when the slave girl arrived on the beach in fine clothes, pretending to be the princess, the surf bird squawked, "K-No!"

Son-of-Great-Whirlpool-Maker was far too terrified of the bird to go against its wishes. So he too squawked, "K-No!"; though he couldn't see why he was refusing to marry such a beautiful princess.

Slender-One had ten slave girls. So ten times her relatives dressed one of them in fine clothes and escorted her, with much ceremony, down to the beach. Ten times the surf bird squawked, "K-No!" And ten times Son-of-Great-Whirlpool-Maker also squawked, "K-No!"; though he still couldn't see why he was refusing to marry such a beautiful princess.

"What can we do?" Slender-One's relatives wailed to one another. They did not want the princess to marry into that family. But how could a seagoing people dare to offend a family with a hat that could release a power that could suck down even the greatest of the great northern canoes as if it were no more than a bit of driftwood? "What can we do?" they wailed.

It was what they had already done that enraged the surf bird. Suddenly, it started spinning around. The magical water beneath it began to whirl. And when the bird flew off, suddenly, the released power started a mighty whirlpool offshore. On shore, it started a whirling of pebbles and driftwood and even canoes.

The people were terrified.

So was Son-of-Great-Whirlpool-Maker. For pebbles and driftwood and even canoes were hurtling around his muddled head. "Do something! Do something!" he yelled at the surf bird, who was calmly watching proceedings from the top of a totem pole.

Naturally, the people thought he was yelling at them. So they did something. They fled into the house, grabbed the princess and brought her out, with her ten slave girls.

At once the whirling stopped. And the surf bird settled itself once more on the magical hat.

With more haste than ceremony, her relatives escorted the princess down to the beach and fled back into the house. So they did not even see which way the canoe went.

And they did not see how the next great whirling started, or where. They only heard a few thumps against the planks of the big cedar house. And when they finally dared to venture out into the quiet that followed the thumps, they found only a bit more damage than there had been before.

There was no sign of the sealskin canoe. No sign of the princess. No sign of the ten slave girls.

The princess had vanished.

A wild wailing rose up from the beach, where Slender-One's relatives began mourning the loss of their beautiful princess.

Then someone saw the hat, the magical hat.

It was on top of a totem pole.

The wailing was lost in the stunned quiet of dismay.

Blown from a muddled head by the whirlwind it had created somewhere offshore, the terrifying hat had landed on the totem pole. And there it sat, with the living surf bird at the top.

Like a beached whale, the hat was now theirs. Sent to them by the spirits, in return for the princess they had given to a spirit being?

People looked at one another in dismay. By the custom of the Coast, the hat was now theirs. But who wanted a hat topped by a bird no one knew how to handle? Who wanted a hat that had already wrecked their beach?

There was one wild hope.

Great-Whirlpool-Maker would undoubtedly want it back.

"Perhaps we can give him back the hat," Slender-One's mother dared to hope. "And he will give us back the princess." After all, the obligation of a gift was a law of the Northwest. If the villagers gave Great-Whirlpool-Maker the magical hat, he had to give them something of even greater value. His pride demanded it, and his prestige among his peers. And in this case, it would mean getting rid of something they certainly did not want—the hat—in return for something they certainly did want—the princess.

But, who would dare to touch the hat? And risk annoying the surf bird? Even if someone did dare to touch it, who would dare to take it to Great-Whirlpool-Maker, who had a taste for human beings? And even if someone did dare to take it to him, who knew where he lived?

People eyed the surf bird, who was calmly watching proceedings from the top of the totem pole. And their eyes were uneasy. Something had to be done.

But what?

Clearly, there was only one way to find out.

A shaman put on a dancing apron that clattered with fringes of bird beaks. He put a crown of grizzly bear claws over his long straggly gray hair. He picked up his medicine rattle and his white eagle tail feather. Then, as wooden batons and padded hands drummed on hollow cedar, he began to circle the fire in a wild leaping dance. The dance grew faster and wilder, faster and wilder, faster and wilder until, suddenly, the shaman collapsed and lay as though dead.

People hushed themselves. For now the shaman's spirit-self had left its body to make the spirit journey in search of Great-Whirlpool-Maker's house. And who knew what it would find on such a journey? Almost holding their breath, the people waited.

At long, long last the shaman seemed to stir. So the people began to chant softly, luring his spirit-self back to its body.

The shaman sat up. And his eyes were a wild glitter.

"The house is on an island to the north," he said in his cracked old voice. "An island with three bony trees high on a rock. Great-Whirlpool-Maker is wild with anger at the loss of his magical hat; for his power is in that hat. His son does not know where it went. And the princess is lying as though dead in a cave near the house." He held up a scrawny hand to silence the gasps. "Slender-One's mother must go there. Only she must go. And without the hat."

"Without the hat?" People widened their eyes in dismay. The terrible hat was going to stay on in their village? As one, they turned toward the princess's mother.

Slender-One's mother shrank back for one instant. Then, being a great lady, she squared her shoulders to do what must be done. She rose quietly and summoned a slave paddler.

"Take this!" the shaman said; and he gave her an ancient charm shaped like a killer whale. "Tie it to a spear. And cast the spear at a giant killer whale that will surface near your canoe."

The lady tied the charm to a spear. She went off in a small canoe with her slave paddler. And no sooner had they rounded the point to the north than a giant killer whale surfaced near their canoe. The woman cast the spear at it. It seemed to catch the spear in its great mouth. Then it raced northward with the canoe in tow. It went like a storm wind. And, it seemed, before they had really caught their breath again, they were nearing a remote island with three bony trees high on a rock.

The supernatural killer whale made straight for a small lonely beach on the island. It spat out the spear, and vanished.

And there on the beach, appearing as if from nowhere, stood a tiny old woman.

"Mouse Woman!" Slender-One's mother gasped in great relief. For it was well known that Mouse Woman was a friend to the distressed. She always turned up when a princess had vanished.

"You have woolen ear ornaments?" the tiny being asked; though her eyes were already coveting the mother-of-pearl trimmed tassels.

Trembling with haste, the lady took them off and handed them to the little old woman, whose ravelly fingers began at once to tear them into a lovely, loose, nesty pile of mountain sheep wool. Then, having received her favorite gift, Mouse Woman properly proceeded to give her favorite giving—advice.

"Follow me with great stealth," she advised. And she led the way to the cave where Slender-One lay as though dead, without her slave girls. "Leave her there until the hat is returned," Mouse Woman advised.

Then she led the way, by a back entrance, into a great cedar house. She cautioned silence to the two human beings as they cowered back into a dark corner. For, as everyone knew, the huge man by the fire had a taste for human beings. And a keen nose to smell them out.

"I smell human beings!" he cried out. And the two trembled with terror, as Mouse Woman had intended that they should. For it was always a good thing to make a dangerous situation clear to people. Then they were willing to act in the proper manner. And let her handle things.

"I SMELL HUMAN BEINGS!"

"Of course you smell human beings," Mouse Woman answered, marching boldly up to the huge man. "The least breath of air stirs the robes of the ten slave girls you ate." She pointed to the ten shredded-cedar-bark robes hanging on the wall. "The smell of the girls lingers."

Great-Whirlpool-Maker considered that explanation. It seemed to almost satisfy him. But he did keep glancing about. And he did keep sniffing in a way that was most disconcerting to the two human beings cowering back in the dark corner.

"I have word of the hat," Mouse Woman announced in her squeaky little voice.

"The hat?" Great-Whirlpool-Maker roared in a voice that made the two human beings jump. He leaped to his feet. "Bring my hat to me!"

"It is not mine to bring," Mouse Woman calmly informed him. "Neither is it yours to demand. For the spirits have given it to a human family."

"What family?" he demanded; and his voice was like a clap of thun-

der. For his power was in that hat. Without it he was nothing in the world
of supernatural beings.

"It is enough for me to know what family," Mouse Woman calmly told
him. "Since I will conduct the negotiations."

"Negotiations?" Now his voice was like a long roll of thunder.

"Certainly. Negotiations," said the tiniest but most proper of the narnauks.* "Now, if the family were willing to give you the magical hat, what
could you give them in return?"

Hope sprang up in his eyes. "My son?" he suggested.

Mouse Woman dismissed that suggestion with a twitch of her nose.
So his glance began to range over the treasures in his house.

But Mouse Woman stopped that. Quickly. Before he should peer into
a certain dark corner. "You have a princess," she suggested. It was well
known that she had a feeling for princesses.

"The princess!" His eyes brightened. His tongue licked his big lips.

"A princess alive and in good condition," the tiny negotiator said, to
take his mind off his taste for human beings. "Perhaps the family would
be willing to accept a princess—IF she were alive and in good condition."

"They can have her," he agreed. In fact, he would be glad to be rid of
the human being his son was determined to marry. For the princess's tender flesh was a terrible temptation. It was such a temptation that he had
thought grease into the girl's mind to keep her as though dead, well away
from his nose. For even he could not eat his own daughter-in-law.

"Do nothing until I return!" Mouse Woman ordered. He had thought
grease into the girl's mind; and only he could think it out again. But she
did not want him going near the princess until she was there to handle
things. "Do nothing until I return!" she ordered again. Then she vanished.

Back once more in the corner with the two human beings, she took a
cautious glance at Great-Whirlpool-Maker. But he was rubbing his
hands in excitement. He was lost in thoughts of the magical hat. So she
whisked the two out the back entrance and led them to their canoe.

She got on board with them. "Only I can handle this situation," she
told them with proper pride. And when the slave paddler had taken them
out into deep water, she took a strange little fish charm out of her hand-
basket. She tied it to the bow of the canoe and then threw it into the sea,
ahead of them.

At once the canoe raced southward. As if it were being towed by a
supernatural sea serpent.

* *Narnauk,* supernatural being.

They stopped once on the way to the village, at a rocky point where four mice were waiting.

"Fetch Great-Charmer to Slender-One's village!" Mouse Woman called out. And the four mice vanished as if they were four wisps of sea mist. "Great-Charmer is one of my best friends," Mouse Woman explained. "And she has agreed to help us." She did not explain how Great-Charmer was going to help them.

The canoe sped southward to the village. And there, Slender-One's mother told the people what had happened.

All eyes turned admiringly on valiant little Mouse Woman.

"We will go for the princess tomorrow," the tiny narnauk announced. She indicated Slender-One's mother and two brothers and three uncles. All six swallowed when they thought of what was waiting with the princess.

"And we will take the hat," Mouse Woman went on.

Now everyone swallowed. For who would dare to touch the hat to get it off the totem pole? And who would dare to carry it across the sea, when, at any moment, its living surf bird might spin about, fly off, and release the power that could suck down even the greatest of the great northern canoes as if it were no more than a bit of driftwood?

They all went into the house, where they ate little and talked even less.

Suddenly, the room seemed to brighten. Yet no one had stirred up the fire or thrown on grease to make it flame up.

"Great-Charmer!" Mouse Woman announced in her loudest, proudest squeak. For her best friend was a tall, dazzling lady. And she was wearing the HAT.

People caught their breath. And few slept well that night. For what if the surf bird spun round while they were sleeping, sending firebrands and maybe even people whirling about the great house? What if even the house itself were whirled out to sea, with them in it? When they finally did sleep, they dreamed of carved chests and hot-stone baskets and painted screens flying about their heads.

They were thankful for morning. And never had every last person in the village been so helpful about getting a group out to sea. Never had they watched a departing canoe with more anxious eyes. And never had they seen a being as dazzling as Great-Charmer, sitting serenely in the great, high-prowed canoe with the terrifying hat on her head. Never had they watched a bird with such concern for its movements.

As before, Mouse Woman tied her fish charm to the bow. As before, she cast it into the water, ahead of the canoe. And exactly as before, the canoe sliced through the water as if it were being towed by a supernatural sea serpent.

Almost, it seemed, before they had caught their breath, the travellers stood off the remote island with three bony trees high on a rock. But this time they stood off the spot where Great-Whirlpool-Maker waited.

He peered at them with his bad eyes. And he almost danced with frustration at being so near the magical hat, and yet so far from it. He watched Great-Charmer step up onto the plank with the hat swirling up above her head to the top, where the living surf bird was enjoying the proceedings.

The first voice to break the tense silence was a small squeaky voice. "Send out a small canoe!"

Great-Whirlpool-Maker raised his hand in a signal. A sealskin canoe moved itself out to the great painted canoe.

Slender-One's two brothers got into it. And, as if silently commanded, the sealskin canoe took them to the beach, where they immediately made for the cave where their sister was lying as though dead.

Great-Whirlpool-Maker's eyes were still peering out at the dazzling lady with the hat. He still almost danced with frustration. For without that hat he was nothing among the supernatural beings.

It was Mouse Woman's imperious squeak that made him finally glance over to where the brothers were now carrying their limp sister. He licked his lips at sight of three delicious young people.

"No princess, no hat!" Mouse Woman thundered as well as a small squeaky voice could thunder. And her nose twitched.

He glared at the little busybody. But he understood her. If he were given the hat he wanted so much, then he must give, in return, something the giver wanted quite as much. His pride demanded it.

"A princess in good condition!" Mouse Woman reminded him.

He glared again at her. But he understood her. If he were given something of great value, prestige demanded that he return something of great value. And, in her present condition, the princess was of little value.

He glared one last time at the little busybody, who could be counted on to spread the word of his behavior. Then, covering his eyes with both hands, he thought the grease out of Slender-One's mind.

There was a gasp of pleasure from the big canoe as the princess stirred and then embraced her brothers.

There was no gasp from Great-Whirlpool-Maker or his stupid son. One was too busy licking his lips to gasp; while the other was too busy blinking his eyes as he tried to understand what was happening around him.

Then Son-of-Great-Whirlpool-Maker, like his father, fixed his gaze on the dazzling lady. For he saw that Great-Charmer was much more beautiful than a human princess. He even saw that his father would not always be licking his lips over such a daughter-in-law; for she was not a human being. He didn't even bother to watch the brothers lift his intended bride into the sealskin canoe and then hand her tenderly over to her mother and to her three uncles.

Great-Charmer still stood on the plank, with the magical hat on her head. Great-Whirlpool-Maker still kept his gaze on the hat. And now beads of moisture stood out on his huge forehead. For that hat held his power. And a tiny, meddling busybody was keeping it from him.

He glared at Mouse Woman. He had given a gift of great value, hadn't he? Now didn't the receivers' pride demand that they give him something of great value? Wasn't the obligation of a gift the law of the Northwest? A matter of pride! A matter of prestige!

He almost held his breath as Mouse Woman readied her fish charm.

Slender-One and her family, also, almost held theirs. Would Mouse Woman risk giving that inhuman monster his power while they were still near him?

Still almost holding their breath, they watched her nod to Great-Charmer, who stepped lightly into the sealskin canoe, still wearing the magical hat. And they would have seen what happened next if Mouse Woman hadn't chosen that very moment to toss her fish charm into the sea and set them racing homeward.

They let out their breath in a great sigh of relief. Of course! They should have known that Mouse Woman would honor the obligation of a gift, on their behalf. Of course she would do the proper thing. It was why she was such a power in the world. It was why even the biggest of the narnauks eyed her with respect.

That night, grease flamed up the fire in the great cedar house in Slender-One's village. Delicious whiffs of food tickled people's noses. And fringes of bird beaks and deer hooves clattered as dancing blankets and dancing aprons whirled around the fire.

Then on a signal from the High Chief, the house hushed itself. And with great ceremony, Slender-One's two brothers approached Mouse Woman with a small dancing apron, beautifully patterned in the Chilkat way. They dropped it around her shoulders, where it became a dancing blanket—a dancing blanket that whirled and clattered as she did a merry, scurrying dance around the leaping fire.

Then she vanished.

No one saw her reappear near a small tidal pool on the beach. No one saw her stoop down to look closely into the small circle of water. No one heard her delighted sigh at seeing the pool hold the whole great starry world in its smallness.

Then, alone with the starry night and the shining water and the deep, deep shadows of the crowding forest, Mouse Woman did another little dance. For it was all strangely satisfying. Through her alert care for young people, the princess was safe. And through equally alert care for proper behavior, the whole village was properly in awe of the mighty world of spirits. With Great-Whirlpool-Maker once more in possession of his magical hat, even the brashest of young paddlers would not dare to spit into the sea or to do anything else that might offend the ocean spirits. As the tiny pool held the whole great starry world in its smallness, so SHE held the balance of the vast green wilderness in her ravelly fingers.

Suddenly they began to almost nibble at the beautifully woven wool of her dancing blanket.

And that, too, was strangely satisfying.

A powerhouse of propriety and a friend to the distressed, a meddling busybody to those on the wrong side of the law, Mouse Woman holds "the balance of the vast green wilderness in her ravelly fingers." She's a mouse who boldly confronts the giant Great-Whirlpool-Maker. Her power is not physical. She's a combination of the American advice champion, Abigail Adams, and the manners expert, Emily Post. Mouse Woman's actions and advice incorporate the society's spoken and unspoken rules of behavior. She is a great power in the world because it is understood that she will do the proper thing.

Mouse Woman conducts negotiations with a shrewd understanding of the personalities involved. The humans must be properly scared into letting her handle things. As for Great-Whirlpool-Maker who wants to eat the three young people, "No princess, no hat!" Mouse Woman thunders. She demands that Great-Whirlpool-Maker uphold the rules of the society, those same rules that will return his hat to him.

The Great-Whirlpool-Maker's wild craving for human flesh is kept in check by another of Mouse Woman's valuable characteristics, typically attributed to women, her gossiping. "He glared one last time at the little busybody, who could be counted on to spread the word of his behavior."

Like so many women, this little heroine maintains the structure of the society with its traditions, rules, and balance. "Through her alert care for young people, the princess was safe. And through equally alert care for proper behavior, the whole village was properly in awe of the mighty world of spirits."

The Lytton Girls Who
Were Stolen by Giants

Salishan People[53]

Once some people were camped on the hills near Lytton, and among them were two girls who were fond of playing far away from the camp. Their father warned them against the giants, who infested the country.

One day they rambled off, playing as usual, and two giants saw them. They put them under their arms, and ran off with them to their house on an island in a large river, a long distance away. They treated them kindly, and gave them plenty of game to eat. First they brought them grouse, rabbits, and other small game; but when they learned that the girls also ate deer, they brought to them plenty of deer, and the girls made much buckskin. The giants were much amused when they saw how the girls cut up the deer, how they cooked the meat and dressed the skins.

For four days the girls were almost overcome by the smell of the giants, but gradually they became used to it. For four years they lived with the giants, who would carry them across the river to dig roots and gather berries which did not grow on the island.

One summer the giants took them a long distance away, to a place where huckleberries were very plentiful. They knew that the girls liked huckleberries very much. They left them to gather berries, and said they would go hunting and come back in a few days to take them home. The elder sister recognized the place as not many days' travel from their people's home, and they ran away.

When the giants returned for them, they found them gone, and followed their tracks. When the girls saw that they were about to be overtaken, they climbed into the top of a large spruce-tree, where they could not be seen. They tied themselves with their tumplines.* The giants, who had lost their tracks, thought they must be in the tree, and tried to discover them. They walked all around and looked up, but could not see them. They thought, "If they are there, we shall shake them out." They shook the tree many times, and pushed and pulled against it; but the tree did not break, and the girls did not fall down. Therefore the giants left.

---

* *Tumpline*, a sling formed by a strap slung over the forehead or chest for carrying a pack on the back.

After they had gone, the girls came down and ran on. The giants were looking all around for their tracks, when at last they came to a place where the girls had passed. They pursued them; and when the girls saw that they would be overtaken, they crawled, one from each end, into a large hollow log on a side-hill. They closed the openings with branches which they tied together with their tumplines. The giants lost their tracks again, and thought they might be in the log. They pulled at the branches, but they did not move. They peered in through some small cracks, but could not see anything. They tried to roll the log down the hill, to shake out whatever might be inside, but it was too heavy. After a while they left.

When they were gone, the girls ran on as before, and after a time reached a hunting-camp of their own people in the mountains. During their flight they had lived on berries and fool-hens.* Their moccasins were worn out, and their clothes torn. They told the people how the giants lived and acted. They were asked if the giants had any names besides Tsawanē´itEmux, and they said they were called Stsomu´lamux and TsekEtinu´s.

    Like the Nez Percé, the Salishan People lived on the plateau between the Coast Range and the Rocky Mountains in the northwest United States and southwest Canada.

    After four years of living behind enemy lines, these two girls make their hair-raising escape. They bring back important information about how the giants lived and acted, and they bring back the giants' names. Being able to name something often suggests having power over it.

---

* *Fool-hen,* a grouse that exhibits little alertness or fear of man.

The Legend of the Coppermine River

Inuit[54]

A long time ago a young girl named Itiktajjak left her home to go in search of some firewood. While she was walking along, a brown bear picked up her scent and began to follow her. Realizing that the bear was on her track the young girl immediately fell to the ground, stiffened her muscles and pretended to be dead. The bear came upon his prey but thought that the young girl had frozen solid. Without hesitation he heaved her upon his back and started to carry her to his cave where his family was waiting.

It happened that the path taken by the bear led through tall willow bushes. Thinking that she might hinder the bear's progress, Itiktajjak hooked her stiffened arms around the branches and forced the bear to slow his pace. The bear struggled and fought to free his burden from the bushes but the harder he tried the more tired he became.

He arrived at his cave to find his two devilish cubs playing on the large platform that served as their bed. Mother bear was asleep. Father bear was exhausted by his difficult journey and lay the girl on the floor saying to his cubs, "Here is something for you to eat."

On hearing these words the cubs performed a joyful dance around Itiktajjak who still appeared to be quite frozen. Father bear wanted to rest. His children wanted to play. In exasperation the old bear motioned the cubs to be quiet. "Later on you will have some of the girl to eat," he told them.

Hearing the excitement the mother bear awoke, climbed out of bed and with an axe in her hand went to examine this piece of game lying on the floor. Finding the girl to be very stiff she laid the axe on the floor near Itiktajjak and went back to bed.

When Itiktajjak sensed that both mother and father had gone to sleep, she opened her eyes for the first time. The two cubs, ever watchful of the young girl's movements, cried, "Father! She has thawed! She opened her eyes!"

But the old bear would not be disturbed and growled, "Let her open her eyes, but let me be! She has tired me out already by gripping the willow branches." The bear quickly fell into a deep sleep.

Itiktajjak continued to pretend to be dead. She had noticed the axe lying close by, but before she opened her eyes once again she wanted to be certain that all of the bears were asleep. Very soon thereafter all was quiet in the cave. The cubs, tired from their play, had fallen asleep.

Sensing that it was safe to open her eyes, the young girl quickly got up, grabbed the axe and hit the mother bear a blow on the ear. Immediately the cave was filled with the old bear's cries of pain. Itiktajjak glanced quickly about her and saw that the father bear was awakening. She fled from the cave, pursued by the male bear who was now fully aroused.

Knowing only that she must run as quickly as she could, Itiktajjak ran until she came to a small stream. She jumped across, then paused briefly on the other side. She took her little finger and with it traced a line through the water. While so doing she repeated the magic words, "River, river, make your path cross here." The words were barely uttered when the stream swelled to a torrent of water, separating Itiktajjak from the old bear.

"What can I do now?" thought the bear. "There isn't any way for me to get across this raging river." With these thoughts the bear paced up and down the bank on his side of the river. Finally he called out to the girl, "How did you manage to cross this river?"

Without a moment's hesitation Itiktajjak replied, "I put my nose in it and drank until the water disappeared and a dry path appeared."

The father bear thought that he could do the same so he began to lap up the water as quickly as he could. He drank and drank and the more he swallowed, the fatter he became. Finally, with one last swallow, he exploded and the water from his body spread a heavy mist over everything.

Itiktajjak watched all of this happening and noticed that clouds were beginning to form from the mist. Never before had clouds been seen in this area. From these clouds water was soon to fall into the river which had been created when the young girl drew her finger through the waters. This river has come to be known as the *Qorlorloq* or Coppermine, the river whose course is scattered with waterfalls.

"Inuit" designates the indigenous peoples of northern Canada. The Coppermine River is in the southern part of Canada's Kitikmeot Region, northeast of Great Bear Lake.

Many folktales deal with serious problems. Frequently, the problem is poverty. In this story the problem is abduction. The girl's vulnerability is real, but she comes up with several ingenious stratagems. She plays dead, but grabs onto branches to tire the bear. She uses magic to make the stream grow into a river. She also simply runs away, like the future queen of England, Eleanor of Aquitaine did. On two separate occa-

sions, Eleanor of Aquitaine had to gallop away into the night to escape would-be abductors. This folktale has taken a serious problem and helped to explore solutions, probable and improbable. True to form, the ending is happy.

The Huntress

Inuit[55]

A long time ago in the village of Tikeraq, there lived a man and his
wife. They had a daughter who was a great huntress and whose
endurance and strength were exceptional. When she went on hunting
trips by kayak she would travel far away and leave the other hunters
behind. Often she would wait until the other hunters had disappeared
from her view before she would set out. Then, rowing quickly, she would
catch up to them in a very short time.

She used a long, two-seated kayak. Her father was happy to steer while
she rowed and threw the harpoon. One day father and daughter left home
in their kayak. They hunted for some time and then decided to return
home. On their way back, a beast appeared from the sea and came toward
them, snarling furiously. When the beast neared the kayak, the girl threw
her harpoon. In the same instant she fell into a faint.

When she regained consciousness and opened her eyes she found herself kneeling on an unknown shore. She looked all around, not knowing
where to go. At last she set out in a westerly direction, following the
coastline. She stopped several times to look for signs that would reveal
the presence of people, but there was nothing, not even the faintest signs
of habitation.

After a long walk she came upon some wood cuttings. From that point
onward she frequently found other pieces of wood and they appeared to
be increasingly fresher. She knew that soon she would encounter people.

A little further on she came upon a kayak which had been left on the
shore. She was glancing about for its owner when a voice said, "My kayak
has trapped someone. If it is a man, I shall kill him. If it is a woman, she
will live." No sooner had the girl heard these words than the owner of the
kayak came running up to her. Taking her by the arm, the man led her to
his igloo and made her his wife.

This man often went hunting, rising very early in the morning and
travelling long hours in his kayak. He was a shaman who could take this
marvelous kayak over land as well as water. When he was away hunting,
his wife remained in the igloo occupying her time with various household
tasks.

Each time she was left alone like this, a poor boy came to visit her. She
never saw him approach, nor was she able to determine where he came

from. One moment he wasn't there; in the next instant he was standing beside her. When the young woman noticed his presence and had finished her work, she always gave the boy a small piece of meat. Taking the food the boy would then disappear as quietly as he had come. By watching him leave one day the young woman was able to discover his home. The poor boy lived in his grandmother's igloo which was in fact close by, but which was so hidden from view that the young woman had not noticed it.

One morning, when her work was done and she had given the little orphan some food, he spoke: "Grandmother wants you to come."

Immediately the girl followed him to the old woman's igloo. As soon as she saw her, the grandmother began talking.

"You have made my grandson's life happy by giving him something to eat. He is grateful to you. This is why I want to warn you that a great danger awaits you. This man whom you have taken as your husband is tired of you. Soon he is going to kill you. He has already had many wives and when he became weary of them he killed them. When he returns from his trip it will be your turn. His storehouse is filled with the flesh of his dead wives.

"Alone you have no chance to escape him. He will kill you too. Those other women never valued my grandson. They never gave him any food. That is why I never did anything for them. But I want to help you. You will come back here tomorrow. It will not be easy for me to save you from this danger, but I will try. Now hurry home before your husband comes back!"

The woman returned home. When her husband came in from hunting she noticed that he had changed. He was irritable; he did not even glance at her. It was as if he were completely disgusted with her. The fact that he refused to look her in the face confirmed her suspicions and convinced her that what the old woman had said was true. The next morning, when her husband had departed and as soon as her housework was done, she went to the old woman's igloo.

The grandmother immediately announced: "He will try to kill you when he returns at dusk. I haven't much which will protect you from him. All I have is a small pail. I know of nothing else that can save you from this danger."

The old woman continued to speak in vivid terms as if she could visualize the scene she described. "Here is your husband who is preparing to return to his igloo to kill you. When he arrives, remain here. He is on his way now. Take this pail which is made from seal skin and which has something in the bottom of it."

The movements and the words of the grandmother were those of a shaman. One would have sworn that she was beside the man and was imitating everything he did. "He is at his igloo. He enters. He looks for you. He thinks you have disappeared. He goes outside. He looks for you around the igloo. He gets into his magic kayak. He comes here. Take this pail in your hand!"

Saying this, the shaman gave the magic bucket to the girl. "Look outside; when the bow of the kayak appears throw the pail on top of it. Here he comes! In a moment he will appear in the entrance way. There he is!"

The bow of the marvelous kayak was barely in the entrance when the girl threw the bucket on it. Immediately she lost consciousness and no longer knew what was going on around her.

When she revived, she found herself once again kneeling on a strange shore, not knowing where to go. She set out to walk along the edge of the sea. From time to time she stopped to rest. Eventually she came to an igloo and entered.

Inside, all alone, was a woman. The woman did not offer her visitor any food. Rather, she excused herself by saying, "I am not offering you anything to eat because I am afraid of what my older brother will say."

The young woman from Tikeraq remained but a short time. When she was ready to go the woman of the igloo offered this advice: "Do not look back when you depart. Only when you have gone some distance can you turn your head if you wish."

The girl followed these directions. After walking for some time she looked back and saw a huge wild animal, the like of which she had not seen before, lying on the ground beside the igloo.

Walking on, she saw in the distance another igloo. Several people lived there and here they gave her food and let her sleep. The next morning after another meal, one of the men questioned her: "Are you going to stay with us?"

"No," she replied, "I am going on."

"In that case, where are you going?"

"That way toward the west; that is the direction in which I am going."

The man then told her: "In that place where you want to go there are beings which kill men. They are not far from here. You, being a woman, will be killed without hesitation. Just recently our child was murdered. You have no weapon with which to defend yourself. Here, take this. With this you will be able to get away from them."

The man took a short-handled knife from his belt. The handle was so short that it could only be held with difficulty. However its small size made the knife easy to conceal in a pocket or a belt. It was a magic weapon which had the power to kill terrible things. "Here," declared the man, "is a weapon which will save you from danger."

To teach the young woman how to use it, the man moistened the blade with spittle and lodged its handle in the igloo wall beside him. Despite herself the girl now found herself being drawn irresistibly toward the sharp copper blade. Try as she might she could not stop herself from being drawn to the blade. Having demonstrated its powers, the man took the knife and gave it to her saying, "Here, take this and carry it with you."

Taking her leave the girl walked on until she arrived at the igloos of the beasts she had been warned of. She was met by the servant of one of the ogres who led her by the arm to the igloo of his master. Seeing the girl the ogre spoke: "A woman! This is one who doesn't have much longer to live."

After a short silence the girl replied: "Yes, I am but a woman. I do not have much longer to live."

The ogre spoke again: "This is a woman with a glib tongue. She doesn't have much longer to live."

Once more the girl replied: "Yes, I have a glib tongue and I don't have much longer to live."

At this point the ogre prepared to jump at the girl. She cried out: "Look, I am but a woman and I have not much longer to live." With that, she pulled the knife from her belt, wet the blade with spittle and stuck the handle in the snow on her side of the igloo. The magic of the knife drew the ogre toward the blade. He stamped his feet and tried to resist but his efforts were wasted. Faster and faster he was drawn to the knife. Despite himself he was thrown upon the weapon. The wound was fatal.

When the news of the ogre's death was known, the village people came to thank the girl for ridding them of this menace. Thinking that more man-killers might be in the area the girl asked: "Where must I go now to find more like him?"

"Here, there are no more," replied the people, "and we are very happy because we have been so afraid. Over there at Tikeraq, however, there is an ogre who kills travellers. We have heard this from people who live on the land and who go there to get seal oil."

This news made the girl think back over the past. She wondered how this could be in her own village of Tikeraq which had never been plagued by such beasts. "The reports must be true. I remember that in days gone by the land people came to our settlement, to Tikeraq, to get their oil." Thinking these thoughts, she resumed her journey.

When she arrived in sight of the igloos of Tikeraq she was met by another ogre's servant who took her to his master's home. Entering the igloo the girl was immediately recognized by those present. Her father, more than the others, was full of joy.

"Since you disappeared, I have done nothing but kill people. I myself have become a man-killer. From now on, that is finished. I shall kill no one else."

The daughter then repeated the adventures that had befallen her since the day she had fainted in her father's kayak. When she had finished her story, her father explained what had happened to him and his people.

"We were the only ones who ate the meat of the terrible beast that you harpooned that day. There is still some left. We gave no one else any of it. Perhaps it was the meat that made me into an ogre. But with you gone we had no one to hunt for us. I killed those who came here for meat."

The young woman took out her knife, moistened it and put it beside her. Her father and the other people in the igloo were drawn to it and would have been stabbed had not the girl removed it in time. "It was this blade that saved me," she said. "I used it to kill the ogre."

The father was frightened by this demonstration but he was happier to have his daughter back. He declared he would never kill again.

The Huntress lives in the cold, harsh reality of the extreme north. Her survival depends on her ability to haul a walrus up onto the beach, to accurately throw a harpoon, and to paddle a kayak into the wind through rough icy water. She is a great huntress and fearlessly harpoons a monster.

With the shaman, she changes, she becomes docile. "Taking her by the arm, the man led her to his igloo and made her his wife." The neighboring grandmother places the responsibility for the relationship on the young woman. The grandmother says, "This man whom you have taken as your husband . . . . " Even then, the young woman doesn't contradict her. While she is the man's wife, the heroine assiduously does household tasks. When she finds that she has married an Inuit Bluebeard with his own room filled with the flesh of his dead wives, the young woman makes her escape—as soon as her housework is done.

The Huntress re-emerges. Magic knife in hand, she saves one village from an ogre. Then she saves her own village from her father-turned-ogre. Her father stops eating human flesh not only because she frightens him, but more importantly because he no longer has to. The provider of the household, his daughter the Huntress, has returned. At different times in our lives, we express different parts of ourselves. This woman is as completely a huntress as she is a homemaker.

Story of a Female Shaman

Reindeer Chukchee[56]

There was a female shaman. She had an only son who fell sick. In the meantime she left her home and went to some other people who lived on the very end of the sea, beyond the margin of the sky. Her husband said, "You are a bad mother. Your only son is suffering, and you leave him and go to the others." "Indeed," said she, "I merit your blame. Still those people beyond the limit of the sky want me so. Their only son is also suffering."

She set off, but while she was on her way the other boy died. She came there. "Oh, he is dead." They had not carried him out into the open because they were waiting for her arrival. She said, "And what payment are you going to give me?"—"Two reindeer teams."—"What kind of reindeer?"—"One grey one, spotted black, and the other a grey one, spotted white."—"All right, I will try."

She struck her drum and restored the boy to life. She spent a year there, and in the meantime her own son died. She went home the next year in the fall. "Where is the boy? Let him come out and look at the reindeer."—"He is asleep."—"Ah, you may awaken him and let him have a look at the reindeer." The father said, "He fell asleep just now. I will not awaken him."

Then she understood and said, "Open him." They opened him. She felt the skin on his arms and it was all rotten, for he had been dead since the summer. Then she said, "I want to have a rest." The husband said, "Why should you have rest? Are you not a shaman? Do something."—"I must have rest," she said.—"You are a shaman. You don't need rest." She struck the drum, but could not find the boy. Then she said, "Rather kill me. I could not find his soul."—"I will not kill you."—"Ah, I could find nothing on the sea. So you must kill me. When I am killed I shall take these reindeer, which were brought from a dead boy in the other world."

So the husband killed her. Then he tied the body on the driving sledge and slew also the grey spotted reindeer team. They went to sleep, and heard a clatter outside. The killed female shaman departed to the sky. She met a raven and the raven said, "I envy you your reindeer team."— "Yes?" said the woman. She drove on and met an eagle. He was chopping wood. He said, "Ah, what a beautiful team."—"Yes, I will give you the other one left at home."—"A female monster carried off your boy. When

147

you come there, you must look well for his clothes. The female monster has taken all his clothes off his body, his coat, cap, and boots. Now you may go away."

She rode away and her bells jingled. She came to the house of the female monster and looked down the vent-hole. The soul of her son was there, tied fast to a pole with arms and legs spread asunder. He asked his mother, "Why do you come here?"—"I come to fetch you home."—"We shall both be killed."—"Did I come to seek life?" She untied the son's soul and carried him off.

The female monster came home and he was not there. "Ah," said she, "I will catch them. Then I will break their bones and swallow both of them." The son's soul told the mother, "Ah, we are pursued." The female shaman called all her assistant spirits to help her, but no one came, all were afraid. The son said, "Leave me alone. Let me fall down."—"I will not. Let her kill us both together." Then she called for the last of her spirits, who was the diver spirit. Two diver spirits came in answer to her call. The female shaman said to one of the diver pair, who also was a female, "And where are your companions? I called for them all and no one came." The female diver said, "Now you must look at the sky. If much blood is spilled and the sky reddens, you may know that the monster has been killed."

The divers flew away. After a while the sky reddened as if the whole world were covered with blood. "Ah," said the female shaman, "so they have killed her." They came home. She called loud, "There, get up." The people awoke. She beat her drum and after a while both creatures she had met on the way, the raven and the eagle, came there and took places by the sides of the corpse. She drummed on. The skin of the body grew fresh and sleek as if on a living body. She snatched the soul and put it into the body. "Wake up. You have slept enough."

Dawn was breaking. The boy awoke. Then only, the mother went to sleep. First she ordered, "Slaughter both the reindeer teams that I brought lately." One team was for the raven and the other for the eagle.

This is a story about being a mother and having a second job as well. Not only is this heroine overloaded with work, every step she takes receives a critique from society. Her child is sick, but she has to go to work. "You are a bad mother." She comes home tired, "I want to have a rest." "You don't need rest," the husband says. The mother/shaman even lets herself be killed to bring her son back to life. (Death is obviously not much of a barrier in this culture!) Only after she has snatched her son's soul and returned it to his refurbished body, "Then only, the mother went to sleep." Like so many working women, this woman is the farthest thing from a bad mother—she is Supermom.

The Magic Eagle

Timotean People, Venezuela[57]

One day long, long ago, god Ches left his home in the sky and came to Earth to bestow on his favorite chieftain a rare and beautiful gift. It was an eagle made of solid gold. So skillfully designed was this bird that it seemed to be almost alive.

The chieftain took the eagle in his strong hands. He looked at it in awed silence. Overwhelmed, he could find no proper words with which to thank the god for favoring him over the chieftains of other tribes.

God Ches understood the chieftain's silence and said, "Because of your goodness and wisdom, you alone are worthy of this honor. This golden eagle is not only beautiful, but it has magical powers that will bring your tribe victory in battle and good fortune in times of peace. Guard the eagle and keep it safe until I ask for its return."

The chieftain answered humbly, "Oh, great God Ches, I hope my tribe and I shall always deserve your kindness! When you want the eagle back, only give us a sign and the golden bird will be returned at once."

And so it came to pass that for generation after generation, the god's gift brought victory and good fortune to the tribe. The golden eagle was passed on from one noble chieftain to the next.

Years passed, and still the god Ches had not asked for the return of this cherished possession.

Finally, an unusual event took place. It had never before happened in this tribe's history. A young and beautiful princess became the ruler, for it was the law of the Timotean Indians that a daughter could succeed her father if there were no sons.

Because the princess was wise and beautiful, she was accepted by both the men and women of her tribe. They were proud of her just rule. They loved her kind and gentle ways.

Although she looked fragile, she was as strong as the little hummingbird whose dainty wings can carry it on long flights. Though her close friends sometimes worried about her frailty, they were sure that no harm could ever befall their beloved princess.

Nevertheless, she had not ruled for many moons before she became ill—so ill that the witch doctors were powerless to drive away the terrible affliction that threatened her life. They spent hours making special brews and medicines, while priests burned sacrifices to god Ches on the altar.

In desperation the people painted their bodies red and danced until they fell from exhaustion. They pleaded with god Ches to spare their princess.

Still there was no answer, and the tribe sat helplessly as the princess grew weaker each hour.

One morning, long before sunrise, the princess awakened from a restless sleep. She called weakly to her dearest friend and companion.

"Mistafá," she whispered, through fever-parched lips, "god Ches has given me a message in my sleep. He asks that the golden eagle be returned at once to his temple on the mountain peak."

Mistafá was certain that the fever had caused the princess to be confused. However, to soothe her, she answered, "It was only a dream, dear princess."

"No, no," cried the princess, "it was no dream! But I am too weak to return the eagle myself, so it is you who must go for me. When it is returned to god Ches, I shall be cured."

Poor Mistafá! She was filled with doubts and fears. Even if what the princess said was true, how could she dare to approach the sacred temple? Only the chieftain could visit the mountain peak. How would she find her way through the forests and canyons?

So she sobbed to the princess, "But how can I find my way?"

The princess held out her hand weakly and replied, "Do not be afraid, dear friend, for god Ches will protect you and show you the way. Now take the eagle from beside my bed and go at once. When you reach the mountain peak, bury the bird at the side of the temple and call three times to god Ches. He will hear and give an answer."

Mistafá saw the princess close her eyes.

"I do not wish you to die, my princess," she cried, "and though I fear for my life I'll gladly go and deliver the eagle."

The princess looked at her friend and smiled. "Do not fear, for we shall both be saved."

Mistafá took courage from these words and, with the precious eagle wrapped in a soft woven cloth of black and gold, she started on her journey.

Each mile her burden grew heavier, until she had to rest more and more often to catch her breath. But each time she arose with renewed strength. When at last Mistafá saw the mountain peak in the distance, her spirit danced within her and suddenly her feet seemed to carry her like wings up the steep road to the top. Only then did she sink down on a rock to rest her weary legs.

The journey had taken most of the day and Mistafá was eager to do her errand and return to the princess before darkness came.

"I must hurry," she said to herself.

Using a sharp rock, she dug a hole at the side of the temple. With tears streaming down her face, she buried the precious eagle that had been her tribe's dearest possession over the long years. Would she ever see it again?

She thought of the dying princess and called loudly three times, "God Ches! God Ches! God Ches! Oh great spirit, receive the golden eagle which the princess asked me to return to you, and spare her life."

Mistafá prostrated herself on the ground, overcome by her emotions and by this sacred place. All was quiet.

When she finally lifted her head, Mistafá saw that it was dark and realized that she had fallen asleep.

"How long have I slept?" she asked herself fearfully. "I dare not venture down the mountain until daybreak or I shall lose my way. Besides, I must wait for a sign from god Ches."

She found protection between two large boulders. She wrapped herself in the black and gold cloth in which she had carried the golden eagle. Safe and warm, she fell asleep once more.

When daylight came, she awakened with a start. For a moment she could not remember where she was. Then she saw an unusual sight.

There, in the spot where she had buried the eagle, was a fully grown bush with green leaves and purple blossoms. As she approached the plant, Mistafá was startled to hear a voice coming from the bush.

"Gather my leaves in the black and gold cloth and bring them to the priests of your tribe. Instruct them to make a strong hot tea and serve it to the princess."

"It is the sign from god Ches," Mistafá cried joyfully.

Without a moment's delay, she picked dozens of leaves from the plant, but did not disturb the flowers. She left those to beautify the temple.

She gathered the cloth together in careful folds, and held it tightly under her arm as she descended the mountain. She ran through the forest without stopping to rest. At last she could see the homes of the villagers.

Mistafá hurried the rest of the way until she fell at the feet of the princess, to whom she told what had happened.

The princess called the priests, who wasted no time in preparing the strong brew.

All through the night the princess took sips of the tea. By morning her lips had regained their color and her eyes were as sparkling as ever. The fever was gone.

In just a few more days she had regained her health and was able to make the journey to the temple to thank god Ches for the new plant that had restored her health.

Before they died out, the Timotean People lived in the Andes mountains in Venezuela. Women were allowed to become chiefs and warriors, but only men could become priests. The main god, Ches, was male.

It seems to be no coincidence that the woman who makes the journey to the mountain peak leaves the gold and returns with herbal medicine. For thousands of years, village wisewomen and midwives have upheld the important tradition of searching the earth for useful herbal medicines.

"I'm Tipingee, She's Tipingee, We're Tipingee, Too"

Haiti[58]

There was once a girl named Tipingee who lived with her stepmother. Her father was dead. The stepmother was selfish, and even though she lived in the girl's house she did not like to share what she earned with the girl.

One morning, the stepmother was cooking sweets to sell in the market. The fire under her pot went out. Tipingee was in school, so the stepmother had to go herself into the forest to find more firewood. She walked for a long time, but she did not find any wood. She continued walking. Then she came to a place where there was firewood everywhere. She gathered it into a bundle. But it was too heavy to lift up onto her head. Still, she did not want anyone else to have any of the firewood. So standing in the middle of the forest she cried out: "My friends, there is so much wood here and at home I have no wood. Where can I find a person who will help me carry the firewood?"

Suddenly an old man appeared. "I will help you to carry the firewood. But then what will you give me?"

"I have very little," the woman said, "but I will find something to give you when we get to my house."

The old man carried the firewood for the stepmother, and when they got to the house he said, "I have carried the firewood for you. Now what will you give me?"

"I will give you a servant girl. I will give you my stepdaughter, Tipingee."

Now Tipingee was in the house, and when she heard her name she ran to the door and listened.

"Tomorrow I will send my stepdaughter to the well at noon for water. She will be wearing a red dress, call her by her name, Tipingee, and she will come to you. Then you can take her."

"Very well," said the man, and he went away.

Tipingee ran to her friends. She ran to the houses of all the girls in her class and asked them to wear red dresses the next day.

At noon the next day the old man went to the well. He saw one little

153

girl dressed in red. He saw a second little girl dressed in red. He saw a third girl in red.

"Which of you is Tipingee?" he asked.

The first little girl said: "I'm Tipingee."

The second little girl said: "She's Tipingee."

The third little girl said: "We're Tipingee, too."

"Which of you is Tipingee?" asked the old man.

Then the little girls began to clap and jump up and down and chant:

> I'm Tipingee,
> She's Tipingee,
> We're Tipingee, too.
>
> I'm Tipingee,
> She's Tipingee,
> We're Tipingee, too.

Rah! The old man went to the woman and said, "You tricked me. All the girls were dressed in red and each one said she was Tipingee."

"That is impossible," said the stepmother. "Tomorrow she will wear a black dress. Then you will find her. The one wearing a black dress will be Tipingee. Call her and take her."

But Tipingee heard what her stepmother said and ran and begged all her friends to wear black dresses the next day.

When the old man went to the well the next day, he saw one little girl dressed in black. He saw a second little girl dressed in black. He saw a third girl in black.

"Which of you is Tipingee?" he asked.

The first little girl said: "I'm Tipingee."

The second little girl said: "She's Tipingee."

The third little girl said: "We're Tipingee, too."

"Which of you is Tipingee?" asked the old man.

And the girls joined hands and skipped about and sang:

> I'm Tipingee,
> She's Tipingee,
> We're Tipingee, too.
>
> I'm Tipingee,
> She's Tipingee,
> We're Tipingee, too.

The man was getting angry. He went to the stepmother and said, "You promised to pay me and you are only giving me problems. You tell me Tipingee and everyone here is Tipingee, Tipingee, Tipingee,

Tipingee. If this happens a third time, I will come and take you for my servant."

"My dear sir," said the stepmother, "tomorrow she will be in red, completely in red, call her and take her."

And again Tipingee ran and told her friends to dress in red.

At noon the next day, the old man arrived at the well. He saw one little girl dressed in red. He saw a second little girl dressed in red. He saw a third girl in red.

"Which of you is Tipingee?" he asked.

"I'm Tipingee," said the first girl.

"She's Tipingee," said the second girl.

"We're Tipingee, too," said the third girl.

"WHICH OF YOU IS TIPINGEE?" the old man shouted.

But the girls just clapped and jumped up and down and sang:

> I'm Tipingee,
> She's Tipingee,
> We're Tipingee, too.
>
> I'm Tipingee,
> She's Tipingee,
> We're Tipingee, too.

The old man knew he would never find Tipingee. He went to the stepmother and took her away. When Tipingee returned home, she was gone. So she lived in her own house with all her father's belongings, and she was happy.

Many folktales contain a message that might be considered subversive by the status quo. Tipingee and her large network of friends gaily present a united front against the old man and stepmother who would do Tipingee harm. A community of little, seemingly powerless, people works together to defy the big guy.

The Innkeeper's Wise Daughter

Jewish-American[59]

Many years ago, in a small village in Russia, there were two friends, a tailor and an innkeeper. One day, as they were drinking glasses of tea, they began to talk about their philosophies of life. As their discussion went on, they began to argue more and more intensely—each one claiming to know more about life than the other one—and they almost came to blows. They realized that neither one would win the argument, so they decided to bring the matter to the local nobleman, who was respected for his wisdom and honesty and who often served as a judge in disputes. The two friends finished their tea in silence and set out to see the nobleman.

When the nobleman heard the case, he said to the two men, "Whoever answers these three questions correctly will be the one who knows more about life: What is the quickest thing in the world? What is the fattest in the world? And what is the sweetest? Return in three day's time with your answers and I will settle your disagreement."

The tailor returned home and spent the three days thinking about these riddles, but found no answers to them. When the innkeeper returned to his home, he sat down holding his head in his hands. Just then, his daughter saw him and cried out, "What's wrong, Father?" The innkeeper told her about the three questions. She answered, "Father, when you go back to the nobleman, give him these answers: The quickest thing in the world is thought. The fattest thing is the earth. The sweetest is sleep."

When three days had passed, the tailor and the innkeeper came before the nobleman. "Have you found answers to my questions?" he asked. The tailor stood there silently.

But when the innkeeper gave his answers, the nobleman exclaimed, "Wonderful! Those are wonderful answers! But tell me, how did *you* think of those answers?"

"I must tell you truthfully that those answers were told to me by my daughter," replied the innkeeper.

"Since your daughter knows so much about life, I will test her further. Give her this dozen eggs and see if she can hatch them all in three days. If she does so, she will have a great reward."

The innkeeper carefully took the eggs and returned home. When his

156

daughter saw him carrying a large basket, and she also saw how he trembled, she asked him, "What is wrong, Father?" He showed her the eggs and told her what she must do in order to receive a reward and prove her wisdom again.

The daughter took the eggs, and she weighed them, each one, in her hands. "Dear Father, how can these eggs be hatched when they are cooked? Boiled eggs indeed! But wait, Father, I have a plan as to how to answer this riddle." The daughter boiled some beans and waited three days. Then she instructed her father to go to the nobleman's house and ask permission to plant some special beans.

"Beans?" asked the nobleman. "What sort of special beans?" Taking the beans from his pocket, the innnkeeper showed them to the nobleman and said, "These are boiled beans, your honor, that I want to plant."

The nobleman burst out laughing and said, "Well, you certainly are not wise to the ways or the world if you don't even know that beans can't grow from boiled beans—only from seeds."

"Well then," replied the innkeeper, "neither can chickens hatch from boiled eggs!"

The nobleman immediately sensed the clever mind of the innkeeper's daughter in the answer. So he said to the innkeeper, "Tell your daughter to come here in three days. And she must come neither dressed nor undressed, neither walking nor riding, neither hungry nor overfed, and she must bring me a gift that is not a gift."

The innkeeper retured home even more perplexed than before. When his daughter heard what she had to do in three days' time, she laughed and said, "Father, tomorrow I will tell you what to do."

The next day, the daughter said to her father, "Go to the marketplace and buy these things—a large net, some almonds, a goat, and a pair of pigeons." The father was puzzled by these requests, but as he loved his daughter and knew her to be wise, he did not question her. Instead he went to the marketplace and bought all that she had requested.

On the third day, the innkeeper's daughter prepared for her visit to the nobleman. She did not eat her usual morning meal. Instead, she got undressed and wrapped herself in the transparent net, so she was neither dressed nor undressed.

Then she took two almonds in one hand and the pair of pigeons in the other. Leaning on the goat, she held on so that one foot dragged on the ground while she hopped on the other one. In this way, she was neither walking nor riding.

As she approached the nobleman's house, he saw her and came out to greet her.

At the gate, she ate the two almonds to show she was neither hungry nor overfed.

Then the innkeeper's daughter extended her hand showing the pigeons she intended to give as a gift. The nobleman reached out to take them, but just at that moment the young woman opened her hand to release the pigeons—and they flew away. So she had brought a gift that was not a gift.

The nobleman gave a laugh of approval and called out, "You are a clever woman! I want to marry you, but on one condition. You must promise never to interfere with any of my judgments."

"I will marry you," said the innkeeper's daughter, "but I also have one condition: If I do anything that will cause you to send me away, you must promise to give me whatever I treasure most in your house." They each agreed to the other's condition, and they were married.

Some time passed, and one day a man came to speak with the young wife, who had become known for her wisdom, "Help me, please," the man begged, "for I know you are wise and understand things in ways your husband does not."

"Tell me what is wrong, for you look very troubled, sir," she answered. And the man told her his story.

"Last year," said the man, "my partner and I bought a barn which we now share. He keeps his wagon there, and I keep my horse there. Well, last night my horse gave birth to a pony under the wagon. So my partner says the pony belongs to him. We began to argue and fight, so we brought our dispute to the nobleman. The nobleman judged that my partner was right. I protested, but to no avail. What can I do?"

The young woman gave him certain advice and instructions to follow. As she had told him to do, he took a fishing pole and went over to the nobleman's well and pretended he was fishing there. The nobleman rode by the well, just as his wife had predicted, and when he saw the man, he stopped and asked, "What are you doing?" The man replied, "I am fishing in the well." The nobleman started to laugh. "Are you really so stupid that you do not know that you can't catch fish in a well?" "No sir," said the man, "not any more than I know that a wagon cannot give birth to a pony."

At this answer, the nobleman stopped laughing. Understanding that his wife must be involved in this case after all, he got out of his carriage and went looking for his wife. When he found her he said, "You did not keep your promise not to interfere with my judgments, so I must send you back to your father's home."

"You are right, my husband. But before I leave, let us dine together one last time." The nobleman agreed to this request.

At dinner, the nobleman drank a great deal of wine, for his wife kept refilling his cup, and, as a result, he soon became very sleepy. As soon as he was asleep, the wife signaled to the servants to pick him up and put him in the carriage next to her, and so they returned to her father's home.

The next morning, when the nobleman woke up, he looked around and realized where he was. "But how did I get here? What is the meaning of this?" he shouted.

"You may remember, dear husband, that you also made an agreeement with me. You promised that if you sent me away, I would be able to pick whatever I treasured most in your house to take with me. There is nothing that I treasure more than you. So that is how you come to be here with me."

The nobleman laughed, embraced his wife, and said, "Knowing how much you love me, I now realize how much I love you. Let us return to our home."

And they did go home, where they lived with love and respect for many happy years.

This folktale deals with a problem many women face: give their talents free rein, thus competing with or even eclipsing the talents of their husbands, or suppress their talents to keep from threatening their husbands. This heroine passes test after test of her intelligence, but her real wisdom comes to the fore when she answers her husband's marriage condition with a condition of her own. From the beginning of the marriage, this heroine realizes that her husband admires her wisdom only as long as he can control it and keep it from challenging his own. She realizes that this will cause problems and from the outset provides herself with an escape route. When the nobleman sends the heroine home, she doesn't enter into the ego-driven competition over who is wiser. Instead, she defuses the conflict. "I love you," she says in a way that makes her husband realize how much he loves her. At the same time, she makes him laugh in appreciation of her intelligence. She has solidified the love in their relationship and has also laid the groundwork for the next step, teaching him to accept her as an intellectual equal.

Molly Cotton-Tail Steals Mr. Fox's Butter

African-American[60]

"Aunt Nancy," said Janey, "do you know any more stories about Mis' Molly Cotton-tail? I think she's almost as smart as Mr. Hare, and I like to hear about her almost as much."

"Almost as smart! *Almost* as smart! Well if that don't beat all!" said Nancy, throwing up her hands in affectation of indignant surprise. "Let me tell you that when a woman starts out to be tricky, she can beat a man every time, because her mind works a heap faster and she sees all around and over and underneath and on both sides of a thing while he's trying to stare plumb through it."

"Didn't you say she was his wife?" asked Ned. "I should think they would have called her Mrs. Hare always, instead of Molly Cotton-tail. Why do you suppose they didn't?"

"Lord! honey," she answered, "don't come asking me such little foolish questions as that. How do you reckon I'm going to know all the why's and wherefore's of all the old-time doings? I can't specify the reason of her being called Molly Cotton-tail sometimes, but it comes to me just now that maybe the married women didn't take their husband's name in those days like they do now. Anyhow, I know she's called Mis' Molly Cotton-tail and not just wholly and solely the wife of Mister Hare. She isn't the sort of woman to settle down and be just plain Missus Hare all her days, and stay home and listen to the children cry and wash their faces and comb their hair and cook their vittles, year in and year out. Huh-uh! Mis' Molly she's got too much get up and go in her for that. She makes old man Hare stay at home and mind the children now and then, and he doesn't dare to say no, either. Let me see, now, where was I? If I'm going to tell you any more tales, you mustn't come at me that-a-way with questions, unless you want to put the tales out of my head. I just had my mouth fixed to tell you one when you all broke in on me about the name. Let's see, what *was* that tale about, anyhow?"

"Well, I asked you for another one about Mis' Molly Cotton-tail," said Janey; "so maybe it was about her."

"Sure enough, sure enough," said Aunt Nancy. "Apparently I'm getting feeble in the mind as well as in the joints, to go forgetting that-a-way. Yes, the tale was about one time when Mis' Molly and Mister Fox go to make a visit to Mister Fox's brother who lived across the swamp

160

and down in the hollow. He was right friendly with her about that time and invited her to go with him. She was all dressed up in her good clothes and her good manners, going along making herself mighty agreeable, talking about this and that, cutting her eye up at him real sweet and sticking as close as a burr to a cow's tail."

"Why, I didn't suppose they would ever be good friends again after the tricks she played him," said Janey.

"Um! Child," she answered, "this happened so long after that old Fox plumb forgot they ever had any fallings-out. You better not pester me any more I might forget the tale, clean as a whistle. Well, they went on, him helping her over the foot-logs, might mannerly, and running on and cracking jokes with her, and at last they got to the house. Mister Sly-fox's brother which they called 'Hungry Billy,' because he was all the time eating up folks' chickens, he invited them in and told them to make themselves at home and asked them to stay as long as they can. Mis' Molly she took off her hat and shawl and the ridicule* from her arm and lay them on the bed. Then she said, 'Mister Hungry Billy, I'm so industrious I can't bear to be idle even when I'm off on a visit; so please, sir, let me get the supper, instead of sitting here holding my hands.'

"Billy told her he didn't care, so she whirled in and set the table and drew the pine'tag° tea and made the ash-cakes, and Hungry Billy he showed her where to get the butter, down at the spring. While they were at supper along came a neighbor and told them that old Mister Gray Fox was dying and had sent for Billy to sit up with him. So Billy excused himself and asked them to take care of the house until he came back and make themselves right at home. Then he went off with the neighbor.

"That night, when Mister Fox got to nodding and snoging by the fire, Mis' Molly she slipped out to the spring and ate up the butter down to the very last smidgin, and then set to and licked the crock until it was clean as if it had been scoured. Then she licked her mouth and whiskers clean, and came in and sat down by the fire again before Fox had time to wake up and miss her. She sat there looking as innocent as a lamb, going on with her knitting and humming a tune, just as if she had never had butter on her mind nor in her mouth.

"Next morning, Hungry Billy came back, cross and sleepy from the sitting-up and when he went down to the spring to get the butter for breakfast, there sat the crock, empty as a gourd. I let you know he was mad. He came a-huffing and a-puffing up to the house, and he says, says

---

* *Ridicule*, reticule; a woman's small drawstring bag used as a pocket book, workbag, or carryall.
° *Pine'tag*, the dried needle of the pine.

he, 'This here is a nice howdy-do! Y'all call yourselves respectable folks and come here and squat down on me and then when I turn my back you eat up every rap and scrap of butter you can find in the place. I've been thinking y'all were folks and now I find you are hogs!' And with that he turned his back on them both and went flouncing out the door.

"They followed him up, declaring they don't know anything at all about the butter, and Mis' Molly she did enough talking for both, she did. She says, says she, 'It wasn't me, sir, indeed it wasn't! I cross my heart! What would I want with your butter, anyways? I've got me plenty of butter at home; I don't have to go to the neighbors for every little old snack or vittles I want. Besides that, I've got a might delicate stomach, and I can't eat any butter unless I make it myself, because I'm not sure if the folks have been right clean and careful in the making of it.'

"That made Hungry Billy madder than before, and he says, says he, 'Well, maybe my butter wasn't clean; I don't know about that, but I do know about *this*: it's *clean gone*, and what's more, one of you two is the person who 'goned' it. I'm going to keep you both right here until I find out which is the thief.'

"Molly she thought a little, and then she says, says she, 'Mister Billy, I'm very sorry this happened, indeed I am. But what's done can't be undone, and so the only thing now is to prove which of us took your butter. If I'm not deceiving myself, I know the sure and certain way to find out which is the thief. Just you go along about your work and let me and Mister Sly-fox lay down yonder in the sun all day, and when you come back this evening I bound* you can tell which of us done ate the butter.'

"'How come?' says Hungry Billy, says he.

"'That's as easy as rolling off a log,' she says. 'The heat of the sun is going to strak° through and draw the grease out, so when you come back all you have to do is to rub your fingers over our stomachs and then you'll know in a jiffy who done swallowed your butter.'

"Mister Slickery Sly-fox agreed to this, because he knew he hadn't taken the butter, so he wasn't afraid it would be proved to be him. Hungry Billy he said it looked mighty reasonable and he agreed to it, too, and went off across the swamp to tend to his work, and left them both there laying in the sun.

"After a while she says, says she, blinking and batting her eyes like she can't keep them open, 'Um-umph! Mister Fox, that sun makes me powerful sleepy, please excuse me, sir, but I'm just naturally obliged to take a

* *Bound*, bet.
° *Strak*, strake, streak, stroke.

little nap.' Fox said he believed he'd take one himself, and he shut his eyes and put his nose down between both jaws and gave his tail a whip or two to drive away the flies, and pretty nigh he was fast asleep.

"Mis' Molly she watched him out of the corner of her eye, and when she saw he was good and sound asleep she lit up from that without making no noise and struck out for a neighbor's spring and got her a handful of butter. She came tiptoeing back and stooped down and rubbed the butter all over Mister Fox's stomach, so softly that he couldn't feel it, and then she went and licked her paws clean and laid down in her place again and kept one eye on him. About the time when she suspected Hungry Billy home, she shut her eyes and snored so loudly he heard her clean across the hollow. When he came up to them they were apparently fast asleep, and Billy he reached down and ran his hand over Mis' Molly's stomach. Dry as a bone! Then he tried Mister Slickery Sly-fox, and he brought up his hand covered with grease and smelling loud of butter.

"Billy was in a terrible taking* and made such a fuss that he woke Mister Fox and fell to accusing him of taking the butter. Old Fox was so suprised to find his stomach covered with butter that he couldn't say anything at all. About then Mis' Molly Cotton-tail began to stretch and rub her eyes and pretend like she just woke up. She listened to all the goings-on a minute and then she commenced to make great admiration. 'Lord-a-mercy!' she said, 'I couldn't believe this if I hadn't seen it with my own eyes. I'm certainly scandalized that a friend of mine has taken to stealing, most specially on a visit. I declare to goodness my feelings are so hurt that I can't rightly express myself, and what's more, I can't stay here associating with a common thief. I've got my young family to think about. So long, Mister Hungry Billy. I hope you're going to give that man a good walloping, because he certainly earned it, coming here putting up on you and then cleaning out your butter. Next time you get me to go visiting with you, Mister Slickery Sly-fox, you'll be a heap older and smarter than what you are this minute.' With that she went scooting, because she feared if she stayed longer she might get found out somehow or another.

"Hungry Billy he thought a little while and then he said to Mister Fox, 'Well, I'm going to let you off this time, because you are my kin and I don't want to disgrace you; I don't want to let folks know I've got a thief for a brother. But don't let me catch you in these parts any more, or I'm going to set to work and lam° the butter out of that greasy hide of yours; you hear me talking!'

---

* *Taking,* a state of violent agitation and distress.
° *Lam,* to beat soundly.

"Fox he declared and sweared that he wasn't the thief, but Billy didn't pay any attention to him. Then he had half a mind to tell old Hungry Billy about all those henroosts he'd robbed but Billy was so mad already that he kind of feared to do it, so he went slinking off with his ears down and his tail dragging, and they tell me there was a great coolness that sprang up in that family that lasted for some several years, all because of that crock of butter. I let you know, children, it doesn't take much to start a family quarrel, but it takes a heap of time and trouble to patch one up, just the same as it does with those holes where little Master Ned snagged in his britches, and it never seems the same after the patching either."

Arch trickster and feminist, Molly Cotton-tail—NOT Mrs. Hare—rivals her famous male counterpart, Brer Rabbit, for artful cunning and brazen impudence. More powerful than a locomotive, "She makes old man Hare stay at home and mind the children now and then, and he doesn't dare to say no, either." Faster than a speeding bullet, "she sees all around and over and underneath and on both sides of a thing while he's trying to stare plumb through it." Molly Cotton-tail swipes cookies from the cookie jar with impunity.

Tales
from
Asia

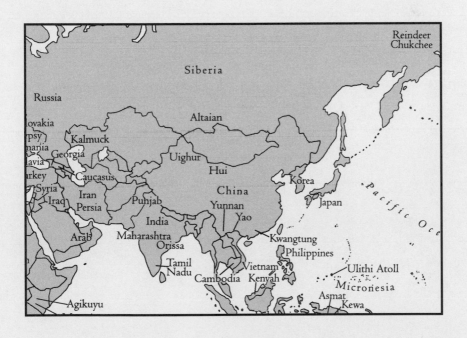

A Rani's Revenge

Orissa, India[61]

In olden times, there were a number of independent states in Orissa. Banki and Khurda were two such states which had a common boundary. There were frequent border disputes between the two states. Sometimes, these disputes even led to war.

Dhanurjaya, the Raja of Banki, was a renowned warrior who had fought many hard battles. He was a skilful archer and swordsman. His Rani, Shuka Dei, was no less a warrior than her husband. Her skill in horse-riding was well-known everywhere.

Banki was a smaller state than Khurda. Her resources in men and materials were poor. But Dhanurjaya's courage was such that he would yield to none and much less to the Raja of Khurda. Once the Raja of Khurda forcibly occupied some villages on the border. Bravely, Dhanurjaya marched forward with his army to fight the invader. That day a severe battle was fought and many were killed. In the end, the small army of Banki could not resist the pressure of a heavy attack. Dhanurjaya fought bravely, but fell into the hands of the enemy and was killed. When they found their ruler slain, the soldiers of Banki gave up the battle as lost and fled from the battlefield.

Soon report of the death of her husband reached Rani Shuka Dei. Her grief knew no bounds, yet her eyes had no tears but flashed fire. Her cousellors came up to her and declared in one voice, "Our Raja is dead. Now there is no hope for us. Let us surrender to the enemy."

"Are we *Kshatriyas** or cowards?" she cried out in anger.

"No Madam," replied her minister, "we are not cowards. But our state is small and our army smaller. We can never expect to win against Khurda. Our Raja is no more and you, O Rani, are only a woman and Prince Dayanidhi is merely a lad. It is wise to give up now a bit of our territory rather than lose the entire state. This may satisfy the Raja of Khurda."

"What? Yield to the enemy! True, I am a woman but do not forget I am a *Kshatriya* and *Kshatriya* blood runs in my veins," cried the Rani in anger.

Turning to her *Senapati*° she continued, "I will fight, and if need be, die

---

* *Kshatriyas*, warrior class.
° *Senapati*, general.

fighting like a *Kshatriya*, but never will I yield even a small strip of land to the enemy."

Feelingly she asked, "Did you not all run away from the battlefield? Tell me, did my husband run away? Bravely, he fought and died in the battlefield. If you are afraid, you may go and hide yourselves in your homes. I am going to the battlefield to fight again. If none of you comes with me, let it be known that I, a woman, will alone march forward and fight against Khurda."

Then she added, "Only those who are not afraid of death, need come with me. Let this be known, to my people."

These brave words of a woman put courage in their hearts and they declared, "If you are going to the battlefield, can we stay behind? We can't let you go alone." They added, "We have asked the Raja of Badamba for help, and may be, he will help us."

The Rani's undaunted courage encouraged the soldiers and soon a great army, with the Rani at the head, marched forward against Khurda.

In the meanwhile, the Raja of Khurda was celebrating the victory. When the news of this fresh attack reached him he could not believe it.

"Impossible," he said. "The Rani of Banki attacking us? Dare she, a widow, take up such a foolish venture, and that too so soon after the death of her husband? Impossible!" However, he instructed his *Senapati* to make preparations for the war.

Great was the surprise of the Raja to see Shuka Dei leading an army against him. Soon a fierce battle raged near the boundary. The Rani's unusual courage gave spirit to her soldiers and they fought bravely. Many deeds of courage were seen on the battlefield and in the end the *Senapati* of Khurda was caught and killed by the Banki army. Thereafter, panic prevailed in the Khurda camp and soon the Raja of Khurda was captured by the Rani's soldiers.

Bound with chains and guarded by the soldiers of Banki, the Raja was brought before Rani Shuka Dei. He was greatly ashamed when he was brought as a prisoner before a woman, and that too a woman whose husband he had so recently killed.

"Was not death in the battlefield a thousand times better than this disgrace? Surely, revenge is in the Rani's heart and she will not spare my life," thought the Raja.

The Rani looked at her soldiers and ordered, "Take off the chains and set free the Raja." Then looking at the Raja, she gently said, "You may now return to your own state. No one here will do you any harm."

The Raja was astonished at the unexpected turn of events. "What," he thought, "she, whom I had taken to be my enemy seeking revenge, now orders my freedom!" With his head bowed he humbly said, "I never imagined that you could show me such mercy."

The Rani rejoined, "Sir, you are my prisoner and if I like I can have your head cut off. But what good would such an act produce? I am a widow. I have a woman's heart. My husband is dead and my grief is too heavy to bear. How could I inflict such a suffering on another woman? No, no, I cannot do this to the Rani of Khurda! I fought with you only to bring back the lost prestige of Banki and not for revenge."

Deeply moved the Raja stood stunned. After a while, he humbly said, "Madam, you got victory over me in the battlefield today, and now you have won a second victory over me by showing such magnanimity. What could my grateful heart say or give you? I remain forever indebted to you and as a token of my gratitude, I surrender to you the entire Kusapala *pargana** of Khurda. I vow, that never more shall the sword of Khurda be raised against Banki."

Later, a pillar was raised at Kusapala, to mark the heroism and magnanimity of Rani Shuka Dei. The pillar still stands.

The mercy and compassion of the Rani appealed to me but left my six-year-old daughter bemused. She didn't know what to make of this story. When the lazy husband in "The Vampire Skeleton" (p. 101) was killed by the monster, I felt sorry for him, but my daughter shrugged her shoulders and said, "Well, he wasn't so good, you know." This difference in our world views reminded me of a quote by G. K. Chesterton: "Children are innocent and love justice; While most of us are wicked and prefer mercy."[62]

---

* *Pargana*, a group of villages.

How Parvatibai Outwitted the Dacoits

Maharashtra, India [63]

In the middle of the last century, areas on the outskirts of Maharashtra were full of thugs and dacoits.* They used to raid the villages, terrorise the people and take away their valuables. The police could not protect the people. The people had to defend themselves by forming their own groups. But many times they fled from their homes to save their lives.

A notorious dacoit chief spread his activities, from villages to the near-by towns. He had now become so bold that he used to send advance intimation to the people as to when he would raid and which houses he would loot. If an effort was made to remove the valuables from the houses or call the police, the victims had to face more severe reprisals. There was thus no way out but to allow oneself to be plundered or offer whatever resistance one could by mustering men who were ready to fight. But the dacoits would always succeed in the end.

One day a rich man named Bapurao received word that his house would be attacked that night. He was also given the usual warning: "If you try to deceive by removing the ornaments from your house or inform the police, you will be given a blood-bath."

Bapurao turned pale when he heard it. He had a big *haveli*° and a brigade of servants working in his house. His coffers were full. He was afraid, but his wife Parvatibai was a courageous and clever woman. When he broke the news to her she asked him: "What do you propose to do?"

"Surely I am not going to yield to these plunderers! I will collect men from the town and along with the servants give them a fight. What do you think?"

"I think there is no use giving an unequal fight. After all the dacoits are better armed, and more used to fighting. They will overpower you in no time."

"But what else can we do?" asked Bapurao.

"I think we should outwit the dacoits by some plan," said Parvatibai thoughtfully.

"But how? Should we hide your jewelbox somewhere . . . say in the dung-heap in the cattleshed?"

---

* *Dacoit*, one of a class of criminals in India and Burma who rob and murder in roving gangs.
° *Haveli*, villa, a large residence of a wealthy person, usually containing garden(s) and servant quarters.

"Let me think," she said, "till then you do whatever you think proper. I will fight them in my own way. Don't worry."

Bapurao felt a little reassured and he went about the town in search of men to help him, while Parvatibai sat a long time thinking. Soon it was evening. Bapurao came back and told his wife: "I have collected some twenty men. We will hide in the woods near the village border and attack the dacoits before they can enter the village."

Saying this he took four servants and several weapons and went away.

It was now dark and the whole village was silent.

Parvatibai then called her maidservants and the two cooks and ordered them: "Prepare a royal meal for fifty persons. Time it in such a way that it should be ready to be served hot by about midnight."

The servants were surprised but they went their way and set to work. Parvatibai supervised the preparations. When the meal was almost ready and the plantain leaves and seats for fifty persons were laid for supper, she put on a new sari, and except the *mangalsutra*,* took off all her ornaments and arranged them in a *thali*° along with her other jewellery. She then sat waiting.

When it was midnight she heard the distant noise of horses' hoofs and sabre-rattling. Soon the noise came closer. Suddenly there was a loud knock on the door. Her heart almost stopped beating, but the next moment wearing a calm and eager expression on her face, she hurriedly went to the door and opened it. Before her stood a large man with a ferocious look, a naked sword in his hand. Parvatibai was scared but with courage she said sweetly:

"Come on brother. Please do come in."

The dacoit was taken aback by this address. But before he could open his mouth Parvatibai said:

"I have been waiting for you and other brothers since I received your message this morning." The dacoit stood staring at her, surprised at this unusual welcome.

"Please come in. And don't waste time. Wash your hands and feet. The supper is ready. Have a hearty meal before you do your work."

The dacoit-chief was still hesitating. But she made them sit on the seats and ordered the servants to serve them hot food. While they were eating, she personally attended to each one and pressed them to eat some more, and not feel shy. When they finished their supper, she brought the plateful of ornaments and placing them before the dacoit-chief told him:

---

* *Mangalsutra*, necklace worn by married Hindu women.
° *Thali*, tray.

"Brother, this is all that I have got, but I have kept back only one piece for myself." She indicated towards the *mangalsutra* on her neck and said: "It is a sacred marriage token which I wear for the long life of my husband and I pray that you should spare it."

The dacoit-chief could contain himself no more. With emotion in his voice he said:

"Of course I will spare it. We have eaten your salt and we are never unfaithful to those whose salt we eat. What's more, you have called me brother and given me a brother's welcome. From today you are my sister and I will see that no harm comes to you." Saying this he returned the plate of ornaments to her and ordered his fellow-dacoits to bring her husband in who was lying on the roadside along with others tied hand and foot. He then set them free and departed.

The villagers were greatly surprised when they heard the story next morning. Since then no dacoit attacked Parvatibai's house, and even today her story is narrated to children.

"I will fight them in my own way," Parvatibai says. She is a champion of lateral thinking. Parvatibai considers the problem from all angles, around and over and underneath, while her husband attacks it head-on. She dismisses the obvious approach, "I think there is no use giving an unequal fight." Not only does Parvatibai give no fight, she accepts, even welcomes, the dacoit. She defuses the confrontation by greeting him as a brother and serving him a banquet. Her welcome turns the dacoit's attack into friendship and he responds with gratitude. Parvatibai successfully changes a win-lose situation into a win-win situation.

The Close Alliance: A Tale of Woe

Punjab, India[64]

One day a farmer went with his bullocks to plough his field. He had just turned the first furrow, when a tiger walked up to him and said, "Peace be with you, friend! How are you this fine morning?"

"The same to you, my lord, and I am pretty well, thank you!" returned the farmer, quaking with fear, but thinking it wisest to be polite.

"I am glad to hear it," replied the tiger cheerfully, "because Providence has sent me to eat your two bullocks. You are a God-fearing man, I know, so make haste and unyoke them."

"My friend, are you sure you are not making a mistake?" asked the farmer, whose courage had returned now that he knew it was merely a question of gobbling up bullocks; "because Providence sent me to plough this field, and, in order to plough, one must have oxen. Had you not better go and make further inquiries?"

"There is no occasion for delay, and I should be sorry to keep you waiting," returned the tiger. "If you'll unyoke the bullocks I'll be ready in a moment." With that the savage creature fell to sharpening his teeth and claws in a very significant manner.

But the farmer begged and prayed that his oxen might not be eaten, and promised that if the tiger would spare them, he would give in exchange a fine fat young milch cow, which his wife had tied up in the yard at home.

To this the tiger agreed, and, taking the oxen with him, the farmer went sadly homewards. Seeing him return so early from the fields, his wife, who was a stirring, busy woman, called out, "What! lazybones!—back already, and my work just beginning!"

Then the farmer explained how he had met the tiger, and how to save the bullocks he had promised the milch cow in exchange. At this the wife began to cry, saying, "A likely story, indeed!—saving your stupid old bullocks at the expense of my beautiful cow! Where will the children get milk? and how can I cook my pottage and collops* without butter?"

"All very fine, wife," retorted the farmer, "but how can we make bread without corn? and how can you have corn without bullocks to plough the

---

* *Collops*, a small piece or slice of meat.

fields? Pottage and collops are very nice, but it is better to do without milk and butter than without bread, so make haste and untie the cow."

"You great gaby!"* wept the wife, "if you had an ounce of sense in your brain you'd think of some plan to get out of the scrape!"

"Think yourself!" cried the husband, in a rage.

"Very well!" returned the wife; "but if I do the thinking you must obey orders; I can't do both. Go back to the tiger, and tell him the cow would-n't come along with you, but that your wife is bringing it."

The farmer, who was a great coward, didn't half like the idea of going back empty-handed to the tiger, but as he could think of no other plan he did as he was bid, and found the beast still sharpening his teeth and claws for very hunger; and when he heard he had to wait still longer for his din-ner, he began to prowl about, and lash his tail, and curl his whiskers, in a most terrible manner, causing the poor farmer's knees to knock together with terror.

Now, when the farmer had left the house, his wife went to the stable and saddled the pony; then she put on her husband's best clothes, tied the turban very high, so as to make her look as tall as possible, bestrode the pony, and set out to the field where the tiger was.

She rode along, swaggering and blustering, till she came to where the lane turned into the field, and then she called out, as bold as brass, "Now, please the powers! I may find a tiger in this place; for I haven't tasted tiger's meat since yesterday, when, as luck would have it, I ate three for break-fast."

Hearing these words, and seeing the speaker ride boldly at him, the tiger became so alarmed that he turned tail, and bolted into the forest, going away at such a headlong pace that he nearly overturned his own jackal; for tigers always have a jackal of their own who, as it were, waits at table and clears away the bones.

"My lord! my lord!" cried the jackal, "whither away so fast?"

"Run! run!" panted the tiger; "there's the very devil of a horseman in yonder fields, who thinks nothing of eating three tigers for breakfast!"

At this the jackal sniggered in his sleeve. "My dear lord," said he, "the sun has dazzled your eyes! That was no horseman, but only the farmer's wife dressed up as a man!"

"Are you quite sure?" asked the tiger, pausing.

"Quite sure, my lord," repeated the jackal; "and if your lordship's eyes had not been dazzled by—ahem!—the sun, your lordship would have seen her pigtail hanging down behind."

* *Gaby*, simpleton.

"But you may be mistaken!" persisted the cowardly tiger; "it was the very devil of a horseman to look at!"

"Who's afraid?" replied the brave jackal. "Come! don't give up your dinner because of a woman!"

"But you may be bribed to betray me!" argued the tiger, who, like all cowards, was suspicious.

"Let us go together, then!" returned the gallant jackal.

"Nay! but you may take me there and then run away!" insisted the tiger cunningly.

"In that case, let us tie our tails together, and then I can't!" The jackal, you see, was determined not to be done out of his bones.

To this the tiger agreed, and having tied their tails together in a reef-knot, the pair set off arm-in-arm.

Now the farmer and his wife had remained in the field, laughing over the trick she had played on the tiger, when, lo and behold! what should they see but the gallant pair coming back ever so bravely, with their tails tied together.

"Run!" cried the farmer; "we are lost! we are lost!"

"Nothing of the kind, you great gaby!" answered his wife coolly, "if you will only stop that noise and be quiet. I can't hear myself speak!"

Then she waited till the pair were within hail, when she called out politely, "How very kind of you, dear Mr. Jackal, to bring me such a nice fat tiger! I shan't be a moment finishing my share of him, and then you can have the bones."

At these words the tiger became wild with fright, and, quite forgetting the jackal, and that reef-knot in their tails, he bolted away full tilt, dragging the jackal behind him. Bumpety, bump, bump, over the stones!—crash, scratch, patch, through the briars!

In vain the poor jackal howled and shrieked to the tiger to stop,—the noise behind him only frightened the coward more; and away he went, helter-skelter, hurry-scurry, over hill and dale, till he was nearly dead with fatigue, and the jackal was quite dead from bumps and bruises.

Moral—Don't tie your tail to a coward's.

The wife takes command. She tells her husband that if she does the thinking, he has to obey orders. She boldly carries out an ingenious plan and scares the wits out of the tiger. Egged on by the jackal, the tiger mounts a second attack. Instantly the wife sizes up the jackal's ploy and the tiger's fear of betrayal.

The title and ending indicate that this story is told from a male point of view. The title, "The Close Alliance," refers to the alliance between the tiger and the jackal, two male characters. The subtitle "A Tale of Woe" reflects the jackal's perspective not the wife's. Seen from the wife's point of view, this is certainly not a tale of woe. When I tell this story to my daughters, I end with the heroine's perspective: "The jackal goes bumpety, bump, bump over the stones and the woman puts her hands on her hips and laughs and laughs and laughs."

The Barber's Clever Wife

Punjab, India[65]

Once upon a time there lived a barber, who was such a poor silly creature that he couldn't even ply his trade decently, but snipped off his customers' ears instead of their hair, and cut their throats instead of shaving them. So of course he grew poorer every day, till at last he found himself with nothing left in his house but his wife and his razor, both of whom were as sharp as sharp could be.

For his wife was an exceedingly clever person, who was continually rating* her husband for his stupidity; and when she saw they hadn't a farthing left, she fell as usual to scolding.

But the barber took it very calmly. "What is the use of making such a fuss, my dear?" said he; "You've told me all this before, and I quite agree with you I never *did* work, I never *could* work, and I never *will* work. That is the fact!"

"Then you must beg!" returned his wife, "for I will not starve to please you! Go to the palace, and beg something of the King. There is a wedding feast going on and he is sure to give alms to the poor."

"Very well, my dear!" said the barber submissively. He was rather afraid of his clever wife, so he did as he was bid, and going to the palace, begged of the King to give him something.

"Something?" asked the King; "what thing?"

Now the barber's wife had not mentioned anything in particular, and the barber was far too addle-pated to think of anything by himself, so he answered cautiously, "Oh, something!"

"Will a piece of land do?" said the King.

Whereupon the lazy barber, glad to be helped out of the difficulty, remarked that perhaps a piece of land would do as well as anything else.

Then the King ordered a piece of waste, outside the city, should be given to the barber, who went home quite satisfied.

"Well! what did you get?" asked the clever wife who was waiting impatiently for his return. "Give it me quick, that I may go and buy bread!"

And you may imagine how she scolded when she found he had only got a piece of waste land.

* *Rate*, to rebuke angrily or violently; scold, upbraid

"But land is land!" remonstrated the barber; "it can't run away, so we must always have something now!"

"Was there ever such a dunderhead?" raged the clever wife. "What good is ground unless we can till it? and where are we to get bullocks and ploughs?"

But being, as we have said, an exceedingly clever person, she set her wits to work, and soon thought of a plan whereby to make the best of a bad bargain.

She took her husband with her, and set off to the piece of waste land; then, bidding her husband imitate her, she began walking about the field, and peering anxiously into the ground. But when anybody came that way, she would sit down, and pretend to be doing nothing at all.

Now it so happened that seven thieves were hiding in a thicket hard by, and they watched the barber and his wife all day, until they became convinced something mysterious was going on. So at sunset they sent one of their number to try and find out what it was.

"Well, the fact is," said the barber's wife, after beating about the bush for some time, and with many injunctions to strict secrecy, "this field belonged to my grandfather, who buried five pots full of gold in it, and we were just trying to discover the exact spot before beginning to dig. You won't tell any one, will you?"

The thief promised he wouldn't, of course, but the moment the barber and his wife went home, he called his companions, and telling them of the hidden treasure, set them to work. All night long they dug and delved, till the field looked as if it had been ploughed seven times over, and they were as tired as tired could be; but never a gold piece, nor a silver piece, nor a farthing did they find, so when dawn came they went away disgusted.

The barber's wife, when she found the field so beautifully ploughed, laughed heartily at the success of her stratagem, and going to the corn-dealer's shop, borrowed some rice to sow in the field. This the corn-dealer willingly gave her, for he reckoned he would get it back threefold at harvest time. And so he did, for never was there such a crop!—the barber's wife paid her debts, kept enough for the house, and sold the rest for a great crock of gold pieces.

Now when the thieves saw this, they were very angry indeed, and going to the barber's house, said, "Give us our share of the harvest, for we tilled the ground, as you very well know."

"I told you there was gold in the ground," laughed the barber's wife, "but you didn't find it. I have, and there's a crock full of it in the house, only you rascals shall never have a farthing of it!"

"Very well!" said the thieves; "look out for yourself to-night. If you won't give us our share we'll take it!"

So that night one of the thieves hid himself in the house, intending to open the door to his comrades when the housefolk were asleep; but the barber's wife saw him with the corner of her eye, and determined to lead him a dance. Therefore, when her husband, who was in a dreadful state of alarm, asked her what she had done with the gold pieces, she replied, "Put them where no one will find them,—under the sweetmeats, in the crock that stands in the niche by the door."

The thief chuckled at hearing this, and after waiting till all was quiet, he crept out, and feeling about for the crock, made off with it, whispering to his comrades that he had got the prize. Fearing pursuit, they fled to a thicket, where they sat down to divide the spoil.

"She said there were sweetmeats on the top," said the thief; "I will divide them first, and then we can eat them, for it is hungry work, this waiting and watching."

So he divided what he thought were the sweetmeats as well as he could in the dark. Now in reality the crock was full of all sorts of horrible things that the barber's wife had put there on purpose, and so when the thieves crammed its contents into their mouths, you may imagine what faces they made and how they vowed revenge.

But when they returned next day to threaten and repeat their claim to a share of the crop, the barber's wife only laughed at them.

"Have a care!" they cried; "twice you have fooled us—once by making us dig all night, and next by feeding us on filth and breaking our caste.* It will be our turn to-night!"

Then another thief hid himself in the house, but the barber's wife saw him with half an eye, and when her husband asked, "What have you done with the gold, my dear? I hope you haven't put it under the pillow?" she answered, "Don't be alarmed; it is out of the house. I have hung it in the branches of the *nîm* tree outside. No one will think of looking for it there!"

The hidden thief chuckled, and when the housefolk were asleep he slipped out and told his companions.

"Sure enough, there it is!" cried the captain of the band, peering up into the branches. "One of you go up and fetch it down." Now what he saw was really a hornets' nest, full of great big brown and yellow hornets.

So one of the thieves climbed up the tree; but when he came close to

---

* *Caste*, in India, a rigid system of hereditary classes, which dictates rules, restrictions, and special customs. Breaking caste is when one breaks one of the rules associated with one's class.

the nest, and was just reaching up to take hold of it, a hornet flew out and
stung him on the thigh. He immediately clapped his hand to the spot.

"Oh, you thief!" cried out the rest from below, "you're pocketing the
gold pieces, are you? Oh! shabby! shabby!"—For you see it was very dark,
and when the poor man clapped his hand to the place where he had been
stung, they thought he was putting his hand in his pocket.

"I assure you I'm not doing anything of the kind!" retorted the thief;
"but there is something that bites in this tree!"

Just at that moment another hornet stung him on the breast, and he
clapped his hand there.

"Fie! fie for shame! We saw you do it that time!" cried the rest. "Just
you stop that at once, or we will make you!"

So they sent up another thief, but he fared no better, for by this time
the hornets were thoroughly roused, and they stung the poor man all over,
so that he kept clapping his hands here, there, and everywhere.

"Shame! Shabby! Ssh-sh!" bawled the rest; and then one after another they climbed into the tree, determined to share the booty, and one after
another began clapping their hands about their bodies, till it came to the
captain's turn. Then he, intent on having the prize, seized hold of the
hornets' nest, and as the branch on which they were all standing broke at
the selfsame moment, they all came tumbling down with the hornets' nest
on top of them. And then, in spite of bumps and bruises, you can imagine what a stampede there was!

After this the barber's wife had some peace, for every one of the seven
thieves was in hospital. In fact, they were laid up for so long a time that
she began to think that they were never coming back again, and ceased to
be on the look-out. But she was wrong, for one night, when she had left
the window open, she was awakened by whisperings outside, and at once
recognised the thieves' voices. She gave herself up for lost; but, determined not to yield without a struggle, she seized her husband's razor,
crept to the side of the window, and stood quite still. By and by the first
thief began to creep through cautiously. She just waited till the tip of his
nose was visible, and then, flash!—she sliced it off with the razor as clean
as a whistle.

"Confound it!" yelled the thief, drawing back mighty quick; "I've cut
my nose on something!"

"Hush-sh-sh-sh!" whispered the others, "you'll wake some one. Go
on!"

"Not I!" said the thief; "I'm bleeding like a pig!"

"Pooh!—knocked your nose against the shutter, I suppose," returned
the second thief. "I'll go!"

But swish!—off went the tip of his nose too.

"Dear me!" said he ruefully, "there certainly is something sharp inside!"

"A bit of bamboo in the lattice, most likely," remarked the third thief. "I'll go!" And, flick!—off went his nose too.

"It is most extraordinary!" he exclaimed, hurriedly retiring; "I feel exactly as if some one had cut the tip of my nose off!"

"Rubbish!" said the fourth thief. "What cowards you all are! Let *me* go!"

But he fared no better, nor the fifth thief, nor the sixth.

"My friends!" said the captain when it came to his turn, "you are all disabled. One man must remain unhurt to protect the wounded. Let us return another night."—He was a cautious man, you see, and valued his nose.

So they crept away sulkily, and the barber's wife lit a lamp, and gathering up all the nose tips, put them away safely in a little box.

Now before the robbers' noses were healed over, the hot weather set in, and the barber and his wife, finding it warm sleeping in the house, put their beds outside; for they made sure the thieves would not return. But they did, and seizing such a good opportunity for revenge, they lifted up the wife's bed, and carried her off fast asleep. She woke to find herself borne along on the heads of four of the thieves, whilst the other three ran beside her. She gave herself up for lost, and though she thought, and thought, and thought, she could find no way of escape; till, as luck would have it, the robbers paused to take breath under a banyan tree. Quick as lightning, she seized hold of a branch that was within reach, and swung herself into the tree, leaving her quilt on the bed just as if she were still in it.

"Let us rest a bit here," said the thieves who were carrying the bed; "there is plenty of time, and we are tired. She is dreadfully heavy!"

The barber's wife could hardly help laughing, but she had to keep very still, for it was a bright moonlight night; and the robbers, after setting down their burden, began to squabble as to who should take first watch. At last they determined that it should be the captain, for the others had really barely recovered from the shock of having their noses sliced off; so they lay down to sleep, while the captain walked up and down, watching the bed, and the barber's wife sat perched up in the tree like a great bird.

Suddenly an idea came into her head, and drawing her white veil becomingly over her face, she began to sing softly. The robber captain looked up, and saw the veiled figure of a woman in the tree. Of course he was a little surprised, but being a good-looking young fellow, and rather vain of his appearance, he jumped at once to the conclusion that it was a fairy who had fallen in love with his handsome face. For fairies do such things sometimes, especially on moonlight nights. So he twirled his moustaches, and strutted about, waiting for her to speak. But when she went on singing, and took no notice of him, he stopped and called out, "Come down, my beauty! I won't hurt you!"

But still she went on singing; so he climbed up into the tree, determined to attract her attention. When he came quite close, she turned away her head and sighed.

"What is the matter, my beauty?" he asked tenderly. "Of course you are a fairy, and have fallen in love with me, but there is nothing to sigh at in that, surely?"

"Ah—ah—ah!" said the barber's wife, with another sigh, "I believe you're fickle! Men with long-pointed noses always are!"

But the robber captain swore he was the most constant of men; yet still the fairy sighed and sighed, until he almost wished his nose had been shortened too.

"You are telling stories, I am sure!" said the pretended fairy. "Just let me touch your tongue with the tip of mine, and then I shall be able to taste if there are fibs about!"

So the robber captain put out his tongue, and, snip!—the barber's wife bit the tip off clean!

What with the fright and the pain, he tumbled off the branch, and fell bump on the ground, where he sat with his legs very wide apart, looking as if he had come from the skies.

"What is the matter?" cried his comrades, awakened by the noise of his fall.

"*Bul-ul-a-bul-ul-ul!*" answered he, pointing up into the tree; for of course he could not speak plainly without the tip of his tongue.

"What-is-the-matter?" they bawled in his ear, as if that would do any good.

"*Bul-ul-a-bul-ul-ul!*" said he, still pointing upwards.

"The man is bewitched!" cried one; "there must be a ghost in the tree!"

Just then the barber's wife began flapping her veil and howling; whereupon, without waiting to look, the thieves in a terrible fright set off at a run, dragging their leader with them; and the barber's wife, coming down from the tree, put her bed on her head, and walked quietly home.

After this, the thieves came to the conclusion that it was no use trying to gain their point by force, so they went to law to claim their share. But the barber's wife pleaded her own cause so well, bringing out the nose and tongue tips as witnesses, that the King made the barber his Wazîr, saying, "He will never do a foolish thing as long as his wife is alive!"

This intelligent and resourceful heroine plows the land without a plow, defends her crock of gold against a whole band of persistent thieves, rescues herself when she is abducted, and pleads her own case brilliantly before the court.

The title and ending of this tale indicate that it was told from a man's point of view. The woman is defined only in regard to her husband, she is the barber's wife. At the end, the king makes the heroine's husband his advisor. The value resides in the woman, the recognition goes to the man. Women's contributions are often devalued or overlooked. When the British Empire had holdings all over the world, many British women took an interest in collecting folktales. Thanks to these women we have turn-of-the-century folktale collections from New Zealand, Australia, China, and India. "The Barber's Clever Wife" and "The Close Alliance" were both collected by Flora Annie Steel during winter tours through the districts of the Punjab of which her husband was the Chief Magistrate.

A Wonderful Story

India[66]

Once there lived two wrestlers, who were both very very strong. The stronger of the two had a daughter called Ajit; the other had no daughter at all. These wrestlers did not live in the same country, but their two villages were not far apart.

One day the wrestler that had no daughter heard of the wrestler that had a daughter, and he determined to go and find him and wrestle with him, to see who was the stronger. He went therefore to Ajit's father's country, and when he arrived at his house, he knocked at the door and said, "Is anyone here?" Ajit answered, "Yes, I am here"; and she came out. "Where is the wrestler who lives in this house?" he asked. "My father," answered Ajit, "has taken three hundred carts to the jungle, and he is drawing them himself, as he could not get enough bullocks and horses to pull them along. He is gone to get wood." This astonished the wrestler very much. "Your father must indeed be very strong," he said.

Then he set off to the jungle, and in the jungle he found two dead elephants. He tied them to the two ends of a pole, took the pole on his shoulder, and returned to Ajit's house. There he knocked at the door, crying, "Is any one here?" "Yes, I am here," said Ajit. "Has your father come back?" asked the wrestler. "Not yet," said Ajit, who was busy sweeping the room. Now, her father had twelve elephants. Eleven were in the stables, but one was lying dead in the room Ajit was sweeping; and as she swept, she swept the dead elephant without any trouble out of the door. This frightened the wrestler, "What a strong girl this is!" he said to himself. When Ajit had swept all the dust out of the room, she came and gathered it and the dead elephant up, and threw dust and elephant away. The wrestler was more and more astonished.

He set off again to find Ajit's father, and met him pulling the three hundred carts along. At this he was still more alarmed, but he said to him, "Will you wrestle with me now?" "No," said Ajit's father, "I won't; for here there is no one to see us." The other again begged him to wrestle at once, and at that moment an old woman bent with age came by. She was carrying bread to her son, who had taken his mother's three or four thousand camels to browse.

The first wrestler called to her at once, "Come and see us wrestle." "No," said the old woman, "for I must take my son his dinner. He is very hungry." "No, no; you must stay and see us wrestle," cried both the wrestlers. "I can not stay," she said; "but do one of you stand on one of my hands, and the other on the other, and then you can wrestle as we go along." "You carry us!" cried the men. "You are so old, you will never be able to carry us." "Indeed I shall," said the old woman. So they got up on her hands, and she rested her hands, with the wrestlers standing on them, on her shoulders; and her son's flour-cakes she put on her head. Thus they went on their way, and the men wrestled as they went.

Now the old woman had told her son that if he did not do his work well, she would bring men to kill him; so he was dreadfully frightened when he saw his mother coming with the wrestlers. "Here is my mother coming to kill me," he said and he tied up the three or four thousand camels in his cloth, put them all on his head, and ran off with them as fast as he could. "Stop, stop!" cried his mother, when she saw him running away. But he only ran on still faster, and the old woman and the wrestlers ran after him.

Just then a kite* was flying about, and the kite said to itself, "There must be some meat in that man's cloth," so it swept down and carried off the bundle of camels. The old woman's son at this sat down and cried.

The wrestlers soon came up to him and said, "What are you crying for?" "Oh," answered the boy, "my mother said that if I did not do my work, she would bring men to kill me. So, when I saw you coming with her, I tied all the camels up in my cloth, put them on my head, and ran off. A kite came down and carried them all away. That is why I am crying." The wrestlers were much astonished at the boy's strength and at the kite's strength, and they all three set off in the direction in which the kite had flown.

Meanwhile the kite had flown on and on till it had reached another country, and the daughter of the Raja of this country was sitting on the roof of the palace, combing her long black hair. The princess looked up at the kite and the bundle, and said, "There must be meat in that bundle." At that moment the kite let the bundle of camels fall, and it fell into the princess's eye, and went deep into it; but her eye was so large that it did not hurt her much. "Oh, mother! mother!" she cried, "something has fallen into my eye! come and take it out." Her mother rushed up, took the bundle of camels out of the princess's eye, and shoved the bundle into her pocket.

The wrestlers and the old woman's son now came up, having seen all

* *Kite*, a small hawk.

that had happened. "Where is the bundle of camels?" said they, "and why do you cry?" they asked the princess. "Oh," said her mother, "she is crying because something fell into her eye." "It was the bundle of camels that fell into her eye, and the bundle is in your pocket," said the old woman's son to the Rani: and he put his hand into her pocket and pulled out the bundle. Then he and the wrestlers went back to Ajít's father's house, and on the way they met his old mother, who went with them.

They invited a great many people to dinner, and Ajít took a large quantity of flour and made it into flat cakes. Then she handed a cake to the wrestler who had come to see her father, and gave one to everybody else. "I can't eat such a big cake as this," said the wrestler. "Can't you?" said Ajít. "I can't indeed," he answered; "it is much too big." "Then I will eat it myself," said Ajít, and taking it and all the other cakes she popped them into her mouth together. "That is not half enough for me," she said. Then she offered him a can of water. "I cannot drink all that water," he said. "Can't you?" said Ajít; "I can drink much more than that." So she filled a large tub with water, lifted it to her mouth, and drank it all up at a draught.

The wrestler was very much astonished, and said to her, "Will you come to my house? I will give you a dinner." "You will never be able to give me enough to eat and drink," said Ajít. "Yes, I shall," he said. "You will not be able to give me enough, I am sure," said Ajít; "I cannot come." "Do come," he said. "Very well," she answered, "I will come; but I know you will never be able to give me enough food."

So they set off to his house. But when they had gone a little way, she said, "I must have my house with me." "I cannot carry your house," said the wrestler. "You must," said Ajít. "If you don't, I cannot go with you." "But I cannot carry your house," said the wrestler. "Well, then," said Ajít, "I will carry it myself." So she went back, dug up her house, and hoisted it on her head. This frightened the wrestler. "What a strong woman she must be!" he thought. "I will not wrestle with her father; for if I do, he will kill me."

Then they all went on till they came to his house. When they got to it, Ajít set her house down on the ground, and the wrestler went to get the dinner he had promised her. He brought quantities of things—all sorts of things—everything he could think of. Three kinds of flour, milk, dhall,* rice, curries, and meat. Then he showed them all to Ajít. "That is not enough for my dinner," she said. "Why, that would be hardly enough for my mice!"

The wrestler wondered very much at this, and asked, "Are your mice

* *Dhall*, pigeon peas.

so very big?" "Yes, they are very big," she answered; "come and see." So he took up all the food he had brought, and laid it on the floor of Ajít's house. Then at once all the mice came and ate it up every bit. The wrestler was greatly surprised; and Ajít said, "Did I not tell you true? and did I not tell you, you would never be able to get me enough to eat?" "Come to the Nabha Rájá's country," said the wrestler. "There you will surely get enough to eat."

To this she agreed; so she, her father, and the wrestler went off to the Nabha Rájá's country. " I have brought a very strong girl," said the wrestler to the Nabha Rájá. "I will try her strength," said the Rájá. "Give me three elephants," said Ajít, "and I will carry them for you." Then the Rájá sent for three elephants, and said to her, "Now, carry these." "Give me a rope," said Ajít . So they gave her a rope, and she tied the three elephants together, and flung them over her shoulder. "Now, where shall I throw them?" she said to the astonished Rájá. "Shall I throw them on to the roof of your palace? or on to the ground? Or away out there?" "I don't know," said the Rájá. "Throw them upon my roof." She threw the elephants up on to the roof with such force that it broke, and the elephants fell through into the palace.

"What have you done?" cried the Rájá. "It is not my fault," answered Ajít. "You told me to throw the elephants on to your roof, and so I did." Then the Rájá sent for a great many men and bullocks and horses to pull the elephants out of his palace. But they could not the first time they pulled; then they tried a second time and succeeded, and they threw the elephants away.

Then Ajít went home. "What shall I do with this dreadful woman?" said the Nabha Rájá. "She is sure to kill me, and take all my country. I will try to kill her." So he got his sepoys* and guns into order, and went out to kill Ajít. She was looking out of her window, and saw them coming. "Oh," she said, "here is the Nabha Rájá coming to kill me." Then she went out of her house and asked him why he had come. "To kill you," said the Rájá. "Is that what you want to do?" she said; and with one hand she took up the Rájá, his guns, and his sepoys, and put them all under her arm: and she carried them all off to the Nabha Rájá's country. There she put the Rájá into prison, and made herself Rání of his kingdom. She was very much pleased at being Rání of the Nabha country; for it was a rich country, and there were quantities of fruits and of corn in it. And she lived happily for a long, long time.

* *Sepoy*, a native of India employed as a soldier in the service of a European power, especially one serving in the British Army.

Ajít is one strong woman. She sweeps out elephants with the rest of the dust, hoists her house onto her head, tucks the Rájá and his army under her arm, and makes herself Rání. Stories about physically powerful women like Ajít are not anomalies, they are found in many cultures. They contrast sharply with the dominant popular image of passive, helpless women in folktales.

The Importance of Lighting

Tamil Nadu, India[67]

Once there was a big businessman. He had a son and a daughter. Both were happily married. The brother and the sister had great regard for each other. They decided that in case a daughter was born to one and a son to another, they would marry them to each other so that their family bonds continued. The son had three sons and the daughter had three daughters. The businessman became old and one day he passed away. As he was in debt, the creditors took away a large portion of his money, with the result that his son became poor.

The businessman's daughter was married to a rich man. He prospered in his business. He gave two of his daughters in marriage to two businessmen who were rolling in wealth and both the husband and wife were busy in settling the marriage of their third daughter. At that time, the third daughter reminded her parents of the promise they had made to her uncle. She also told that all her cousins were refusing to marry till she also got married and that she would marry one of her cousins only.

When her mother heard this she was stunned. She said, "Both of your sisters have married in rich families. If you marry a poor man, who will give you only *Kuya*,* how will they respect you?" She further said, "If you insist on marrying your cousin, I will push you in their house and will never think of you."

The girl did not give in. She had decided to marry one of her cousins only.

The girl's mother had no other way out. She sent word to her brother that she will give her youngest daughter in marriage to one of his sons. When her brother heard this, his happiness knew no bounds. He made all arrangements and the marriage was celebrated. His other two sons were married in poor families. The youngest daughter's parents never came to see her or enquired about her welfare.

She was very happy in the poor man's family and never acted as if she was from a rich family. All the three brothers earned their living by stitching banyan leaves and selling them in the market. In this way they were passing their days in extreme poverty.

---

* *Kuya*, Ragee, barley porridge, powdered and cooked in water. A little salt is added to give taste. It is eaten along with red chillies.

The king of that place was one day having his oil bath. He had taken off his ring and had kept it on the floor. Suddenly an eagle came and took away the ring and dropped it in the house of the businessman's son. At that time only the youngest daughter-in-law was in the house. She picked up the ring and tied it to the edge of her sari and did not tell anyone about it.

The King saw the eagle taking away his ring. He made an announcement by beat of drum that whosoever brings the ring and gives it back to him will be rewarded with whatever he asks for. The youngest daughter came to know of this announcement. She went and told her husband about it and said, "Let us go and give it to the King. One thing I may tell you that I will never ask for riches. Whatever I ask from the king, you must be satisfied with that and will never get angry with me." Her husband agreed, and both of them went to the palace and gave the ring to the King.

The King was happy to find his ring and he asked them what they wanted. The lady said, "Your majesty! I do not want riches. My only wish is that on one Friday, nobody should light lamps in their houses. Even in the palace there should be no lamp. Only I will light lamps in my house." The King agreed to this. An announcement was made throughout the town that no one should light his house on the following Friday, and if he did so his eyes will be plucked out.

The youngest daughter, as soon as she got permission from the king to light her house on the following Friday, told her brothers-in-law to bring at least two *varakan** on loan and that the whole house had to be lighted the next Friday. She also asked one brother-in-law to stand near the front door and the second one to stand near the back door. She told them that if anyone wanted to enter the house they should let him do it only on the condition that he would not come out and in case anyone wanted to go out of the house they should let him go out only on the condition that he would not come in again.

All the three brothers went out to bring some money. Both the younger brothers kept their eldest brother in mortgage and borrowed two varakan. They bought oil, earthen lamps and cotton, to illuminate the whole house.

The long awaited Friday came. The youngest daughter along with her two sisters-in-law observed a fast that day and during the night she lit the whole house.

The whole town was in complete darkness because of the king's order. Goddess *Lakshmi*° went from house to house but could not find even a

---

* *Varakan*, One varakan is equal to nearly three and a half rupees.
° *Lakshmi*, goddess of wealth.

ray of light anywhere. In the end she came to the youngest daughter's house. There she saw the brother-in-law standing in front of the house. She took his permission to go in. The brother-in-law enquired who she was, and let her go in only after ascertaining from her that she will not come out.

As Goddess *Lakshmi* could not find light anywhere in the town, she accepted his condition and entered the house. No sooner had she entered the house than Poverty, Goddess *Lakshmi's* sister, could no longer continue to live in the same house and had to leave the place. She quickly came out and asked the brother-in-law's permission to leave the house. The brother-in-law then was reminded of his sister-in-law's words. He enquired who she was and that she should promise that if she left the house she would not enter it again, only then he would allow her to leave. She promised that she would not come back again and left the house through the back door.

The next morning when all the three brothers and their wives got up they found all the vessels, trunks, almirahs full of gold coins. Poverty had disappeared altogether and they became rich. The youngest daughter's parents and her sisters started visiting her house thereafter.

Do you know that from that day onwards people light their houses on Friday and perform *pooja** to invite Goddess Lakshmi.

To rescue her family from poverty, the youngest daughter goes straight to the heart of the matter—replacing the Goddess of Poverty with the Goddess of Wealth. Most people would simply ask for money or land but she knows that since the Goddess of Poverty is living in the house, riches would soon disappear and a job or land would soon be lost.

This heroine needs more than lucid understanding to save her family. To carry out her plan, she must enlist the cooperation of her husband, who may not understand her unconventional idea. She knows that her position in society results in an underestimation of her capabilities. She anticipates his objections and clearly states, "Whatever I ask from the king, you must be satisfied with and will never get angry with me." This young woman reminds me of Mouse Woman, a heroine of the Northwest Coast American Indians (see stories on pp. 116 and 126). Mouse Woman has such wisdom and power that humans and supernatural beings alike respect her. Yet even Mouse Woman finds it necessary to frighten humans before going into a dangerous situation. She has to forcefully remind them to let her handle things because her size makes people underestimate her abilities. Both of these heroines foresee and honestly face this lack of trust.

---

* *Pooja*, religious rites.

The Child of Death

Vietnam[68]

Just a month before she was to have become a mother, a young peasant woman was carried away by a sudden illness to the Land of the
Dead.

A few moments before her death, the young wife had looked steadily
at her husband, with a directness that was contrary to her customary
reserve. And, even though there were friends in the room with them, he
could not help leaning close to see what she wanted.

He heard her murmur: "The baby . . . our child . . . " And then she
was silenced by death.

The bereaved husband uttered a cry of deep anguish, became terribly
distressed, and cried out, sobbing.

Such an unusual display of violent grief astonished his friends. In this
land of Vietnam, you see, people are accustomed to misfortunes, especially when they are not rich, and they usually accept whatever comes
their way with stoic resignation. And everyone must work hard; there is
little time left over for complaining and bemoaning one's fate. Even this
poor peasant soon had to dry his tears. And the day after his wife's burial he was again in his fields, behind his water buffalo and his plow.

A few days later an old woman of the neighborhood who was almost
blind and who sold betel* and other small provisions at a straw hut near
a culvert in an open field was approached by a young woman who some
how seemed vaguely familiar. The woman came to the hut and bought a
few coins' worth of honey. After the customer had gone, the old woman's granddaughter trembled and said the woman had looked exactly like
the young peasant wife who had recently died.

The very next day the same young woman came again, asking for more
honey. To a question from the proprietress, she answered: "It's for my
baby, for I have no milk."

At a signal from her grandmother, the little girl followed the young
woman with her eyes and saw her disappear in the direction of her tomb.

The shopkeeper advised the husband of this strange event. Next day,
going to get some water, he stopped at the straw hut and waited. Toward

---

* *Betel*, a climbing pepper whose leaves are wrapped around or mixed with a whole betel nut and chewed
  as a stimulant.

evening, observing his wife approach, he thrust himself in front of her and spoke to her. She appeared not to hear him, and, lowering her head, she ran away. He hastened in pursuit, but she suddenly disappeared completely.

Dissolved in tears, the husband ran like a crazy man to the tomb and threw himself against it with cries of despair. He remained there, motionless and prostrate, while his tears continued to flow.

Then suddenly he thought he heard a child's cries coming from the tomb. He cupped his ear to the stone and heard the cries distinctly.

He ran to his home, returned with a spade, and began to dig down to the coffin. When he opened it, he saw an infant boy lying on the stomach of his dead mother and moving feebly. On the corners of his mouth, the infant bore traces of honey. The woman's body was cold but unblemished, and it seemed to her husband that her serene, still face was almost smiling, rather than painfully contracted as it had been at the time of her death.

The young father carried the child back to his house. Then the neighbors helped him to reclose the coffin and the tomb.

In the village the father sought some woman willing to nurse his son. But everyone was afraid and stole away from him when he approached. For a time he had to feed the baby on rice gruel, but gradually the compassionate hearts of his neighbors overcame some of their fears, and after several days one of the neighborhood women volunteered to serve as a wet nurse.

The child grew up normally from that time, and his subsequent life revealed nothing out of the ordinary at all.

As for the mother, no one ever saw her again. Her husband revisited the tomb a number of times, but always found nothing. And even though he also went periodically to the whole area she had traversed, including the straw hut of the merchant, his wife never appeared before him again.

Many times he went to the pagoda to pray for his wife's return, sometimes even spending the whole night there in prayer. But all was in vain: he never saw her again, not even in his dreams.

It might be assumed that the poor wife's strength and determination had sustained her even beyond the grave, but only to the point where she could fulfill her destiny by giving birth to her son and feeding him for the first few days. Such efforts of themselves must have so exhausted her that the remnants of life that customarily permit dead spirits to visit the sleep of the living for some time were, in her case, no longer present.

 "In this land of Vietnam . . . people are accustomed to misfortunes, especially when they are not rich, and they usually accept whatever comes their way with

stoic resignation." This exceptional young mother does not accept the death of her child with stoic resignation. She refuses to let her own death cause the death of her baby. With great strength and determination she fulfills her destiny—she gives birth. Then the young mother rallies the remnants of life that permit dead spirits to visit the living. She buys honey and keeps the baby alive until help arrives. She successfully overcomes the boundary of death to give life to her child.

The Story of Princess Amaradevi

Cambodia[69]

In a small kingdom of Kampuchea, there once lived a wealthy princess by the name of Amaradevi who was an educated and talented young woman. Now, there were four old grand ministers of the palace who unfortunately had no appreciation of Amaradevi's many accomplishments, but, being attracted by her riches, they all wished to marry her. Princess Amaradevi kindly rejected their proposals, choosing instead to marry a fine young man whose name was Mahoseth Pandide.

Amaradevi and Mahoseth loved and respected each other. They lived happily together in peace and harmony. But the four grand ministers were very bitter and resentful. Whenever they spoke to Mahoseth, they tried to be as insulting and offensive as possible. They even started vicious rumors throughout the palace, claiming that Mahoseth Pandide was disloyal to the king. Then they began to whisper to the king himself that Mahoseth was dishonest and deceitful. The gentle king, who loved his daughter and her husband, urged the ministers to be more reasonable and cautious in their accusations. But the more the king urged, the more determined the ministers became to destroy Mahoseth.

One day, they decided to tell the king that Mahoseth Pandide was plotting to kill him and take the throne. This time, their arguments and false proofs were so convincing that the king believed them. Without even giving Mahoseth Pandide a chance to defend himself, the angry king ordered him to leave the country immediately and never return.

The four ruthless ministers were satisfied with the result of their schemes. Delighted with their success, they congratulated each other and began plotting their next steps. "Of course," First Grand Minister Senak advised, "we do not know which one of us Amaradevi will wish to marry. We must each ask her, one at a time. Then after she chooses and marries one of us, we will divide her riches equally. But now, she must be mourning for her foolish husband. So let us wait two weeks from today before we talk with her."

Meanwhile, with her husband banished from the kingdom forever, Amaradevi passed the days in sorrow. She blamed herself for not being able to save her husband. She had known that the powerful grand ministers had wanted to marry her for her money. She had known that the ministers had plotted against her beloved husband. So each day as she paced

195

back and forth in her palace rooms, she relived her own stupidity and tried to think of a way to prove to the king that Mahoseth had always been loyal and that the four ministers had been the real evil plotters.

"Oh, you greedy, wretched monsters!" she would cry to herself. "I will find a way to punish you. I will never be your rich puppet-wife. I will find a way to have my Mahoseth returned to me. I will find a way to teach you to respect and honor a woman's mind and heart."

Two weeks after Mahoseth Pandide's banishment, First Grand Minister Senak came to visit Amaradevi with his proposals of love and marriage. Amaradevi listened to him quietly and slowly replied, "Yes, my dear Senak, I am quite lonesome. Perhaps I could love you and marry you. If you wish to visit with me, why not return later this evening, at seven o'clock?"

First Grand Minister Senak was delighted. He bowed excessively and promised to return at the appointed time.

During the same morning, Amaradevi was surprised by the visits of the other three ministers. It seemed that almost as soon as one left, another appeared. They all praised her beauty, professed their love, and begged her to marry them. Amaradevi was polite to all of them. As they left, she graciously invited each one to visit with her that same evening. The second grand minister, Pakkos, she told to come at eight o'clock. The third grand minister, Kapindu, she told to come at nine o'clock. And the fourth grand minister, Devin, she told to come at ten. But all that morning, as Amaradevi had been listening quietly to the four unscrupulous ministers, she had been trying to think of a way to entrap them and prove their treachery to the king. Now, Amaradevi had been educated not only in music, painting, and the fine art of poetry but also in government, law, the sciences, and engineering construction. Being so talented, she was quite capable of planning a clever strategy that would ensnare the false-hearted ministers and at the same time legally prove their villainy to the king.

Soon after the last grand minister left, Amaradevi summoned her servants to her palace rooms. First she instructed them on how to dig a huge pit under the floor of her small back parlor, and how to prevent it from caving in. Next, she told them how to make a special mixture of mud, hot water, and sticky rice in a large caldron. The servants then poured this mixture into the pit, filling it halfway. Finally, Amaradevi skillfully taught the servants how to construct a trap door to cover the large hole. The trap door was operated by a rope secretly hidden behind a curtained recess.

When the construction work was finished, Amaradevi dismissed the servants and sent for her personal maid. She ordered her maid to bring all of her precious jewels and pile them carelessly on a table near the trap door in the small back parlor. When that was done, Amaradevi told the maid to expect the visits of the four grand ministers. The maid was to welcome them respectfully and ask them politely to wait for the princess in the small back parlor. The maid bowed obediently, and Amaradevi continued, "When each man arrives and is in the small back parlor, please come to me."

That evening, promptly at seven o'clock, First Grand Minister Senak arrived. The maid graciously greeted him and led him to the small back parlor. Then she walked softly to her mistress's rooms. Amaradevi rose quickly, saying to the maid, "Follow me quietly and do as I tell you."

The maid followed after Amaradevi to the small back parlor. They slipped silently behind the curtained recess, waited, and watched. First Grand Minister Senak was bending over the table of glistening jewels. He put his hand out to touch one. Then he quickly pulled his hand back to his side and stepped back. He paced the room a bit and slowly returned to the table, putting his hand out once more, then down again. The jewels were like magnets, pulling his hands to them. He just must touch one. He looked around the room and through the doorway. Then, quickly reaching out, he grabbed a huge ruby and stuffed it deep into his pocket. At that moment, Amaradevi signaled her maid. Both women pulled hard on the rope. The trap door opened, throwing First Grand Minister Senak screaming into the large pit of warm mud and sticky rice. Then the heavy trap door closed neatly and tightly, muffling the wretched man's shouts.

The three other grand ministers arrived at their appointed times. Each in turn was politely greeted by the maid. Each in turn was asked to wait for the princess in the small back parlor. And each in turn became bewitched by the table of shimmering rubies, emeralds, and diamonds. None of them could resist the temptation of stuffing at least one of the jewels into his pocket. As each grand minister stuffed his pocket, the two women pulled the trap-door rope, throwing another wretched man into the deep pit filled with warm mud and sticky rice. As each grand minister fell into the pit, the mud and sticky rice rose higher and higher until the men could barely breathe. As they thrashed about trying to escape, they almost choked on the drying mud and swelling rice.

Amaradevi kept the trap door tightly closed all night. The next morning, she told her servants to take the mud-caked ministers out of the pit, bind their hands, and lead them to the royal court. In solemn dignity, she followed behind them. When they reached the throne room, the princess bowed before her father. With great restraint, she spoke. "Your Majesty, I ask your permission to prove to the royal court the perfidy of these four grand ministers of the palace."

The king nodded, and Amaradevi continued. "The grand ministers all asked for my hand in marriage because they were greedy for my riches. When I refused their proposals and married the good Mahoseth Pandide, they plotted against him, finally convincing the royal court that he was disloyal and dishonest. Now the ministers have come to me again with proposals of love and marriage. But the only thing that they really love is our royal jewels. I trapped them as they were stealing our sacred treasures from my apartments. I will prove this to you. Now you will know who the guilty traitors really are."

Amaradevi signaled her maid. The woman reached into each grand minister's pocket, pulled out a precious royal jewel, and held it up before everyone's eyes.

The king was both saddened and furious. He ordered the palace guards to tie the mud-caked ministers to elephants and drag them through the streets for all the people to see.

Amaradevi bowed to the king and returned to her palace rooms.

Amaradevi's wealth does not protect her or earn the respect of others. Instead it attracts four ruthless, greedy ministers. Luckily, "Amaradevi had been educated not only in music, painting, and the fine art of poetry but also in government, law, the sciences, and engineering construction." She is resourceful in addition to being well-educated. Amaradevi devises a plan. She designs a trap and trap door and oversees its construction. Amaradevi teaches the wicked ministers to respect a woman's mind and heart, and she wins back her husband.

A good education can be vital to protect one's interests. For example, there is an association between high death rates in pregnancy and childbirth and low levels of education for women. Despite the value of education, in 1986 less than one half of the eligible girls in 76 countries were enrolled in secondary education.[70] These girls are now semi-literate women facing a complex world, without Amaradevi's education.

The Tale of the Oki Islands

Japan[71]

Many hundreds of years ago—about the year 1320 to be exact—the Emperor Hojo Takatoki ruled Japan with absolute power. A samurai, a noble soldier by the name of Oribe Shima, accidentally displeased the ruler and was banished from the land. Oribe was sent to a wild rocky group of islands off the coast of Japan called the Oki Islands. There he led a lonely, miserable life, for he had left behind his beautiful young daughter, Tokoyo, and he missed her terribly. She, too, felt unbearably sad, and at last, unable to stand the separation any longer, decided to try to reach her father or die in the attempt. She was a brave girl and knew no fear. As a child she had loved to dive with the women whose job it was to collect oyster shells deep down under the sea. She risked her life as they did, though she was of higher birth and frailer body.

After selling all her property, Tokoyo set out for the coast and at last reached a place called Akasaki, from where on clear days the islands of Oki could be seen. She tried to persuade the fishermen of the town to take her to the islands, but no one would, for it was a long and difficult journey. Besides, no one was allowed to visit those who had been banished there.

Although discouraged, Tokoyo refused to give up. With the little money she had left, she bought some food. Then, in the dark of night, she went down to the sea, and finding a light boat, she set sail all alone for the islands. Fortune sent her a strong breeze, and the current also helped her. The following evening, chilled and half dead, she arrived at the rocky shore of one of the islands. Scrambling out of the boat, she made her way up the beach to a sheltered spot and lay down to sleep for the night. She awoke in the morning quite refreshed, and after eating the rest of her food, she decided immediately to search for her father.

On the road she met a fisherman.

"Do you know my father?" she asked. Then she told him her story.

"No," said the fisherman, "I have never heard of him." Then he cautioned her earnestly. "Take my advice and do not ask for him. Your questions may get you into trouble, and may send your father to his death."

After that, Tokoyo wandered from place to place, hoping to hear word of her father, but fearful of asking anyone about him. She managed to stay alive by begging food from kindly people she met here and there along the way.

One evening she came to a shrine which stood on a rocky ledge. After praying to Buddha to help her find her father, she lay down in a small grove near by and went to sleep. In a little while she was awakened by the sound of a girl's sobs, and a curious clapping of hands. She looked up into the bright moonlight and was startled to see a beautiful young girl of about fifteen crying bitterly. Beside her stood a priest, who clapped his hands and murmured over and over:

"*Namu Amida Butsu's.*"

Both were dressed in white gowns. After the prayer was over, the priest led the girl to the edge of the rocks and was about to push her into the sea when Tokoyo ran out and caught hold of her just in time to save her from falling over the cliff.

The old priest was completely astonished, but in no way cross.

"I judge from this action," he said, "that you are a stranger to this island. Otherwise you would know that this ceremony is not to my liking. Unfortunately, on this island we are cursed by an evil god called Yofune-Nushi. He lives at the bottom of the sea, and each year demands that we sacrifice one girl under fifteen years of age to his kingdom. We make this offering on June thirteenth, the Day of the Dog, between eight and nine o'clock at night. If we do not appease him, the evil god becomes angry and causes great storms at sea and many of our fishermen drown."

Tokoyo listened gravely, then spoke.

"Holy monk, let this young girl go and I will take her place. I am the sad daughter of Oribe Shima, a noble samurai who has been banished to these islands. It is in search of my father that I have come here; but he is so closely guarded, I cannot get to him, or even find out where he is. My heart is broken and I no longer wish to live. Let me sacrifice myself. All I ask is that you deliver this letter to my father if you can find him."

After she had finished speaking, Tokoyo removed the white robe from the girl and placed it on herself. She then knelt at the shrine and prayed for courage to kill the evil god, Yofune-Nushi. Upon rising, she withdrew from her clothes a beautiful dagger that belonged to her family, and placing it between her teeth, she dived into the roaring sea and disappeared. The priest and the young girl stood at the ledge looking after Tokoyo, overcome with wonder at her courage.

Tokoyo, an excellent swimmer, headed straight downward through the clear water, which was illuminated by the moonlight. Down, down she swam, passing schools of silvery fish, until she reached the very bottom. There she found herself opposite an enormous cave which glittered with marvelous shells. Peering in, she thought she saw a man seated in the cave. She grasped her dagger, and bravely entered the cave, planning to battle and kill the evil god. When she got close, she was surprised to see that what she thought was a man was only a wooden statue of Hojo Takatoki, the emperor who had exiled her father. Angry and disappointed, she started to strike the statue, but then she changed her mind. "What good would it do? I'd rather do good than evil," she thought to herself. Deciding to rescue the statue, Tokoyo undid her sash and tied the statue to herself. Then she began swimming upward.

As she came out of the cave, an enormous glowing snakelike creature covered with horrible scales and waving tiny legs swam up in front of her. Its fiery eyes convinced Tokoyo that she was face to face with the evil sea god that terrorized the island. Determined to kill the dreadful monster, Tokoyo courageously swam close and with her dagger struck out his right eye. The evil god, surprised with pain, tried to re-enter his cave, but because he was so enormous and at that moment half-blind, he could not find his way. Swiftly taking advantage of the situation, Tokoyo struck him in the heart. With monstrous gasps and heavings the evil beast slowly died.

Tokoyo, happy to have rid the island of the dreadful god which demanded the life of a young girl each year, decided that she must raise the monster to the surface so that the island people would know once and for all he was dead. Struggling slowly and painfully, she at last managed to swim to the top, bringing along also the wooden statue of the emperor.

The priest and the girl, still lingering at the ledge, were astonished to see Tokoyo emerge suddenly from the water.

Rushing down to greet her, they cried out in amazement when they saw what she carried with her. Carefully they led the exhausted girl to a dry spot of beach where she lay down.

When assistance came, everything was brought to town—the body of the evil god, the wooden statue of the emperor, and Tokoyo herself. Word had already spread in the village, and the brave young girl was given a heroine's welcome. After that there were many ceremonies celebrating her extraordinary courage. The lord who ruled the island informed the Emperor Takatoki directly of what had passed.

The Emperor, who had long been suffering from an unknown disease, suddenly found himself well again. It was clear to him that he had been laboring under the curse of someone to whom he had behaved unjustly—someone who had carved his figure, cursed it, and sunk it in the sea. Now that the statue had been raised, the curse was over and he was well again. When he discovered that the person who had freed him from his spell was none other than the daughter of Oribe Shima, he immediately ordered the release of the noble samurai from the island prison.

Tokoyo and her father, once again happily reunited, went back to their native village, where they were hailed and feted. Oribe Shima's lands were returned to him and he was soon as prosperous as ever.

On the islands of Oki a shrine was built to commemorate the wonderful event, and all across Japan the name of Tokoyo became forever famous.

Tokoyo risks her life diving for pearls, undertakes a quest to find her father, and plunges into the sea to battle a monster. When she finds a statue of the emperor who has condemned her father, she starts to strike it but changes her mind, "I'd rather do good than evil." Had she vented her anger on the statue, she might not have had the strength to kill the monster. Tokoyo's choice to act constructively enabled her to combat the real enemy at hand.

Although Tokoyo says that she no longer wants to live and that she's willing to sacrifice herself, we never doubt that she will live and succeed. When she clenches the dagger between her teeth and dives into the roiling sea, there is adventure and danger but never doubt. My daughters pleaded eloquently for heroines who didn't die. Frightening monsters, robbers, riddles, insurmountable obstacles to overcome, all of these were fine, in fact the more the better. All was well as long as my daughters were sure of a successful heroine and a happy ending.

The Monkey Bridegroom

Japan [72]

In a certain place there lived an old man. One day he went out to dig up *gobo* roots,* but he couldn't dig out a single one. Just as he was wondering what to do, a monkey came along and called out, "Grandfather, grandfather, shall I help you pull up *gobo* roots?"

"Yes, please help me. If you will dig up some roots for me; I'll give you one of my daughters as your wife."

"Will you really do that!" the monkey cried. "Then I shall come to claim her in three days."

The old man, thinking that the monkey surely would never come to claim one of his daughters, agreed to all he said.

While they were talking, the monkey began pulling up *gobo* roots and soon had a large pile of them. "The monkey certainly has pulled up a lot of roots; perhaps he really intends to come for one of my daughters," the old man thought to himself, beginning to get a little worried.

Finally the monkey had pulled up every *gobo* root in the field. "Well," he said to the old man, "I shall surely come for your daughter." Then he scampered off.

The old man thought to himself: "He must really intend to come. Why did I ever tell him that I'd give him one of my daughters? What shall I do? What shall I do? I don't think that any of my girls will agree to become his wife. I must try to persuade one of them." The old man walked sadly home, talking to himself.

When he got home, he called his eldest daughter and, after telling her what had happened, said, "When the monkey comes in three days, will you go to be his bride?"

"What!" she cried. "Who would ever want to become a monkey's wife!" and she refused even to consider it.

The old man then called his second daughter and asked her the same thing.

"Why," she cried, "what a fool you are! Who would ever make a promise like that? I may be older than our youngest sister, but I'm not going to become that monkey's bride. I don't think anyone would do it," and so she refused completely.

* *Gobo roots,* burdock, a staple vegetable in rural Japan.

"Since the other two have refused," the old man thought to himself, "I don't think that the youngest will agree either. However, I'll have to ask her; there's nothing else to do." He went to his youngest daughter and told her what he had promised and that the monkey would be coming in three days to get his bride. "Your sisters have both refused. Will you please go and be his bride." His face paling, the old man made his request.

The girl thought for a while, then replied, "Yes, father, since you have promised, I will go."

Upon hearing this, the old man was overjoyed, crying, "Really! Will you really go?"

"I will go because of my duty to you," said the girl, "but you must give me three things to take with me."

"What things do you want?" he asked. "I will give you anything you request."

"Please give me a very heavy mortar, together with a heavy maul for pounding rice and one *to** of rice."

"What!" he cried, "is that all you want! If so, you shall have them," and he soon brought them to her.

On the third day the monkey came as he had promised. The youngest daughter said to him: "I am to become your bride, but when we go back to the mountains, we will want to eat rice *mochi*, so let's take this mortar, maul, and bag of rice with us. You can carry it all on your back."

The monkey loaded everything on his back. It was very, very heavy, but since his bride had requested it, he did not want to refuse, and they set off up the mountain, the monkey carrying his heavy load.

It was just the beginning of April, and on both sides of the road the cherry trees were in full bloom. They traveled along until they came to a place where the road went close to the edge of a deep canyon. At the bottom of the canyon there was a river. At this point the branches of the cherry trees fell over into the canyon, making such a beautiful scene that the girl stopped, saying to the monkey, "Oh, such a lovely cherry tree. Won't you please climb up and get me a branch of those cherry blossoms."

Since this too was a request of his bride, the monkey agreed and began to climb up into one of the trees. "Please get some flowers from the topmost branch," the girl cried from below, so the monkey continued to climb higher and higher. "Isn't this about right?" he asked, but the girl urged him higher and higher until he had climbed up to where the branches were very small and weak.

* *To*, about 50 pounds.

The load on his back was very heavy, and the branch he was on was very small; suddenly it broke, and the monkey fell headlong into the canyon below, landing with a splash, *dossun*, in the river. As he sank from sight with the heavy mortar on his back, he sang this song:

> I do not regret my death,
> But oh, how sad for my poor bride.

And he soon disappeared from view.
The girl was very happy and returned to her home.
Naa, mosu mosu, komen dango. "Well, hallo, hallo, rice cakes."

Loss of face is particularly important in Japan. The youngest daughter who saves her father's honor by agreeing to marry the monkey is comparable to Beauty of "Beauty and the Beast," who saves her father's life by agreeing to marry a beast. The concept of "giri" strictly governs every give-and-take in Japanese society; gifts and reciprocal gifts are kept track of meticulously. Both the monkey and the father know that the monkey's offer of help has strings attached. When the monkey accepts the daughter, he breaks two rules. He accepts more than he can ever repay and he has presumed to transgress the strong hierarchical divisions of Japanese society. The monkey's willingness to pick the cherry blossoms further reveals his improper behavior because as the old proverb says, "Only a fool plucks the cherry blossom."[73] The youngest daughter saves herself from this improper marriage by setting up a situation in which the monkey suffers the consequences of his pretensions. Pride goeth before a fall.

In many folktales the father gives away his daughter to a monster. This "Beauty and the Beast" type of tale can represent arranged marriages where young girls were given to older, physically unattractive, but rich men. Beauty is given to the Beast, the youngest daughter in "East of the Sun and West of the Moon" is given to a bear. The women submit to the authority of their fathers and are convinced to sacrifice themselves for the good of the father and/or the family. Although we have been influenced to sympathize with and think romantically of the Beast it is important to remember that these women are being asked to give their spiritual love and physical love, to a beast, a bear, a monkey, with absolutely no guarantee that it will turn into a wonderful man in the end.[74]

The Mirror of Matsuyama:
A Story of Old Japan

Japan [75]

Long years ago in old Japan there lived in the Province of Echigo, a very remote part of Japan even in these days, a man and his wife. When this story begins they had been married for some years and were blessed with one little daughter. She was the joy and pride of both their lives, and in her they stored an endless source of happiness for their old age.

What golden letter days in their memory were those that had marked her growing up from babyhood; the visit to the temple when she was just thirty days old, her proud mother carrying her, robed in ceremonial *kimono*, to be put under the patronage of the family's household god; then her first dolls' festival, when her parents gave her a set of dolls and their miniature belongings, to be added to as year succeeded year; and perhaps the most important occasion of all, on her third birthday, when her first *obi** of scarlet and gold was tied round her small waist, a sign that she had crossed the threshold of girlhood and left infancy behind. Now that she was seven years of age, and had learned to talk and to wait upon her parents in those several little ways so dear to the hearts of fond parents, their cup of happiness seemed full. There could not be found in the whole of the Island Empire a happier little family.

One day there was much excitement in the home, for the father had been suddenly summoned to the capital on business. In these days of railways and *jinrickshas*° and other rapid modes of travelling, it is difficult to realise what such a journey as that from Matsuyama to Kyoto meant. The roads were rough and bad, and ordinary people had to walk every step of the way, whether the distance were one hundred or several hundred miles. Indeed, in those days it was as great an undertaking to go up to the capital as it is for a Japanese to make a voyage to Europe now.

So the wife was very anxious while she helped her husband get ready for the long journey, knowing what an arduous task lay before him. Vainly she wished that she could accompany him, but the distance was too great for the mother and child to go, and besides that, it was the wife's duty to take care of the home.

*Obi, broad brocade sash.
° *Jinricksha*, a small light, two-wheeled passenger vehicle drawn by one man.

All was ready at last, and the husband stood in the porch with his little family round him.

"Do not be anxious, I will come back soon," said the man. "While I am away take care of everything, and especially of our little daughter."

"Yes, we shall be all right—but you—you must take care of yourself and delay not a day in coming back to us," said the wife, while the tears fell like rain from her eyes.

The little girl was the only one to smile, for she was ignorant of the sorrow of parting, and did not know that going to the capital was at all different from walking to the next village, which her father did very often. She ran to his side, and caught hold of his long sleeve to keep him a moment.

"Father, I will be very good while I am waiting for you to come back, so please bring me a present."

As the father turned to take a last look at his weeping wife and smiling, eager child, he felt as if someone were pulling him back by the hair, so hard was it for him to leave them behind, for they had never been separated before. But he knew that he must go, for the call was imperative. With a great effort he ceased to think, and resolutely turning away he went quickly down the little garden and out through the gate. His wife, catching up the child in her arms, ran as far as the gate, and watched him as he went down the road between the pines till he was lost in the haze of the distance and all she could see was his quaint peaked hat, and at last that vanished too.

"Now father has gone, you and I must take care of everything till he comes back," said the mother, as she made her way back to the house.

"Yes, I will be very good," said the child, nodding her head, "and when father comes home please tell him how good I have been, and then perhaps he will give me a present."

"Father is sure to bring you something that you want very much. I know, for I asked him to bring you a doll. You must think of father every day, and pray for a safe journey till he comes back."

"O, yes, when he comes home again how happy I shall be," said the child, clapping her hands, and her face growing bright with joy at the glad thought. It seemed to the mother as she looked at the child's face that her love for her grew deeper and deeper.

Then she set to work to make the winter clothes for the three of them. She set up her simple wooden spinning-wheel and spun the thread before she began to weave the stuffs. In the intervals of her work she directed the little girl's games and taught her to read the old stories of her country. Thus did the wife find consolation in work during the lonely days of her husband's absence. While the time was thus slipping quickly by in the quiet home, the husband finished his business and returned.

It would have been difficult for anyone who did not know the man well to recognise him. He had travelled day after day, exposed to all weathers, for about a month altogether, and was sunburnt to bronze, but his fond wife and child knew him at a glance, and flew to meet him from either side, each catching hold of one of his sleeves in their eager greeting. Both the man and his wife rejoiced to find each other well. It seemed a very long time to all till—the mother and child helping—his straw sandals were untied, his large umbrella hat taken off, and he was again in their midst in the old familiar sitting-room that had been so empty while he was away.

As soon as they had sat down on the white mats, the father opened a bamboo basket that he had brought in with him, and took out a beautiful doll and a lacquer box full of cakes.

"Here," he said to the little girl, "is a present for you. It is a prize for taking care of mother and the house so well while I was away."

"Thank you," said the child, as she bowed her head to the ground, and then put out her hand just like a little maple leaf with its eager widespread fingers to take the doll and the box, both of which, coming from the capital, were prettier than anything she had ever seen. No words can tell how delighted the little girl was—her face seemed as if it would melt with joy and she had no eyes and no thought for anything else.

Again the husband dived into the basket, and brought out this time a square wooden box, carefully tied up with red and white string, and handing it to his wife, said:

"And this is for you."

The wife took the box, and opening it carefully took out a metal disc with a handle attached. One side was bright and shining like a crystal, and the other was covered with raised figures of pine-trees and storks, which had been carved out of its smooth surface in lifelike reality. Never had she seen such a thing in her life, for she had been born and bred in the rural province of Echigo. She gazed into the shining disc, and looking up with surprise and wonder pictured on her face, she said:

"I see somebody looking at me in this round thing! What is it that you have given me?"

The husband laughed and said:

"Why, it is your own face that you see. What I have brought you is called a mirror, and whoever looks into its clear surface can see their own form reflected there. Although there are none to be found in this out of the way place, yet they have been in use in the capital from the most ancient times. There the mirror is considered a very necessary requisite for a woman to possess. There is an old proverb that 'As the sword is the soul of a samurai, so is the mirror the soul of a woman,' and according to popular tradition, a woman's mirror is an index to her own heart—if she keeps it bright and clear, so is her heart pure and good. It is also one of the treasures that form the insignia of the Emperor. So you must lay great store by your mirror, and use it carefully."

The wife listened to all her husband told her, and was pleased at learning so much that was new to her. She was still more pleased at the precious gift—his token of remembrance while he had been away.

"If the mirror represents my soul, I shall certainly treasure it as a valuable possession, and never will I use it carelessly." Saying so, she lifted it as high as her forehead, in grateful acknowledgment of the gift, and then shut it up in its box and put it away.

The wife saw that her husband was very tired, and set about serving the evening meal and making everything as comfortable as she could for him. It seemed to the little family as if they had not known what true happiness was before, so glad were they to be together again, and this evening the father had much to tell of his journey and of all he had seen at the great capital.

Time passed away in the peaceful home, and the parents saw their fondest hopes realised as their daughter grew from childhood into a beautiful girl of sixteen. As a gem of priceless value is held in its proud owner's hand, so had they reared her with unceasing love and care: and now their pains were more than doubly rewarded. What a comfort she was to her mother as she went about the house taking her part in the housekeeping, and how proud her father was of her, for she daily reminded him of her mother when he had first married her.

But, alas! in this world nothing lasts for ever. Even the moon is not always perfect in shape, but loses its roundness with time, and flowers bloom and then fade. So at last the happiness of this family was broken up by a great sorrow. The good and gentle wife and mother was one day taken ill.

In the first days of her illness the father and daughter thought that it was only a cold, and were not particularly anxious. But the days went by and still the mother did not get better; she only grew worse, and the doctor was puzzled, for in spite of all he did the poor woman grew weaker day by day. The father and daughter were stricken with grief, and day or night the girl never left her mother's side. But in spite of all their efforts the woman's life was not to be saved.

One day as the girl sat near her mother's bed, trying to hide with a cheery smile the gnawing trouble at her heart, the mother roused herself and taking her daughter's hand, gazed earnestly and lovingly into her eyes. Her breath was laboured and she spoke with difficulty:

"My daughter, I am sure that nothing can save me now. When I am dead, promise me to take care of your dear father and to try to be a good and dutiful woman."

"Oh, mother," said the girl as the tears rushed to her eyes, "you must not say such things. All you have to do is to make haste and get well— that will bring the greatest happiness to father and myself."

"Yes, I know, and it is a comfort to me in my last days to know how greatly you long for me to get better, but it is not to be. Do not look so sorrowful, for it was so ordained in my previous state of existence that I should die in this life just at this time; knowing this, I am quite resigned to my fate. And now I have something to give you whereby to remember me when I am gone."

Putting her hand out, she took from the side of the pillow a square wooden box tied up with a silken cord and tassels. Undoing this very carefully, she took out of the box the mirror that her husband had given her years ago.

"When you were still a little child your father went up to the capital and brought me back as a present this treasure; it is called a mirror. This I give you before I die. If, after I have ceased to be in this life, you are lonely and long to see me sometimes, then take out this mirror and in the clear and shining surface you will always see me—so will you be able to meet with me often and tell me all your heart; and though I shall not be able to speak, I shall understand and sympathise with you, whatever may happen to you in the future." With these words the dying woman handed the mirror to her daughter.

The mind of the good mother seemed to be now at rest, and sinking back without another word her spirit passed quietly away that day.

The bereaved father and daughter were wild with grief, and they abandoned themselves to their bitter sorrow. They felt it to be impossible to take leave of the loved woman who till now had filled their whole lives and to commit her body to the earth. But this frantic burst of grief passed, and then they took possession of their own hearts again, crushed though they were in resignation. In spite of this the daughter's life seemed to her desolate. Her love for her dead mother did not grow less with time, and so keen was her remembrance, that everything in daily life, even the falling of the rain and the blowing of the wind reminded her of her mother's death and of all that they had loved and shared together. One day when her father was out, and she was fulfilling her household duties alone, her loneliness and sorrow seemed more than she could bear. She threw herself down in her mother's room and wept as if her heart would break. Poor child, she longed just for one glimpse of the loved face, one sound of the voice calling her pet name, or for one moment's forgetfulness of the aching void in her heart. Suddenly she sat up. Her mother's last words had rung through her memory hitherto dulled by grief.

"Oh! my mother told me when she gave me the mirror as a parting gift, that whenever I looked into it I should be able to meet her—to see her. I had nearly forgotten her last words—how stupid I am; I will get the mirror now and see if it can possibly be true!"

She dried her eyes quickly, and going to the cupboard took out the box that contained the mirror, her heart beating with expectation as she lifted the mirror out and gazed into its smooth face. Behold, her mother's words were true! In the round mirror before her she saw her mother's face; but, oh, the joyful surprise! It was not her mother thin and wasted by illness, but the young and beautiful woman as she remembered her far back in the days of her own earliest childhood. It seemed to the girl that the face in the mirror must soon speak, almost that she heard the voice of her mother telling her again to grow up a good woman and a dutiful daughter, so earnestly did the eyes in the mirror look back into her own.

"It is certainly my mother's soul that I see. She knows how miserable I am without her and she has come to comfort me. Whenever I long to see her she will meet me here; how grateful I ought to be!"

And from this time the weight of sorrow was greatly lightened for her young heart. Every morning, to gather strength for the day's duties before her, and every evening, for consolation before she lay down to rest, did the young girl take out the mirror and gaze at the reflection which in the simplicity of her innocent heart she believed to be her mother's soul. Daily she grew in the likeness of her dead mother's character, and was gentle and kind to all, and a dutiful daughter to her father.

A year spent in mourning had thus passed away in the little household, when, by the advice of his relations, the man married again, and the daughter now found herself under the authority of a step-mother. It was a trying position; but her days spent in the recollection of her own beloved mother, and of trying to be what that mother would wish her to be, had made the young girl docile and patient, and she now determined to be filial and dutiful to her father's wife, in all respects. Everything went on apparently smoothly in the family for some time under the new regime; there were no winds or waves of discord to ruffle the surface of every day life, and the father was content.

But step-mothers are proverbial all the world over, and this one's heart was not as her first smiles were. As the days and weeks grew into months, the step-mother began to treat the motherless girl unkindly and to try and come between the father and child.

Sometimes she went to her husband and complained of her step-daughter's behaviour, but the father knowing that this was to be expected, took no notice of her ill-natured complaints. Instead of lessening his affection for his daughter, as the woman desired, her grumblings only made him think of her the more. The woman soon saw that he began to show more concern for his lonely child than before. This did not please her at all, and she began to turn over in her mind how she could, by some means or other, drive her step-child out of the house. So crooked did the woman's heart become.

She watched the girl carefully, and one day peeping into her room in the early morning, she thought she discovered a grave enough sin of which to accuse the child to her father. The woman herself was a little frightened too at what she had seen.

So she went at once to her husband, and wiping away some false tears she said in a sad voice:

"Please give me permission to leave you to-day."

The man was completely taken by surprise at the suddenness of her request, and wondered whatever was the matter.

"Do you find it so disagreeable," he asked, "in my house that you can stay no longer?"

"No! no! it has nothing to do with you—even in my dreams I have never thought that I wished to leave your side, but if I go on living here I am in danger of losing my life, so I think it best for all concerned that you should allow me to go home!"

And the woman began to weep afresh. Her husband, distressed to see her so unhappy, and thinking that he could not have heard aright, said:

"Tell me what you mean! How is your life in danger here?"

"I will tell you since you ask me. Your daughter dislikes me as her step-mother. For sometime past she has shut herself up in her room morning and evening, and looking in, as I pass by, I am convinced that she has made an image of me and is trying to kill me by magic art, cursing me daily. It is not safe for me to stay here, such being the case; indeed, indeed, I must go away, we cannot live under the same roof anymore."

The husband listened to the dreadful tale, but he could not believe his gentle daughter guilty of such an evil act. He knew that by popular superstition people believed that one person could cause the gradual death of another by making an image of the hated one and cursing it daily; but where had his young daughter learned such knowledge?—the thing was impossible. Yet he remembered having noticed that his daughter stayed much in her room of late and kept herself away from everyone, even when visitors came to the house. Putting this fact together with his wife's alarm, he thought that there might be something to account for the strange story.

His heart was torn between doubting his wife and trusting his child, and he knew not what to do. He decided to go at once to his daughter and try to find out the truth. Comforting his wife and assuring her that her fears were groundless, he glided quietly to his daughter's room.

The girl had for a long time past been very unhappy. She had tried by amiability and obedience to show her goodwill and to mollify the new wife, and to break down that wall of prejudice and misunderstanding that she knew generally stood between step-parents and their step-children. But she soon found that her efforts were in vain. The step-mother never trusted her, and seemed to misinterpret all her actions, and the poor child knew very well that she often carried unkind and untrue tales to her father. She could not help comparing her present unhappy condition with the time when her own mother was alive only a little more than a year ago—so great a change in this short time! Morning and evening she wept over the remembrance. Whenever she could she went to her room, and sliding the screens to, took out the mirror and gazed, as she thought, at her mother's face. It was the only comfort that she had in these wretched days.

Her father found her occupied in this way. Pushing aside the *fusama*, he saw her bending over something or other very intently. Looking over her shoulder, to see who was entering her room, the girl was surprised to see her father, for he generally sent for her when he wished to speak to her. She was also confused at being found looking at the mirror, for she had never told anyone of her mother's last promise, but had kept it as the sacred secret of her heart. So before turning to her father she slipped the mirror into her long sleeve. Her father noting her confusion, and her act of hiding something, said in a severe manner:

"Daughter, what are you doing here? And what is that that you have hidden in your sleeve?"

The girl was frightened by her father's severity. Never had he spoken to her in such a tone. Her confusion changed to apprehension, her colour from scarlet to white. She sat dumb and shamefaced, unable to reply.

Appearances were certainly against her; the young girl looked guilty, and the father thinking that perhaps after all what his wife had told him was true, spoke angrily:

"Then, is it really true that you are daily cursing your step-mother and praying for her death? Have you forgotten what I told you, that although she is your step-mother you must be obedient and loyal to her? What evil spirit has taken possession of your heart that you should be so wicked? You have certainly changed, my daughter! What has made you so dis-obedient and unfaithful?"

And the father's eyes filled with sudden tears to think that he should have to upbraid his daughter in this way.

She on her part did not know what he meant, for she had never heard of the superstition that by praying over an image it is possible to cause the death of a hated person. But she saw that she must speak and clear herself somehow. She loved her father dearly, and could not bear the idea of his anger. She put out her hand on his knee deprecatingly:

"Father! father! do not say such dreadful things to me. I am still your obedient child. Indeed, I am. However stupid I may be, I should never be able to curse anyone who belonged to you, much less pray for the death of one you love. Surely someone has been telling you lies, and you are dazed, and you know not what you say—or some evil spirit has taken possession of your heart. As for me I do not know—no, not so much as a dew-drop, of the evil thing of which you accuse me."

But her father remembered that she had hidden something away when he first entered the room, and even this earnest protest did not satisfy him. He wished to clear up his doubts once for all.

"Then why are you always alone in your room these days? And tell me what is that that you have hidden in your sleeve—show it to me at once."

Then the daughter, though shy of confessing how she had cherished her mother's memory, saw that she must tell her father all in order to clear herself. So she slipped the mirror out from her long sleeve and laid it before him.

"This," she said, "is what you saw me looking at just now."

"Why," he said in great surprise, "this is the mirror that I brought as a gift to your mother when I went up to the capital many years ago! And so you have kept it all this time? Now, why do you spend so much of your time before this mirror?"

Then she told him of her mother's last words, and of how she had promised to meet her child whenever she looked into the glass. But still the father could not understand the simplicity of his daughter's charac-ter in not knowing that what she saw reflected in the mirror was in real-ity her own face, and not that of her mother.

"What do you mean?" he asked. "I do not understand how you can meet the soul of your lost mother by looking in this mirror?"

"It is indeed true," said the girl; "and if you don't believe what I say, look for yourself," and she placed the mirror before her. There, looking back from the smooth metal disc, was her own sweet face. She pointed to the reflection seriously:

"Do you doubt me still?" she asked earnestly, looking up into his face.

With an exclamation of sudden understanding the father smote his two hands together.

"How stupid I am! At last I understand. Your face is as like your mother's as the two sides of a melon—thus you have looked at the reflection of your face all this time, thinking that you were brought face to face with your lost mother! You are truly a faithful child. It seems at first a stupid thing to have done, but it is not really so. It shows how deep has been your filial piety, and how innocent your heart. Living in constant remembrance of your lost mother has helped you to grow like her in character. How clever it was of her to tell you to do this. I admire and respect you, my daughter, and I am ashamed to think that for one instant I believed your suspicious step-mother's story and suspected you of evil, and came with the intention of scolding you severely, while all this time you have been so true and good. Before you I have no countenance left, and I beg you to forgive me."

And here the father wept. He thought of how lonely the poor girl must have been, and of all that she must have suffered under her step-mother's treatment. His daughter steadfastly keeping her faith and simplicity in the midst of such adverse circumstances—bearing all her troubles with so much patience and amiability—made him compare her to the lotus which rears its blossom of dazzling beauty out of the slime and mud of the moats and ponds, fitting emblem of a heart which keeps itself unsullied while passing through the world.

The step-mother, anxious to know what would happen, had all this while been standing outside the room. She had grown interested, and had gradually pushed the sliding screen back till she could see all that went on. At this moment she suddenly entered the room, and dropping to the mats, she bowed her head over her outspread hands before her step-daughter.

"I am ashamed! I am ashamed!" she exclaimed in broken tones. "I did not know what a filial child you were. Through no fault of yours, but with a step-mother's jealous heart, I have disliked you all the time. Hating you so much myself, it was but natural that I should think you reciprocated the feeling, and thus when I saw you retire so often to your room I followed you, and when I saw you gaze daily into the mirror for long intervals, I concluded that you had found out how I disliked you, and that you were out of revenge trying to take my life by magic art. As long as I live I shall never forget the wrong I have done you in so misjudging you, and in causing your father to suspect you. From this day I throw away my old and wicked heart, and in its place I put a new one, clean and full of repentance. I shall think of you as a child that I have borne myself. I shall love and cherish you with all my heart, and thus try to make up for all the unhappiness I have caused you. Therefore, please throw into the water all that has gone before, and give me, I beg of you, some of the filial love that you have hitherto given your own lost mother."

Thus did the unkind step-mother humble herself and ask forgiveness of the girl she had so wronged.

Such was the sweetness of the girl's disposition that she willingly forgave her step-mother, and never bore a moment's resentment or malice towards her afterwards. The father saw by his wife's face that she was truly sorry for the past, and was greatly relieved to see the terrible misunderstanding wiped out of remembrance by both the wrongdoer and the wronged.

From this time on, the three lived together as happily as fish in water. No such trouble ever darkened the home again, and the young girl gradually forgot that year of unhappiness in the tender love and care that her step-mother now bestowed on her. Her patience and goodness were rewarded at last.

This mother and daughter share a powerful love for each other. Together they create an atmosphere of love and support that permeates the household. This great love even touches the stepmother's jealous heart enabling her to break the evil stepmother stereotype and become a good stepmother. For generations mothers and daughters have shared this kind of love. For generations the act of connection, support, and care through deep love has remained an unsung heroism. Like the beating of our hearts, we rely on it so completely, we forget to acknowledge it.

The Tiger and the Coal Peddler's Wife

Korea[76]

Deep in the mountains lived a young couple who supported themselves by digging and selling coal. It was a hard life and a lonely one for their nearest neighbor was thirty *ri** away. Still they were very happy and anxiously awaited the birth of their first child, which was due any time.

Early one morning the man headed out to the nearest village, where it was market day, to sell a load of coal and buy some supplies. However, because of a sudden rainstorm, there were not many shoppers so he went from one remote house to another peddling his coal. By the time he had sold all of it and returned to the village to buy the much needed supplies, it was too late for him to return home.

Meanwhile, his wife gave birth. And, ironically, their dog gave birth to three puppies.

The woman lay in bed, cuddling the baby and dozing. It became dusk and she began to worry. Knowing she must eat something to be able to nurse the baby, she got up out of bed and began preparing seaweed soup.

She heard something outside and, thinking it was her husband, threw open the door and found herself staring into the eyes of a very large tiger.

She was overcome with fear but, thinking of her newborn baby, she tried to stay calm. Out of the corner of her eye she saw the puppies. "Here's some meat for you!" she shouted, grabbing up one of them and tossing it out the door.

The tiger caught the puppy in its mouth, gulped it down and looked at the woman hungrily.

"Here! Take this!" she shouted, throwing it another puppy.

The tiger gulped it down and stared at the woman.

She looked at her faithful dog and its remaining puppy. She couldn't bring herself to give the puppy to the tiger. Glancing around she noticed some cotton. She quickly wrapped it around a hot coal from the cooking fire and tossed it to the tiger.

As with the puppies, the tiger caught it in its mouth and quickly gulped it down. Its eyes became big and it opened its mouth as though choking. It ran a few steps this way and that. Then it fell forward on its

---

* *Thirty ri*, about ten miles.

front legs and then over on its side. The woman watched its body shake and become still.

Her husband returned home early the next morning and was alarmed to see a dead tiger in front of his house. But his alarm turned to relief when his wife met him at the door with their newborn son in her arms.

The man sold the tiger skin for a lot of money and from then on they lived more comfortably.

"Thinking it was her husband, [she] threw open the door and found herself staring into the eyes of a very large tiger." What follows is frenetic thought and desperate action. Yet in the midst of these frantic moments, this young mother has a flash of empathy with another mother. Instead of throwing the last puppy, the heroine kills the tiger.

The Plucky Maiden

Korea[77]

Han Myong-hoi was a renowned Minister of the Reign of Se-jo (A.D. 1455–1468). The King appreciated and enjoyed him greatly, and there was no one of the Court who could surpass him for influence and royal favour. Confident in his position, Han did as he pleased, wielding absolute power. At that time, like grass before the wind, the world bowed at his coming; no one dared utter a word of remonstrance.

When Han went as governor to Pyong-an Province he did all manner of lawless things. Any one daring to cross his wishes in the least was dealt with by torture and death. The whole Province feared him as they would a tiger.

On a certain day Governor Han, hearing that the Deputy Prefect of Son-chon had a very beautiful daughter, called the Deputy, and said, "I hear that you have a very beautiful daughter, whom I would like to make my concubine. When I am on my official rounds shortly, I shall expect to stop at your town and take her. So be ready for me."

The Deputy, alarmed, said, "How can your Excellency say that your servant's contemptible daughter is beautiful? Some one has reported her wrongly. But since you so command, how can I do but accede gladly?" So he bowed, said his farewell, and went home.

On his return his family noticed that his face was clouded with anxiety, and the daughter asked why it was. "Did the Governor call you, father?" asked she; "and why are you so anxious? Tell me, please." At first, fearing that she would be disturbed, he did not reply, but her repeated questions forced him, so that he said, "I am in trouble on your account," and then told of how the Governor wanted her for his concubine. "If I had refused I would have been killed, so I yielded; but a gentleman's daughter being made a concubine is a disgrace unheard of."

The daughter made light of it and laughed. "Why did you not think it out better than that, father? Why should a grown man lose his life for the sake of a girl? Let the daughter go. By losing one daughter and saving your life, you surely do better than saving your daughter and losing your life. One can easily see where the greater advantage lies. A daughter does not count; give her over, that's all. Don't for a moment think otherwise, just put away your distress and anxiety. We women, every one of us, are under the ban, and such things are decreed by Fate. I shall accept with-

219

out any opposition, so please have no anxiety. It is settled now, and you, father, must yield and follow. If you do so all will be well."

The father sighed, and said in reply, "Since you seem so willing, my mind is somewhat relieved." But from this time on the whole house was in distress. The girl alone seemed perfectly unmoved, not showing the slightest sign of fear. She laughed as usual, her light and happy laugh, and her actions seemed wonderfully free.

In a little the Governor reached Son-chon on his rounds. He then called the Deputy, and said, "Make ready your daughter for to-morrow and all the things needed." The Deputy came home and made preparation for the so-called wedding. The daughter said, "This is not a real wedding; it is only the taking of a concubine, but still, make everything ready in the way of refreshments and ceremony as for a real marriage." So the father did as she requested.

On the day following the Governor came to the house of the Deputy. He was not dressed in his official robes, but came simply in the dress and hat of a commoner. When he went into the inner quarters he met the daughter; she stood straight before him. Her two hands were lifted in ceremonial form, but instead of holding a fan to hide her face she held a sword before her. She was very pretty. He gave a great start of surprise, and asked the meaning of the knife that she held. She ordered her nurse to reply, who said, "Even though I am an obscure countrywoman, I do not forget that I am born of the gentry; and though your Excellency is a high Minister of State, still to take me by force is an unheard-of dishonour. If you take me as your real and true wife I'll serve you with all my heart, but if you are determined to take me as a concubine I shall die now by this sword. For that reason I hold it. My life rests on one word from your Excellency. Speak it, please, before I decide."

The Governor, though a man who observed no ceremony and never brooked* a question, when he saw how beautiful and how determined this maiden was, fell a victim to her at once, and said, "If you so decide, then, of course, I'll make you my real wife."

Her answer was, "If you truly mean it, then please withdraw and write out the certificate; send the gifts; provide the goose; dress in the proper way; come, and let us go through the required ceremony; drink the pledge-glass, and wed."

The Governor did as she suggested, carried out the forms to the letter, and they were married.

She was not only a very pretty woman, but upright and true of soul—

---

* *Brook*, to put up with, tolerate, endure.

a rare person indeed. The Governor took her home, loved her and held her dear. He had, however, a real wife before and concubines, but he set them all aside and fixed his affections on this one only. She remonstrated with him over his wrongs and unrighteous acts, and he listened and made improvement. The world took note of it, and praised her as a true and wonderful woman. She counted herself the real wife, but the first wife treated her as a concubine, and all the relatives said likewise that she could never be considered a real wife. At that time King Se-jo frequently, in the dress of a commoner, used to visit Han's house. Han entertained him royally with refreshments, which his wife used to bring and offer before him. He called her his "little sister." On a certain day King Se-jo, as he was accustomed, came to the house, and while he was drinking he suddenly saw the woman fall on her face before him. The King in surprise inquired as to what she could possibly mean by such an act. She then told all the story of her being taken by force and brought to Seoul. She wept while she said, "Though I am from a far-distant part of the country I am of the gentry by ancestry, and my husband took me with all the required ceremonies of a wife, so that I ought not to be counted a concubine. But there is no law in this land by which a second real wife may be taken after a first real wife exists, so they call me a concubine, a matter of deepest disgrace. Please, your Majesty, take pity on me and decide my case."

The King laughed, and said, "This is a simple matter to settle; why should my little sister make so great an affair of it, and bow before me? I will decide your case at once. Come." He then wrote out with his own hand a document making her a real wife, and her children eligible for the highest office. He wrote it, signed it, stamped it and gave it to her.

From that time on she was known as a real wife, in rank and standing equal to the first one. No further word was ever slightingly spoken, and her children shared in the affairs of State.

The plucky maiden comforts her father, "Why should a grown man lose his life for the sake of a girl? . . . A daughter does not count." Obviously the daughter doesn't believe it. When the Governor comes to take her, she stands there with a knife and says, No way! This heroine wages a determined battle for her honor. She is ready to die for the respect to which she is entitled as gentry by birth. She continues to fight until she has guaranteed her children a respectable position in the society.

The Phoenix and Her City

Hui People, China[78]

According to legend, the city of Yinchuan was at one time called "Phoenix City." Today, if you mention the Phoenix City to old people, they will tell you that the Gaotai Temple east of Yinchuan, by the Yellow River, is the head of the Phoenix; the two wells by the Gaotai Temple are its eyes; the Drum Tower at the center of the city is the heart of the Phoenix; the West Tower and the North Tower are its claws; the trees, flowers, and grass in Zhongshan Park are the tail of the Phoenix— which used to be so long as to extend all the way to the Helan Mountains.

Why is Yinchuan called the "Phoenix City?" It is a long story. Do you by chance know anything about the Phoenix herself? She is the Bird of Happiness. Wherever the Phoenix is, there happiness is.

Seven Phoenix sisters lived on a high mountain peak south of the Chang Jiang (Yangtze) River. They lived there to bring happiness to people. So the place where they lived was very beautiful, with turquoise hills and clear bodies of water. Everywhere was the fragrance of flowers. Rows of trees stood there. The people were good looking and strong. Each year brought them an abundant harvest of the five cereals. People there lived prosperous lives. They had nothing to worry about. They lived together joyfully and pleasantly.

At the same time the Ningxia Plain, to the north was a land of poor soil, and the people there lived under great hardships. Though the Yellow River flowed past them in the east, the water was so shallow that it could not be channeled into the fields. The Helan Mountains in the west could not keep out the cold air currents which blew in from Siberia. The Liupan Mountains in the south could not keep the sands of the Tengger Desert in check. Nonetheless, the Hui, the Mongol, and the Han people did not lose heart; diligently they continued working on this stretch of land. But though the people's muscles were nearly torn to shreds from hard work, and their blood was nearly desiccated, they could not ease their poverty. Sadly they sang:

> Though the river is wide
> And the mountains are high
> Ningxia—an endless wasteland!

When news of the Bird of Happiness reached Ningxia, all the Hui,

Han, and Mongol peoples were looking forward to her arrival in Ningxia, every day and every month. They looked forward to her arrival with so much devotion that their eyes turned red from the strain (and they recited this verse):

> Though the river is wide
> and the mountains are high,
> Ningxia—its people hungry and nothing to wear!

The wild goose learned about this and was deeply moved by the sincere desire of the Ningxia people. She volunteered to fly southward to visit the Phoenix sisters and to communicate the genuine wish of the Ningxia people in detail. There, in the woods, the seven Phoenix sisters deliberated. The youngest insisted that she would go to Ningxia to have a look. The remaining six sisters agreed. They knew her habit—that, once she had decided on a course of action, no one could make her change her mind anymore. But they told her to return home as early as possible.

And so the youngest Phoenix began her journey, immediately. All the birds in the woods came to send her off. Some were playing on flutes and others were singing, while still others frolicked in dance. It was a very thrilling sight. The people from around there also came to see her off. They brought with them many presents, some for the young Phoenix and some for the people of Ningxia.

The six Phoenix sisters, and the lark, sent their little sister across the Chang Jiang river. After bidding farewell to her sisters and her friends, the young Phoenix flew to Ningxia trailing the wild goose who led the way. Riding a red cloud in the blue sky, she arrived in the Liupan Mountain area in almost no time at all. There she was received by Hui people who welcomed her with warm greetings. To them it seemed rather auspicious to have a red cloud in the sky. The Phoenix alighted happily by the Yellow River, between the Helan and the Liupan mountains.

Many tents, huts, and yurta were set up along both banks of the Yellow River. Hui, Han, and Mongol peoples lined the river banks to welcome the Phoenix. Birds arrived from the Liupan and Helan mountains. Cattle, sheep, camels, and horses came from the grasslands to welcome her. They all chanted songs of welcome to the limits of their voices. Their songs resounded through the skies. Even the water of the Yellow River echoed as they sang.

After the Phoenix arrived in Ningxia she flew here and there without resting. When she saw the Yinchuan Plain she thought to herself, "What a vast expanse of dry land they have here!" She turned toward the Yellow

River and, all around, she drew many lines. These lines became irrigation canals which, at their mouths, accepted water from the Yellow River.

The next morning the Phoenix rose very early and began flying about. She was so busy that she hardly took time to wipe away her sweat. The Phoenix scattered her presents all over the Liupan and Helan mountains, and all over the Yinchuan Plain. Flowers, trees, and crops sprang up instantly everywhere across the Yinchuan Plain. Herds of cattle appeared on the grassland. The Liupan Mountains cast off their worried frown and put on a green dress. The Helan Mountains discarded their white hair and covered themselves instead with green trees.

Ningxia altered its appearance completely. People were grateful to the Phoenix, for the happiness as well as for the lush southern scenery which she had brought. Since that time Ningxia has been known as the "Land of Prosperity beyond the Great Wall."

Well watered by irrigation canals the crops grew well. People harvested rich bounties every year, and they sang with joy:

> At both ends Ningxia Plain is pointed.
> Yellow River east and Helan Mountains west,
> The Liupan Mountain range stands south.
> Land well irrigated, rich harvests, year after year.

Ningxia had become a place as beautiful as the southlands. "The people around here are kind and hard working. It is now as beautiful around here as is my native place." This the Phoenix thought. "I will remain here!"

And so she regarded Ningxia as her home. Together with the people of Ningxia she worked hard to cultivate the land and to raise cows, horses, camels, and sheep.

At that time there lived, far to the west of Ningxia, a tribe of people of a different race. And one year the chief of this tribe, together with his men, pushed into Ningxia like a cruel beast of prey. They burnt crops and killed people. The Phoenix became very angry. She changed herself into a city to contain all the people inside her, with four city gates tightly sealed. No matter how hard the enemies tried, they could not break her open. The battle raged for three months. In the end the enemy ran out of food and was forced to withdraw. Ever thereafter, whenever an enemy came, the people would withdraw into the city for protection. As soon as the enemy withdrew they would re-emerge to resume farming and herding animals.

Now that the Phoenix had changed herself into a city she asked the wild goose to carry a message to her sisters in the south, telling them that she would not return home anymore. On that account it has become the task of the wild goose to carry a message to the southland once every year. Each autumn, when the crops are ripe, the wild goose flies south. And with the arrival of spring, the next year, the wild goose will fly back again with best regards to the Phoenix, from her six sisters.

Many years passed. A tribal chief appeared. Later came the emperor, the warlords, the bureaucrats, and finally the landlords. The face of Ningxia changed. The masses of people were exploited and oppressed by a small number of people. The mountains became barren and the fields were left uncultivated. The Ningxia Plain became a stretch of dry land again. Cattle, sheep, and camels were dying from hunger. Even the Liupan and Helan mountains were covered with ominous dark clouds.

One year the emperor sent an official with a pockmarked face to Ningxia. Upon his arrival he had a palace built at a place southeast of the Phoenix City. He conscripted young men for military service and robbed the people of their belongings. The Hui, Han, and Mongol peoples suffered a lot under this greedy official. When he learned that there was a gold pony sunk in Heiquan Lake, he decided to steal it.

One night he sat in the government office and thought to himself, "I can steal the gold pony without all the people here knowing it. But how can I hide the truth from the Phoenix?"

He continued thinking, "Ever since the Phoenix has come to Ningxia, the people are increasingly becoming more educated and capable. I have done many evil deeds, so that, if I might run out of luck some day the gold pony will fall into the hands of others."

As he thought in this fashion, he suddenly gnashed his teeth and said to himself, "I must take preventive measures. I must kill the Phoenix first."

He searched out the Phoenix before the night was over. When he found her he cut open her throat with his sword. But, even though the Phoenix died, her heart remained alive. She was still thinking about the people of Ningxia. There appeared a canal which carried the flow of her blood. Her blood flowed from one village to another into the thirsty fields.

The next morning many people were surprised to find a newly dug canal winding its way in front of their houses. When news of the canal spread, the inhabitants came running to see for themselves. They were all puzzled: Why! Can it be possible that the Milky Way in heaven has fallen to the ground?"

As they admired the water flow, they discovered some red threads in it. Some old men recognized it as blood, and they began shouting, "Ah, there is blood in the water!"

Just then an old ahong came running, as if he had gone mad. He elbowed his way through the crowd. Then, with his eyes fixed on the water he cried with deep sorrow, beating his breast and stamping his feet: "Oh my Allah! It is true!" The people surrounded him and asked what was the matter.

After a pause the old ahong began to murmur, "I dreamt I saw the Phoenix last night. She told me that she was being killed by someone. She could not tear herself from us. Therefore she made a canal with her blood for us to irrigate the land."

Upon hearing what the old ahong told them, the people were overcome with grief. Some shed tears of sadness and others wept in sorrow. Still others broke out into loud crying. They cried and cried for nine days and nine nights until the sky was cloudy, the trees were yellow, and the mountains were bald. The people lamented and chanted:

> The melon clings to the vine.
> A baby clings to its mother.
> How can the Ningxia people live
> Without the Phoenix to protect them?

On the tenth day the Phoenix once more appeared to the old ahong in a dream. She informed him that her heart was still alive, that after another ninety-nine years she would rise again. Many capable people would appear then. Ningxia would become a paradise on earth.

She told the ahong, "Wait patiently for me. The Phoenix will return when a red cloud appears over the Liupan Mountain range."

The people were no longer sorrowful, and all things on earth resumed their former state. In memory of the Phoenix, people called the city of Yinchuan the "Phoenix City." The canal that was made by the blood of the Phoenix they called the "Red Flower Canal."

The people of Ningxia and the Phoenix together change a wasteland into the "Land of Prosperity beyond the Great Wall." The people are grateful for the Phoenix's help and the Phoenix respects them for being kind and hard-working. She comes to live with them. The Phoenix and the people fight the greedy official who defines the problem thus: "Ever since the Phoenix has come to Ningxia, the people are increasingly becoming more educated and capable."

In 1894 Mary McDowell moved from the rich Chicago suburb of Evanston to Packingtown. Packingtown was one of the neediest areas of Chicago, bordered by slaughterhouses, the city dump, and a creek carrying sewage and refuse from the slaughterhouses. Mary McDowell lived in Packingtown for forty-two years until her death. She established a settlement house and began to organize the people so they could act as a whole. Together the people of Packingtown and Mary McDowell took on the city and gained concessions such as public parks and the right to city garbage service so they could use the dump they lived next to. They unionized and took on the tricky problem of addressing the irresponsibility of the industry for which most of the people in Packingtown worked.[79] *The Phoenix and Mary McDowell crossed the rich-poor boundary and working together with people changed the lives of thousands for the better.*

Sailimai's Four Precious Things

Hui People, China[80]

Sailimai's father-in-law, Ali, was conscripted to do repair work in the palace for the emperor. One day, when Ali had been working till midday, the hard work made his head swim. This gave him a pain in the back and caused his hands to shake. Quite unexpectedly he knocked over one of the emperor's precious vases. It broke into pieces. When the emperor heard of it he opened his eyes so wide that it seemed as though sparks would fly from them.

He drew his sword and was about to kill Ali. Being tired and hungry, and seeing that the emperor was about to kill him, he was too scared to think. Panic-stricken he implored, "Forgive me, your Majesty! I will pay for it. I will pay for it."

The emperor said with scorn, "Ah! Such a poor old Hui even talks big! You will pay for it?"

A minute later he spoke again: "All right, Ali, I will not ask you to pay for my precious vase. I only ask four things of you: The first, something more black than the bottom of a pan; the second, something clearer than a mirror; the third, something which is harder than steel; the fourth, something that is as large as the sea. You must have these four things in ten days, or I will chop off your head."

Even though Ali had avoided death at that moment, he felt sick as he went home. All day long he was depressed and unable to eat or fall asleep. Sailimai saw all this with her eyes, and she asked, "Father, what is the trouble? Do not depress yourself like this."

The deadline set by the emperor was drawing nearer. Ali wanted to speak about it, but he thought it useless to tell her and only gave forth a long sigh. But Sailimai did not give up and persuaded him with all the words she could muster: "Just tell me. Maybe we can find a way."

Ali could not refuse her repeated questions. With tears in his eyes he told her the entire story, exactly as it happened. After hearing the story, Sailimai said, "Father, do not worry! I have all these four things. When the emperor comes tomorrow, I shall present them to him myself."

Ali reckoned that Sailimai was just trying to comfort him, and said, "Do not be a fool, Sailimai. There are no such things anywhere in the world. The emperor made his request of these things deliberately difficult for me!"

Still, Sailimai said, "Father, I really have these four things. You can see tomorrow even if you do not believe me now."

The next day the deadline for having the four things had come. The emperor wondered why Ali did not appear. He went to punish the crime himself, followed by a troop of soldiers. Ali and Sailimai were just waiting at home. When the emperor entered he asked ferociously, "Ali, have you got the four things ready? It is high time now!"

Sailimai stepped forward and said, "Your Majesty, the four things are ready. Please name them, one by one."

The emperor said, "The first thing I want is that which is more black than the bottom of a pan."

Sailimai said, "Yes, I have it. A bottomless heart with avarice is more black than the bottom of a pan."

The emperor was shocked. Hmm! Initially I wanted to put him on the spot, and now I lose! How sharp she is! And so the emperor spoke again: "The second is something clearer than a mirror. Do you have that?"

Sailimai answered quickly, "Yes. Knowledge in one's mind is more clear than a mirror."

The emperor could hardly believe that a rural woman had spoken these words. He cleared his throat and said, "Something that is harder than steel—do you have anything like that?"

Sailimai answered loudly, "Yes I do, it is the unity of the brothers."

The emperor for a long time remained speechless, and dumbfounded. He blushed scarlet with shame. And after that he asked, "Do you have something as large as the sea?"

Sailimai said, "Yes, a virtuous woman's heart is as large as the sea."

The idea had never occurred to the emperor that Sailimai could come up with the four things. And she did it so well. He shouted at his soldiers who stood about, "Get out!" Then he left dejected and surrounded by his men.

Since that time the story about the wise Sailimai spread far and wide.

As the wise Sailimai answers the riddles, she teaches the emperor to understand his own misdoings. What is "more black than the bottom of a pan?" the emperor wants to know. In her answer, Sailimai refers to the Emperor's own heart so filled with avarice that he is willing to kill a man over a vase. The emperor continues, "What is clearer than a mirror?" "Knowledge in one's mind." Such is Sailimai's knowledge as she responds to the riddles so clearly. What is "harder than steel?" Sailimai talks about people who unify against injustice, just as she is doing by standing up for her father-in-law. What is as "large as the sea?" "A virtuous woman's heart." Sailimai has such a heart. Her virtue defeats the emperor's cruelty.

A Woman's Love

Uighur People, China[81]

If a woman has won true love, it lasts her life and never fails. Nothing on earth can spoil it. But, if it be untrue, nothing can help her. Now I'm going to tell you about the love of a woman. This woman lived a poor life in the countryside, but she was clever and beautiful. Her skill at embroidering flowers was second to none.

She fell in love with a man when she was a little girl. Like her own family, that man had only a single room for a home. He had scarcely anything he could call his own. But he laboured hard with his hands, and never went hungry. He wasn't smart or wise. He was just an ordinary man. Everyone in the district knew he was straight as a die. He never told a lie, and he believed whatever he was told. The girl understood all this, but she loved him just the same. Her parents liked him too, and so the couple were engaged to be married.

It was common knowledge in the countryside that a good girl couldn't stay unnoticed. Talk of her would spread till it came at last to the king's ears. With this girl it was the same. The king hadn't seen her. Though he was the leader of the country, he never went into the countryside. But he heard about her, and that was enough.

This is how it happened. Some of the toadies who tried to please the king by doing little services for him, showed him the girl's embroidery. He knew at once she must be a special girl. So he thought, she may be beautiful: then she would amuse me for quite a while. And if she is ugly or silly, I can just throw her aside and look for another one to play with.

Soon the king's minister arrived at the girl's home. "Good luck has come to the girl," he announced. "Our king wants to marry her."

The father said, "My daughter is already engaged. The marriage was her own choice. Don't bother me. Go and ask her."

The minister went to see the girl. Well, being a king's messenger, he had a tongue like a nightingale. He said a great number of good things, but the girl wasn't taken in. She said in a firm voice, "Go back. Please convey my thanks to the king. I don't want to marry him. You know I am a girl from a poor home. I want to marry a working man. I don't want to live in a palace and do nothing. A king, to marry a village girl from a poor family! Oh, it's no good at all. I would ruin his reputation." The minister was at a loss to find suitable words to answer her speech. With a heavy heart he reported it to the king.

The king was full of anger. "I'll get her sooner or later."

The girl married the poor man. They worked hard and made plans for their home. Gradually they saved eight silver coins. The girl said, "We mustn't waste this money. Take it to town and buy some cotton thread."

The man bought some cotton thread, and day and night the girl worked to embroider four ribbons. Her nimble hands made exquisite pictures. They sold the four ribbons for sixteen silver coins. The man used twelve coins to buy food, and four to buy more thread. The girl worked harder still, making beautiful ribbons. Soon they had earned forty coins. The girl said, "Buy me some coloured thread and I'll embroider a colourful bedspread."

When the bedspread was ready, she sent the man to sell it in town. "You must sell it for twenty silver coins. There are forty streets in our town and you may sell it in any street you like. Bring it back home if nobody wants to buy it. Remember this: You must not go to the forty-first street."

This bedspread was a rare and precious thing. People made a circle round it in the street, and jostled to see it. But though many admired it, none could pay twenty silver coins. It was hard to find a man rich enough to afford twenty coins for a bedspread. The husband walked up and down and nobody wanted to buy it. Late in the afternoon he thought of going home, but he was troubled as he thought how his wife had spent so much time on it and now nobody wanted to buy it. She will be very sad, he thought to himself. In order not to let her down, I should think of a way to sell it, and return home a little later than usual. He forgot what his wife had told him and stepped into the forty-first street.

The forty-first street was full of handsome buildings, but there wasn't a soul about. Now he realized why he was forbidden to come here. It must be where the palace officials lived. Just as he was about to turn back, a crowd of people spilled into the street through the gates. They were all dragging dogs or carrying eagles on their wrists. They looked powerful and proud. The king was riding a horse. As soon as he saw the man, he said, "What are you doing here? Don't you know this is the forty-first street?" His voice boomed like an ancient bell.

The man said, "Sorry, I didn't know. Here, I'll be off right away." But as he turned to go, the king caught sight of the bedspread.

"What's that in your hand?"

He answered, "Nothing. It's only a bedspread."

"Let me see," said the king.

The man unfolded the bedspread, and a pack of trouble with it. The king had seen the girl's handiwork once before, and this beautiful bedspread was obviously embroidered by her. It couldn't be denied. The king looked at the man standing beside him and hated him very much. "Who embroidered this?"

The man didn't know what to say. Instead of replying with a smart lie, he just opened and shut his mouth. Then he said, "I embroidered it." All the people around laughed, and he grew even more worried and awkward.

The king said, "Tell me the truth. You needn't be afraid. Who made it?"

He said, "It was made by my sister."

"I know this man," said one of the courtiers. "He has no sister."

The king's face turned serious. "I want no more of your nonsense. Speak out the truth. Quick, man!"

It was impossible to lie. He had to tell the truth. "My wife made it."

The king nodded, smiling. "A wonderful bedspread it is. How much do you want?"

He answered, "Twenty silver coins."

The king took the bedspread and paid him twenty coins saying, "Tomorrow I'm going to hunt in the woods and I plan to take a rest when I pass your village. You must prepare something for me to eat."

On his way home, the more he thought the more the man regretted neglecting his wife's words. He asked himself many times why he had to go to the forty-first street; why he had to sell it there . . .

He handed all the money to his wife but he looked so unhappy she knew something unusual must have happened. She asked, "My dear, what makes you so sad?"

The man couldn't hide the truth, and he told her the whole story. After hearing it all, she was upset, and complained, "I told you not to go there, and you turned a deaf ear. Now, as you see, more trouble will come." The man was so distressed. He blamed himself. His eyes were filled with tears of shame. On seeing this, the girl forgave him, and she comforted him, "Never mind. I'll hide myself when they come tomorrow. Say, 'She has gone out,' if they want to see me."

The next day the king truly came to their village and entered their house, calling loudly for tea to be served. He thought the lady of the house would have to come and make him the tea, but it was the man who came. The king said, "Tell your wife to make tea. I have more to ask you."

He replied, "My wife has gone away."

The king's face turned angry. Then he realized it was a simple trick. Certainly, she was hiding. So she thought she could run away from his hands? He turned kind. "Never mind, come here. Let's drink some wine together." The man thought the king was sincere. And as it was a rude thing to refuse a king's offer, he drank the wine, which was specially strong. Soon he was as drunk as a lord, and would not wake up for three or four days.

An order was given to search the room. Their home was only a single, narrow room. There weren't many hiding places. She was soon found.

The king was amazed at her beauty. No wonder people talked about her everywhere. Whoever saw her would fall in love with her. Naturally the king wanted her. He talked very big, and offered to do so many good things for her, but the girl refused him completely. "I am married. My husband is still living and I love him. I'll never change my mind to love another man, even if you kill me."

The king was very angry. He could do nothing except order his followers to tie her on horse-back by force. He thought he could have everything he wanted. As for the girl, she only thought of her drunk husband. How would he find her when he woke up, if they took her away? An idea appeared in her mind. She said to the king, "You have to grant me a favour if you are determined to marry me."

The king was very pleased. "Oh, tell me quickly. It needn't be just one favour. You are welcome to ask as many favours as you like."

The girl said, "It is the custom in our village that any woman who leaves her husband for another has to put cakes and water by the wayside for the spirits. If we neglect it, bad luck will come."

The king said, "Certainly, certainly. Do everything as you wish."

Then the girl made some special cakes, and left a few in front of her husband, with a secret mark pointing the direction she was forced to go. Next to the cakes she placed a bowl of water. The king took her away. But at intervals until they reached the king's palace she left cakes and water by the road.

Three days later, the man woke up and found himself alone. He knew the king had made a fool of him. His wife was kidnapped. But when he saw the secret mark on the cakes, he knew what to do. He ate the cakes and drank the water, and then set out to look for her. He walked the whole way, stopping to eat the cakes and drink the water on the route, and following the secret marks. They led him straight to the king's palace.

The walls of the palace were very high, and guards watched the gate all the time. It was hard to get in. For days and nights he did nothing but wander about the high walls. Then he met an old woman who asked him what he was looking for. The old woman looked kind and friendly, so he told her the truth. She said, "I'll give you a coin with which to buy some things girls need—thread, needles, looking-glasses, combs. Stand by the gate and cry your wares. You might chance to meet her."

The king wanted to marry her as soon as they got to the palace. But the girl said, "Waiting sharpens desire. Give me some time. You mustn't come to my room. There is no hurry." She gave the king a look which took away his speech.

A few days later, while the king was out hunting, the girl heard a hawker crying his wares by the gate. It was her husband's voice. She went to the gate. She was so happy to see him, but he couldn't recognize her, for her face was covered by a veil. She told him to come closer, so she could see what he had for sale. She looked at his trinkets, and let him know who she was. Then, at a moment when there was nobody nearby, she whispered, "Take these two coins and use them to buy two horses. Wait for me in the evening outside this wall in three days' time." She handed him the money, and whisked back through the gate. It was done secretly. No one saw them.

Returning from the hunt, the king paid her a visit, but she was not pleased. "Who has offended you?" asked the king.

The girl made an ugly pout. "It is you! You carried me off, but why am I here? I haven't the least authority here."

The king took out forty-one keys there and then, and said, "Here you are. Now you have charge of everything." She took the keys and began to smile a little smile. The king said, "Well, how much longer must I wait?"

The girl replied, "Just three more days. Be patient."

Next day when the king was again out hunting, she took her chance, unlocked the stable door and, choosing two good horses, ordered a servant to sell them at the market. Her husband bought them with his two silver coins.

The third day came. That evening, the husband brought the horses and waited for her outside the palace wall. The more he waited the more he worried. Where was she? He got so tired with waiting and worrying that he fell asleep beneath the wall.

Just then, the infamous bald-headed man of the town staggered by, and paused at the unusual sight of a sleeping man with two horses at midnight. The drunken bald-headed man was about to wake the sleeper and question him when two parcels dropped down from above, followed by a lithe figure. It was the king's new lady! The bald-headed man thought, Something is up.

She was in such a whirl she didn't look closely at the man standing by the horses, just told him to hurry up and tie the parcels to the saddle. She jumped up and rode off, and the bald-headed man rode just behind her.

The moon shone brightly to light their way as they fled far from the king's palace.

After a long time they took a rest. The girl let her horse idle as she tidied her hair. She asked, "Did everything go all right?" The bald-headed man mumbled in reply. He was afraid to answer in a loud voice. The girl knew something had gone wrong. She peered at her companion. Oh! Instead of her husband, she was frightened to see the infamous bald-headed man of the town. She blamed herself for setting off so recklessly. She had only escaped into the hands of another bad man.

The girl wasn't downhearted. As they rode, she thought of many ways to cope with the situation. When dawn came, she said to him, "I've been thinking. To be blunt, I'd made up my mind to go off with the first man I saw, but I must tell you the truth. I don't like your bald head. It's ugly and a disgrace. Take these five coins and fetch me a big pan of oil. Hot oil is a sure cure for baldness. As soon as your hair grows again, we'll get married. How is that?"

The bald-headed man was overjoyed. He was in luck! He was going to marry a beautiful woman and get his hair back too. Immediately he bought a big pan full of oil at the nearest village. He gathered some fire-wood and heated the oil. When he sat with his bald head uncovered for the cure, the girl picked up the pan and poured the boiling oil on it, and killed him.

The girl rode on alone for some distance, till she met four hunters. As soon as they saw her, they began to argue. This one said, "I will marry her." That one said, "No, I will." And the others said, "Let me." "Let me."

The girl stopped them all. "What's the use of arguing with one another? No matter how you shout, I can't marry all of you. Let me see. Give me a bow and some arrows. I'll fire in four directions, and he who brings back an arrow first will marry me."

The hunters were very glad to settle their dispute with this race. Each of them was confident of success. They said, "That is very good. All right. Fire away."

The girl took the bow and shot four arrows as far as she could. But when those four hunters brought the arrows back, she was a long way off. All they won was sore feet.

She rode on and on again, till she met four gamblers. They too quarrelled, and all insisted on marrying her. The girl said, "Now listen to me. I'll give you a bowlful of wine each. He who drinks it all in one gulp but doesn't get drunk will marry me." The gamblers were well used to drink, and all agreed. But she gave them the king's strong wine, and they all fell fast asleep. All they won was sore heads.

Now the girl knew that it was a hard thing for a girl to travel alone. So she opened one of the parcels she had brought from the palace, and took out some men's clothes to disguise herself as a gentleman. Then she rode on safely till she came to a city.

It was a queer place. All the people were dressed in colourful clothes and looking up at the sky. They were all carrying big pieces of meat. They were pushing and shoving and running up and down. She asked one of them, "What has happened, and what are you all doing?"

He explained, "Our king has died. His 'Bird of Happiness' has been released today. We are looking for the bird in the sky. The man on whom the bird chooses to land will become our new king. The meat is to tempt it."

As the man was speaking, the Bird of Happiness swooped low. People began to cheer, all hoping that the bird would bring them happiness, but after circling the crowd, the bird alighted on the shoulder of the girl dressed up as a man. All the people threw away their meat and shouted hurrah! Of course they all begged her to enter the palace.

Well, she had never thought that such a thing could happen to her. Truly she had never dreamed it. She didn't wish to do it, but their invitation couldn't be refused. They said that this custom had been handed down from generation to generation. Anyone who objected to it would be thrown into prison.

She became their king. Theirs was a big and powerful nation. Even that bad king who had kidnapped her was under its rule.

The girl received people's congratulations and set out learning how to rule. She dealt with everything fairly, and relied on common sense not clever arguments. All admired her. People said, "How happy we are now with such a good king." It was she who had brought happiness to the common people. So the people hoped she too would find happiness of her own. They said, "Our king, you are still single. It would be well for you to find a girl and get married."

She replied, "There is no hurry about that. It's early yet for me to get married. I'll let you know when I find the right girl." So the question of the king's marriage was left aside.

One day as she was studying something in her office, a high minister came to her, and said, "Four hunters have come to appeal to you, saying that a lady promised to marry them, but then ran away. Now they want to know whether she came here. What do you think?"

The king said, "The first thing is to put them in prison, and then wait until we find the lady." The minister did as she said.

A few days passed, and the minister came to report another case.

"Another four men came to appeal to you, also saying a certain lady agreed to marry them but cheated them in the end by making them drunk."

The king said, "Let's wait. Put them in prison. We can't do anything till we find the lady."

A few days later, the bad king who was under the new king's rule arrived. Usually with the lesser kings, she would receive them pleasantly. But she knew who this little king was. Oh, she was full of hatred and anger. The bad king said, "There's a little matter on which I'd like your help."

The king said, "I'm too busy. Tell my minister what you want." She showed him the door.

A little while later the minister found her and said, "He told me that a lady promised to marry him, but she escaped. He was told that she came to this country."

The king said angrily, "Oh, nothing but looking for a lady all the time. I'm tired of it. Put him in prison. He can cool his heels there till we find the lady."

The minister was surprised to hear this decision. He thought that to throw a neighbouring king into prison wasn't a nice thing; but the king sounded so determined that he couldn't question it. And so the minister did just as she had ordered.

A few days passed. The minister reported, "Today again another man has come looking for a lady. He is young and poor. Shall I put him in prison too?"

The king said, "Wait. Bring him to me here."

The minister could not understand all this, but he did as she said. The king glanced at the man, and saw he was just the man she had been longing for every day and every night. That young poor man was the man whose absence had robbed the king's food of savour and her sleep of restfulness. It was her husband. But though the king knew him, the young man couldn't recognize his wife.

All the courtiers were asked to leave the room. Then the king said to the young man, "I know you are looking for your wife. But can you tell me what marks she has on her body?"

The young man replied, "Of course. I know her very well. There is a black spot on her breast."

The king undid her shirt and asked, "Look! Is this the mark?"

The man looked straight at her, and cried, "Oh! How . . . " The king made a gesture. "Be quiet. I'm going to release you. Tomorrow you must dress up as a lady and go to an eating house."

The king let the young man go. "That settles that case," she said to her minister. He was afraid to ask her what she meant.

Next day, the king went for a walk with her ministers. Suddenly the king stopped at the entrance to an eating house. There was a young lady at a table. The king looked at her for quite a long time, motionless. Then turning to the ministers, the king said, "Did you not want me to get married? Now I want you to know that I've found the young lady for me. She is now eating inside there. She is a good girl. I wish I were married to her."

When the ministers heard this, they all offered their congratulations. The marriage was settled without the least trouble. As for the wedding, it was as grand as could be.

When they were married, the king taught her husband every day how to handle affairs of state. She gave him some king's clothes to wear, to see how they felt. She taught him how to speak and walk like a real king. Gradually he learned everything. Soon he was good enough to appear in public. Then she said to him, "It's not good to keep up this lie. What's the use of pretending? Let's call a meeting of our people and let them know our secret. It's high time to decide how to punish those men I put in prison."

Next day all the gossip of the court was about the king's face. It was so changed. Most people thought he must be seriously ill. As they whispered to each other, a palace gong sounded many times. It was the special signal for the whole city to gather together. So the chief minister, and the lesser ministers, the workers and the wastrels all hurried to the main gate of the palace. The whole city was there. After a short time, the king appeared. He was very changed. Beside him was his wife. She too was very changed. Not until the girl began to tell them the story of her past sufferings, in the familiar voice of the king, did the people realize what had happened. The people were moved to tears by her pain. They clamoured to punish the wrong-doers. But the girl who had been king declared, "Let the gamblers go. They wouldn't have done anything wrong if I had not fallen into their hands. A spell in prison was quite enough. The four hunters are just common people. There couldn't be any grudge between us. So just let them go. But as for that so-called 'king', let's keep him in prison for ever and ever, lest he do harm to our ladies and young girls."

In this story, the heroine's beauty becomes a disadvantage when it attracts the attention of an unscrupulous king. This intelligent woman, however, knows how to use men's predictability to turn the tables on them. The king is proud of his power; he assumes he can have anything he wants. When the woman pretends that he will also have her, she gets permission to leave a path for her husband and the keys to the household. She suggests a competition to the overconfident hunters. They all run off for arrows and she escapes. The gamblers are proud of their ability to hold alcohol. She gets them drunk on the king's strong wine. In this society a woman alone is fair game, so she dresses herself as a man and gains freedom and a kingdom. In each case the woman prevails because of her ability to recognize the assumptions of her adversary and to base her actions on this knowledge. When she is king, her abilities benefit others as well. She brings happiness to the common people, punishes the evil king who had abducted her, and reunites herself with her much beloved husband.

Maiden Liu, the Songster

Yao People, China [82]

In antiquity the Seven Star Cliff in the Kao Yao district had no human habitation. Only fierce animals roamed about the wild countryside until the Yao tribe migrated there. Then they bravely subdued the animals, got rid of the snakes and diligently planted crops on the hilltops. The people lived a very simple life. They liked to sing and dance, and gradually became known for these talents. The happy love songs of the young people reverberated throughout the mountain valleys. During their festivities, flutes and drums mingled with their singing and the dances often lasted from dusk to dawn. However, life was hard for them, and to make matters worse, the Yao did not get along with the Han officials. The Han armies were often sent to oppress them; soldiers burned their villages, and plundered the cows and sheep. There were many misunderstandings, so the Yao people just kept to themselves.

There was a Han maiden named Liu San Mei, living nearby the Yao villages. She was a farmer's daughter, compassionate, brave and beautiful. Her hair was dressed in a topknot resembling a curled cloud. She had shiny red cheeks and dark, sparkling eyes that looked like two drops of morning dew on a lotus leaf. Besides, she was an expert songster, and her name was known to the country-folk far and near.

She once organized an open singing contest that brought people from all parts of the countryside. Some traveled several days and nights to get there. As was customary, she sang in verse and then a participant rapidly replied. Whoever could remain singing the longest was the winner. One by one, competitors dropped out, unable to cope with her endless repartee. She seemed to have a veritable spring of fresh songs that came from her heart.

An elderly scholar, well-known for his profound knowledge of the classics heard about her, and said with disdain, "This girl is only a village maiden. She could not have studied the classics or books of song. Who is she anyway?" He decided to challenge her, and shame her into silence. Hiring a boat that he loaded with classic books of song, he headed for her place. When he reached the village, he saw a lovely young girl washing laundry by the bank of the river. "Call your Maiden Liu here. I am a scholar who has come with a boatload of books to compete with her," he announced proudly.

The old scholar in the boat piled high with books was a comical sight to Liu San Mei who answered by singing in a vibrant voice,

> Washing laundry at the riversides
>   is Liu San Mei.
> Sing your mountain songs,
>   if you have any to come,
> For mountain songs
>   come only from the heart.
> Whoever heard of songs laden in a boat,
>   by river to come?

The old scholar realized that she was the maiden he sought. He had come to expose her lack of knowledge and now she was poking fun at him! He was very upset as he tried to recall her song. Hurriedly he began opening his books to find the source, for he believed all songs could be traced to the classics. Laughter and insulting remarks came from the crowd that had gathered along the bank when he failed to find her verse. They stood half the morning without hearing him utter a single verse. The old scholar was so humiliated, he ordered the boatmen to turn around and shove off.

Everyone throughout the countryside heard what had happened, and respected Maiden Liu more than ever. She loved to sing the songs of the Yao tribe and even learned their dialect. She was truly loved by the Yao people who asked her to compose many songs for their tribe. When the Yao maidens sang their love songs during the spring festival, this one was always heard:

> How learned our Liu San Mei!
> Gifted in singing and composing songs.
> The songs, she composed
> Handed down to posterity.
> Just mention her name
> Our hearts too, burst with song.

The tales of Maiden Liu spread from one person to ten, from ten to a hundred until they reached the ears of the magistrate. He strongly condemned her behavior and pronounced her singing immoral.

Then one day while Liu San Mei was working in the fields, a group of young men saw her and began to compete with her in song. One verse was answered by the other's until the whole valley echoed with their songs. People stopped to listen, unable to tear themselves away. Pathways were blocked by young and old who tarried to enjoy the wit and ability of Liu San Mei.

It so happened that the magistrate was being carried through in his sedan chair, but despite the shouts of his chair-bearers, they could not pass. The magistrate stepped down and angrily ordered the maiden to cease singing. He scolded her roundly saying, "Study the classics and sing proper songs. A dutiful maiden doesn't go about stirring up trouble."

Breaking into song, she answered lightheartedly,

> When rooster crows, he pats his chest;
> I sing to lighten my heart.
> Stuffed with classics, mute in song,
> Like covering a lantern with cowhide.

Having no suitable rebuke, the magistrate mounted his chair and ordered his men to retreat.

The Han officials not only hated her songs, they were dissatisfied with her friendship with the Yao, and tried to think of ways to destroy it. But the brave maiden overcame all obstacles. She traveled throughout the countryside where she was welcomed by the Yao, and treated as one of them.

By and by she met a young man from the White Crane Cave district of the Yao tribe. He was a diligent cowherd and a talented singer. Whenever he sang, his rich, warm voice touched the inner springs of her heart. She would burst into song to express her admiration, and they became close, beloved companions.

At one of the annual Yao festivals when drums were beaten and cymbals clashed in the villages gaily festooned with myriads of decorations, the young men wearing new dress and a beautiful bird's feather in their turbans, came together with the maidens who likewise put on their best embroidered blouses and skirts, and wrapped their legs to endure long hours of dancing. They assembled at dusk near Seven Star Cliff to sing to their hearts' content. As evening wore on people noticed in the moonlight, the silhouette of a young man and a maiden on top of the cliff. Maiden Liu and her lover could be clearly recognised. The most melodious songs ever heard, drifted from the clifftop like a crystal waterfall. Countless people listened to their singing which continued for seven days and nights. Finally, amidst the most melodious song, the couple was transformed into stone images. It was said that they became Celestial Spirits.

Her stone image and an altar for people to worship the maiden are still in the waterfall cave of the Seven Star Cliff. Every year during the spring festival, multitudes visit the cave to pay homage to the beloved songster. Many folk worship her as a Goddess Protector of Crops.

Cowherds around the Seven Star Cliff area still sing this ballad—

> Liu San Mei,
> Send us the wind.
> Where is the wind?
> In the Yellow Weed forest.
> Push away the Yellow Weed:
> Let the wind pass.

The Yao people protected themselves by concealing their true thoughts from the Han officials. Wind stood for freedom. The Yellow Weed was a derogatory term for the hated Han oppressor. Yellow was the Chinese imperial color, and used when issuing orders that were written on yellow paper or cloth.

> You give the sun,
> I, the crop;
> I give the mountain valley
> For your herd to roam.

In the last stanza, the sun was symbolic of man, the male principle. Woman produced the crops, the growth-children. Woman gave as the mountain valley for the cowherd to be nourished and his tribe to increase.

Liu San Mei possessed spirit and courage. She dared to fight for freedom on behalf of the Yao people. In fact, she stood as a symbol of friendship between the Yao and Han. Although she was a Han, she rebelled against the oppressions of the Han rulers. Her songs are eternal, remembered by all.

There are many tales about Liu San Mei told in the border regions of the Kwangtung and Kwangsi provinces in southern China.[83] Liu San Mei, a Han maiden, crossed the strong social boundary between Han and Yao people to protest her own people's oppressive treatment of the minority, the Yao. Today the Han people make up about 93 percent of the population of China. Fifty-five minority nationalities distributed over 50 to 60 percent of the territory make up the remaining 7 percent of the population.

There is a striking modern example of women crossing strong social boundaries to aid the oppressed. Jane Goodall, Dian Fossey, and Biruté Galdikas revolutionized the study of primates. For many years these women endured life in the wilds where they studied primates in their natural habitats. These women identified emotionally with the apes they studied. A groundbreaking paper of Jane Goodall's was returned to her because she used sex-appropriate pronouns, "she" and "he" instead of "it" to identify the chimpanzees she studied. Dian Fossey was killed trying to save the mountain gorillas. These women taught us about chimpanzees, mountain gorillas, and orangutans on a scientific and an emotional level. They have founded organizations to enlist our aid in keeping these species from extinction. Like Liu San Mei, these women are protesting their own people's oppression of another group.[84]

The Festival of Pouring Water

Yunnan, China[85]

> Year after year there is the Festival of Pouring Water.
> Let us see who pours upon whom

This is an old saying of the Thai people. From generation to generation to the present day, everybody throws water upon everybody else on this festival day. This is not because it is so hot, nor because people are dusty. What then is the reason? Let me tell you the story from its beginning.

Formerly there was a goblin king who was terribly cruel. If it came to his mind to kill someone, he killed him—he did whatever came to his mind. The earth has four regions, and he wanted to rule over all four of them. He had great abilities. When he was submerged in water, he was not drowned; when he was burned in fire, he did not die. No arrow, spear, or dagger could wound him. From time to time he went out to plunder and to get gold, silver, slaves, and beautiful girls, and nobody dared to stop him. He already had six wives, one more beautiful than the other; but this was still not enough for him, and so he kidnaped a seventh girl. He liked her very much, since she was even more beautiful than all the others.

One night, when he was especially delighted with her, she dared to ask him, "I have heard that you have great abilities, that water cannot drown you, fire cannot burn you, arrows, spears, and daggers cannot wound you. Does this mean that you will live forever on this earth?"

"Not necessarily so, because I too have a weak spot," the goblin king said.

"What are you afraid of, with all your abilities?" she further questioned him.

"This I will tell only you alone," he said in a low voice. "What I am afraid of is that somebody might take a hair from me and strangle me with it."

"You are not afraid of heaven, not afraid of earth. How can you be afraid of a single hair?" she asked even more daringly.

"Do not think a hair is weak. It really can strangle me," he said to her in a low voice.

When she had learned the secret, she thought, "If he really could be strangled by a hair, and if thus we could get rid of the goblin king, this

245

would be fine. We could save many more people from being mistreated by him. I will try to do it." Thus she waited until, after his pleasures, he fell into a deep sleep. Then she pulled a hair from his head, wrapped it around his neck, tied it well, and his head fell off. At this she was filled with joy.

Very soon the head of the goblin king began to roll by itself on the earth. Wherever it rolled, fire sprang up from the earth, and out of the flames numerous ghosts arose. Then the seventh wife became extremely frightened and began to scream aloud. When the other six wives heard her screaming, they all came running. One of them, a very clever girl, quickly lifted the head up. Strangely enough, once the head ceased to touch the earth, the fire and the ghosts disappeared. From then on, they did not dare to lay the head down again for fear it might roll around again. So they carried the head, one after the other in turns, each for a year. As long as the head was not completely dead, blood dripped from it.

Therefore, when after the end of a year one girl handed the head to the next one, everybody poured water over the girl in order to wash away from her body the old blood and also in order to prevent the head from starting fires again.

So it was done once every year. They poured seven times. When every girl had carried the head once, the head finally died. From then to the present day, people pour water over one another, and this is called the Festival of Pouring Water.

Working together, these women save their people. The first girl severs the head. The second girl snatches it up. The third girl carries the head for the third year. The fourth girl, the fifth girl, the sixth and the seventh, carry the head for their years. Without each and every one of these women, the goblin king would not have been conquered. These women support and help one another and in doing so create a better world.

A Polite Idiosyncrasy

Kwangtung, China[86]

An old woman went to visit a married daughter who lived with her husband's mother. She found all the family absent, except her daughter, and her daughter's mother-in-law. The mother was invited to stay and take supper with the other two women, and just after nightfall, the three sat down to take their evening meal together. They were barely seated at the table, when a gust of wind blew out the lamp and they were left in darkness. The mother-in-law said: "Sit still, both of you, and I will go and light the lamp." But while she was speaking the daughter took the lamp and went away to light it.

The mother, supposing that the mother-in-law had gone, and that her daughter sat beside her in the dark, hastened to say that, during meals, a guest should be served with the choicest of the viands. That side of the platter holding the tenderest portions of the meat, and that side of the dish on which lay the ripest of the fruit, should be turned toward the guest, so that the best might be taken, without an appearance of greediness. If the guest were one's own mother, then filial piety, as well as hospitality, required that these attentions should be scrupulously bestowed. She had scarcely given these instructions when the light reappeared, and she discovered that she had been talking, not to her daughter, but to her son-in-law's mother! Horrified by her mistake, she at once cast about in her own mind for a way of recovering the mother-in-law's respect, and then said: "I have a curious peculiarity which has afflicted me all my life. If, at any time, the light suddenly goes out, and I am left in the dark, my mind wanders and I talk without purpose till the light reappears." "Ah," responded the mother-in-law, "I wholly understand a peculiarity of that sort, for I myself have a somewhat similar one. Whenever the lamp goes out in the evening, I at once become stone-deaf, and only recover my hearing after the lamp is again lighted!"

When taken at face value, this simple conversation between two women elicits a shrug of the shoulders. Yet underneath this conversation, the effort that women make to keep relationships alive in families and communities swells like the incoming tide.

The Young Head of the Family

Kwangtung, China[87]

There was once a family consisting of a father, his three sons, and his two daughters-in-law. The two daughters-in-law, wives of the two elder sons, had but recently been brought into the house, and were both from one village a few miles away. Having no mother-in-law living, they had to appeal to their father-in-law whenever they wished to visit their former homes, and as they were lonesome and homesick they perpetually bothered the old man by asking leave of absence.

Vexed by these constant petitions, he set himself to invent a method of putting an end to them, and at last gave them leave in this wise: "You are always begging me to allow you to go and visit your mothers, and thinking that I am very hard-hearted because I do not let you go. Now you may go, but only upon condition that when you come back you will each bring me something I want. The one shall bring me some fire wrapped in paper, and the other some wind in a paper. Unless you promise to bring me these, you are never to ask me to let you go home; and if you go and fail to get these for me, you are never to come back."

The old man did not suppose that these conditions would be accepted, but the girls were young and thoughtless, and in their anxiety to get away did not consider the impossibility of obtaining the articles required. So they made ready with speed, and in great glee started off on foot to visit their mothers. After they had walked a long distance; chatting about what they should do and whom they should see in their native village, the high heel of one of them slipped from under her foot, and she fell down. Owing to this mishap both stopped to adjust the misplaced foot-gear, and while doing this the conditions under which alone they could return to their husbands came to mind, and they began to cry.

While they sat there crying by the roadside a young girl came riding along from the fields on a water-buffalo. She stopped and asked them what was the matter, and whether she could help them. They told her she could do them no good; but she persisted in offering her sympathy and inviting their confidence, till they told her their story, and then she at once said that if they would go home with her she would show them a way out of their trouble. Their case seemed so hopeless to themselves, and the child was so sure of her own power to help them, that they finally accompanied her to

248

her father's house, where she showed them how to comply with their father-in-law's demand.

For the first a paper lantern only would be needed. When lighted, it would be a fire, and its paper surface would compass the blaze, so that it would truly be "some fire wrapped in paper." For the second, a paper fan would suffice. When flapped, wind would issue from it, and the "wind wrapped in paper" could thus be carried to the old man.

The two young women thanked the wise child, and went on their way rejoicing. After a pleasant visit to their old homes, they took a lantern and a fan, and returned to their father-in-law's house. As soon as he saw them he began to vent his anger at their light regard for his commands, but they assured him that they had perfectly obeyed him, and showed him that what they had brought fulfilled the conditions prescribed. Much astonished, he inquired how it was that they had suddenly become so astute, and they told him the story of their journey, and of the little girl that had so opportunely come to their relief. He inquired whether the little girl was already betrothed, and, finding that she was not, engaged a go-between to see if he could get her for a wife for his youngest son.

Having succeeded in securing the girl as a daughter-in-law, he brought her home, and told all the rest of the family that as there was no mother in the house, and as this girl had shown herself to be possessed of extraordinary wisdom, she should be the head of the household.

The wedding festivities being over, the sons of the old man were to return to their usual occupations on the farm; but, according to their father's order, they came to the young bride for instructions. She told them that they were never to go to or from the fields empty-handed. When they went they must carry fertilizers of some sort for the land, and when they returned they must bring bundles of sticks for fuel. They obeyed, and soon had the land in fine condition, and so much fuel gathered that none need be bought. When there were no more sticks, roots, or weeds to bring, she told them to bring stones instead; and they soon accumulated an immense pile of stones, which were heaped in a yard near their house.

One day an expert in the discovery of precious stones came along, and saw in this pile a block of jade of great value. In order to get possession of this stone at a small cost he undertook to buy the whole heap, pretending that he wished to use them in building. The little head of the family asked an exorbitant price for them, and as he could not induce her to take less, he promised to pay her the sum she asked, and to come two days later to bring the money and to remove the stones. That night the girl thought about the reason for the buyer's being willing to pay so large a sum for the stones, and concluded that the heap must contain a gem. The next morning she sent her father-in-law to invite the buyer to supper, and she instructed the men of her family in regard to his entertainment. The best of wine was to be provided, and the father-in-law was to induce him to talk of precious stones, and to cajole him into telling in what way they were to be distinguished from other stones.

The head of the family, listening behind a curtain, heard how the valuable stone in her heap could be discovered. She hastened to find and remove it from the pile; and when her guest had recovered from the effect of the banquet he saw that the value had departed from his purchase. He went to negotiate again with the seller, and she conducted the conference with such skill that she got the price originally agreed upon for the heap of stones and a large sum besides for the one in her possession.

The family, having become wealthy, built an ancestral hall of fine design and elaborate workmanship, and put the words "No Sorrow," as an inscription over the entrance. Soon after, a Mandarin passed that way, and, noticing this remarkable inscription, had his sedan-chair set down, that he might inquire who were the people that professed to have no sorrow. He sent for the head of the family, and was much surprised on seeing so young a woman thus appear, and said: "Yours is a singular family. I have never before seen one without sorrow, nor one with so young a head. I will fine you for your impudence. Go and weave me a piece of cloth as long as this road."

"Very well," responded the little woman; "so soon as your Excellency shall have found the two ends of the road, and informed me as to the number of feet in its length, I will at once begin the weaving."

Finding himself at fault, the Mandarin added, "And I also fine you as much oil as there is water in the sea."

"Certainly," responded the woman; "as soon as you shall have measured the sea, and sent me correct information as to the number of gallons, I will at once begin to press out the oil from my beans."

"Indeed!" said the Mandarin. "Since you are so sharp, perhaps you can penetrate my thoughts. If you can, I will fine you no more. I hold this pet quail in my hand; now tell me whether I mean to squeeze it to death or to let it fly in the air."

"Well," said the woman, "I am an obscure commoner, and you are a famed magistrate; if you are no more knowing than I, you have no right to fine me at all. Now I stand with one foot on one side of my threshold and the other foot on the other side; tell me whether I mean to go in or to come out. If you cannot guess my riddle, you should not require me to guess yours."

Being unable to guess her intention the Mandarin took his departure. The family lived long in opulence and good repute under its chosen head.

At the end of this story, the young head of the family is tested by an angry magistrate. In replying to him, the young woman understands his most basic assumption and uses her knowledge to outwit him. She understands that he assumes he is superior to her. She states his opinion: "I am an obscure commoner, and you are a famed magistrate . . . " She carries it one step further: "if you are no more knowing than I, you have no right to fine me at all." This young head of the family has the ability to understand assumptions. She is able to get to the heart of the situation without rancor.

As far back as I remember, I was encouraged to be nice, polite, and good like Cinderella. My opinions and ideas were so caught up in obeying these social injunctions that I lost the ability to get to the heart of a situation. I became threatened and angry when faced with a situation where the image of what I "should" be conflicted with who I felt I "was." The key to overcoming the resulting feeling of helplessness lay in understanding the assumptions that went into the situation. When one has gotten to the heart of the matter, then like this heroine, one can agree to make the cloth once the Mandarin has measured the road.

Altyn-Aryg

Altaian People, Siberia[88]

Once there lived a tsar named Kara-Kan, who, while he had many subjects and herds, possessed but one daughter, Altyn-Aryg. When this tsar grew old he said, "I have no sons and my strength is leaving me; my daughter cannot govern a numerous people, and will not be able to look after so many cattle. Let the underground father take for himself half my people and half my herd." The daughter retorted, "Why cannot I rule all the people and manage the whole herd?" "The task is too great." "If you will not give me my people and my herd, I will not live with you; I will depart to another land."

Setting forth, despite her parents' grief, she arrived at the kingdom of a certain hero, and called at his house. They greeted one another, and the hero said, "Tell me whose daughter you are?" The maiden answered, "I am the daughter of Kara-Kan and by name Altyn-Aryg; and what is your name?" The hero answered, "Maiden, I am called 'The Well-meaning Altyn-Kan.' Whither are you going?" The maiden replied, "I have come a long way and will go further; I must find and kill the Tsar-snake. If he is fated to die, he will die; if I am fated to die, I shall die. He, the Tsar-snake, is strong and has overcome many tsars; he collects tribute from many lands; foreign heroes fear him, and weep and pay him tribute." Sooner or later Altyn-Aryg reached the domain of the Tsar-snake and caught sight of him in an uninhabited valley. The tip of the Tsar-snake's lower jaw lay on the ground and the tip of his upper jaw reached the sky.

Altyn-Aryg, like the others, approached and entered the jaws, within which she saw many live persons and birds and beasts. Having reached the Tsar-snake's heart, she turned to the heroes, said, "How could one kill him?" One of them answered, "Lady, we cannot kill him, but will you not test your strength?" The girl called for a sword and a hero handed her one. Then she struck at the Tsar-snake's heart, but did not kill him, because the sword broke. Taking out her own sword, she cried to the heroes, "See what will be!" With these words she struck and the Snake died, whereupon she issued forth from his jaws, the birds flew away and the wild beasts ran off. When the heroes came out they said, "Your life will be indestructible and your grave renowned! You have done a beneficent action, and saved us; we will pay you tribute." The girl answered, "Heroes! I do not require your tribute. Go and resume your former lives."

Altyn-Aryg took away with her the herdsmen and the cattle, and returned to the home of her father and mother, who, at the moment of her arrival, were celebrating a feast; eating and drinking and making merry. The father said, "Where have you been, my daughter?" She related how she had slain the Tsar-snake. Praising her highly, the father said, "It is well that you have used your strength to free the souls of birds and beasts and heroes. I give you now my people and my herds, for I am weak and expect to die." The maiden received the full inheritance, and when her father died she buried him and had a funeral repast; then, weeping and sobbing, she grieved over her loneliness. After some time had elapsed a hero approached and, greeting her, said "Will you be my wife?" She replied, "What sort of person are you and have you a father and a mother?" The answer came, "I have neither father nor mother and my name is 'Katkauchyl, the rider of the lion-horse.'" Altyn-Aryg agreed to the proposal, but after a banquet the hero confessed that he had no domain; however, he would be willing to live on his wife's estate. The wife replied, "My people and my property will be at your disposition." And they began to live.

Altyn-Aryg demands her inheritance and won't take half for an answer. "If you will not give me my people and my herd, I will not live with you. . . ." She proves herself better than all the heroes who went before her into the Tsar-snake's jaws. The full inheritance is hers in the end.

On August 31, 1962, an African-American woman, Fannie Lou Hamer, walked into the registrar's office in Indianola, Mississippi, and demanded her right to vote. As a result, she and her family were evicted from their home and shot at, but Fannie Lou Hamer continued her walk into the monster's jaws, she became a civil rights activist. Women have fought and continue to fight for their rights.[89]

The Wife Who Stole a Heart

Kalmuck People, Siberia[90]

In former times there ruled over a great kingdom called Iksvakuvardhana a khan known as "The Enlightened." After his death he was succeeded on the throne by his son, a valiant and handsome youth, endowed with both power and splendour, and married to the daughter of a khan ruling a southerly district. But the young khan did not love his wife. At the distance of a mile a bewitching girl of womanly form was dwelling with her father, and for her the young ruler developed the warmest feelings of love. Thus it came to pass that after his long continued friendship the object of his devotion was likely to become a mother. But, in consequence of a severe illness, the khan passed out of her life, and the girl was ignorant of what had happened to him. Once, well after nightfall, when the moon's rays relieved the darkness, there was a knock at the maiden's door. The girl, with a beaming countenance, looked up and saw the young khan, who had discarded his usual attire. Experiencing supreme joy, she went forward to greet him, took him by the hand and led him into her room. After he had refreshed himself with rice spirit and bread and the other food which she set before him, he said, "Wife, come outside," and when she followed him he called again, "Come further." He gradually enticed her further and further with his conversation, and they approached near to the khan's town, from the interior of which came loud sounds of clashing cymbals and of kettledrums. The maiden asked what the noise meant. He answered, "Do you not know? They are preparing my death-sacrifice." "Preparing your death-sacrifice? What has happened to the young khan?" "He is dead, and you will be," he continued, "delivered of a son in my elephant stall. In the palace my mother and my wife are in conflict on account of a precious stone, which lies concealed under the sacrificial table. Give it to my wife and send her back to her relations! My mother and you should together seize and hold the reins of government, till our little son has grown up." After these words he vanished.

The astonished and afflicted girl fell down in a faint; but, recovering, rose and cried in a loud voice, "Khan, khan!" Soon the pains of labour fell upon her and she dragged herself into the elephant stall, and during the night bore a son. In the morning the elephants' attendants arrived and said, "This will not do! A woman has entered the khan's elephant stall! Her coming will interfere with the elephants." But the woman said to one of them, "Go to the khan's mother and request her presence here." The man acted accordingly, and the princess-mother came. The woman related to her the whole story. "Ah," cried the princess, "the desire for posterity is astounding! Let us make our way to the house," and she took the woman with her and tended her carefully and showed her all honour. As the jewel was discovered in the spot indicated by the girl, the princess put confidence in her, and giving the precious stone to the former wife, sent her back to her relatives. The mother and the new wife now worked together for the success of the kingdom.

Every month, on the fifteenth, the khan came to his wife and stayed with her till dawn, when it was his custom to disappear. She related this to his mother, who replied, "It is not true; if it is true, exhibit a proof of it." When the wife produced indubitable evidence, the princess-mother said, "Daughter, see whether you can arrange an opportunity for us, mother and son, to speak with one another."

When, on the fifteenth day of the month, the khan appeared, his wife said to him, "It is well for us to meet on the fifteenth of every month; but, I am bold enough to say, it is unfortunate that we do not live more completely united," and she burst into a fit of weeping. The khan replied, "If you have courage to undertake a hazardous enterprise, a steady union will be possible; but for a woman perseverance is difficult and irksome." The wife exclaimed, "I have already shown that I could run risk; if in this life a constant mutual happiness be possible for me and you, I will over-come all obstacles; I will even allow my flesh to be torn from my bones." "Very well," said the khan, "if upon the fifteenth day of next month, when the moon augments her light, you will go about a mile in a southerly direction, you will find an iron old man, who, after he has swallowed molten metal, will cry out, 'I have a terrible thirst!' Give him rice-spirits. A little further on you will come upon two rams in conflict; give them yeast cakes. Continuing on your way, you will meet a troop in coats of mail; give them meat and cakes. If you walk forwards, you will arrive at an enormous black building, whose floor is soaked with blood. A banner made of human skin is waving over it and at the gate stand two bloody and hairy servants of the Judge of the infernal regions; give each of them a bloody sacrifice! Further in the interior of the edifice is, in the middle of a circle formed of eight fearful magicians, a magical enchanter, sur-rounded by nine hearts. 'Take me, take me!' eight old hearts will say; but 'Take me not!' a new heart will say. Without fear or trepidation, take the new heart! Then if you, casting no look backwards, retreat immediately it is possible that we shall remain for ever in this life united." Such were his words.

The wife fixed them in her mind, and, on the night of the fifteenth, when the moon was increasing the force of her beams, she stepped forth, unnoticed, toward the south. She gave the dues to the various beings on the way, and reached the interior of the building. When she had taken the new heart, which called out "Take me not," she fled, holding the pulsating heart. Two magicians pursued her, and called to the servants who guarded the gate, "A theft has been made of a heart; hold her fast!" But the two servants replied, "This woman has given us a bloody sacrifice," and they let her pass. When the magicians called next to the troop of armed men to secure her, the men answered, "She has given us meat and cakes," and did not molest her. When the pair of rams were appealed to, they refused to interfere, saying, "She gave us yeast cakes." Lastly, when the magicians appealed for assistance to the iron old man and shouted to him, "Seize her, she has carried off a heart!" he replied, "She gave me strong drink," nor did he impede her progress. The woman ran fearlessly and, reaching home and opening the khan's door, beheld her husband, the khan, in ravishing attire. All had happened as the pair desired, and they fell on each other's necks with passionate embraces.

A mistress ousts the wife, becomes the recognized wife, and rules the kingdom with her mother-in-law. Against high odds, she has assured the posterity of her child. I identified strongly with the displaced first wife but had to admit the valor of the heroine when she faces an iron old man who swallows molten metal, servants standing on a bloody floor under a banner of human skin, and eight fearful magicians. I don't like to think of myself as competing with other women, but, to get my wonderful husband, I did compete.

For years, theories of evolution strongly linked male competition with evolution. Males have the capability to produce many offspring, therefore male competition was seen as the determining factor in evolution. It was assumed that females consistently had as many offspring as they could and were too busy with their babies to contribute to the social organization. Reacting to the focus on male competition, but using the assumption of female noncompetition, some women conceived of an idealized matriarchical society where women ruled a rational, peaceful world. Primatologist Sara Hrdy insists that competition between females has always existed and is an important element in the continuing evolution of human beings.[91]

Tales
from
the Pacific

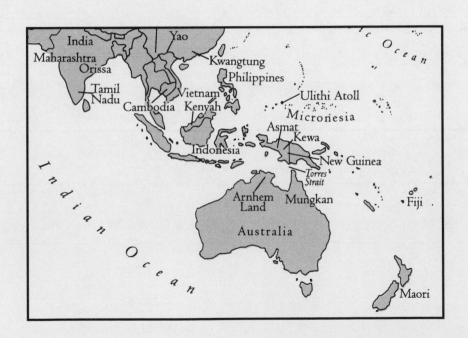

Hiiaka Catching a Ghost

Hawaii[92]

Hiiaka, the sister of Pele, and the goddess of ferns, and their new friend Wahine-omao, were hastening through the forests above the bay of Hilo. They came near a native house. Two girls were lying on a mat near the doorway. The girls saw the strangers and with hearts full of hospitality cried: "O women strangers, stop at our house and eat. Here are dried fish and the kilu-ai (a-little-calabash-full-of-poi, the native food)." It was all the food the girls had, but they offered it gladly. Hiiaka said: "One of us will stop and eat. Two of us will pass on. We are not hungry." The truth was that Wahine-omao of the light skin needed food like any one not possessing semi-divine powers.

So Wahine-omao stopped and ate. She saw that the girls were kupi-likia (stirred-up-with anxiety) and asked them why they were troubled.

"Our father," they said, "went to the sea to fish in the night and has not returned. We fear that he is in trouble."

Hiiaka heard the words and looked toward the sea. She saw the spirit of that man coming up from the beach with an ipu-holoholona (a-cal-abash-for-carrying-fish-lines, etc.) in his hands.

She charged the girls to listen carefully while she told them about their father, saying: "You must not let tears fall or wailing tones come into your voices. Your father has been drowned in the sea during the dark night. The canoe filled with water. The swift-beating waters drove your father on to the reef of coral and there his body lies. The spirit was returning home, but now sees strangers and is turning aside. I will go and chase that spirit from place to place until it goes back to the place where it left its house—the body supposed to be dead. Let no one eat until my work is done."

Hiiaka looked again toward the sea. The spirit was wandering aimlessly from place to place with its calabash thrown over its shoulder. It was afraid to come near the strangers and yet did not want to go back to the body. Hiiaka hastened after the ghost and drove it toward the house where the girls were living. She checked it as it turned to either side and tried to dash away into the forest. She pushed it into the door and called the girls in. They saw the ghost as if it were the natural body. They wept and began to beseech Hiiaka to bring him back to life.

She told them she would try, but they must remember to keep the bundle of tears inside the eyes. She told them that the spirit must take her to the body and they must wait until the rainbow colors of a divine chief came over their house. Then they would know that their father was alive. But if a heavy rain should fall they would know he was not alive and need not restrain their cries.

As Hiiaka rose to pass out of the door the ghost leaped and disappeared. Hiiaka rushed out and saw the ghost run to the sea. She leaped after it and followed it to a great stone lying at the foot of a steep precipice. There the heana (dead body) was lying. It was badly torn by the rough coral and the face had been bitten by eels. Around it lay the broken pieces of the shattered canoe. Hiiaka washed the body in the sea and then turned to look for the ghost, but it was running away as if carried by a whirlwind.

Hiiaka thrust out her "strong hand of Kilauea." This meant her power as one of the divine family living in the fire of the volcano. She thrust forth this power and turned the spirit back to the place where the body was lying. She drove the ghost to the side of the body and ordered it to enter, but the ghost thought that it would be a brighter and happier life if it could be free among the blossoming trees and fragrant ferns of the forest, so tried again to slip away from the house in which it had lived.

Hiiaka slapped the ghost back against the body and told it to go in at the bottom of a foot. She slapped the feet again and again, but it was very hard to push the ghost inside. It tried to come out as fast as Hiiaka pushed it in. Then Hiiaka uttered an incantation, while she struck the feet and limbs. The incantation was a call for the gift of life from her friends of the volcano.

> "O the top of Kilauea!
> O the five ledges of the pit!
> The taboo fire of the woman.
> When the heavens shake,
> When the earth cracks open (earthquakes)
> Man is thrown down,
> Lying on the ground.
> The lightning of Kane (a great god) wakes up.
> Kane of the night, going fast.
> My sleep is broken up.
> E ala e! Wake up!
> The heaven wakes up.
> The earth inland is awake.
> The sea is awake.
>   Awake you.
>   Here am I."—Amama (The prayer is done).

By the time this chant was ended Hiiaka had forced the ghost up to the hips. There was a hard struggle—the ghost trying to go back and yet yielding to the slapping and going further and further into the body.

Then Hiiaka put forth her hand and took fresh water, pouring it over the body, chanting again:

> "I make you grow, O Kane!
> Hiiaka is the prophet.
> This work is hers.
> She makes the growth.
> Here is the water of life.
> E ala e! Awake! Arise!
> Let life return.
> The taboo (of death) is over.
> It is lifted,
> It has flown away."—Amama.

—These were ancient chants for the restoration of life.—

All this time she was slapping and pounding the spirit into the body. It had gone up as far as the chest. Then she took more fresh water and poured it over the eyes, dashing it into the face. The ghost leaped up to the mouth and eyes—choking noises were made—the eyes opened faintly and closed again, but the ghost was entirely in the body. Slowly life returned. The lips opened and breath came back.

The healing power of Hiiaka restored the places wounded by coral rocks and bitten by eels. Then she asked him how he had been overcome. He told her he had been fishing when a great kupua* came in the form of a mighty wave falling upon the boat, filling it full of water.

The fisherman said that he had tried to bail the water out of his canoe, when it was hurled down into the coral caves, and he knew nothing more until the warm sun shone in his face and his eyes opened. Hiiaka told him to stand up, and putting out her strong hand lifted him to his feet.

He stood shaking and trembling, trying to move his feet. Little by little the power of life came back and he walked slowly to his house.

Hiiaka called for the glory of a divine chief to shine around them. Among the ancient Hawaiians it was believed that the eyes of prophets could tell the very family to which a high chief belonged by the color or peculiar appearance of the light around the individual even when a long distance away. Thus the watching anxious girls and the friends of Hiiaka

---

* *Kupuas*, legendary monsters that could change themselves into human beings at will. They were always ready to destroy and often devour any strangers passing near them. Peculiar rocks, trees, precipices, waterfalls, or birds might be given human and supernatural power and called kupuas.

knew that the ghost had gone back into the body and the fisherman had been brought back to life.

Hiiaka is a goddess of great power but she is also intimately connected to the world. Hiiaka leaps after the escaping spirit, drives it to the side of the body, and orders it to enter. She doesn't simply command, she physically slaps the ghost back against the body. Her incantation is only one part of this resurrection. Again and again she slaps and pounds the ghost into the body. It is hard work. Finally, the ghost leaps up to the mouth and eyes and life returns; Hiiaka has raised the fisherman from the dead. The story does not finish with this amazing accomplishment. To stop here would leave the focus on the goddess's power, but Hiiaka's motivation, her compassion, is equally as important. She considerately uses her healing powers to restore the parts of the body torn by the rough coral and bitten by eels. She takes the time to make an emotional connection with the fisherman and asks him to tell his story, even though she already knows every detail of what happened. As they walk slowly toward the fisherman's house, Hiiaka causes the glory of a divine chief to shine around them. She does this not only as a sign of her power, but also to relieve the anxiety of the fisherman's daughters. Hiiaka's compassion is intimately connected with her power.

Hiiaka and the Seacoast Kupuas

Hawaii[93]

Makaukiu

Hiiaka, the sister of Pele, the goddess of volcanoes, by her magic power was able to find and destroy many of these mysterious monsters (kupuas). She had two companions as she journeyed along the eastern coast of the island Hawaii. Their way was frequently very wearisome as they climbed down steep precipices into valleys and gulches and then had to climb up on the other side.

In one valley beautiful clear sea-water invited the girls to bathe. Two of them threw aside their tapa* clothes and ran down to the beach. Hiiaka bade them wait, telling them this was the home of Makaukiu, a very ferocious monster. But the girls thought they could see any evil one, if living in that pure, clear water, so they laughed at their friend and went to the edge of the water. Hiiaka took some fragrant ti-leaves,° made a little bundle and threw it into the sea. The girls made ready to leap and swim, when suddenly Makaukiu appeared just below the surface, catching and shaking the leaves.

The girls fled inland to higher ground, but Hiiaka stood at the edge of the sea. The sea monster tried to catch her in his great mouth. He lashed the water into foam, trying to strike her with his tail. He tried to wash her into the sea by pushing great, whirling waves against her, but Hiiaka struck him with the mighty forces of lightning and fire which she had in her magic skirt. Soon he was dead and his body floated on the water until the tide swept it out to sink in the deep sea. The place where this monster was slain was given his name and is still called "The Swimming-Hole of Makaukiu."

Mahiki

The Hawaiians say that the desire for battle was burning in the heart of Hiiaka and she longed to kill Mahiki, who lived near Waipio Valley—one of the most beautiful of all the valleys of the Hawaiian Islands.

---

* *Tapa*, a coarse cloth made in the Pacific islands from the pounded bark of certain plants, usually decorated with geometric patterns.
° *Ti*, a woody plant with terminal tufts of elongated leaves.

Mahiki was a whirlwind. When he saw the girls coming he fled inland, hiding himself in a cloud of dust. Whenever the girls came toward him he fled swiftly to a new place. They could not catch and destroy him.

As they were following the whirlwind they heard some one calling. They stopped and found two persons without bones—the bodies were flesh, soft and yielding, yet of human form. Hiiaka had pity on them, so she took the ribs of a long leaf and pushed them into the soft bodies, where they became bones. Then the two could stand. After a time they could use their new bones in their legs and walk.

Pili and Noho

Hiiaka remembered that there were two dragons in the river Wailuku, a river of swift cascades and beautiful waterfalls near Hilo, so she turned back filled with the wish to destroy them and free the people from that danger.

At the place where the people crossed the river were two things which looked like large, flat logs tossing in the water. Any person wishing to cross the river would lay fish, sweet potatoes, and other kinds of food on the logs. When these things disappeared the logs would act sometimes as a bridge and sometimes as a boat, taking those who had given presents across the river. These logs were the great tongues of the dragons Pili-a-moo and Noho-a-moo, i.e., the dragon Pili and the dragon Noho.

Hiiaka and her two companions came to the river side. The travellers called for an open way across.

One dragon said to the other, "Here comes one of our family."

The other said: "What of that? She can cross if she pays. If she does not give our price, she shall not go over in this place."

Hiiaka ordered the dragons to prepare her way, but they refused. Then she taunted them as slaves, ordering them to bring vegetable food and fish. The dragons became angry and thrashed the water into whirlpools, trying to catch the travellers and pull them into the river. The people from far and near gathered to the place of this strange conflict.

A chief laughed at Hiiaka, saying, "These are dragon-gods, and yet you dispute with them!"

Hiiaka said, "Yes, they are dragon-gods, but when I attack them they will die."

The chief offered to make any bet desired that she could not injure the dragons.

Hiiaka said, "I have no property, but I wager my body, my life, against your property that the dragons die."

Then began a great conflict along the banks and in the swift waters.

Hiiaka struck the dragons with her magic skirt in which was concealed the divine power of lightning. They tried to escape, but Hiiaka struck again and again and killed them, changing the bodies into blocks of stone. Then she called the chief, saying, "I have made the way safe for your people and you; I give back your property and the land of the dragons."

Hiiaka and her friends turned north again and hastened to Waipio Valley to catch Mahiki—the demon of the whirlwind. He ran down to meet her and threw dust all over them, then fled inland to the mountains. Hiiaka chanted:

> "I am above Waipio,
> My eyes look sharply down.
> I have gone along the path
> By the sea of Makaukiu,
> Full flowing like the surf.
> I have seen Mahiki,
> I have seen that he is evil,
> Evil, very evil indeed."

Moo-Lau

Then Hiiaka thought of Moo-lau, who was the great dragon-god of the district Kohala. He had a great multitude of lesser gods as his servants. Hiiaka clearly and sweetly called for the dragon-gods to prepare a way for her and also to bring gifts for herself and her companions. Moo-lau answered, "You have no path through my lands unless you have great strength or can pay the price."

Then began one of the great legendary battles of ancient Hawaiian folklore. Hiiaka, throwing aside her flower-wreaths and common clothes, took her lightning pa-u (skirt) and attacked Moo-lau. He fought her in his dragon form. He breathed fierce winds against her. He struck her with his swift-moving tail. He tried to catch her between his powerful jaws. He coiled and twisted and swiftly whirled about, trying to knock her down, but she beat him with her powerful hands in which dwelt some of the divine power of volcanoes. She struck his great body with her magic skirt in which dwelt the power of the lightning. Each pitted supernatural powers against the other. Each struck with magic force and each threw out magic strength to ward off deadly blows. They became tired, very tired, and, turning away from each other, sought rest. Again they fought and again rested. Hiiaka chanted an incantation, or call for help:

> "Moo-lau has a dart
> Of the wood of the uhi-uhi;

A god is Moo-lau,
Moo-lau is a god!"

This was a spirit-call going out from Hiiaka. It broke through the clouds hanging on the sides of the mountains. It pierced the long, long way to the crater of Kilauea. It roused the followers of the fire-goddess. A host of destructive forces, swift as lightning, left the pit of fire to aid Hiiaka.

Meanwhile Moo-lau had sent his people to spy out the condition of Hiiaka. Then he called for all the reptile gods of his district to help him. He rallied all the gnomes and evil powers he could order to come to his aid and make a mighty attack.

When the battle seemed to be going against her, suddenly the Ho-ai-ku men and the Ho-ai-ka women, the destructive gnomes from the crater, broke in a storm upon Moo-lau and his demons. Oh, how the little people from the pit devoured and destroyed the dragon army! The slaughter of the reptile horde was quickly accomplished and Hiiaka soon saw the body of her enemy the dragon-god trampled underfoot.

When the god Mahiki saw that Moo-lau was slain and his army defeated he raised a great cloud of dust and fled far off around the western side of the island. The whirlwind was one of the earth-monsters which even the sister of the goddess of volcanoes could not destroy.

Many were the evil demi-gods who tried to hinder Hiiaka in her journey along the east coast of the island Hawaii. Sharks fought her from the seas. The gnomes and dragons of valley and forest tried to destroy her. Even birds of evil omen came into the fight against her, but she conquered and killed until the land was freed from its enemies and the people of the districts along the sea could journey in comparative safety.

Pau-o-palae, the goddess of ferns, met the chief of this land which had been freed from the power of the dragon. She saw him swimming in the sea and, forgetting her companions, leaped in to sport with him. They at once decided to be married. Then she turned aside to his new home, leaving Hiiaka and Wahine-omao to go on after Lohiau.

"Yes, they are dragon-gods, but when I attack them they will die." Hiiaka wields the forces of lightning and fire; the desire for battle burns in her heart. She has the kind of power normally associated with more famous male gods. But she is not like the Norse god, Thor, or the Greek god, Zeus, who often used their lightning bolts to display their power. Hiiaka is raw power motivated by compassion. Primed for battle with the destructive whirlwind, the goddess drops everything to help two boneless people. Hiiaka throws her lightning bolts to help others. She frees the land from evildoers and makes the land safe for people.

A Calabash of Poi

Hawaii[94]

One of the disguises which Pele, the goddess of fire, was fond of assuming was that of an aged hag. In fact, it was hardly a disguise at all, for Pele was as old as the hills themselves; besides her quick temper and natural jealousy had furrowed her face with deep, hard lines, which a bitter disposition imprints upon a face, quite irrespective of its age. On this day Pele was intent upon a secret mission, and, taking a gnarled branch of the *koa*-tree for a cane, she trudged at a rather brisk pace down the mountain-side. Only on approaching two Hawaiian houses of varying pretensions did she slacken her speed and finally pause at the outer palisade of the first.

It was a sizable house,—or *hale*,—as Hawaiian houses go, perhaps fifty feet long with its side thatched with *ti*-leaves—a sign of rank. Its only window, a small aperture about a foot square, looked out on a carefully planted *taro* patch, while rows of tasselled cocoanut palms and fruit-laden banana plants made a pretty background to the setting.

Pele paused for a moment to make a mental summary of the growing crop, and then grasping her cane, hobbled to the threshold.

"Aloha," she said to the small group of people sitting within the doorway.

"Aloha," was the reply in a not over-cordial tone of voice.

Pele waited—apparently there was to be no invitation to enter or to refresh herself.

"I have walked many miles," she said finally, assuming a small and feeble voice. "I am very hungry. Perhaps you have as much as a calabash of *poi**** for me."

"We are very sorry, but we have no *poi*," said the Hawaiian chief, for such was the master of the house. "Besides our evening meal is *pau*."°

"Then, perhaps, a small piece of salted fish?"

"No, nor fish," was the short rejoinder.

"Then, at least, some ripe *ohelo*† berries for I am parched with thirst."

---

* *Poi*, a paste made of bread-fruit or sweet potatoes, baked, pounded, and mixed with a little water and left to slightly ferment. It is then mixed with more water until it has the consistency of a mucilaginous paste.

° *Pau*, finished.

† *Ohelo*, Hawaiian blueberry with a shining red or yellow berry.

"Our berries are all green, as you can see for yourself, providing your eyes are not too dimmed by age."

Pele's eyes were far from dim! She suppressed with an effort the flashes of fire that ordinarily blazed in their black depths at a moment's provocation and, bowing low, made her way in silence to the gate. Passing a few steps further down the hard road, she entered a smaller and less thrifty garden and paused on the threshold of a small hut. The work of the day as well as the evening meal was over, and the family of bronzed-skinned boys and girls played about the man and woman who sat watching in rapt attention the last golden rays of the sun sinking in a riot of color behind the gentle slopes of Mauna Loa.

"Ah, I see your evening meal is past," sighed Pele. "I am sorry for I am both tired and hungry, and had hoped for a little refreshment after a day's walk down the steep mountain."

"Neither fish nor *awa** have we," promptly said the poor fisherman, "but to such as we have you are most welcome."

Almost before he had concluded these few words, his wife had risen, motioned Pele to a place on the mat and set before her a large calabash of *poi*.

Pele did not wait for a further invitation but fell to eating with much relish. Dipping her fore-finger in the calabash, she raised it dripping with *poi*, waved her finger dexterously in the air wrapping the mucilaginous *poi* about it, and placed it in her mouth. She seemed to finish the entire contents in no time and, looking up, remarked:

"I am still hungry. Would it be too much to ask for another calabash?"

Again the woman arose and placed before her a second calabash of *poi* not perhaps as large as the first but filled to the brim.

Again Pele emptied the calabash with great relish. Wishing to test the extent of their patience and generosity, she sighed as she finished the last mouthful, calling attention to the empty calabash in her lap.

This time a third calabash smaller than the second—but quite full, was placed before her.

Pele finished half of the third calabash, arose heavily to her feet, and, pausing before the chief, she uttered these words:

"When your neighbor plants *taro*, it shall wither upon its stem. His bananas shall hang as green fingers upon the stalk, and the cocoanuts shall fall upon his favorite pig. When you plant *taro* at night, you may pull it in the morning. Your cane shall mature over night and your

---

* *Awa*, an intoxicating drink.

bananas ripen in one day's sunshine. You may have as many crops as there are days in the year!"

Saying these words, Pele trudged out of the gate and was seen to disappear toward Ha-le-mau-mau in a cloud of flame.

When the astonished fisherman passed beyond the threshold of his hut on the following morning, yellow bananas hung on the new plants, the full grown *taro* stood ready to be pulled, and the cane-cuttings reached to the eaves of his house. Looking across at his rich and powerful neighbor, he saw that, indeed, the curse of Pele had already descended upon him. In place of the rich man's prosperous acres stood the sun-parched remnants of but yesterday's proud crop.

"There, children," said Alec, the old half-breed guide, "Whether you'se believes in the ole lady Pele or not, don't you ever forgit to be nice to the ole folks. It just might be Pele. You'se can't always tells."

Similar stories appear in Europe. Someone like Jesus or St. Peter disguises himself, tests a rich person and a poor person and judges them on their responses. Jesus and St. Peter are not the heroes; they are the hero-makers. They set the standards for the hero's test. They are part of the structure of the tale, the background; it is simply assumed that they are powerful and just. In this Hawaiian story, the judge—the goddess Pele—is female. Because she is powerful and just, she sets the standards. Yet, it was so unusual to have a woman in the role of divine judge, I viewed Pele as the heroine. To me she was not simply part of the structure, the background. I felt relief and freedom when I identified with the person in control rather than the person having to measure up. This gender reversal of the judge made me recognize how implicit the male's power is and how much influence this assumption has had on my subconscious.

Rau-Whato

Maori People, New Zealand[95]

The story of Rau-whato goes back some two hundred years. She was the wife of Turi-roa, a descendant of Tu-wharetoa, the great founder of the Taupo tribe. The young couple lived happily with their people in the Poniu pa on the northern shore of Lake Taupo. One night the pa* was surprised by a raiding party of Ngati-raukawa. The taua° fell on the unsuspecting pa, most of the defenders were killed, and a few were taken as slaves. In the darkness and confusion Turi-roa led his wife and young son down to the beach and along the shore to a shallow cave in the headland. It was a poor refuge, but there was no other way of escape. The canoes had been destroyed by the Ngati-raukawa, whose chief knew of the existence of the cave in the cliff. It was only a short respite that the fugitives could hope to enjoy.

"I cannot escape," Turi-roa told his wife. "But you must try for the sake of our son. You are a strong swimmer. I will tie the boy on to your back and you must try to cross the lake to your mother's home."

Rau-whato removed her waist cloth, and Turi-roa folded it and bound it firmly on her shoulders as a pad. The child was lashed tightly to it. A last embrace and the young woman slipped into the chilly water and began her long swim. Barely had she left the shore than the leader of the raiding party and some of his men surrounded the cave. Turi-roa inquired why they had raided Poniu pa. He was told the reason and submitted to the inevitable. As he gave up his life he knew that his wife and son had escaped undetected.

The kindly atua† protected the courageous young woman. After five long miles of exhausting toil she felt a flat rock under her hands and drew herself wearily on to it. She had reached the shore close to the pa where her mother lived. She was taken in and warmed and comforted, but her only thought was for the lad for whom she had risked her life. He was rubbed and warmed by the fire and fed; and later was given the name Te Urunga (the pillow) as a reminder of the folded garments which had been strapped on his mother's back, and which had kept his head above the waves.

* *Pa*, village.
° *Taua*, hostile expedition, war party.
† *Atua*, god.

Rau-whato felt the pull of the depths beneath. She mourned the loss of her husband and felt her precarious solitude amidst the expanse of water. Fighting the currents and with difficulty seeing over the waves, numbed by the cold and carrying her precious child, Rau-whato swam. She saved the life of her child.

How Pulap Acquired
the Art of Navigation

Ulithi Atoll, Micronesia[96]

There was a bird, a *kulung* or golden plover, living on the island of Ponape. He was very big and a *legaselep*, or man-eating spirit.

After eating all the people on Ponape he went to Truk and ate all the people on Truk, too. After eating all the people on Truk he went to Wólúl and did the same thing there—he killed all the people. He left Wólúl and tried to reach Pulap but was unable to get there and reached Pulusuk instead. The reason that he did not get to Pulap was that Pälülop was there and caused the island not to be seen by the bird. He tried and tried to get to the island but did not succeed. From Pulusuk he tried again to find Pulap. He returned. Then he again tried but could not find it.

Once while he [the plover] was flying to Pulusuk, Pälülop said to his daughter, "You must prepare some food for the *legaselep* and take it to the end of the island of Pulap and leave it there. Wait for the *legaselep* and when he comes give him the food." Pälülop made *felsü*, or magic, for the *legaselep* so he could find the island of Pulap. The *legaselep* came and he saw the island as well as the girl near the food. She saw the *legaselep* and said to him, "Here is your food," and he looked at the food and said, "I am not satisfied with this food." She told him to try it and see what happened. He ate the food but after putting it in his mouth, other food took its place. As he ate, the food was replenished. He ate like that and was satisfied with the food, but the food was still there. He said to the girl, "I am very satisfied with this food and I thank you very much. But I will teach you something. I will teach you the art of navigation." He started teaching the girl how to be a navigator.

After she knew what navigation was she asked the *legaselep*, "How can I see the islands?" and the *legaselep* told the girl, "You must climb that coconut tree, then look over and see all these islands." She climbed the tree and while she was nearing the top of the tree, the tree went up a little bit more. She climbed again and the coconut tree got still taller. She was very high up and looked at all the islands. The girl knew, by calculating from the tree, the direction of this island and that, and she climbed down from the tree. The plover said to her, "Now I know that you know all these things, so I will leave you." The girl said, "No, you must stay and I will collect some food for you." So she made a lot of baskets and filled them with food. She hung the baskets on the bird and the plover flew toward Truk, but he did not succeed in reaching the island because he was tired and fell into the water and drowned.

That is why the people of Pulap are the lords of navigation.

The Ulithi Atoll is a group of coral islands with a total land area of 1.8 square miles in the Federated States of Micronesia. A detailed map of the area reveals tiny island dots in the open ocean 1,000 miles east of the Philippines and 900 miles north of New Guinea. With so few islands and so much ocean, navigation is a crucial skill for the Ulithi islanders. A noble god, the Titan Prometheus, brings fire to the people of Greece; a brave but human girl brings navigation to Pulap. She dares to feed the man-eating golden plover. An apt student, she understands the art of navigation: recognizing wind and wave patterns and keeping a heading by reading the swells made by the dominant wind pattern. She realizes that to apply this theoretical knowledge to the real world, she needs to see the relationship between the islands. She asks the pertinent question, "How can I see the islands?" After destroying the flesh-eating plover who has been plaguing the islands, this brave and intelligent heroine returns home to teach her people the art of navigation.

Rola and the Two Sisters

Ulithi Atoll, Micronesia [97]

There were two sisters living on Mogmog. A *legaselep*, or man-eating spirit, also lived on Mogmog and his name was Rola. He used to go about catching people to eat. He killed all the people on the island except these two girls. One day he performed some *bwe*, or knot divination and discovered that two more people were on the island. He searched for them and they hid in the woods. They found a big *kell*, or tropical almond tree, and tried to climb it but the younger one could not. The older one climbed it and as she went up she kept taking the bark off the tree until she reached the highest part. Then she took some coconut oil and applied it to the trunk so that if the *legaselep* came and saw her he would not be able to climb up.

Rola came looking around and saw the younger one. He took her to his place. She was too small for him to eat so he fed her. After she was about twelve years old she used to cook for both of them. One day when the *legaselep* went fishing the girl cooked some food for them and took some of it to her sister. She sang a song:

> "Ionama itino!"

The older sister answered,

> "U-u-u!"

The younger sister then sang:

> "Ionama itȯ lai talo!"

The older sister answered her with:

> "I do not want to come   "I tewe bwioibwioi
> Because I am afraid of Rola, Rola"   Bwȯ i metȯkh Rola, Rola"

The younger sister sang:

> "Rola is not here   "Ta meli Rola
> Because he went fishing   Bwȯ elafitä
> For a fish meal, a fish meal."   Täliela, täliela."

Thereupon she [the older sister] came down and ate the food that the younger sister had brought her. She finished eating and they cried together. Then the younger sister went back to the *legaselep*'s place.

Rola came back from fishing and asked her what was wrong with her eyes. She told him that it was because she looked in the smoke as she was cooking and it got in her eyes. Rola believed her. Next morning Rola went again to fish and she cooked some food and took some of it to her sister. The same thing happened as before. When Rola came back from fishing he asked her if she had been crying and she answered, "No, it is because the smoke got in my eyes while I was cooking." The same thing happened again, for a third time.

The fourth time Rola suspected that something had happened to her, so he told her he was going fishing, but instead of fishing he put a driftwood log on the canoe to make it look as if someone were on the canoe. Then he returned to the island. He watched her cook food and take some to her sister. Both the girls sang the same songs as before. The older sister came down and ate the food her sister had brought and when she was finished they both cried on one another. The younger girl then returned to Rola's house and the older sister climbed up the tree again.

The *legaselep* came and sang the song that the younger sister would sing, but his voice was a little different.

"Ionama itino!" [Sung low, like a man]

The girl knew that the sound was not like that of her sister, so she did not answer. The *legaselep* changed his pitch to be like that of the younger sister, and he sang like she:

"Ionama itino!"

The older sister answered him and she came down. He seized her and swallowed her. He went back to his house and the sister knew that he had eaten her sister.

She took two *khilikhil* or stalked barnacle shells and placed them under her tongue. Rola came and demanded, "Bring me food!" and she answered "Bring me food!" Rola said, "I told you to bring me my food because I want to eat," and the girl answered, "I told you to bring me my food because I want to eat." He said, "I told you what to do but you are just saying the words I am saying. I am going to come and kill you." She repeated what he said. He said, "I told you these things but if you do not obey I will come and get you." She again repeated what he had said. Thereupon the *legaselep* seized her and swallowed her.

But both she and her sister were alive inside his stomach. The younger girl took out two shells from her mouth and gave one to her sister so that each had one. They started to cut his stomach. He felt his stomach hurting and he sang:

I eat fish,   I mehoi ikh
My stomach does not hurt.   Tei methakh sahai.

I eat coconut meat,	I mehoi cho,
My stomach does not hurt.	Tei methakh sahai.
I drink palm toddy,*	I ül hachi,
My stomach does not hurt.	Tei methakh sahai.
I eat a baby,	I hangi chökh seri púkh,
I eat my child,	Wel lai sa methäkh,
My stomach hurts.	Sahai.

After he had finished singing his stomach broke open. The girls came out from his stomach and went to take a bath, and they went back to the *legaselep*'s house and lived there.

One day they went to Sorlen and Potangeras and told all the people that the *legaselep* was dead. They returned to Mogmog and became the chiefs of that island.

 Unlike Little Red Riding Hood, these two sisters don't need a woodcutter to cut them out of the monster's belly. They do it themselves with barnacle shells!

* *Toddy,* the fresh or fermented sap of various palms.

The Old Woman and the Giant

Philippines[98]

In a cave near the village of Umang, there once lived a wicked and greedy giant. He would kill and eat anyone who happened to pass by the cave. That was why everybody tried to avoid the place.

But one day, an old woman, who had gone to the woods to gather fuel, lost her way and found herself near the giant's cave. Seeing her, the giant shouted, "Now, I'm going to kill and eat you, unless you can show me that you can make a louder noise than I."

This frightened the old woman. But being wise and shrewd, she kept her head.

"What good will it do you if you eat a skinny old woman like me?" she asked the giant. "But if you let me go, I'll fetch my daughter, who's young and stout. Then, if you can make more noise than the two of us together, you may kill both of us. And you'll really have something good to eat."

The giant's greed was aroused. And so he told the old woman, "All right, you may go. But be sure to come back and bring your stout daughter with you."

The old woman went home and returned as she had promised, bringing her daughter with her. She had a drum with her, while her daughter had a bronze gong.

As soon as they neared the cave, the old woman began to beat her drum. At the same time, the daughter beat her gong. The noise that they made was so great that the giant could not hear his own voice, no matter how hard he shouted.

When he could no longer stand the noise, the giant covered his ears with his hands. Then he dashed blindly out of the cave. And he fell into a great big hole.

That was the end of the wicked and greedy giant. And the people of the whole countryside rejoiced at his death.

This old woman turns the tables on the giant by using her ability to understand his assumptions and predict his responses. She knows he is greedy so she dangles before him the prospect of eating both her and her stout, young daughter. This convinces him to let her go. The giant proposes a battle of noise. The old woman understands that the giant is proud of his voice and so blinded by his arrogance that he doesn't even see the need to specify what kind of noise. The old woman doesn't waste time arguing, she agrees to the spoken rules but when she comes back with her daughter, she has ingeniously interpreted the implicit rules of the game to include drums and gongs. An appropriate moral might be: If you have to play, play by your own rules!

The Magic Coin

Philippines[99]

Years ago a poor couple who lived in a small barrio set up a little store. They got ready their goods: rice, fish, sugar, soap, and clay pipes.

They waited all day, but it seemed that the people in the barrio did not need anything. They bought nothing from the store.

At the end of the day, Cata, the wife, held out a few miserable centavos to her husband, saying in a pitiful voice, "Pecto, how can we live on this?"

At noon the next day, three beautiful women stopped at the store. Across the street, under a tree some men were standing, doing nothing. By the side of the store was a group of children playing tubig-tubig.

Cata was astonished when the three beautiful ladies asked for clay pipes but she said nothing. She handed each lady a clay pipe.

One of the ladies spoke, "How much for the three clay pipes?"

"Ten centavos," replied Cata hoping that they would not ask for a bargain.

The ladies gave her an old ten-centavo piece, nicked at the edges. "Nevertheless it is money," thought Cata and accepted the money gratefully.

She watched the ladies walk down the street, "What are you staring at?" inquired Pecto looking over her shoulder.

"Those three ladies. Look, there they are." Cata replied pointing down the street.

"Where? I don't see anybody. Are you seeing things?" asked Pecto crossly.

"How blind can you be? Now they are turning around the bend. Look! Now they're gone," Cata answered.

"I've no time for jokes, Cata," Pecto was very angry.

Cata called out to the loafers, "Kulas, Takyo," she called, "Pecto says I'm seeing things. Tell him that three beautiful ladies stopped and bought clay pipes from my store."

"What beautiful ladies?" they asked surprised. "We saw no one here."

"But surely," she began confusedly, "you were looking here. The children . . . Children you saw the ladies? didn't you?"

"What ladies?" the children spoke in unison.

They all looked at Cata strangely and hurried away whispering among themselves. Cata herself began to wonder if she had been seeing things. Then she remembered the ten-centavo piece.

"Here is the crooked ten-centavo piece to prove they were here," she mused aloud. She was about to show it to Pecto but changed her mind. She tucked the coin into the corner of her little trunk.

The following day when Cata opened her store, she was surprised to find several barrio people waiting to buy things from her. They bought, paid, and left. Hardly had she attended to the last customers when another one entered. There was a steady stream of customers the whole morning.

In the evening she had to go to town to replenish her goods. She added other items that she had not had before.

Business was brisk the next day and every day after that. Soon Cata found her store becoming too small to hold all her merchandise. So she built a larger store. She bought a large stock of supplies, but these supplies too, were gone in a very short time. Their store flourished and grew bigger and bigger and they became richer and richer.

One day while Cata was tending the store, three beautiful ladies appeared. She recognised them at once to be the ladies who had bought the clay pipes.

"Here are the pipes. We don't need them anymore. Give us back the ten centavos we gave you," said one of the ladies.

Cata went swiftly to her little trunk, this time stowed away in a deep locker. She took the crooked ten-centavo coin and gave it to the ladies.

"Here's your ten-centavo piece, thank you. I have used it well," said Cata.

She watched the ladies walk down the road until they disappeared around the bend.

"Perla," she called to her helper, "did you see me talking to three beautiful ladies?"

"Mana, Cata," Perla smiled, "you are joking. You were just standing there doing nothing."

Cata smiled. To herself she said, "Of course, you couldn't see them because they were fairies. The ten-centavo piece they gave me has made us rich. They got it back, but no matter I'm more than content with what we have."

And so Cata and Pecto continued to prosper, getting richer and richer every day.

It is an old, crooked coin, nicked at the edges, but Cata senses its importance. She doesn't spend it, although she and her husband are poor. Cata tucks the coin away, and when the fairies come to reclaim their magic coin she is able to return it to them. Because she trusts and believes her feelings, Cata properly assesses the whole inter-

action. Neither her husband, nor her helper, nor the children saw the fairies, but Cata refuses to be pushed into self-doubt by peer pressure. Her deed is simple. She kills no dragons, she outwits no thieves, she simply saves a coin. However, her ability to recognize the importance of the coin comes from a strong belief in her own impressions. Cata's heroism resides in her strength of character, something so basic that it lies under the surface and gently readjusts rather than shatters the world.

The Creation of Lake Asbold

Asmat People, Irian Jaya, Indonesia[100]

Hidden high in the cloud-shrouded cordillera* of Central Irian lies an isolated lake. However, it was not always a lake. The people of Bokondini tell of the time it was a fertile valley where their ancestors built their beehive-shaped houses and cultivated their yam gardens. Unkindness toward a lowly mongrel dog seems to have brought about the end of this valley community.

It was pig feast time for the inhabitants of the valley. Scores of people lined the bank of the Kambo River. They were washing the entrails of the many pigs that had been slaughtered. A mangy, starving dog meekly approached the first person and begged for a small scrap of intestine to ease his gnawing hunger. The person refused with a curse, as did the next one and the next one and so on down the line. The people not only refused him a scrap of food, but kicked him and threw stones in order to drive him away. Still, the poor scrawny creature begged, hoping to find someone with a kind heart.

After many rebuffs, the outcast dog humbly approached the last person on the river bank. It was an old woman whose face showed signs that she herself had suffered some hard times. With his tail between his legs and his body tense, prepared for the pain of another stone or kick, the dog begged for a morsel of meat. Pity filled the woman when she saw what the poor dog had already suffered. She offered the dog some pieces of meat with the same sympathy a mother might show to her own child. As he ate he forgot his pains and aches and he was filled with gratitude toward the woman.

That night when she returned home she allowed the mangy dog to follow her and decided to keep him and always feed him so that he would never have to be hungry again. When they reached the house she was astonished when the dog began to speak to her. He said, "In a few days a heavy downpour will begin and it will cause the Mabiyogup River to flood. In order to be safe you must take your family and all your possessions and go high up on Mount Biambaga."

She quickly went and told her husband what the dog had said, but he

---

* *Cordillera,* a group of mountain ranges forming a mountain system of great linear extent often consisting of a number of more or less parallel chains.

didn't believe it. Instead, he was furious with her for having brought home the scrawny, mangy animal. Nevertheless, the woman took her small son and their most important possessions and found a safe place high up on the mountain.

Then the sky opened with a deluge such as the valley had never before experienced. The flood waters surged over the huts so quickly that no one had time to escape. The kindly woman, her son and a humble dog that talked were the only survivors of that community that had once been so prosperous. When you go there now all you will see are the clear, cool, sparkling waters of Lake Asbold.

Compare the heroine of this story to Noah of the biblical flood myth. This old woman is the last, lowly person on the riverbank. Her face shows signs of hard times; she is poor. Noah has the resources to build and provision an ark large enough to save two of each kind of animal in the whole world. This old woman takes pity on an outcast dog and gives him food instead of kicks. A compassionate heart is her salient characteristic. Noah is just and righteous, perfect in his generation. When the grateful dog warns the old woman of the flood, she tries to save her husband but he refuses to listen. She must be content to save herself, her son, and the dog. Noah's wife and sons, their wives, and all the animals obey him and are saved. Noah is a man who walks and talks with God, his story is in the Bible. This kind-hearted old woman talks to a mangy dog. Her story was found in a little book sandwiched between two thick volumes in a dusty corner of an anthropology library.

Senan and Aping

Kenyah People, Sarawak, Malaysia[101]

Making his way to the village of Tevau Na'a Pigan one day was a stranger who made himself known to the people there as Aban Aet. Tevau Na'a was almost deserted and quiet at that time for all its men were away at war. The only ones who remained to care for the house were the womenfolk. On that day some of these women were sitting here and there along the gallery. Then this Aban Aet came climbing up a ladder at one end of the longhouse and was soon met by a girl called Kalabang Eot Pelang.

To her Aban Aet recited a verse. In it he told her that he, Aban Aet, was there to seek for a girl as wife to a widower. When Kalabang Eot Pelang refused, Aban Aet went on further meeting a succession of girls namely Kalabau Ngam Njau, Nau Peu Bunyau, Laong Keyong, Usun Sigau, then Awing Nyaring and Bungan Lisu, but in each case he met with a mocking refusal. "You ought to rid your mind of that silly idea," they told him. "Don't you have enough sense to see for yourself that you are too old now?" Walking away Aban Aet made the last attempt, this time it was to Aping, the younger sister of Bungan Lisu. Shocking the rest of the girls, Aping accepted the man's wish as she indicated him to sit down to smoke while she went to prepare some rice for him. The time was short enough for the smoke to rise over the rice-pot before the rice was cooked and ready for serving. After eating Aban Aet told Aping to get ready since night was near. Therefore, the girl took out her valuable beads, her spare raiments, a hat and a basket and set off with the stranger. "Oh, she is going to marry Aban Aet," exclaimed the others in amazement. To this Aping replied that she had to agree for pity's sake. After covering a weary distance the two arrived at a strange building; the longhouse of Alo Lae, Aban Aet's abode. In spite of its length and hugeness the house was deserted and neglected, and not a single soul could be seen anywhere. Tangling and matting the house planks were trailing plants, and the surroundings were covered with dense weeds and shrubs so that the paths which led to the house were obscured by them. The inmates had been killed by giants. Into this curious building they entered and when it was evening they sat down to dinner. That night Aping was ordered to make her choice of a bedroom for herself and this she did. The next morning she did the household chores. On going to feed what few pigs they had,

Aping could not stand seeing the house surrounded by the thick grass any longer. So she decided to clear the place. When Aban Aet saw her engaged in the work he cautioned her that they were going to run a risk if she did so. For all the other inmates of the house were killed by giants, and if these giants saw the place was cleared they would suspect the presence of humans within the house and they would then go to seek for the occupants.

Hiding himself inside a large jar close to the house top was a young man, Senan, who was the son of Pa Lenjau. This Pa Lenjau was no other than the man whom they called Aban Aet, for Aban Aet was the name he once assumed in order to disguise himself. Due to the unhappy circumstances, Senan told his father how sympathetic he was to Aping since the girl had been deprived of her happy life at home to share their constant fear of being attacked by the giants. But the father replied that life would be more miserable for them if there was nobody to manage the domestic chores for them. And therefore Senan had to accept Aping as his wife.

Thus, at the dead of each night Senan would creep from within the little space of the jar to sleep in his room below while Aping was soundly asleep. And each morning as Aping got up she found some clues that betrayed the presence of a man in the house during the night. One of these clues was a broken leg-band lying on the floor. It suggested that the mysterious visitor was someone other than Pa Lenjau for Pa Lenjau did not wear any leg-bands. Curious to know who the man was, Aping hit upon a plan. She asked the old man whether he had any ginger, and the old man replied that he would go to the field to fetch some for her since none was available in the house. When the old man left for the farm, Aping decided to go along with him. After taking the ginger and some sugar-cane, they made for home. As they walked back Aping was eating the sugar-cane, dropping the skin along the path as she did so. "Be careful where you drop these skins," the old man cautioned her, "or else the giants, on finding them, will know we are still alive and will then come to hunt for us." Back at home Aping crushed the ginger which she then put in her mouth that night to keep her awake as she lay in bed. As the night drew darker the young man glided down. Although Aping was awake and was aware of his coming she kept calm and pretended not to know. Then as Senan was falling asleep she got up and went to cast a spell upon him under which he slept soundly till sunrise. After Aping had done the morning chores she went to see the sleeper. By that time he was awake but he did not dare to stir for he was sure that he had been observed or would be observed. Thus, under the staring gaze of the damsel he was petrified with embarrassment and was compelled to admit that he had been trying to make his existence known to her since he was ashamed of her reception into the house during such sad circumstances. But finally he got up and became calmer as the three gossiped over their breakfast. After breakfast Aping was busy clearing the vines which matted the house top, and for the second time she was reminded by the old man that to get rid of the vines would give evidence of their presence to the giants. But Aping was reluctant to cease working. After working she played on a mouth-harp and a flute. When the piercing sound reached the ears of the two lolling giants they were eaten up with a desire to chase after the person who played the instruments.

As Senan and Aping were sitting on the verandah the giant's hunting dog appeared but it succumbed to death after receiving a venomous dart from Aping's blow-pipe. Immediately they went to hide the carcass. As the sound of heavy foot-steps was heard Aping told Senan to go into the room and soon after that the giant came in view. It was a male giant. "Oh, I just heard human sounds coming from here," he growled. As he advanced nearer, Aping greeted him with a grin with the intention of displaying her set of black teeth. When the giant saw the teeth he expressed his admiration of them and insisted on Aping blackening his too. "You will experience a terrible pain as you undergo the process," Aping told the giant, "but if you want your teeth to be beautifully black you must endure it no matter how painful it will be." When everything was settled Aping lit a big fire and told the giant to lie down nearby. And as the monster opened its huge mouth Aping kept on pricking his fleshy gums with poisonous darts. "If you are sweating, stop fearing any danger for that is a sign of its efficacy," said Aping to the giant. After some time the giant grew weaker and fell dead. Then they carried the body to a place for hiding. When the giant did not show himself, his wife was in a rage and she left immediately and followed the path her husband had taken. As she reached the longhouse Aping greeted her again with a grin, but she was not as easy to lure as her husband. In fact she chided the girl and condemned her black teeth. Then she went and made a careful inspection of the place. At last she came upon the corpse of her dead husband. So furious was she then that she challenged Aping to fight. Accepting the invitation Aping donned herself with her husband's apparel and armed herself with his sword, shield and spear. Then fighting like a maniac, the two moved uphill and over crags in the struggle. After a time Aping was apparently defeated. After she had invoked her spirit to give aid, a magpie-robin came to her help just in time and told her to strike constantly at the giant's great toe (the vulnerable spot). And when she smote at the part the giant collapsed and died.

As the giant lay dead on the ground Aping called for Senan from his hiding place. Fearful expressions faded from the latter's face, as he spoke his version of the fight. "I was in fear of your life," he gasped, "but if you, a woman can kill a giant I am sure that your men at Tevau Na'a can do mightier deeds." The three made merry over the captured heads of the two giants that night. And to commemorate the happy event they erected a *balawing* near the longhouse on the following morning before they set off on their way to the giants' house. As they approached the great building they saw pineapples and bananas laid by the paths as allurements for their human prey. But none of them was tempted to sample the fruits for they knew that they were laid out as bait. As they came to the pond of the giants they saw emaciated bodies of human beings supporting the rock above the pond. Some were laid on a platform by the water. Among them was Senan of Ra Pungon Iman. In compassion they helped them to stand up. "How is it that you are coming?" Senan asked them, "The giants may be back soon from hunting." "Oh, don't worry both of them are dead now," answered Aping. As they walked further up the house they saw Padan Me and Jalong Buse of Ra Pungon Iman guarding the entrance to the house. And while they were ascending the steps the two sentries were attempting to trip them on a revolving log into a trap. When they were asked why they did that to their fellow beings they replied that they had to do their duty for the sake of their lives. On being told that the giants were dead they left their work immediately and said to themselves:

SA PE KUN DULU URAN
KUN BA'AN DULU PATAPAN
LEPO TEMABU NA'A PINGGAN
KEMBAU NA'A SULAU LAWAN.

By which they meant that it was not a wonder, for the people of Tevau Na'a were always spoken of as being courageous and strong.

When Aping and Senan entered the house they met Ulau Pangeta, the daughter of the giant. "Dare you come here?" she asked in mixed pity and surprise. "My parents are away hunting but their return is expected," she added again. "What is there to worry about, since we are akin?" they lied to her. Ulau Pangeta accepted them then with much hospitality. After cooking she served them their meal and asked them not to avoid the food for it was not of human flesh but of meat and fish as she herself was not a man-eater like her parents. While they were eating Aping asked Ulau Pangeta whether it was against her wish if anybody killed her parents. "I am glad if they are killed and got rid of," replied the daughter, "for the sight of those human beings whom they roast over the hearth and those whom they secured to the house-beams is so pitiful," she remarked as she gestured to them. "All is well for us, since I have killed them both," Aping said, breaking the news much to the delight of Ulau Pangeta.

Then Aping asked her concerning some barns in the distance. "That one contains 'telang ading' (a liquid with the power of bringing the dead to life), the second contains fans (devices used by the giants to attract those who flee from them), the third contains hooks (for them to catch hold of those who try to escape), the fourth contains man's vitality (buan laset) and the rest contain 'abang' rice, 'lasak' rice, and 'bura' rice," said Ulau. Then Aping and Senan took the "telang ading" and sprinkled it over the skeletons and emaciated bodies of the captives who at that instant came to life to resume their works. "Who brought us to life?" some of them asked. Aping of Tevau Na'a replied the others. After that, they left for home, followed by Ulau Pangeta. Thus Senan and his widowed father were again happily united with Pa Bawin and Bungan, Senan's mother and sister respectively.

After some time Pa Bawin and her husband, Lenjau, decided to arrange the marriage of Senan and Aping. In preparation they pounded some rice and went to fish and hunt. When the "borak" (rice-wine) had been fermented, the fish and meat properly cooked, Senan beat the gong summoning their guests. Hearing the sound the people of Tevau Na'a guessed that Aping was going to wed to Aban Aet. So they set off to Alo Lae bringing "borak" and rice as presents. When they arrived at Alo Lae they saw for themselves that the man to whom Aping was to marry was not Aban Aet but a handsome youth whom they recognised as Senan, the son of the man whom they knew as Aban Aet. Some of the girls from Tevau Na'a were envious of Aping's good fortune. Bungan suggested to Aping that she would like to exchange homes with her, but when Aping refused she again asked her if she would agree to exchange necklaces and again she was disappointed as Aping refused for the second time. But later Aping mentioned to Senan that Bungan was the girl whom his father had requested to be his bride and to make things easy for them then it would be better for him to marry Bungan instead of her (Aping). But Senan replied that earlier Bungan had repudiated his father's request, and to change her mind and intervene just before the wedding was too late.

Thus, on the morning of the wedding day a pig was to be slaughtered. Ulau Buring then went to feed the pig with much fussing as the people were trying to catch the animals. Utan Buring made the first attempt but she failed; then some young men tried and they, too, could not get a good grip on the pig for it was too slippery. At last Aping decided to volunteer but she tried to avoid being seen while doing so. Lucky for her, Utan

Kaluro was at that time giving birth. And while the people were crowding around the newly-born baby Aping caught the pig.

When everything had been settled Aping and Senan dressed themselves in their wedding attire.

> Like the trailing bodies of glow-worms were the tassels of bead-strings that dangled from Aping's ears.
> And like bunches of the "palal" fruit were the clusters of her earrings, layer upon layer beneath her hair.
> Like the stem of a tender shoot, the whole length of her lower arms were covered with ivory bracelets.
> Like a fresh mushroom which springs to life after the rain was the appearance of Senan of Alo Lae.
> His ear ornaments of tiger's fangs were the shape of the crescent moon.
> As the black stripes of the hornbill's tail-feathers was the raven hair of Senan in contrast to his complection.

Then they went to the gallery and settled themselves on a gong to receive the bestowal of divine favour as Pa Lenjau was reciting an incantation to the Spirit which they believed dwelt in the pig that lay before him.

The incantation was as follows: To the spirit of this pig which we are to kill for the ceremony we ask favour so that we, the people of this house may have good strong young men and dutiful girls who will one day be our leaders.

The feast lasted for two days and then the people from Tevau Na'a left, paying their last tribute to the couple.

A woman's strengths often go unappreciated until circumstances spotlight them. In this story, Aping's power becomes more and more obvious. An unassuming girl, Aping marries out of pity. The next morning, the image of tractability, she does the housework. However, she doesn't cower before the threat of the giants. She dares to drop sugar cane skins on the path and she stubbornly insists on cleaning outside the house. Aping plays her mouth-harp, practically challenging the giant to come. When the giants appear, she takes full responsibility. Aping fells the giant's dog with a dart from her blowpipe. She kills the giant with a ruse and the giant's wife in a pitched battle. She even restores life to the skeletons of the giants' captives. Never underestimate a woman.

Ubong and the Head-Hunters

Kenyah People, Sarawak, Malaysia[102]

It was evening time in the longhouse of Lepo Tau. The women and children were coming back from bathing in the river carrying on their backs baskets containing water in bamboo tubes. A few men, who had returned from their farms, were trying to tie their boats at the river banks. They had brought with them some vegetables and a wild boar which they had caught at their farm. High over the roofs of the house of Lepo Tau, wisps of grey smoke were curling up in the sky. A few swallows were still busy dipping down over the river taking their evening meal of insects. Now and again one would dip into the water leaving behind drops of water like a stream of pearls. On the verandah of the longhouse sat an old lady with silver hair. In the dying light of the day she was busy with her beads, threading them carefully on to a string. She wanted to make a bead hat to present to her granddaughter who was soon to be married. A few of the children gathered around the old lady watching her intently. She looked up from her work and her face was sorrowful but still kindly and in her eyes were sorrow and joy mixed together. One of the little children asked her to tell them a story. The old lady put down her beads and the hat she was making and she told them a story.

Long, long ago before any of your parents were born, we people of Lepo Tau came and settled on the Baram river. We had to come here from the Usun Apau because of the famine there and after many wanderings we found this lovely spot at the mouth of the Moh river. The leader of the people in those days was my husband. He was a very fine warrior called Balan. That year we were just harvesting and my husband was spending the night in the farm. I stayed at home because we were about to have our first child. All the other people were out in the farms. Suddenly as I sat on the verandah of the house I heard a tremendous noise and people were shouting, "Ayau! Ayau! Head-hunters! Head-hunters!" Suddenly onto the verandah rushed a host of Bakong people. We were always terrified of the Bakong people because they had been our enemies for a long time. I rushed into my room and hid myself in a corner. The men came and they searched and said they were looking for a particular man. "Have you seen him?" they asked. I could hear them asking the people outside on the verandah. "No," said one to the other. These men then rushed out to the other side of the house brandishing their swords and spears. I dared not venture out to the verandah but stayed in my room all night. The next morning I was waiting for my husband to turn up. He had promised to come back because I was about to give birth. After some time I heard a few people from the river bank and I could hear the sounds of mourning. "Who could it be?" I thought. I rushed out and down the ladder down to the river bank and there an old man came up to me and said, "I have terrible news for you. Last night the Bakong people killed your husband." Now Balan was a very fine man. His hair was sleek black like the back of a snake. He was strong and straight and his limbs were tough. No one among the whole of the Bakong people could fight with him, so strong he was, but then I heard the story.

That night my husband was sleeping soundly in a leaf hut far away from the longhouse. Because it was harvest time he was protecting the rice from the hungry squirrels, deers and the wild boars. Suddenly out of the jungle and the gloom a party of Bakong warriors threw down the door of the hut and cut off the head of the sleeping man. For months and months they had been hunting for a particular man in retaliation for what he had done to them. Unfortunately they got the wrong man and the noblest of the Kenyahs, a man who was renowned for peace-keeping lay a victim of their savage revenge. There was great mourning in the house for eight days and afterwards we buried my husband and you can see his monument upriver.

After some time my child was born and he was given the name of Oyau because his father was dead. After a year many of the people of the house asked me to marry again but I resolved that I would remain faithful to my dead husband and join him later in Alo Malau. The Lepo Tau people were filled with hatred for the Bakong people and they set off up the Moh river and followed the enemy into their own country. Year after year the fighting went on between our two tribes but I have no thought for revenge. Every year I thought to myself, why should our people go on fighting like this, killing one another and wasting all their man-power. It was senseless this eye for eye revenge, this never ending blood feud. I reminded the people of the great qualities of their dead leader, of his courage, of his prowess at hunting, his pride in his mountain padi field. I used to talk to the young men and tell them to be brave hunters and to hunt for animals but not for men. On the wall of my room I kept the sharp parang* with delicately carved hilt, a plumed helmet of my husband, with its gleaming shower of feathers of the hornbill and the string of precious blue beads. I was Balu, a widow and though free to marry and still young and beautiful I refused to take anyone in marriage.

* *Parang*, a short sword, cleaver, or machete.

After some years I decided on a plan to make peace with the Bakong people. One time I heard that a party of men were coming down river in a long boat and our people were getting ready to ambush them but that night I called a meeting and because I was a princess I was allowed to speak to them. "Look here, you people, how foolish you are. All these years you have been fighting with the Bakong people and the Bakong people are also Kenyahs. Why should we fight our own kith and kin? Tomorrow when the Bakong people come I am going to invite them up to the house and make a feast and in that way show them that we want to live peacefully with them." To this all the people of Lepo Tau agreed because they, too, were tired of the endless war and blood feud. The whole night long there was sounds of merriment and of festivity in the house. Chickens were killed, wild pigs were roasted and rice wine was prepared in great earthen ware jars. Early in the morning when the mist was still hanging above the river the sound of a long boat was heard. The Bakong people were about to pass stealthily past the house of the Lepo Tau people. Just as they were passing the headman of the Lepo Tau people hailed them and called them to come up. Shyly the men moored their boats and they came up to the long gallery of the longhouse. To their astonishment they were invited to partake of the peace meal. They sat down with their backs to the river and after they had eaten, the headman offered rice-wine to them and in their songs they asked that they would live at peace with the Lepo Tau people and be friendly with them forever after. In reply the headman of the Bakong people offered rice-wine to the headman of the Lepo Tau. He asked for mercy from them, saying that they had done great wrong and that they were brothers and they promised from henceforth they would no longer go to war with their relatives, the Lepo Tau people. Everyone praised the courage of Balu Ubong, the faithful widow who preached mercy and forgiveness and love.

The children listened to her story and as they watched they saw the old lady's eyes grow misty with tears as she remembered her loving husband. From that day onwards the Lepo people and the Bakong people have lived peacefully with one another.

"Ubong and the Head-Hunters" and "Senan and Aping" are from the Kenyah people who live close to the headwaters of the Baram River, the second largest river in Sarawak, Malaysia, on the island of Borneo. Head-hunting was one of their traditions.

Ubong is a woman who has every reason to hate and thirst for revenge; when she was pregnant with her first child, the Bakong head-hunters killed her husband. Her tribe seeks revenge but Ubong does not. Instead, she sees the futility of revenge and the never-ending blood feud that it perpetuates. For years Ubong encourages the young men to hunt for animals, not men. In addition she gives them a positive vision to work toward; she reminds the people of their noble qualities, thus encouraging them to expect a better future. Ubong creates peace because she has had the imagination to envision it and the determination to realize it. Like many folk and fairy tales, this tale carries a utopian message, which crosses the boundaries of time and culture: To make a world with less violence come true, we have to first envision it.

Kumaku and the Giant

Fiji [103]

Kumaku was a healthy, happy little girl with sturdy limbs and an active body, with bright black eyes dancing with fun and shining with happiness. Her straight black hair hung down to her shoulders, and often she'd place a flower above one ear. Like many other small girls she was sometimes as naughty as she was beautiful.

One day when her mother was cooking food for dinner she called to Kumaku.

"Kumaku," she said, "take this coconut shell and bring me some water."

Kumaku took the shell and said, "Do you want fresh water from the spring?"

"Oh no," said her mother, "I want sea water please; then I won't need to put any salt in it, and I have been too busy lately to make salt."

As Kumaku ran down the path her mother called after her, "Keep away from the spiders' webs!"

Kumaku knew what she meant. There were giants on the island of Rotuma. Their presence was always indicated by spiders' webs, which were strung across the path. Unwary travellers were caught in them and captured by the giants and eaten. Kumaku thought she knew better than her mother, as little girls often do, so when she came to a path that led through the bush, and saw the spiders' webs across it, she ran down it, singing a song which she knew the giants would hear. This is the song:

> Kumaku
> Draws water from the sea,
> Come with me, giants,
> Come and help me.

Before she had finished the song two giants sprang out of the bushes, picked her up and carried her down to the sea, where she filled the coconut shell with water.

The giants towered over her, but Kumaku gave a little smile, and as they reached out their hands with their long claws, she sang again:

> Blow, winds from Fiji,
> Blow up the black sand of the sea,
> Fill the giants' eyes

So that they cannot see.
Blow, winds from Tonga,
Blow up the white sea sand,
Dazzle their eyes
While I fly to the land.

These were magic words, because they were part of a magic song. Immediately a strong wind blew in from the sea, carrying with it black sand and white sand hundreds of miles across the ocean, from Fiji and from Tonga. It blew into the giants' eyes so that they were blinded and could not see. They groped for her, but she easily dodged them, ran up the path, and gave the coconut shell full of salt water to her mother just as though nothing had happened.

Like Little Red Riding Hood, Kumaku goes off the path. Her mother warns her to avoid the traps set by flesh-eating giants, but Kumaku thinks she knows better than her mother. Unlike Little Red Riding Hood, who must learn to recognize and deal with wolves, Kumaku already knows how to deal with the dangers in her world. She knows how to bring the giants to her to aid her in her work. She knows how to blow sand into their eyes and make her escape, mischief sparkling in her bright black eyes all the while.

Revival and Revenge

Kewa People, Papua, New Guinea[104]

Abrother and a sister lived alone and looked after their pig, Puramen-alasu. One day an old man came and said he would marry that girl. After he had gone, the brother said to her, "You must go to his house." Again and again the old man returned to the siblings' house, each time saying, "I want to take her with me." The brother was apprehensive about the old man, and he said to his sister, "Let us kill our pig now. Lest he kill the two of us, you must go with him." So they killed the pig, butchered it, and cooked it. Only the back of the pig's neck did the brother keep for himself; the rest, including the two sides and backbone, his sister took with her in her netbag. The old man led her away. As they went, she saw him give the pork away to people they met on the road.

Soon they came to a fork in the path, and the old man told her, "I'll go this way, but you must take the other path." But then he added, "Wait, I'm thirsty. Wait here for me while I get a drink of water." But he was deceiving her, for while she waited he went back and killed and ate her brother, who was sitting at home eating his share of pork. He cut him into pieces and then came back with them. The sister guessed what had happened, and she wept copiously for her brother.

Then the old man told her to go off in the direction he had indicated, on the other path. The path led her onto a fallen log. While she was walking along it, the old man suddenly appeared and shoved her into a deep well underneath. Down and down she tumbled bouncing—kilikili tatatata*—down to the bottom.

She lay at the bottom, her head reeling from her fall. After a while she got up slowly. She heard people groaning: "Don't hold my arm." "Let go of my head." "Get off me." Lying beside her were other young women who had been thrown down there. Some were dead others only half dead.

The sister saw that one young red-skinned girl, who was sitting beneath some casuarinas and pines, appeared to be well. She asked her, "Are all these women alive, or have some died?"

"Some are dead, mostly from hunger; but others are still alive," was the answer.

---

* *Kilikili tatatata*, the Kewa language is rich in imitative words like the "Kilikili tatatata," which represents the sound of the girl falling into the well.

Now, the brother had given his sister many bundles, which she had put in her netbag. She opened one and found some glowing embers; in another were a bushknife and axe. So the sister took the axe, cut a dry *walu* pine, and made fires in different places. Then she asked the other girl to help her put the others by the fires, so they would be warm.

Then the sister took a stake of *kagu* wood, skewered a pig kidney she had brought, and cooked it. Then she shared it out to the other women. She cooked all her pork and gave most of it away. The remainder they recooked later. Those young women's bodies soon fattened up.

Later the sister looked inside the other bundles her brother had given her. In them she found cuttings of sweet potato, *rani* and *padi* greens, and other crops. She planted the cuttings here and there at the bottom of the well, and crops grew from them. Presently all the young women were quite recovered.

One day the sister said to the others, "Listen now, I want to say something." She reminded them about the old man. They should do something in return, she urged. So they chopped down trees and began to make a ladder of forked sticks and crosspieces. They worked their way to the top of the well, laughing and joking all the while.

One day a young man passed by the well and heard the sound of women laughing. He came and listened at the edge. Realizing that the women were engaged in constructing a ladder, the youth put some logs down and climbed downward to see. Then he returned to his village and told others what he had discovered. An old man there said, "Hey, they are mine! Why did you go there? They are mine!"

"Yes," said the youth, "but I did see them there, those women."

When the women had almost reached the top of the hole, the youth returned and climbed down to them. They asked him who he was. "I heard your voices," he answered, "and I've come to tell you that a villager up there is preparing a feast for some people, who will be bringing him pandanus leaves for thatch. And I also heard an old man say you all belong to him." The young women replied that they knew nothing about any of this.

When they had come out of the well and put on their ornaments, the youth advised them to arrive with bundles of pandanus leaves, and he offered them a bushknife and axe to use while collecting them. "We have our own!" the women told him.

They made their way to the ceremonial ground. People were surprised to see all these fine young women approaching. So many of them: could this one old man have thrown so many into that well? The youth heard that old one say with satisfaction, "All these women are mine!"

People were heating the stones for the earth ovens. When smoke had filled the ceremonial ground, the young women ran over to the old man, surrounded him, beat him with their *walu* sticks, and threw him into the fire. The sister took the axe her brother had given her and cut him through the middle. His body burned unnoticed in the smoke.

The young women turned into *kope* leaves, which we use for cooking. Nowadays people still kill one another with axes, and they make scaffolds the way those ones did.

This story presents a picture of women cooperating. Individually each of these women was pushed into the well. United, they grow strong, escape the well, and wreak their revenge on the wicked old man. Led by the sister who heals them and feeds them, the women form a thriving community at the bottom of the well.

Women build community from the most intimate relationships to large scale organizations. Women are usually the ones to remember birthdays, send holiday cards, and babysit grandchildren. Women build communities by chatting with neighbors and exchanging favors. Women are community builders on larger scales as well. Eleanor Roosevelt helped further a world community when she worked hard to pass the United Nations' Universal Declaration of Human Rights. Many popular fairy tales have the configuration of women pitted against other women: Snow White vs. her evil stepmother, Cinderella vs. the nasty stepsisters and stepmother. This story reminds us that women are also excellent community builders and models of cooperation.

Uzu, the White Dogai

Torres Straits, Australia[105]

At the top of Gebin Pad, a hill on the island of Gebar which many people today call Two Brothers Island, there lived inside a stone a *dogai** name Uzu.

Uzu looked like all other *dogai*, tall and skinny, with a face like a flying fox. She had long teeth and big ears; indeed, her ears were so big that when she lay down to sleep, she could use one as a mat and the other as a cover to keep her warm. But Uzu was a good *dogai*, and she was very kind to anyone in trouble.

One day the women and the girls from the village of Gebi went out fishing on the reef, stringing the fish together as they caught them. In the late afternoon they turned back.

Alas, one poor girl, whose name also was Uzu, was stung by a stone-fish. The pain was so bad that she could not walk. She had to sit down and watch her friends disappear from sight around Umai Piti Gizu. The tears streamed from her eyes. There she was, alone, the sun nearly gone down into the sea.

From her home Uzu saw all that had happened, so she made her way towards her namesake.

The girl saw her coming and screamed with fright: "Mother! Mother! The *dogai* is going to kill me!"

But she was quite wrong.

This *dogai*, the white one, the good one, pulled a hair from her head, tied it round Uzu's foot over the wound, put her over her shoulder, and carried her up to her home inside the stone. She made the girl sit down, spread leaves over the sore place on her foot, and told her to sleep. Then she went off to dig *kutai* and *kog* and *boa* (yams).

When the girl woke next morning she was given the best parts of the freshly roasted yams, Uzu the dogai contenting herself with the burnt outside crusts.

Every day this white *dogai* rubbed the girl's foot and dressed it with fresh leaves, and every day she fed the girl well.

---

* *Dogai*, a female witch-like creature, sharp-featured and long-eared. They were always looking for a man to grab as a husband. Dogai lived in stones, trees, or underground, were possibly of sub-human intelligence, but cunning and shrewd. They could impersonate living women. Most dogai were evil and all were feared. The dogai language was a gibberish of the Islanders' tongue.

When the girl's foot was healed, and there was no more pain in it, the good *dogai* took her back to her village, saying, as she left her: "When the men are cutting up dugong* and turtle, set aside a portion for me. Go now, and give your family this present of yams."

The girl ran to her mother and told her the whole story.

And ever after, when the canoes returned from hunting, and the men had butchered their kill, the girl Uzu filled a basket and made her way up the hill. Outside the stone where Uzu, the white *dogai* who did not eat people, had her home, she called: "Aka! Aka! (Granny! Granny!) I have brought your share of meat and fat."

Modern rewritings of folktales tend to change the stories so that the evil witch or fire-breathing dragon is really a nice person. Dogai are usually evil, like witches and dragons. However, Uzu is a good dogai who bandages the girl's wound, cares for her, and feeds her. When the girl's foot is completely healed, Uzu sends the girl back to her family with a present. Uzu breaks down the evil dogai stereotype. Here is a politically correct tale from the Torres Straits, a distant maze of reefs, rocks, and islands in the stretch of water separating the northernmost tip of Australia from New Guinea. Evidently our modern, revisionist folktales aren't so modern after all.

---

* *Dugong*, sea cow, genus of aquatic herbivorous mammals, related to the manatees.

The Black Snake Man and His Wife, the Dove

Muŋkan People, Australia[106]

Min Yúwam, the black snake, and Min Kɔ̧ḷet, the dove, were once man and wife. They lived across the river close by.

They say: "Let's go and stay down-river!"

They find honey and cut it out; lay it on tea-tree bark and go on again. They come to a camp; pick up firewood, light a fire and eat their honey. Then they lie down and go to sleep. They sleep on.

Next morning the husband wakes and calls his wife: "Come along! We'll go now!" They go.

They see honey and cut it. "You go for tea-tree bark!" The wife goes for tea-tree bark and strips it off; carries it back and throws it down. They lay the honey on it and tie it up with string.

"Now let's go!" They travel on and on and on.

The man says: "We'll rest here!" They make camp. They pick up firewood and light a fire. In the evening the man spears a fish and carries it back to camp. The woman says: "We're never hard up for meat, we two!" They grill it in the coals. It cooks and they take it out and eat it.

"Let's camp here!" They sit there yarning, yarning, yarning still.*

"Now let's lie down to sleep!" They lie there. They fall asleep. They lie on there sleeping.

She calls to her husband: "It's daylight, my husband! Let's go now, you and I!"

"Let's sit a while, it's early yet! We need not go just yet!" They sit on a while in the shade.

"Now let's go!" They travel on and on down-river till they come to another camp. They see honey and the man is cutting it out. His wife finds some yams and is digging them out with her yamstick.

Her husband calls: "Which way did you go?"

"Here I am!"

Her husband comes up: "Now let's go!"

"All right!"

They go on again. On and on and on they go!

---

* *Yarning,* to tell a tale or to have a conversation, chat, gossip.

"The roots are heavy; let's stop here!"

"All right! We'll camp here!"

They light a fire; clear the ground, smoothing it over with their feet. They sleep.

Early next morning he says: "Now let's go back up-river to your home!"

"Yes! Let's go home again up-river!"

They turn homewards up-river. They travel, travel, travel, travel, travel. At last they clear a place and sleep soundly.

"We must be going!" He picks up his spears and she picks up her dilly-bag,* her yamstick, tomahawk and honey stick.

"Home we go!" Back up to the home camp they come.

"I'll sit here and rest! The babe inside me is weighing me down heavily! The babe will soon be born now!"

"Yes! You stay! I'll look round for fish and roots!"

"Yes! I'll sit here by myself!"

She sits there. She kneels, sitting on her heels: "Ei´! Ei´! It's taking a long time to be born! Now it comes!" She holds the baby's head and body with her hands in front of her and directs it to the ground as it comes.

"Now it's nearly born!"

"Uŋá'! Uŋá'!"

"Now it's born!"

"Uŋá'!" the baby cries.

"Now I must be holding the cord and calling names for it myself. Who else is there to call for me! Now I hold it myself, calling the names!" She calls names one after the other; calls again, again, again. The cord gives way.

"Yu:mí:tya! Yu:mí:tya!" she is calling as the afterbirth comes away. Yu:mí:tya! is her husband's name.

"All is over!" She lays the baby on tea-tree bark.

The man comes back from fishing. The woman sees her husband there. He sits down in a camp apart.

"I wonder what it is!" he says to himself aloud.

"It's a man-child!" the woman answers, speaking aloud to herself (she speaks indirectly; she may not speak directly to him on account of the birth taboo).

She sits a while by herself, then lies down and sleeps soundly—the babe close beside her. The baby cries. The mother picks it up and puts it to her breast. The milk comes down and the baby drinks.

For five days the woman lies resting; the haemorrhage is not yet fin-

---

* *Dilly-bag,* a mesh bag of native fibers usually with a drawstring.

ished. Her husband keeps bringing her roots, ever the same. Fish is eaten by neither of them. Fish is forbidden lest the baby grow sick and die. Her husband cooks the yams in the fire and when they are cooked, he takes them out and lays them down a little way off from the woman. The woman picks them up from where he has laid them. The man eats some himself. They lie down camping at a distance.

Now the haemorrhage is finished altogether. "I've finished with it!" she says to herself aloud.

Next day the man goes fishing; spears a fish and goes up into the shade with it. Then he picks up firewood, breaks the necks of the fish, cooks and eats a small knight-fish and a small catfish; lays aside some for the evening.

The woman now goes to look for yams for herself. She may not yet eat fish, as the fluid is still coming away.

The man lights his own fire and she lights one for herself and the child. They sleep.

Daylight comes. The man goes off fishing. The woman goes to dig yams.

After six days thus, the fluid has ceased to flow.

The mother and child still lie down alone. She is digging many roots, the baby lying close by her on tea-tree bark. The mother does this every day, whilst the father goes fishing and spearing fish. The woman cannot yet give the yams she is gathering to her husband; he is still taboo to her. Nor can the man give the fish he is spearing to his wife either; she is taboo to him.

Now the woman's menstrual flow begins a little. For three days it comes. Now it is finished altogether.

The wife says to her husband: "I have recovered now, and I would be bringing up the baby to you!"

The husband says: "Yes! bring it up now!"

The woman says: "Very well!"

She puts the yams and some small fish she has collected into her dilly-bag, fills three dilly-bags with yams—right to the top. One dilly-bagful is food for herself, and one for her husband, and the third is for the baby to give to its father. She has made a nice new string apron. She now fastens it on herself and wears it. She smears her face with clay and her body with ashes, putting white clay on her head. Picking up the baby, she rubs it with charcoal all over and smears a streak of white clay down its nose. She breaks off the navel cord (which is now dry) to give her husband. She fastens a beeswax pendant to it, striped with strips of yellow orchid bark, and ties the cord round the baby's neck, ready for its father. Picking up her dilly-bags, she hangs one from her head, slings another across her shoulder and her chest to hang under the other arm, and places another on her head. Gathering up the baby, she carries him across her arms. Thus she carries the newborn baby to its father.

Now she is bringing it to him. The father, sitting with crossed legs in his camp, stretches out his arms from afar to take the baby. The woman brings the baby and lays it in his arms. Together they hold it there—he sitting and she kneeling before him, facing each other.

After a while, the father takes the baby and lays it on his knees and gazes on it. He takes sweat and anoints the baby with it; rubs it over its forehead and face.

"This is my very own son, made by me! I will take care of it always!" He plays with it. Then he takes the navel cord and fastens it round his own neck. The baby cries and he rocks it in his arms.

Thus they sit together facing each other—husband and wife. They sit a while thus.

Then the woman goes for the roots she has gathered and lays them down beside her husband. She picks up a dilly-bag and rubs it across the mouth of her baby, saying: "So that he may not be always crying!"

Then she lays it on his stomach, saying: "So that he shall not run after others for food, but will come running back to us, and we will always keep together!"

By and by the father gets up and lays the baby in its mother's arms, and the mother lays it down on tea-tree bark.

She picks up firewood, lays a fire and clears a place for them to camp. There together in the same camp they lie down to sleep.

The woman says to her husband: "I'll go back to my own place!"

To the man's place up-river the man went, carrying the baby with him. There at Yuːmíːtya they went down into their *auwa*, father and son together.

The mother Min Kɔḷet went down at Kɔḷet'áuwa—"the place of doves."

The birth of Min Kɔḷet's baby takes place in a world where Nature and human spirit coexist in a tangible power. In industrial societies we have detached ourselves; we have constructed a superficial distance from Nature, which encourages disrespect. We have air-conditioned Nature, blinded her with 100-watt light bulbs, and smogged her up in a concrete cloverleaf. We birth babies in hospitals lined with doctors and anesthetists, where the only person not officially working is the sweating, grunting woman pushing out the baby.

"She sits there. She kneels, sitting on her heels: 'Ei´! Ei´! It's taking a long time to be born! Now it comes!' She holds the baby's head and body with her hands in front of her and directs it to the ground as it comes." The language, the cry, the force of this moment catapults us from light bulbs to starry nights. Min Kɔḷet gives birth to her baby.

The *Mogwoi's* Baby

Arnhem Land, Australia[107]

A *mogwoi* * woman set off; carrying her baby under one arm in a paperbark container. She was going to collect some bush foods. As she
went along she called out to her husband, "You go and get fish for us
both! I'll get plant food." She chose a good place to leave the baby, and
set to work. She got some food and put it down. She got more and put
it down. Got more, put it down . . . The baby was crying. "Ah, my baby's
crying! I'll give her milk. There she is, over there." She set off, sat down,
and breast-fed the baby. Then she left her and went to get more food.
This time she was farther away among the grasses, too far to hear.

A human man called Laarnmirndja set off with his dog, to go hunting. The dog smelt something. He sniffed about, smelling, looking
around. He kept on looking about. "What's this I'm smelling, something
for me? An animal? A djanda goanna, maybe?" He went digging about,
digging in a great hurry, around the baby. The man, going along, saw the
baby. "Here's a nice baby for me. I'll take it!" He picked it up, and went
running off. He ran—and *brrr!* He got there. The people living at that
place said, "A baby for us, a nice one!" "Yes, for us! What is it? A girl?
That's good!" they said. "For me, give it here to me!" "No, I've got it, I'm
holding it!" "No, for me! Give it to me! I'll give it milk, breast-milk!"

The *mogwoi* woman was talking to herself. "I'll eat some food first: it's
still early morning." She went to where she had left the baby, and saw it
was gone. She began to abuse whoever had taken it. "Oh, my baby! Some
deformed creature snatched you away, someone with a damaged nose and
a twisted-up mouth! Oh, my dear child! Oh, who snatched you away from
me?" She hurried about, searching. She found the man's tracks and followed them. Human children were talking and calling out. She heard
them, and went running in their direction.

They heard her coming. "She's on the way!" they said. She was waving
a long, thick stick, ready, as she hurried along. "She's the baby's mother,
she's hurrying," they said. "She's on the way, looking for her baby!" She
was going along. Hurry, hurry, hurry! Getting close! "Where's my baby?"
They picked up another baby, one of theirs. "This is your baby!" "No.
This is yours. It's no good!" They gave her another baby. "No. This is

---

* *Mogwoi*, although non-humans, mogwoi share many human customs and some are spirits of the dead.

yours: it's covered with sores!" She threw it away. They gave her another baby. She left it, did not pick it up. "This one's no good, no good at all. Ugly face!" They gave her more, but she did not want them. Then she lifted up the corner of a paperbark cover. "This is my baby, this truly good one!" She picked it up, and ran off. Then they attacked her. They hit her. Many of them; they struck her with stone axes and fighting sticks; they threw spears at her. She ran away. She dived into the jungle. "Husband! Come here!" "What?" "They were all hitting me, they took my 'eye', my baby!" "Come on, wife!" he said. "Let's go to that lot, those people!" They hurried together, the husband carrying his spears, holding them ready to throw. He flung spears at those people. They flung spears back at him. He jumped aside. And again! Men came at them with stone axes. And again! They fought. Then those two rushed off into the jungle, into the jungle of dense trees like banana plants.

Women have always worked multiple part- and full-time jobs. As in many gatherer-hunter societies, the women collect most of the food. It is also the women who bear the responsibility for the children. As the mogwoi woman does one job, she cannot give full attention to her other job; her baby is taken. The mother's cries rend the air, "Oh, my dear child! Oh, who snatched you away from me?" It is the mother who hurries about, searching. It is she who finds the baby. It is she who battles for the baby and reclaims her. The husband lends his support but it is the woman who holds the responsibility for the children as well as for bringing home most of the bacon. Women's work, women's contributions ought to be recognized and valued.

Biriwilg (Told by Women)

Arnhem Land, Australia[108]

Biriwilg set off, coming and camping on the way, looking for honey and meats and vegetable foods. She came to Wiridjeng, where she met Ngalmoban, who was carrying *man-gindjeg*, bitter yams, and asked her, "Where shall we go?" Ngalmoban said, "We'll go this way, north, in search of a place." So they came on together. They camped at Gun-roid-bi-boro, a red-ochre place name, and talked together. Ngalmoban told her, "I'm going higher up, and you go this way. We'll go separately. I'm taking *man-gindjeg* yams." Biriwilg agreed: "I'm going to the Garigen area, I'm not going that way." Ngalmoban went off with her yams. She was throwing them about at different places so they would grow there, and naming the places as she did so.

Biriwilg went on by herself. At Gara-morug on the plain, eating *man-gulaid* nuts, she said, "I'll go north and look for a place to put myself!" She came on, crossing the fresh water at Mula, and settling down for a while at Ngaraid-wodi-daidgeng where White Cockatoo had cut the rock with a boomerang. Still she came on. "I'm looking for a house where I can put myself and stay always." On the way she was eating long yams. "I'll stay here for a while, at Inyalbiri, eating these yams." Then she went on again. At Gun-ngad-bo she gave the place its name, because "here I dug a soak and I drank water." She came on, climbing up, camping on the way, and crossing the water at Yawagara. She said, "I'll go this way, where there is a big stretch of water, and I'll cross over." She crossed a big creek at Wolgal, went on, looked at the place and said, "Here I'll put myself, where the place is good and the cave-house is good, where I'll stay always." She went on, and was digging for soak water. As she dug the ground, she saw that it was only a little hole. She got up, and dug in another place. This time she was digging a big hole. Then she went, and was swimming about in it. When she had finished swimming, she climbed up out of the water and went to the cave. She said, "Here I put myself. I am Biriwilg. I came a long way. Ngalmoban and I came together, then we said farewell to each other. She went on. I came this way, and here I'll stay for ever: I put myself. I stand outside, like a drawing [painting] I stand. But I am a woman. I started off far away. Here the name of the place is Gun-gangin, where I put myself. I stand like a person, and I keep on standing here for ever."

307

According to traditional Aboriginal belief, life began during a mythological period known as Dreamtime. During Dreamtime, the world was formed by spirit beings. The land was soft and malleable and as these beings moved across the land, they often became a part of it. The land was alive. The land is still alive. It speaks: "I am Biriwilg . . . like a drawing I stand. But I am a woman . . . I stand like a person, and I keep on standing here for ever."

Tales
from
Sub-Saharan
Africa

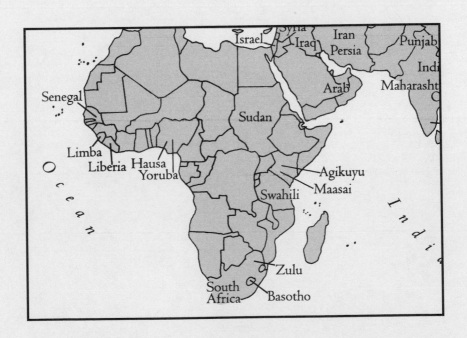

The Woman, Her Husband, Their Children and the Dodo

Hausa People, Nigeria[109]

There was a man and his wife had six children. There came a time of famine, and the woman said "Husband, let us go into the bush to somewhere where we can find some leaves to eat." "Very well, mother of my children" said he.

So they separated and she took a basket and made a paste with some indigo and water and then went off to the bush. There she came across some guinea-fowl. "Guinea-fowl of Egypt" said she "Come and let me do your hair for you and dress it with indigo." The guinea-fowls came to her, and clustered round her, and she would take hold of the head of one and anoint it with indigo. Then another would come and she would wring its neck and then put her foot on it. And she went on doing this till the sun set. Then said she "Off you go, guinea-fowls, go home till tomorrow." Then, filling her basket, she lifted it up and went off home. "Welcome home, mother" said her children; and her husband said "Well done, mother of my children." "Thank-you" said she. Then they plucked the guinea-fowls and cooked and ate them. And next day she again went and dealt with the guinea-fowls in the same way and returned home.

But the next day her husband said "Mother of my children, rest and let me take over the work." "Very well" said she. So away went her husband, and he called out "Guinea-fowl of Egypt, come and let me do your hair for you and dress it with indigo." And along came the guinea-fowls. But as soon as they arrived, he took hold of one and wrung its neck. When the others saw this they flew off and went away, leaving him there. And so from morning to evening he got nothing but just that one guinea-fowl. So he collected some grass and picking up the guinea-fowl, put it in the basket, lifted it up and off he went home. "Welcome, husband" said his wife. "Thank-you" said he. "Welcome, Dad" said his children. "Thank-you" said he. Then they uncovered the basket, and there lay one guinea-fowl. This the children took, but their father took it away from them, saying "There! That's children for you! I'm away in the bush ever since morning, while you're all at home, and I get myself a guinea-fowl— and you have to grab it! Well—I won't let you have it." "Well, husband" said their mother "you've spoilt that market for me."

311

Next day, when it was light, she set off, taking her basket and made for the bush. And, coming to a river, she looked for some bushes and hid herself among them. Presently along came the beasts of the bush—elephant and bush-cow, roan antelope and lion, hyena, leopard, gazelle, duiker, and hare—all came and drank. Then they set off again, back into the bush.

Whereupon the woman got up and said "Hey, elephant! You one-eyed, one-legged, one-eared rascal!" "Do you mean me?" asked the leading elephant. "No" said the woman. "Do you mean me?" said the next elephant. "No" said the woman. And so for the next and the next, until the last one said "Do you mean me?" and the woman said, "Yes." And then that elephant turned and went back, thinking that it was a fish that had spoken.

And, going into the water, [the elephant] began catching fish and throwing them out, saying "And I'll do the same to you tomorrow, if you're rude to me like that." Then she went off.

Then the woman fetched out her basket and began collecting the fish and putting them in the basket. She filled the basket and lifting it up, went off home. "Well done, mother of my children" said her husband, and "Thank-you" says she.

This went on for some days, until the husband said "Mother of my children, let me take over the work from you, and you have a rest." "Very well" says she, and handed it over to him.

So, when it was light, he took the basket and going to the river, hid in the bushes. And all the beasts of the bush came and drank and went on their way. Then he got up and said "Hey, elephant! You good-for-nothing rascal! You one-eyed, one-legged, one-eared thing with a gap in your teeth." And the leading elephant said "Do you mean me?" "Yes" he answered. "That's not a fish, it's a man" said she, "now I'm being insulted like that other elephant was," and getting hold of some fire she kindled the bush. And it caught—and the man only got away by the skin of his teeth.

So he went home and called out "Mother of my children!" but she answered "Bah! Why do you call me? Now you've spoilt that market."

Next day, when it was light, the mother set out, taking her basket, and went into the bush. There she saw a compound, and coming up to it, hid herself to watch. Then she saw a dodo,* who had killed a man and was bringing him home. When he reached the door, he said "Baram" and the door opened, and he took the body in and left it there. And, coming out again, he said to the door "Zarga gungun," and it shut, and away he went.

* *Dodo*, ghoul.

Then the woman came forward and going up to the door said "Baram." Whereupon the door opened. And, entering, she beheld rice and guinea-corn, bulrush-millet, cassava-flour and oil. Then, taking a mortar, she put her basket down on it, and taking from the bulrush-millet, filled her basket with it. Then she spread her cloth and filled that with rice. Next she went and coiled a head-pad. And, lifting the millet on to her head and tying the rice on to her back, she went out through the door. When she got outside, she said to the door "Zarga gungun." The door closed and the woman went off home. And for seven days she went on doing this.

And on the seventh day, when she had been and collected the corn and come home, her husband said "Mother of my children, let me take over the work from you, and you have a rest." "Very well" said she.

So he went and hid and watched the *dodo* bring the man that he had killed. And the *dodo* said to the door "Baram" and the door opened. And he went in and put down the body and came out. Then he said to the door "Zarga gungun" and the door closed.

Then the man came forward and said to the door "Baram" and the door opened. And when he had got inside, he said to the door "Zarga gungun" and the door shut. Then he went into the compound, and saw the millet and the guinea-corn, the rice, the cassava flour and the oil.

Then he took a cooking-pot and put some water on to boil, saying to himself "I won't go until I've cooked some rice and added a little oil and eaten it. Then I can pack up something and take it to them." And there he stayed until the rice was cooked. He had just taken the pot off the fire, when there was the *dodo*!

"Who's there?" said the *dodo*. And the man answered "By God, it wasn't me! It's only today that I've started coming." "That's a lie" said the *dodo*, "Someone's been taking my corn every day." "It wasn't me" said the man, "It was the mother of my children—she's been coming and taking your corn." "I see" said the *dodo*, "Well, you eat that rice that you've cooked. Then I'll mount you and you can take me to the mother of your children." "Certainly" said the man. When he had eaten the rice, the *dodo* said to him "Go and get that saddle over there, that's what I'm going to ride you with." "Yes, yes" said he and fetched it. Then the *dodo* got up, put the saddle on him, mounted him, and away they went till they came to the man's home.

"Mother of my children" he said "come on out to meet me." But she said "My children, today your father has done a bad thing. Just look— he's brought a *dodo* to us!" Then the children rushed to their mother and clung to her. And the *dodo* said "Now then! Out you come! For since you've eaten up my corn, I'm going to eat you up!"

So they came out, and set off along the path till they came to the *dodo*'s home. And the *dodo*, before he set off on his round, said to the mother "Before I get back, you cook me one of your children!" She acquiesced. Presently out came a mouse and said "What are you crying for?" and she answered "The *dodo* told me to cook my child." Says the mouse "Here's a hole. Put your child in here!" And she accepted gratefully.

Then she went and took some of the human flesh, which the *dodo* had been collecting. And she went on doing this in the same way, until all her children had vanished.

Then said the *dodo* to the mother "Before I get back, you cook yourself!" "OK" said she and got up and took some human flesh and cooked it. Then she took some rice and some cassava flour and some oil, and went into the mouse's hole.

When the *dodo* returned, he said "Good-for-nothing woman. Well, I've had my own back for that corn that they ate—I've eaten them up." Then, turning to the man he said "I shan't take you to the bush with me today. Stay here and cook yourself." "Very well" said he, and off went the *dodo*.

"Well" said he "If I've got to cook myself, I may as well cook some rice and eat it first." So he took a cooking-pot—using a large water-storage jar!—and put it on the fire; and another for himself. And he cooked the rice and ate it.

Then he got up and went to get in the pot, but when he felt the water, it was boiling, "Ow!" said he "Oh dear, oh dear! Mother of my children, however did you manage to cook yourself?" and he began to cry. Then he dashed forward, meaning to jump into the pot—and smashed it. So he brought another one, and put that on the fire, and getting some water, poured it in. Says he to himself "Now I'll get into this pot, before the water has had a chance to get hot."

But then the woman felt sorry for him and said "Here, you! Confound you—come on into the hole here!" Then she went and took some meat and put it into the pot. And again helped herself to rice and cassava flour and oil, and so back into the hole.

Along comes the *dodo* "Ha," says he, "Rascals! Now I've eaten them in return for that corn they ate." And there they all were, in the hole. Then the *dodo* went and began to cook his *tuwo*,* and sat there stirring it, and it was very appetizing *tuwo*!

Then the man, coming to the mouth of the hole says "Hey—whoev-

---

* *Tuwo*, the usual evening meal, guinea corn. Its preparation involves pounding and winnowing five or six times, washing, back into the mortar for pounding again, making into balls and putting into boiling water, taking out and pounding again until quite smooth, rolling in flour, putting into a calabash with buttermilk, and mashing.

er's stirring that *tuwo* —when you've finished, give me a lick." The *dodo* looked, and he looked, but he saw no one. So the man went on "You there, stirring the *tuwo*, it's you I'm talking to. I say, when you've finished, spare me a little!"

But just then the mother, taking up a stirring-stick, and aiming at his backside, walloped him hard with it. "Hey, hold on, mother of my children!" says he "I was only asking him to spare a little for me."

Off went the *dodo* to collect all the beasts of the bush to help him, and along they came. "That hole there" says he—"I want the people in it caught and brought out." Then some of them said "Camel." "No" says the camel "Look at the ostrich—she's got a small neck and a small head."

Then the mother took a knife and sharpened it and came to the mouth of the hole. The ostrich stuck her head in, and the mother grasped it and taking her knife to it, slaughtered it. And outside, the ostrich's tail came down to the ground.

Then the beasts of the bush began to say "The ostrich has grabbed something and can't get out." And there they were, all dancing around, when the ostrich suddenly collapsed, headless. Whereupon the whole gathering scattered at full speed. And the hyena's comment was "What a singularly pointless trick to invite us here, just to shorten our heads!"

And the *dodo* said "As for me—I'm leaving this compound. And I'm not coming back!"

Then out came the woman, her husband and her six children, They all helped themselves to corn and rice. Then they went home. And the famine came to an end. Kungurus kan kusu. I ate the rat—he didn't eat me.

The most widely known folktales with heroines end with a beautiful princess marrying a handsome prince and living happily ever after. This story also stereotypes the characters. The mother is a resourceful thinker, good provider, and an extremely patient wife. The father is a bungler. However, they have a loving relationship. They speak to each other politely. He compliments her on her catch and she responds with a gracious, "Thank you." He considerately attempts to give her a day off. Each time he bungles the job, she simply says, "Well husband, you've spoilt that market for me." Even when he leads the flesh-eating dodo to her and the children, she takes it in stride. When the husband tries to cook himself, she takes pity on him and saves him: "Confound you—come into this hole here." It's refreshing to have a heroine love someone who isn't perfect.

Ku-Chin-Da-Gayya and Her Elder Sister and the Dodos

Hausa People, Nigeria[110]

There was once a maiden who declared that she would never marry a man with a scar on his body. And she sent away all the young men who came, saying that they had scars.

But two *dodos** heard of this and changed themselves into men; and set off and travelled till they came to the compound where the girl lived. They made formal greeting, and the girl came out and scrutinized them. "Father" said she, "I've seen some real men." "Have you though?" said he. "Yes" she answered. "That's fine" he said, and the guests were shown to their lodging-places.

Next day when it was light, her father said "Where are these men of yours? Call them here, so that I can see them." So she went and called them, and her father asked "Well—which of the two of them are you going to marry?" One of them said "Me," and "Very well" said her father, and immediately collected all the equipment for a marriage, and they were married. After that they stayed for three nights, and on the fourth day they said that it was time to be going home. "Take your wife with you" said the father, and "Yes indeed" said they.

Now the girl who had been married had a younger sister, and her name was Ku-Chin-Da-Gayya.° Well, they had set off and were already on their way, when Ku-Chin-Da-Gayya came up and said "Take me with you." But her sister answered "My good girl, you don't even know where we are going—how can you ask us to take you with us?" So the girl turned herself into a fly and slipped into some *fura*† they were taking with them.

They travelled for a while until they reached some dense bush, whereupon the husband said to his friend "Tell my wife to give you some water and bring it to me, for us to drink." Accordingly the friend went over to the wife and said "He says you are to give us water" and went back again. Whereupon she began to cry, and out came her sister. Says the younger sister "Go round behind that geza bush, you'll see some water there. Take some,

* *Dodo*, ghoul.
° *Ku-Chin-Da-Gayya*, means roughly "overcome me by trickery."
† *Fura*, the usual morning meal, preferably of millet, mixed with buttermilk and "drunk." Its preparation is similar to that of the evening meal, *tuwo*.

316

and mix up some *fura* for them." She went behind the bush and saw the water; took some and mixed up *fura* and took it to them. And they drank it.

And so they set off again. And when they had travelled some way on into the bush, they decided to stop again. They put down their loads, and the two friends went to some shade and sat down and rested. And the elder sister sat down in a separate patch of shade. Presently the husband said to his friend "Go to that woman and tell her to give you some young beans." "Right" said the other, and coming over said "He says you're to give me some young beans" and he went back over to his friend. Then she began to cry again, saying "Now, in the dry season here in the middle of the bush, how shall I get young beans?" Whereupon her younger sister says "Take some of the fruit of the geza; put it in a calabash and cover it over with a mat-cover, and take it to them." So she did just as she was told and took it to them, and when they uncovered it, there were young beans, cooked! "Fancy that!" they said, "Out here in the bush, in the dry season, the rainy season still distant—however did she get hold of young beans?" And they ate them and again set off, till they came to the compound of the *dodos*.

Along came the other *dodos*, rejoicing that their son had married a human wife and brought her home, and that thus they had meat. That night, when the *dodo* and his human wife were asleep, the *dodo*'s father came. But Ku-Chin-Da-Gayya wasn't asleep. And the *dodo*'s mother came too, saying "Sarma, sarma diddis."* But Ku-Chin-Da-Gayya still wasn't asleep and she said "Who's that saying 'Sarma sarma diddis' to us?" "It's your husband's mother" said the female *dodo*, "Saying 'Sarma sarma diddis' to you." "What do you want that you should say 'Sarma sarma diddis' to us?" "I want some hot coals—that's why I said 'Sarma sarma diddis' to you." "Here you are, take some, but don't let us hear your 'Sarma sarma diddis' again!" Away went the female *dodo* and was followed by her husband, and the girl spoke to him in the same way.

Next morning when it was light, the girl's *dodo* husband said to her "We're off to the farm. When you've finished making the *fura*, give it to Ku-Chin-Da-Gayya to take to us there." "Very well" she answered. So when she finished preparing the *fura*, she gave it to her sister, who picked it up and went off. But when she got near to them, she changed herself into a bird and flew on towards them.

Well, it seemed they weren't hoeing the farm at all, but eating frogs. "Greetings to you, menfolk of my sister" said she. But before she could finish what she was saying, the two *dodos* broke in and began to say to her

* *Sarma, sarma diddis*, presumably dodo language.

"Hullo there, bird! When we've given our little sister-in-law something to eat, we'll give you a leg and a shoulder," and they began to dance. Then she returned to where she had left the *fura*, picked it up and took it to them.

And they, when they saw her coming, changed themselves into men again. And she took them the *fura*, they drank it and she went off home. And in the evening they too returned home. And day after day these events were repeated, until Ku-Chin-Da-Gayya grew quite thin. Then her elder sister asked her "What's the matter with you, that you're getting thin?" "Rather" answered the other, "Should you say 'What's the matter with you, that while I sleep, you watch over me?'" and she went on "For you know, that husband of yours is a *dodo* and his mother and father are both *dodos* too." "Is this true?" asked her sister. "Yes" she answered and left her.

It was night again and they were asleep. Ku-Chin-Da-Gayya took off her sister's cloth and fastened it on to her husband and loosing also the beads from the other girl's neck, put them also on her husband; and so too with the girl's headcloth. Then she lifted her sister and put her down beyond her husband, leaving the husband on the outside. Next she began to dig a hole, and didn't reach the surface till she was inside the hut of the *dodo* mother.

Presently along comes the *dodo* mother, and says "Sarma sarma diddis." She was answered by silence, so she said "They're asleep." Then she came right up to the entrance of the hut and repeated "Sarma sarma diddis." Again there was no reply, so she went in and taking hold of her son, cut his throat. For she did not know it was he, but thought it was his wife. Then she went back to her own hut and to sleep.

Next morning when it was light, the mother *dodo* said "*Now* we shall have meat to eat." But when the girl awoke, she saw her husband, killed and "Oh, oh, oh!" she wailed "What'll become of me?" Now Ku-Chin-Da-Gayya was crouching just inside the hole and she said "What are you crying for? Here, come on into the hole, and follow it right into the hut of the lady of the house." But Ku-Chin-Da-Gayya stayed there, squatting in the mouth of the tunnel. Whereupon presently along came the father and mother *dodo* to eat the flesh of the girl that had been killed. And then Ku-Chin-Da-Gayya spoke, saying "You can eat the flesh of your own son—you're not eating our flesh." And the mother and father began to lament. Then said Ku-Chin-Da-Gayya "You can say goodbye to me" and closing up the tunnel, went off home.

Then the mother *dodo* changed herself into a *kanya** tree, and came near

---

* *Kanya*, the African ebony tree.

to the entrance to the town. And the little boys and girls of the town came to pick her fruit. Ku-Chin-Da-Gayya's mother said to her "Hey, why don't you go and enjoy some *kanya* fruit; all the others are going and picking it and eating it; but you haven't been yet." "I'll go today" she answered. And when she had got there she said "*Kanya.*" No reply. "*Kanya.*" Still no reply. Then said the girl "If you were a *kanya* belonging to our town, you would've answered when I called you." "Yes?" said the *kanya*. But Ku-Chin-Da-Gayya answered "You wicked, good-for-nothing woman—I knew you were the witch all along. You won't eat me. And the tricks I played on you, you won't play them back on me."

So away went the *kanya*, and presently returned as a river. And the children went bathing in it, but Ku-Chin-Da-Gayya did not go. Then someone asked her "Aren't you going bathing?" "All right" she said and went off. When she got there, she said "River." No reply. Again she said "River." Again no reply, three times in all. Then said Ku-Chin-Da-Gayya "If you were a river belonging to our town, and I had called you, you would have answered." "Yes?" said the river, but Ku-Chin-Da-Gayya said "You wicked, good-for-nothing woman, I know you—you're the witch. You'll never repay the trick that I played on you, till the day you die. You may as well go back to your home and settle down there and relax. For whatever you turn yourself into, I'll come along and recognize you." That's all. Kungurus kan kusu.

When Little Red Riding Hood went through the woods, she didn't know what a wicked creature the wolf was. Ku-Chin-Da-Gayya, however, knows a dodo when she sees one. She weaves her way through the multitude of traps set by the flesh-eating dodos and saves herself and her sister. She recognizes and outwits the mother dodo who has changed herself into a tree. Ku-Chin-Da-Gayya recognizes and outwits the mother dodo-turned-river. Ku-Chin-Da-Gayya is a little girl who knows how to protect herself. "I know you—you're the witch. . . . You may as well go back to your home and settle down there and relax. For whatever you turn yourself into, I'll come along and recognize you."

Moremi and the Egunguns

Yoruba People, Nigeria [111]

In the days when Ife was still young there was a distant city called Ile-Igbo. Between the two cities was a forest, and neither one knew of the other's existence. No person of Ife had ever passed through that forest, nor had anyone from Ile-Igbo.

But one day a hunter from Ile-Igbo went out in search of game. He became lost in the forest and wandered many days without knowing which way to go. He began to give up hope, thinking, "The forest has swallowed me. Now I am coming to the end of my life." Then, when his despair had nearly killed him, he emerged from among the trees and there just a little beyond he saw the city of Ife. He looked in wonder, for he had never heard that such a place existed, but he did not approach the city. After he had rested he reentered the forest and, in time, he found his way back to Ile-Igbo.

He told the Oba* of his own city what he had seen. The Oba thought, "As is well known, there is no such city as the one he describes." Nevertheless he sent messengers to check on the hunter's story. The messengers entered the forest. They pressed on. After some days they were saying to one another, "The hunter told our Oba a wild story. There is no city out here in the wilderness." Then they came to the edge of the forest and saw Ife standing there. They saw Ife's fields on all sides. They saw the fertile gardens and the granaries filled with food. They watched the people of Ife come and go, but they did not make their presence known.

The messengers returned to Ile-Igbo and reported to their Oba. They said, "The hunter's words were true. On the other side of the forest stands a prosperous city. Its gardens are full of all kinds of growing things. Its granaries are full of grain. Its market is full of people selling manioc,° corn and yams."

The Oba of Ile-Igbo reflected on what he heard, for while Ife was prosperous his own city was not doing well. The gardens of Ile-Igbo did not grow enough food, and often there were families that had to eat wild roots because their crops were poor. The Oba thought, "Why should

---

* *Oba*, a ruler of any of several African peoples of western Nigeria.
° *Manioc*, cassava.

320

that other city prosper while mine suffers?" He called his counselors together. They discussed the matter. And it was decided to send an expedition to Ife and loot it of food. But Ife appeared to be strong, with many warriors. So the Oba's counselors devised a plan.

Instead of arming themselves with spears and other such weapons the men of Ile-Igbo disguised themselves as Egunguns, messengers from the land of the dead. Some were dressed as Ololu, or Beater, Egunguns and carried clubs. Some were dressed as Alapa-Nsanpa Egunguns and had long arms hanging down at their sides. Some were dressed as Etiyeri Egunguns, with long protruding ears affixed to their heads. All the Egunguns wore masks, and their bodies were covered with *raffia*.* They were fearsome to see, and even the people of Ile-Igbo were terrified.

The Egunguns went through the forest and arrived at the edge of Ife. There they rested for a while. At a signal from their leader they entered the city, dancing, gyrating, singing and making strange sounds.

The people of Ife were struck with fear and ran away into the bush. Then the Egunguns pillaged Ife. They took food from the granaries and the gardens. They took everything that they could carry. After that they disappeared into the forest and made their way back to Ile-Igbo. The Oba was happy. The people were happy. Now there was plenty of food for everyone in Ile-Igbo and there was no need to worry about the crops in the fields.

But the food stolen from Ife did not last forever. A time came when it was gone. And so the Oba met again with his counselors and decided to send another pillaging expedition to Ife. Once again the men dressed in the costumes of Egunguns and went through the forest and caused the people of Ife to flee from their city. Once again they looted the houses, granaries and the gardens and returned home.

The looting of Ife became a way of life for Ile-Igbo, whose people neglected their own gardens even more than before. Whenever Ile-Igbo ran short of food another expedition was sent to Ife. Life in Ife became hard. Though the people there worked industriously they no longer had enough to eat. They planted, gathered their crops, and then the mysterious Egunguns came out of the forest and took everything away.

In Ife there was a woman named Moremi. She went to the Oba of Ife, saying, "These spirits from the forest where do they come from? Where do they go? Why do dead spirits need to consume the food of the living? If things go on this way, Ife itself will die and become a dead spirit. We

---

* *Raffia*, the fiber of the raffia palm used for tying plants and making articles such as baskets or hats.

should find out about these Egunguns. Therefore when they come again I will remain in the city and learn why they continue to harass us."

The Oni, or Oba, of Ife objected, saying that it was taboo for women to watch the Egunguns, that to remain in the city was too dangerous. Moremi insisted. The Oba called on some of the elders of Ife to come and discuss what Moremi proposed. The counselors said, "If things go on this way Ife will dry up and fall away from the face of the earth. Something must be done. Let Moremi do as she wishes." Having heard his counselors, the Oba of Ife agreed.

Moremi went to the sacred brook called Esinminrin. She supplicated the brook, asking for help against the Egunguns. She pledged that if she could save Ife she would give her young son Olu-Orogbo as a sacrifice.

In time the Egunguns again swarmed into Ife. The people fled to the bush, all except Moremi. She remained behind, and when the raiders entered her house they found her there. Not knowing what else to do with her they took her back to Ile-Igbo and brought her to the Oba. The Oba of Ile-Igbo found Moremi beautiful. He made her one of his wives. Little by little Moremi learned about the way Ile-Igbo had been deceiving Ife and reducing it to poverty. The people of Ile-Igbo began to forget that Moremi came from Ife. She waited for an opportunity to escape.

One night when she was with the Oba, Moremi brought him a great deal of palm wine and he drank heavily. Sleep came upon him. Moremi dressed herself in rags so that she looked like a beggar, and in the darkness she made her way to the forest and began the long journey back to Ife. Each night she climbed a tree and slept in the branches to be safe from wild animals. When the sun rose she resumed her walking. At last, after many days and nights, she came again to Ife. There was happiness in the city when she returned. People called out to one another, "Moremi who was carried away by the Egunguns has returned!" They crowded around her house. There was singing and dancing.

Moremi disclosed everything she had learned in Ile-Igbo. Everyone was surprised to hear that the mysterious beings who came out of the forest were not really messengers from the dead, but raiders dressed in masks and raffia. They decided on a way to deal with the Egunguns when they came again.

Life went on. Then one day the Egunguns from Ile-Igbo again emerged from the forest and entered Ife. This time the people did not run into the bush. They went to their fires and lighted torches. As the Egunguns approached the houses the people ran out with their torches and set fire to the raffia costumes of the raiders. Soon all the Egunguns were aflame. They went this way and that in panic, running, falling, crying out. Some were blinded by the smoke and ran into the spears of the Ife warriors. Some died in the flames that enveloped them. Only a few managed to get out of their raffia costumes and escape to the forest. Those who found their way back to Ile-Igbo told the Oba what had happened. It was the last Ile-Igbo pillaging expedition to Ife. The Egunguns never came again.

There was a festival in Ife. The people praised and honored Moremi for her courageous act that had saved the city. But for Moremi it was not yet over. She had pledged that if she saved Ife from the Egunguns she would sacrifice her son Olu-Orogbo to the sacred brook Esinminrin. She carried out her promise. She went to the book with her son, all of Ife walking behind her. There was a ritual, and there at the edge of the running water Olu-Orogbo was sacrificed. The people returned home. Moremi's heart was filled with grief.

But when everyone was gone a strange thing happened at the place of the sacrifice. A golden chain descended slowly from the sky. Olu-Orogbo stood up. He took hold of the chain and was raised into the sky, where he lived on under the protection of the Sky God Olorun.

Ife also lived on.

Amidst the terror of attack and the desperation of famine, one person, Moremi, asks the rational and important questions that lead to the solution: "Why do dead spirits need to consume the food of the living? Where do [they] come from? Where do they go?" She is determined to save her city. Courageously Moremi remains alone to face the Egunguns. Tenaciously she gathers information in the enemy village. Exercising great self-control, she waits for the right moment to escape. Moremi brings the life-saving information back to her people. The next time the Egunguns come, Ife is ready.

The Spider, Kayi, and the Bush Fowl

Limba People, Sierra Leone [112]

The spider and Kayi—they lived in a hut. The spider went and trapped a bush fowl. The bush fowl was killed. He brought it. "Kayi, here is food for sauce. Lay it down." She laid it down. Kayi got up. She pounded millet. She put it down. She took a bowl, she went to the water. When she had gone to the water, the spider got up. He ate the millet, all of it. When his wife came back, she came and put down the water, she went and looked at the millet. "E! Spider." "Yes?" "Who ate the millet?" "The bush fowl ate the millet." "What?" "Yes." "Well, all right."

Later the spider got up, he went to tap his palm tree. When he had gone to tap his palm tree, Kayi got up. She prepared the bush fowl. She boiled it. She cooked the millet. She finished eating it *all!* She sat down. The spider came back. "Kayi, have you kept anything for me?" "No." "What about the millet?" "E! Well, the bush fowl ate up all the millet!" "What about the bush fowl?" "The bush fowl has gone, gone off to the bush."

"The [dead] bush fowl ate the millet," says Kayi's husband. Kayi doesn't complain or yell. Kayi doesn't nag. Kayi knows that two can play that game. When her husband comes back for dinner, he finds that the [dead] bush fowl has not only eaten up all the millet but has also run off back into the bush!

The Story of Two Women

Limba People, Sierra Leone[113]

I, Suri Kamara, I am coming to tell Yenkeni a story of two women who wanted to have children. These two they came to be married to the same husband. They lived there in that marriage. They always asked everyone who came to the village where they were whether they knew a person who understood the medicine for having children. A man came from a journey. He came and told them, "I met a woman, she is in one part of the village. That woman, Kanu came and gave her medicine for having children." The two, each of them, their hearts came and rose up, to go to the woman so that the woman could help them to get the power to have children, so they could have children.

Then one of them came and stood up, the elder. She came to go. When she came to go, she came and found the village. The old woman who understood the medicine for having children was there. When she came and reached there, she told the old woman, "Mother, well, here on the earth I was brought out by Kanu; but right up to this time today, nothing! I am unable to have a child. Well, I, I want to have children. That is why I am bringing you this gift, so that Kanu may grant me to have children, by grace of your power."

Then the old woman said, "Will you be able?" "Yes." "Will you be able?" "Yes." "Will you wash off its filth?" "Yes." "Will you wash off its filth?" "Yes." "Will you allow it to wet on you?" "Yes." "Will you be able?" "Yes." "Will you be able to be vomited on?" "Yes." "Will you like the vomit?" "Yes." "Well, sit down." The woman sat down. She had food cooked for her. She finished eating. The night came.

Now the old woman—those who came to her to ask to have children, she had had a house built for her, and whoever came had to lie down in that house. In the centre of the house was an earth bed. There the person was to lie down.

When darkness came, then the old woman said to the girl who came to find children, "Well, now, here you are to sleep. I will not be able to make you a fire.* You will sleep here alone. Whatever comes to you here, if you want to bear children—don't be afraid! Well, treat the thing well."

---

* To be given no fire for heat or light at night is considered a real hardship if sleeping alone in a house.

Then the girl said, "All right, I agree." She had a mat spread for her on the bed, in the centre of the house. She lay down. The old woman locked the door. When they had slept for long in the first sleep, there the girl saw a great snake coming. The snake—it was huge; it crawled *fuuu!* She the girl, she stayed there. She welcomed the snake. The instant she took hold of the snake as if to put it on her knee, what did she see? A pillow. She took the pillow, and put it at her head. She kissed the pillow, kissed the pillow, kissed the pillow. When the time had gone on for long since she had lain down again, there rats came to her. The rats began to wet on her. She took her cloth, her fine cloth, she opened it out, she covered herself with it so that the rats might wet the cloth.

When the morning came, the old woman went to open the door. The old woman asked her, "When you spent the night here, what did you see?" "Well, when darkness came in, what was the first thing to come to me?—a snake. That snake, it welcomed me and I put it on my knee. What did I see on my knee?—a pillow. Well even though it was a snake that came to me, it was with good intent; that is why I put it on my knee, a pillow. When I put it on my knee, when I saw that it was a pillow, that is why I put it at my head so you would know that I was thinking about the purpose I came to you. The rats too, when they began to wet on me— that is why I also opened out my cloth so that here where you spread for me, the mat would not be spoilt."

Then the old woman said, "All right. Well, wait. Now I am going into the bush, I will say good-bye to you." The old woman went into the bush she went to pick the medicine for giving birth, all of it. She came back, she came and took it, she the old woman. She went alone into the house. She took a basket. In that basket, there she put a child, a girl, one with sores all over her body. She took medicine, with which the girl could cure the child she put in the basket. She put it inside. Then she picked up a little rice and a little of the medicine for having children, she gave it to her. "Well, go. As you go, don't open the basket on the road. As soon as you reach the place, go to the waterside; don't send anyone else! You yourself are to go for the water. The rice—don't husk it. Come and put the cooking pot up on the fire. When you have finished cooking, when you are going to eat the cooked rice, then open the basket. The thing you see there, if it is something, you two, you and it, you are to eat the rice. If you see medicine there, it is that medicine you are to eat with the rice."

The girl took the basket. She slung it over her shoulder. She went for far. She was not satisfied, for she thought "Perhaps the basket will drop by mistake and be lost, and fall on the ground." She took her cloth— which she no longer considered at all—she wrapped the basket in it.

As soon as she reached the place and went to the waterside, she took and put the cooking pot on the fire, she took the little bit of rice and put it in the pot. She cooked it well. She took the cooked rice, she helped it out. She took a pan and began to fan it so that the rice would cool. When the rice had finished cooling, then she sat, then she sat. She opened the basket. As she opened the basket, what did she see inside? A child, with sores, a girl child. She first took the rice, she pushed it to one side. She unloosed the child, she took the child, she put her on her knees. She first lifted up the child and kissed her, kissed her again, kissed her. She took the child, she took her cloth that she had bought with much money, she first spread it out for the child.* She left the child, she ran to the waterside. She came and put water on the fire for the child, she ran into the bush. She went and picked her some leaves for medicine too for her sores. She came and took soap, she scrubbed the child. When she had finished scrubbing the child, she rubbed the medicine on the child. As she was rubbing her with it, then the child said, "Mother. I, I am hungry now." She put the child down, she took oil, she put it where the child was to eat. The child finished eating. She was satisfied. Once she scrubbed the child, the child was cured, the girl child.

That child—it did not take long, the woman conceived, a boy child. In two months she came and bore a child, a boy. It was a boy, a chief! The girl that she got when she was looking for medicine, she became the child's guardian.

Time passed, and the child grew. Then her companion got up, her co-wife. Then she asked her, "Friend. Now we are co-wives, we two only that are married here. You, you went on a journey. When you went on the journey and came back, Kanu came and helped you. You came and bore a chief. I beg you now, don't think about our co-wifehood. Show me now this path where you walked until Kanu gave you a child." Then her companion sat down. She told her all, completely.

Well, she, the one who had borne no child, she was the one that was always the more loved; she was the one who always had clothes bought for her—the best ones, the ones of high price. She got up, she went and told her husband. The husband went and packed for her as the first had been packed for. She went. When she had gone, she came and found the old woman. When she found the old woman, the old woman asked her, "Why have you come?" Then she said, "Mother. I have come to find a way to bear children. I and my husband—we have travelled much, but we

---

* Sometimes old pieces of cloth or rag are used for laying a child on, but this girl uses a precious piece of material.

have not yet got children. That is why we are running here to you, for you to come and help us."

Then the old woman said, "Well I, I have heard. But I have something to ask you. Can you wash off the filth?" Then the girl said, "What! Oh mother, it was not to wash off filth that I came. Look at my body. Does it look like filth? That remark, don't say that to me again!" Then she said, "Well, I won't say that to you again. But what I have to ask you, I, I must ask you. Now, you, will you be able to wash off wet?" Then the girl said, "Oh mother! I did not come here for a quarrel. Stop this! I did not come here to you for you to go and ask me to wash off wet. Look at my body, is that what my body is like? Is it to come and wash off wet? Stop this, don't say that a second time!" Then the old woman said, "Yes, but I have not yet finished asking you. What about you, will you agree to be vomited on? Will you wash off the vomit?" Then she said, "Now, I will not answer you again. If this talk helps me, it is not proper. You are only talking at me. But these words you are saying to me, they are not entering my heart well. My heart is not cool. It is only because you are old——"* Then the old woman said, "Well, all right, sit down now." She was cooked for. She finished eating.

The darkness came in. Then the old woman poked her. "Come." It was to the bed where her companion spent the night, the one who came first. As they reached the place then she said, "Well, I am giving you lodging in this house. When I give you lodging here, everything that comes to you here, embrace it with both hands, whatever thing you see here, since you are calling for children for yourself." "All right, I agree." She lay down. When she had lain down, the old woman locked the door. Not long after, the snake came, the snake that had come before and found her co-wife there. It came again *gbuuuu*. As it came, that instant it went right to her breast. She the girl, as soon as she saw the snake, threw the snake down. The snake went and fell. She took the spoon that was leaning against the bed, she banged it on the snake's head. She struck it again. The snake died. The rats also began to come to wet on her. Then she stood on the middle of the bed, "You, you, you, you! Your habits! Don't spoil my cloth. It was bought for me for a high price by my husband. It was not to you I came. I came to the old woman for her to help me to bear children."

The sun came to rise. As the old woman opened the door *gburu*—she said "Mother! Mother! So that is why you came and spread my bed here for me! The sufferings I have had this night—since I was borne by my parents, I had not ever seen such sufferings. But it is all right! But it is all right!°

---

* that I put up with it.
° She speaks very sarcastically.

Then the old woman said, "Oh, friend, you have finished the night. Kanu said that nothing would hurt you. Now I am coming to say good-bye to you."

Then the old woman went. The old woman did not show unfairness. What she had given her companion, that is what she gave her too. She went and picked medicine, she took a little bit of rice, she took a little medicine, took a basket, took a child and put them inside. But when she had put them inside, she showed her the rule. "When you are going, if you open the basket on the road, what you see there—that will be your portion."

As soon as she went out, as soon as she had left the village, when she had been told good-bye—that instant she said, "A person cannot be given something without looking to see what it is inside." As soon as she opened it a little bit and peeped, she saw a shiny skin—shining. Behold, it was a snake! She tied and tied it in, she went. As soon as she reached there, she went and cooked rice. When she had finished arranging everything as she had been told by the old woman, as she was going to eat she opened the basket. What did she see? A child with sores. Then she took the child, then she went for rags, the rags she wiped her feet on when she wanted to lie down! She went and took the rags, she rammed them into the child's mouth so that the child could not cry, so that the people would not know that the girl had brought a child with sores. She took her, she bound the rags on her giving her pain all over on her sores. She put her back in the basket. She tied it all up, she went. She took the road back. As soon as she arrived, she did not even go right to the old woman's house, she dropped the basket. Then she said, "I did not come to you to beg a child with sores." She went back. As she went back, she died. No sign from her stomach even came to her first.

That is why, since she died, the other women who live now in our country, whoever of them as they are walking round steps on the dust of the girl, the one who did not want children—that woman, right until she dies, Kanu will not give her any sign of bearing a child. From the snake that she killed—from that came death to the children. At the first, no child died; only the old people, they died.

Since I heard that story, and Yenkeni came saying she wanted to hear that story in Limba—that is the story. It is finished.

Before I had children I knew how to pace myself through a full-length ballet. I had the endurance to dance on a set from nine in the morning until midnight. I knew the happiness of being in love. When I became a mother, I had no idea that I was beginning the longest, toughest, most emotion-laden ballet I would ever dance, a permanent performance, which encompasses more pain, more sweat, more patience, more fatigue, and purer joy than anything else I have ever done. Both of the women in the story still reside inside me. I miss the life of dancing, reading, and having beautiful but breakable objects lying around the house, but I gently hold back my daughter's hair when she's vomiting, kiss my daughters when they cry, and clean up the kitchen after my six-year-old chemist.

The Man Killed for a Spinach Leaf

Limba People, Sierra Leone[114]

I am Yaling. I am going to tell Yenkeni a story. A story for you, Yenkeni.

A man once married a wife in a village. The chief there planted leaves for sauce—spinach. He said that no one was to pick that spinach. "If you pick it, I will kill you."

Well, the wet season fell. Now, the people were in the farm there,* the woman with her husband. He said "I am going to go and beg for a spinach leaf." When he came and begged for the spinach leaf, the chief said, "That leaf, if you pick it, I will kill you. Of all those in the village, no one must pick it. It is the 'sacrifice' of the village." The boy said, "All right."

Then what happened? When night came, the boy came from the farm. He came and picked the spinach, one bunch of leaves. That one bunch he took away with him when he went. For if even one bunch of spinach leaves is picked you will eat it for two days while you are in your house. You shred it finely. That is what the boy came and picked—one bunch. He took it away.

When the chief heard this in the morning he looked. He could not see it [spinach]. He sent a servant for the boy. "Go and ask there for the spinach for me—the spinach that he came and picked. If he was the one, let him confess. Let him confess."

When the servant went, he went and asked him. The boy said, "I went and begged yesterday, but he refused. So I went and stole it."

It would have been better for him not to have thought of it. For when the servant came and told the chief after he had left the farm, the chief set out from the village. He took his sword. He sat on his horse. He struck his horse *gbaŋ*! Then he began to go, galloping *raaa*, right to the farm. When he got there he asked. When he asked, he said, "What about that man sitting there? I have come for you. You went today and picked the spinach. That is why I have come for you." When the man wanted to speak, he struck him.

Ah! when he had killed him, there was left his wife, a girl, who was pregnant. The young wife got up. She went far off. She said, "I will not

* i.e., it is implied that they were poor.

331

stay here, here where my husband was killed because of sauce. If I stay on here tomorrow, if I stay my child will be killed." She went far away. She went and stayed there.

When she bore the child, she gave her child the name of Sira. That Sira—she began to bring her up. When the child began to cry then she began to pet her, "Hush, oh, child, hush.* Your father was killed for a spinach leaf." Always, always, always she told that to the child as she suckled her, till she could sit, till she could walk—always she would say that and the child would hear it. Till the child was weaned she told her that; when the child began to cry she said, "Hush, oh, child, hush. Your father was killed for a spinach leaf."

When the child grew and got sense, her breasts were filled—*beredei!* everyone tried to woo her. She refused. When she was grown, she asked her mother. "Mother, where did my father go?" Then her mother said, "Your father was killed for a spinach leaf." "What was the name of that chief?" "Ha! I cannot think of him again. For where I came from is far away, a long way to reach this place." "Well, show me the road to where you came from then." It was the girl that asked. Her breasts were well filled oh! Her mother showed her.

Then she stood up. She put on beads, as far as her navel. She bought a hanging loin cloth, she put it on; she tied her head tie, and bound on a head band of beads, and hung beads on her neck, and covered her wrists with bracelets. She tied her clothes in a bundle. "I must find the one who killed a man for a spinach leaf."

When she set out, she began to go. She came to one village. All the people stood up, to look at such a lovely girl. As she stood there they said, "We will not ask yet about her. She is a fine girl. When you see her, that woman is a perfect woman on earth, beyond all others." They stood up for her.° They welcomed her. She came and entered the compound. She stood there. She was asked, "Any trouble?" "No, no trouble. I am travelling inquiring, seeking the chief who killed a man for spinach. When I hear of that man, he is the man who will marry me."† Ha! all the people there, they wanted her in marriage. But they said, "No, that chief is not here."

She went on. She went for very far. She came to a village. They all welcomed her. She came and stood outside in the compound. They wanted to marry her there. Everyone was standing there, getting ready to put a first gift for her. When she was asked, "Any trouble?" she answered, "No,

---

* The mother sings this refrain as a kind of lullaby to the child.
° i.e., wanting to marry her.
† The girl is depicted as speaking rather slowly and solemnly as if making a public announcement.

no trouble. I am here to make a free marriage with someone." Ha! they all got ready. "I love you." "I love you." She answered. She had marriage gifts brought out for her. The kolas given for her came to one hundred. The money given for her came to £2. They were gifts for marriage.* They were first gifts of all. Everyone was bringing out gifts. Then she said, "For me—all that you have given, I have looked at it all. But the one who is to marry me is the one who killed a man for spinach." They said, "Ah, but it is not here, he is not here."

She went on. She passed through six villages. She asked for him. But he did not come out.

When she came to the village where the chief was—that chief was called Saio—she was welcomed well. She entered. She came right in. She came and stood outside the chief's house. At that moment, the chief's drum was beaten—*gbiŋ, gbiŋ, gbiŋ, gbiŋ, gbiŋ, gbiŋ, gbiŋ*. All the people gathered. The people came to look at her. If you saw that girl—there is no girl like her in the country. When she had had the gifts given to her— well, you know what power is like! they all thought that she had come to live with the chief, to stay in his house with peaceful heart. They brought out kola for her there, as the first gift. The kolas were two hundred. The money was up to £60—as a first gift! She took it. "I have seen the money. It is much. It pleases me. But the one who is to marry me is only if I hear of the man who killed someone for a spinach leaf."

Then Saio stood up from where he was sitting. His heart was eager to marry her. "The woman I love has come, the woman I love has come. She, it is she who will look after me when I am old."

He stood up. He came outside. "Here I am!" He tapped himself. "Here I am. I am the one who killed a man for a spinach leaf. My spinach here it was growing in my compound. That was what he came and cut. That is why I killed him. When he came and begged, I refused. 'My wife is hungry.' At night he went and picked it, one bunch, one bunch. That angered me, that is why I killed him. It was I, I Saio."

The woman said, "All right"—the girl called Sira—"all right, I have found my mate. For he was the one I was seeking. It is you [who] will marry me. I have come to the marriage." Since the day she was born, she had had no husband. Then at that time she was angry.

Then the chief stood up. It was as you usually do—if a wife comes for you, a new wife, you take a hen to make sacrifice for her. It was a sheep he went and bound, saying, "Here is the sacrifice for her." He gathered

---

* The list is given in an excited tone, emphasizing the great amounts that were being brought out for the girl.

all his headmen and announced the news to them. The girl—the one called Sira—said, "It is good. I agree. I came for a marriage; now I have found the marriage. My mother gave birth to me there; they began to woo me there in marriage, they killed a cow for me. But I did not agree. I said I would wait till I heard of a man who killed someone for a spinach leaf. Now I have found the marriage. I am glad. With Saio here I will stay." He was a great, great chief. Ha! He was called "There is no earth." When he came to make the sacrifice, the sheep was killed. The girl was cooked for.

The time came. You know how it is with a new wife.* The chief said to the one who should sleep in his dwelling, "You will not sleep here today. Go out today! Go out today! My new wife, Sira, will sleep here today." She went in, at that time; they spread the bed for her. A new wife, sitting there in all her blackness—well, that is what we call a fine thing! When they had spread the bed for her, he the chief stood up. All the keys—he gave them all to her.° Oh! the owner of the house, she is to get out! "Now you are being left the house. You are the head wife. You will not have to do anything." Everything, everything he could remember, he told her it all. All his powers of magic—he told her all. Sira said, "All right."

When they lay down to sleep, Sira thought, "Behold, this man is the one who killed my father for a spinach leaf. That deed I will revenge."

When they were going to lie down to sleep, they had not yet lain down, he said—for you know how it is with a new wife, how you talk to her; everything you are thinking in your heart you will say—he lifted the sword and he said, "Here is the sword, the sword I killed the man with who stole the spinach. This is that sword." Sira said, "Yes, all right." He leant the sword against the wall. He said, "Do you see that horse outside there? It was on it I rode when I was going for him in the farm." Sira said "Oh."†

When they had lain down to sleep, when the chief fell asleep, then she stood up. She took the sword—she Sira—she struck the chief with it "for you killed my father for a spinach leaf." She struck the chief at once.‡

It was at night. Everyone was asleep. The servants that had been guarding him had been told by everyone, "Don't stand here." They said, "No, all right." "Go to your houses today, a new wife has come to me today."

---

* The audience nodded and murmured in agreement.
° He was making her his chief wife, in charge of the whole houshold, and tells the previous chief wife to go—a dramatically narrated episode.
† Sira is made throughout this episode to speak only in monosyllables, as if shy and obedient—the opposite of the truth.
‡ This was related very quietly, conveying the atmosphere of night, sleep, and stealth.

When she had killed him there, she took the keys. She opened the lock on the door. She went out. Everything she had brought when she was coming she took with her—the gold she had been given, and the golden earrings. She did not leave it. She took everything.

When she had gone off far away, in the night, going to return to her home where she had come from, then the light came.

When the light came they looked for their chief who always wakes early. The light became bright. The servants said, "He will want to be going. Let us go and knock at the door. Oh! but a new wife came to him yesterday. You know what a new wife is like,* it is sweet. He wants to have much talk with her. It is a new marriage, is it not?" So they went away again.

They saw the sun rise higher. Now the sun was hot—very hot. Then the chief's cousin got up. "Ha! let us look. I am going to look at where the chief is lying. Perhaps he is ill. One cannot be sure.

What happened? They went and opened the door. All they heard was the buzzing—*gbuu*—of the flies. They looked—the chief was lying there. He had been struck. The wife had gone.

Then the cousin shouted, "Hey! hey! hey! hey! something has happened. The wife that came yesterday to the chief, she came and killed him."

The drum was beaten—*gbiŋ, gbiŋ, gbiŋ, gbiŋ, gbiŋ, gbiŋ, gbiŋ*. The people gathered. They came and looked—it is the chief lying there, their kind chief, the chief called Saio.

Sara, his son, he was sent off, "Follow the woman." He mounted the horse. *Gbaŋ*, he lashed the horse. It galloped—*raaa*. When he followed the girl, as the sun was coming to the mid point exactly, he came up to the girl—"Hey! you going there, you going there, don't move from where you are, it is you I am pursuing. Stand!" The sword had been given him. "If you meet her, kill her to revenge what she has done to our father, our kind kind chief."

What did the girl do? Before he could reach her, the girl took off all her clothes, she stood there. The man came up to her on his horse— *thadaŋ thadaŋ*°—he turned his eyes, secretly looking.† Ha! the man got off his horse. His heart was pleased with the woman.

"You, you are the one I am pursuing. You killed my father. You killed our chief." Then the girl said, "Yes, it was me. I killed him. Is that why you have come?" "Yes." "Is that why you have come?" "Yes." "To kill me?"

---

* One of the audience interpolated in excitement and ironic sympathy "Behold, the wife had run away!"
° The sound of the galloping.
† This point in the story caused great amusement

"Yes." "But I will ask you a question. Which do you want—to kill me, or to marry me?" The boy—his heart went out to the marriage. The reason he had set out there was spoilt. He said, "Ah, I want to marry you—even if it means I do not go back. If they want to, they can bury him without me. I am not returning—let us go, you and I, to your home. Even if they say that I have to go back with you, we will mount the horse together. I will go and say that you shall not be killed. But I will marry you!" The girl said, "All right. That is good. I accept. But before you marry me, first pick me one leaf from there, for I want to drink, I am thirsty." The boy got down from his horse, he made the horse stand. He hung the whip there. He stuck the sword in the ground. "Am I to climb now?" She said, "Yes. But before climbing take off your gown, and pull your trousers off. Put them down with your cap and go and pick the leaf for me."

The *kuwɔ* tree is very tall. It is tall like that *kusiridi* tree standing by the road. The boy began to climb, for his heart was now turned towards the woman as she stood there now in her blackness with her beads round her loins. That pleased him. He put his arms round the tree, he went up, he came to one leaf. "Is this the one I am to pick?" "No, not that one." He climbed up, he came to another. "Is this the one I am to pick?" "No, it is not that one." He climbed, he came to another one. "Is this the one I am to pick?" "No, not that one; the one on the very top." The boy climbed up to the very top. Then she said "Now you are right up there, now I am going, I who am called Sira."

The girl mounted the horse. She took up the things he had taken off. She took the horse. She took the whip. She took the sword. She lashed the horse, *gbaŋ*, to go to her home. The girl went. She took the horse with her. As she set out from there, she was holding the sword, holding the whip, and the boy's things, that is what she hung over her shoulder.

She came into the village with the horse. She stopped the horse. "Mother." "Yes?" "Here is the sword." The blood was on the sword, the sword she had killed the chief with. "Yes." "This is the sword, the one Saio killed my father with. I went and killed him. Here is the whip he was holding. His son Sara pursued me to kill me. But he was unable. Here are his things."

Then her mother said, "Oh my child, oh my child, I thank you. For what you have done, since you have exacted revenge for what your father suffered, for the spinach leaf,—for that, wherever you stay, may Kanu give you a cool spirit."

Thus you see now, even if someone is called a chief, when people are told that something is forbidden and someone goes out who does not obey that word—even if you are a chief, don't kill him for that.

Since I heard that story, I told it. *Kapoingpoingbang*, you patiently heard me. Saraio, who is sitting there, by your grace too I told the story, I told it to Yenkeni. Since it has ended for me—it is finished.

Unlike Cinderella's passive beauty and unlike Marilyn Monroe's vulnerable beauty, Sira's beauty is an active and powerful weapon. Sira turns her beauty against the chief who murdered her father. She uses it like the biblical Judith used hers. To save her people, Judith put on all her necklaces, bracelets, rings, and earrings. She walked into the enemy camp, drank with the enemy general, Holofernes, then cut off his head. Not only is Sira's beauty a weapon, it is armour. Unlike the heroines who must conceal their femininity with men's clothes, Sira journeys alone, without fear from town to town decked out and flaunting her beauty.

The Leopard Woman

Liberia[115]

Aman and a woman were once making a hard journey through the bush. The woman had her baby strapped upon her back as she walked along the rough path overgrown with vines and shrubbery. They had nothing to eat with them, and as they traveled on they became very hungry.

Suddenly, emerging from the heavily wooded forest into a grassy plain, they came upon a herd of bush cows grazing quietly.

The man said to the woman, "You have the power of transforming yourself into whatever you like; change now to a leopard and capture one of the bush cows, that I may have something to eat and not perish." The woman looked at the man significantly, and said, "Do you really mean what you ask, or are you joking?" "I mean it," said the man, for he was very hungry.

The woman untied the baby from her back, and put it upon the ground. Hair began growing upon her neck and body. She dropped her loincloth; a change came over her face. Her hands and feet turned into claws. And, in a few moments, a wild leopard was standing before the man, staring at him with fiery eyes. The poor man was frightened nearly to death and clambered up a tree for protection. When he was nearly to the top, he saw that the poor little baby was almost within the leopard's jaws, but he was so afraid, that he couldn't make himself come down to rescue it.

When the leopard saw that she already had the man good and frightened, and full of terror, she ran away to the flock of cattle to do for him as he had asked her to. Capturing a large young heifer, she dragged it back to the foot of the tree. The man, who was still as far up in its top as he could go, cried out, and piteously begged the leopard to transform herself back into a woman.

Slowly, the hair receded, and the claws disappeared, until finally, the woman stood before the man once more. But so frightened was he still, that he would not come down until he saw her take up her clothes and tie her baby to her back. Then she said to him, "Never ask a woman to do a man's work again."

Women must care for the farms, raise breadstuffs, fish, etc., but it is man's work to do the hunting and bring in the meat for the family.

The "Leopard Woman" makes a strong case for the separate, complementary roles of women and men. Yet modern women seem to have lost the pride and power of our independent roles. Sarah Hrdy has made an extensive comparison of social behavior among all primates. Throughout the primates, weaker individuals are often victimized by stronger ones, " . . . but never on the scale with which it occurs among people and never directed exclusively against a particular sex after the fashion of female infanticide, claustration of daughters and wives, infibulation, or the suttee . . ." [116] The juxtaposition of these two is jolting: woman's current lack of power and the pride and confidence of the Leopard Woman. Where is our Leopard Woman power? Did women ever have it? How was it lost?

The Midwife of Dakar

Senegal[117]

Everyone in Dakar knows old Fatu. She is the woman who brings all the children into the world, and there is hardly a black woman who has not needed her help at one time or another, when giving birth. Her cabin was a little outside the town, where nowadays one can see nice modern streets, and houses in the fashion of the white man; but at that time this section was just an isolated place.

One night when Fatu was sleeping, she heard a knock on the door. As she was used to being called in the middle of the night, she thought nothing of it, and answered the door. And whom should she see but a big djinn (genie)! She was so scared that she wanted to close the door quickly, but the djinn had foreseen this and seized her hand quickly, pulling her out into the street. He motioned her to follow him, and she did so, trembling all over, not because of the cold, but because of her fear. However, she did not dare to disobey, for everyone knows that you cannot escape from a djinn. So she continued following him through the lonesome roads. Besides, she could soon see that the djinn did not intend to harm her, and so, little by little, Fatu started to feel better about the whole adventure. But she could not recognize where she was, though she thought she knew Dakar inside out. They arrived finally in front of a beautiful palace, bigger and richer than any she had ever seen. Silently she followed the genie through many courts and halls, and arrived in a room where, on a bed, was lying an extraordinarily beautiful woman genie, surrounded by a crowd of others, all very richly adorned. The queen of the genies was about to give birth, and Fatu now understood why she had been summoned.

Without delay, she started on her work, and when a short time after the little genie was born, she received it and bathed it with great care. She had hardly finished her task and handed the baby over to his smiling mother, when everything—palace and people—vanished and, to her great surprise, she found herself no longer in the chamber of the new mother, but in a dark street of Dakar near the old hospital where she had often been before.

She went back home and, upon entering her cabin, she found the table covered with many coins of gold and silver and a necklace of precious stones. She used the money to live in comfort. As for the necklace, however, she would not part with it. Many people, who had heard the story, offered her a big price for it, but she always refused to sell it, and is probably wearing it to this very day, if she is still living on this earth.

It is hard to accept that doctors have taken over the role of midwife, and males now often act like the authorities during the quintessential female act of giving birth.

The labor with my first child was very long. I had been without sleep for two days when a nurse at the hospital said, "I just had a baby ten months ago and look, if we adjust the bed like this, you'll be able to get a little rest and then you'll be able to deliver." She fiddled with the many buttons on the fancy bed and enabled me to catch a few minutes sleep between contractions. Contrast her empathy with the doctor who stitched me up after the delivery. He said, "Stop moving your foot. I can't sew if you move like that."

"It hurts," I answered.

"No, it doesn't."

"It hurts," I repeated.

"It doesn't hurt. You feel some pressure, that's all."

A different male doctor who was walking out the door called back, "She might be right. You could give her a local."

"It does hurt, but I just had a baby, so I can handle this," I thought to myself.

The midwife of Dakar reminded me of the nurse who adjusted my bed. They understood the women they helped.

A Woman for a Hundred Cattle

Swahili[118]

Once upon a time there were a man and a woman. They lived for many days in the land of Pata, and a son was born to them. Their fortune consisted of a hundred cattle. Beyond these they did not have a single calf; they had nothing but the cattle.

As time went by the son grew and became a big child, and when the boy was fifteen years of age, his father died. Several years later, his mother also died. So the young man had a heritage from both his parents—he inherited the hundred cattle which were left to him. He stayed in his home and observed the time of mourning for his parents. When he had finished mourning he felt an urge to look for a woman to marry.

He said to his neighbours, "I want to marry a woman, for my parents are dead and I am all alone now. I cannot stay alone. I must get married."

His neighbours said to him, "Surely, get married, for indeed you are lonely now. We shall look around for you so that you may find a suitable woman to marry."

He said, "Yes, be it so."

Later, he said, "I would like somebody to go out and look for a woman for me."

They said, "If God wills it!"

So one of the neighbours rose and went and looked for a woman whom the young man could marry, until he found one. Then he came and said to him, "I have found such a woman as you want, but she is not from this town."

He asked, "Where, then, does she live?" The neighbour said: "In a different town, pretty far away. I think it takes eight hours of travelling from here to get there."

He asked him, "Whose daughter is this girl?"

And the neighbour said to him, "She is the daughter of Abdallah, and her father is very rich. This woman owns six thousand cattle. The father has no other child, just this one daughter."

When the young man heard this, he was all full of desire to obtain this woman, and he said to his neighbour, "Would you go there tomorrow and carry my answer—which is that I am agreeable."

The neighbour said, "God willing, I will go there tomorrow." And at dawn, the matchmaker rose and travelled until he came to old Abdallah, and he carried the young man's message to him, and related all that had happened.

Finally the father answered him, saying, "I have heard your words, but I desire that anyone who wants to marry my daughter should give me a hundred cattle as a bride-price. If he gives such a bride-price I will give him my daughter for wife."

The matchmaker said, "God willing, I shall go and carry the answer to him."

The father said to him, "Yes, do that!"

The matchmaker rose and went back, and gave the young man the answer. He told him everything that had been discussed.

The young man said, "I have heard your words, but he wants a hundred cattle as a bride-price, and I have just a hundred cattle. If I give them all to him, what will my wife have to live on, if she comes to me? I have no other fortune but these hundred cattle which I have inherited from my father."

Finally his neighbour said to him, "Well now, if you do not want her, tell me so. Then I can go and carry back your reply; or if you want her, tell me so definitely."

The young man bowed his head and meditated and, when he raised his head again, he said, "It does not matter, go and say that I accept. I will go and fetch the hundred cattle and give them to him."

So the matchmaker got up and went to the father of the girl and said to him, "The young man is willing to pay the hundred cattle."

And the father said, "I am willing then that he should take my daughter." They talked over the details, and then someone was sent to bring the young man. The latter came and was amiably received, and they discussed the marriage. So the young man was wedded to the girl and paid the hundred cattle, and the wedding feast was celebrated.

Then the young man took his wife and travelled home. There they remained at first ten days; but when the provisions which they had taken along were used up, the young man had nothing for his wife to eat. Then he said to her, "Dear wife, now I have nothing left to eat. Formerly, I had my cattle. These I milked and thus I had my sustenance; but now I have given my cattle away for you and, therefore, I have nothing left. Dear wife, I will go now to my neighbours and from those who have cows I shall obtain some milk, however little it be, so that we shall have something to eat."

Then the woman said to him, "Yes, dear husband!"

So the young man went out and this now became his occupation. Every day he went out and milked other people's cows, so that he could have something to eat for himself and his wife. This he continued to do every day.

One day his wife went out and placed herself in front of her door just as a very handsome young man passed by. When he saw the woman standing by the door, he was seized with a desire to seduce her. Thereupon he sent a procurer to talk to the woman.

The woman said, "God is my witness that I have heard the message you convey to me, but you must wait a little longer, until I have made up my mind, and then I will let you know. I cannot answer yet." So the procurer rose and went home.

Three months later, the woman's father thought to himself, "I must go and pay a visit to my daughter and her husband." So he started on his journey and went his way until he came to his son-in-law's house. Arrived there, he knocked at the door. The daughter got up and answered, "Who is there?"

The old man said, "It is I, Abdallah."

The daughter rose and said to him, "Will you not come in?"

So he entered and exchanged greetings with his daughter, and she invited him into the hall, and the old man sat down there. The father asked the daughter how she was getting along, and she said, "Pretty well, my father."

Finally the daughter got up, went away from where her father was sitting and went into her room, cogitating and crying profusely, because there was not the slightest bit of food in the house that she could cook for her father. Then she left by the back door, and when she looked behind the yard, she noticed the young man who wanted to seduce her, and he called to her to come nearer. So she went over to him and said to him, "How are you getting along, sir?"

He said, "I once sent someone to you, and you said that you would come to me for a visit, but you have not come. Why are you so wavering? Since I saw you that day when you were standing by the door I have not been able to sleep any more; every day, when I lie down, I dream only of you in my sleep."

The woman answered him, saying, "God be my witness, I shall not harass you any more. If you long for me I shall come without delay. First, however, get a piece of meat for me, so that I can cook something to eat for my guest. I shall come afterward."

The young man asked her, "Who is your guest?"

The woman replied, saying, "It is my father whom I receive as a guest." Thereupon he said, "You wait here, and I will bring you some meat right away."

So he rose and went out, and the woman remained standing there. A little later, he returned with a quarter of beef and said to her, "Here is the meat, but now do not put me off any longer."

She said, "God be my witness, I shall not put you off."

He stretched out his hand and gave her the meat, and the woman took it and went back into her house. Then he who had given her the meat paced up and down outside and waited for the fulfilment of the promise that the woman had made him.

After the woman returned, she took the meat, cut it into pieces, and put it into the pot. As soon as she had placed it in the pot, her husband came back and found his father-in-law sitting in the hall. As he saw his father-in-law sitting in the hall, his blood rose. He could not find a word to say, nor did he know what to do. He went closer until he came to where his father-in-law was sitting. He greeted him according to custom and asked him how he was getting along. After that he went to his wife and found her cooking meat and asked her, "My dear wife, what are you cooking there?"

She said, "I am cooking meat."

He asked, "Where did you get this meat from?"

She said, "I received it from the neighbours; they have given it to me." When her husband heard this he remained silent and became sad because he was so terribly poor.

Then he said to his wife, "My dear wife, what shall we do now that we have not only ourselves to feed but also a guest?"

His wife answered him, saying, "I do not know what we shall do."

Then the man said, "I will go out to the rich people where I milk the cows and tell them, 'I have a guest staying with me now, and I would like you to give me something, whatever it be, to cook for my guest.'" So he rose, went to the rich people where he worked, and apprised them of everything that had happened to him.

These rich people were sympathetic and gave him a little meat and a little milk, which he took. Then he went home.

At his house, in the meantime, his wife had finished cooking the meat that she had received from her would-be seducer. Then her husband returned with the meat, the woman put out her hand, accepted it, and laid it on the floor. Then the husband rose and washed his hands and went into the hall. The woman in the kitchen withdrew the meat from the pot and placed it on the platter from which they were accustomed to eat.

Now the would-be seducer had remained where he was, walking up and down, until he saw that the time, which had been agreed upon with the woman, had passed. Then he said to his heart, "The best thing for me to do is to pass by the front door and look inside. Perhaps I shall see the woman." So he went off and passed by the door, and encountered the woman's husband and the father-in-law sitting and chatting. When the wicked man saw that, he greeted them, and the woman's husband answered the greeting, inviting him to approach. So the wicked man came up and sat down.

Then they conversed together, the woman's husband having no inkling of the stranger's plan and of what he really wanted. Thus they conversed with each other—the woman's father, and the woman's husband, and that impious creature who wanted to disturb the peace of the young man's house. The three men stayed together in the hall.

As soon as the woman inside had placed the meat on the platter, she brought it out into the hall. As soon as her husband rose to be handed the meat, the woman said, "Eat now, you three fools!"

Thereupon her father began, saying, "Well now, wherefore am I a fool?"

His daughter answered him, saying, "Please, father, eat first. Afterwards I shall tell you all about your foolishness."

But the father said, "No, I shall not eat, but you shall first tell me about my foolishness. After that, I shall eat."

Thereupon the daughter rose and said, "My father, you have sold an expensive object for a cheap one."

Her father said to her, "What is it that I have sold too cheaply?"

She said, "It is I, my father, whom you have sold too cheaply."

He said, "Why so?"

She said, "Father, you have no daughter and no child except only me and you went and sold me for a hundred cattle, yet you, father, have six thousand cattle anyhow. You have regarded a hundred cattle as more valuable than me. That is why I have said, 'You have given up a valuable thing for a cheap one.'"

The father answered, "That is true, my child, I was a fool."

Then her husband rose and said, "Now, please, tell me the nature of my foolishness too."

The woman said to him, "You are even a greater fool."

He said, "Why that?"

She said, "You inherited a hundred cattle from your parents; not a single calf more did you inherit. And you took them all and wedded me in exchange for them, in exchange for all your hundred cattle; yet there were so many women in your own town whose bride-price amounted to only ten or twenty cattle. But you did not look at them. Instead, you came and married me in exchange for all your cattle. And now you have nothing, not even anything to eat for me and for yourself, and you have become a servant of others. You go and milk the cows of other people to get something to eat. Had you kept half of your herd of cattle and married a woman with the other half, you would have had something to eat. Therefore, this is your foolishness, my dear husband."

Then the worthless knave asked, "And wherein does my foolishness consist? Tell me!"

Thereupon the woman rose and said, "You are even a greater fool than both the others."

And he asked her, "Why is that?"

She answered him, saying, "You wanted to get with a single quarter of beef what had been bought for a hundred cattle. Are you not, therefore, a fool?"

He jumped up in a hurry and ran away as quickly as he could.

The woman's father stayed with them for two days. On the third day he made his preparation for taking leave and then went home. When he arrived at his house, he unhobbled the cattle which he had received from his son-in-law and sent them back to him. With them he sent another two hundred. Thus his daughter could live in comfort with her husband for many days.

In "Rumplestiltskin" the female protagonist gets bumped around from one obnoxious man to another: a bragging father, who lies that his daughter can spin straw into gold, a greedy king, who threatens her life if she doesn't spin straw into gold, and an unscrupulous rascal, Rumplestiltskin, who spins for her only if she will give him her first-born child. The female protagonist in "Rumplestiltskin" remains a victim throughout and is only saved by happenstance in the end. In "A Woman for a Hundred Cattle," the heroine is also buffeted about by three men, a vain husband, a greedy father, and an unscrupulous rascal. However, the way she deals with the problem presents a strong and plausible woman's solution. Her approach is to get it all out into the open. She places the food and the truth squarely in front of them. Succinctly, she explains to her father and husband how their behavior has brought them to the brink of ruin. By exposing the unscrupulous neighbor, she shames him and gets him out of her life. "A Woman for a Hundred Cattle" gives us a more self-confident and honest role model for the woman in the "Rumplestiltskin dilemma."

Wacu and the Eagle

Agikuyu People, Kenya[119]

A long time ago there was a girl who ate meat in public like a boy. Her name was Wacu and she was the only child in her family. Her father was a rich man with many heads of cattle, many goats, and flocks of sheep. Wacu grazed the sheep and cattle and goats in the fields and milked them in the evening just like boys did. Her father loved her very much and he gave her meat to eat and milk to drink. She developed the habits of a boy. This used to annoy her mother who wanted to bring her up as a good woman and housewife.

The influence of her father dominated Wacu so much that she became ever more boyish and her mother could not easily change her. In the evenings she stayed with her father in *thingira* (father's hut), eating meat and listening to his advice and stories. During the day Wacu grazed the animals and played games like wrestling and long jump with the boys. She was feared by many boys as she defeated many of them. She was widely known throughout the villages as the strong boyish girl who fought and defeated boys.

When Wacu grew up and was initiated into the grown-up age group, as was the custom, she had to give up herding and do domestic work. It was very difficult to rehabilitate her. She could not stop eating meat and drinking milk publicly like a man. For this habit she was shunned by other girls. Friends in her age group got married and Wacu needed to have a husband. A woman of Wacu's habits would find it very difficult to find a lover because Gikuyu custom did not allow women to eat meat publicly.

Wacu's mother complained to her husband that he was spoiling her daughter. He began to realize his mistake too late, for Wacu was widely known as a he-woman. She was strong and hard-working, and above all she was very pretty. Meat eating, hard work, and games had helped to build her body well. But even with these natural physical gifts the boys would not propose to Wacu; they regarded her as a meat maniac.

Wacu gave up the idea of getting married, and went back to her favourite work of herding her father's animals. She continued to eat meat without any secrecy and she even slaughtered sheep whenever she wanted to have meat. She wanted to make the best out of her situation.

One day Wacu visited a relative who lived in a distant part of the

Gikuyu country and while she was there she went to dances in the evenings with other young people. There she met a handsome young man who admired her and proposed to her almost immediately. Wacu accepted him. She returned home and reported the young man's proposal to her parents. They approved. Arrangements were made for the payment of the marriage dowries and the wedding ceremonies and Wacu was quickly wedded before her husband had time to discover her propensity to eat meat.

For some time after her marriage Wacu tried her level best to uphold the manners and customs of a young bride. She would not eat meat, nor would she drink milk or eat fried food. This was too much of a sacrifice for Wacu who was brought up eating all these delicacies. When she could not control herself she bought meat secretly in the market-place, cooked it quietly in her hut and ate it while her husband was at beer parties.

Wacu was a good housewife, hard-working and strong. She bore her husband many children—all boys. When she was sure that she could not get divorced because she had good children she decided to revert to her habit of eating meat publicly without any fear. She did not see why women should be so badly treated by their menfolk. So she declared an open campaign against this injustice of men to women. She became most unpopular with men, and her husband was greatly disturbed because he loved her and her children. He pleaded with her to observe the custom, but it was all useless for Wacu would not be stopped from eating meat.

Wacu's husband went and consulted many witch-doctors to find out what he could do to cure her of this bad habit. They advised him not ever to give her any meat, even if he slaughtered for the customary family religious ceremonies—occasions at which wives were given meat by their menfolk.

Wacu defied this ban. She would buy her own meat from the market and bring it home. When she did not have money to buy any and her husband slaughtered and denied her the right to eat the meat she cried and cursed him:

"Uu-uuuuu!	Uu-uuuuu!
I shall curse;	Ninguga mbu;
This strange homestead;	Mucii uyu wene;
Though I'm betrothed and married;	Nanguritwo;
They have slaughtered;	Naigathinjwo;
And I have not been fed.	Nandiheo.
Uu-uuuuu!"	Uu-uuuuu!"

Wacu knew that this cry was regarded as a bad omen for women to make, and in order to cleanse the homestead a lamb had to be slaughtered and she would be given the meat to quieten the bad spirits. Each time she cried like this the husband slaughtered a lamb and she was given the meat. She really became a nuisance to the whole family, yet she was blessed with so many children that the husband could not bear to see her returned to her father. So she was tolerated.

One day the Gikuyu elders were having a feast of goats and lambs. This feast was held in the field far away from the homesteads. The young men slaughtered and roasted meat while the elders discussed and debated the affairs of the people. Some elders had come with the motions and proposals that women should be given more rights and especially the right to share meat with their menfolk, so that a situation like Wacu's could be avoided in future. Wacu was greatly admired for her hard work, sense of duty, fertility, and beauty, except the one unfortunate characteristic—the love of eating meat. Examples of Maasai women were cited to support the motion, and there was a heated debate. The echo of the noise these elders made could be heard over the hill tops.

While this debate was going on the young men were roasting the meat and when it was well done they put it on green banana leaves to cool a little before the elders could share it. Suddenly an enormous eagle appeared in the sky. It came with such force that it frightened the elders and the young men. It was most strange and quite different from anything men had seen before. The elders and the young men took cover to avoid being carried off by this great eagle.

The eagle came down and with its big claws and beak carried all the roasted carcasses, leaving nothing for the men. Then it disappeared over the hill into the horizon. Some young men ran after it to see if it would drop any meat. They followed it fast over the hill, down the valley, and through a field, and they could see the eagle far away, landing or going low as though it were landing.

They ran faster. The eagle in fact had come to the field where Wacu was weeding. Just a few feet away from her the eagle dropped all the meat and flew away, disappearing into the forest of Kiri-Nyaga. When the young men reached Wacu they found her comfortably sitting down, feasting on the meat. They were surprised and horrified and would not take the meat from her. They returned quickly to the elders to report what they had seen.

The elders came to verify the young men's report, and when they saw that it was Wacu, and that the eagle had dropped all the meat down to her, they all resolved to give their women the right to eat meat in their homesteads, as it was the wish of Mwene-Nyaga that they should have meat. *Ciakorire Wacu mugunda* (Meat found Wacu in the field) is a common joke when one meets some luck without much effort.

Folktales often promise a better life. Cinderella goes from rags to riches, the foolish son makes the princess laugh and receives half the kingdom. However, in almost all cases, the social system that caused the protagonist to be poor and starving in the first place remains intact. The "happy ending" consists of one person, our heroine or hero, moving from the bottom to the top of the heap.

This folktale is unusual in that a challenge to the society is successful. Wacu takes on a part of the system itself. Her strength of character and personal determination bring about an improvement in the lives of all the women in her tribe. She might be compared to other courageous women like Rosa Parks, an African-American working woman in Montgomery, Alabama, in the 1950s. As required by segregation laws, Rosa Parks sat in the back of the public bus. When the bus became so crowded that white people had to stand, she was told to give up her seat to a white man. She refused. She was arrested. Her action sparked a 381-day bus boycott and acted as a catalyst for the Civil Rights Movement in the United States in the 1960s.[120] What Wacu and Rosa Parks have in common is that their courage to stand alone for their rights didn't just move them to the top of the heap, but ultimately changed the system itself.

Elephant and Hare

Maasai People, Kenya[121]

There was once a herd of elephants who went to gather honey to take to their in-laws. As they were walking along, they came upon Hare who was just about to cross the river. She said to one of them: "Father, please help me get across the river." The elephant agreed to this request and said to Hare: "You may jump on to my back." As Hare sat on the elephant's back, she was quick to notice the two bags full of honey that the elephant was carrying. She started eating honey from one of the bags, and when she had eaten it all, she called out to Elephant saying: "Father, please hand me a stone to play with." When she was given the stone, she put it in the now empty bag of honey, and started eating the honey from the second bag. When she had eaten it all, she again requested another stone saying: "Father, please hand me another stone for the one you gave me has dropped, and I want to throw it at the birds." Elephant handed her another stone, and then another, as she kept asking for stones on the pretext that she was throwing them at the birds, until she had filled both bags with stones.

When Hare realised that the elephants were about to arrive at their destination, she said to the elephant which was carrying her: "Father, I have now arrived, please let me down." So Hare went on her way. Soon afterwards, the elephant looked at his bags, only to realise that they were full of stones! He exclaimed to the others: "Oh my goodness! The hare has finished all my honey!" They lifted up their eyes and saw Hare leaping away at a distance; they set off after her. They caught up with Hare within no time, but as the elephants were about to grab her, she disappeared into a hole. But the elephant managed to catch hold of her tail, at which time the skin from the tail got peeled off. Elephant next grabbed her by the leg. Hare laughed at this loudly, saying: "Oh! you have held a root mistaking it for me!" Thereupon Elephant let go of Hare's leg and instead got hold of a root. Hare shrieked from within and said, "Oh father, you have broken my leg!" As Elephant was struggling with the root, Hare manoeuvred her way out and ran as fast as her legs could carry her. Elephant had by this time managed to pull out the root only to realise that it was not Hare's leg. Once more he lifted up his eyes and saw Hare leaping and jumping over bushes in a bid to escape. Elephant ran in pursuit of her once more.

As Hare continued running, she came across some herdsmen and said to them: "Hey you, herdsmen, do you see that elephant from yonder, you had better run away, for he is coming after you." The herdsmen scampered and went their separate ways. When Elephant saw the herdsmen running, he thought they were running after Hare; so he too ran after them. When he had caught up with them, he said: "Hey you, herdsmen, have you seen a hare with a skinned tail passing along here?" The herdsmen answered: "You have passed her along the way as she was going in the opposite direction." While Elephant had been chasing the herdsmen, Hare had gained some time to run in the opposite direction.

Next, Hare came upon some women who were sewing outside the homestead and said to them: "Hey, you mothers who are sewing, do you see that elephant from yonder, you had better run away for he is coming after you." On hearing this, the women scampered for the safety of their houses immediately. But soon the elephant caught up with them and asked: "Hey you, respectable ladies, might you have seen a hare with a skinned tail going towards this direction?" The women answered: "There she goes over there."

Hare kept running and this time she came upon antelopes grazing and she said to them: "Hey you, antelopes, you had better run away for that elephant is coming after you." The antelopes were startled and they ran away as fast as their legs could carry them. But soon the elephant was upon them, and he asked them, "Hey you, antelopes, have you seen a hare with a skinned tail going in this direction?" They pointed out the direction that Hare had followed to him.

Still on the run, Hare next came upon a group of other hares, to whom she said: "Hey you, hares, do you see that elephant coming from yonder? You should all skin your tails for he is after those hares with unskinned tails." There upon all the hares quickly skinned their tails. At the same moment the elephant arrived and asked them: "Hey you, hares, have you seen a hare with a skinned tail going towards this direction?" The hares replied: "Don't you see that all our tails are skinned?" As the hares said this, they were displaying their tails confident it would please Elephant. On noticing that all the hares' tails were skinned, Elephant realized that Hare had played a trick on him. Elephant could not find the culprit, for all the hares were alike. And there ends the story.

The Hare is a trickster. Tricksters are found in folklore traditions all over the world. Anansi in West Africa, Coyote in the southwestern Native American folktales, Brer Rabbit in African-American folklore. All of these famous tricksters are male. In this anthology several less famous, female tricksters are represented: Kayi in West Africa (p. 324), Molly Cotton-tail from African-American folklore (p. 160), and the Hare of the Maasai. Like their male counterparts, each of these female tricksters also has a group of stories associated with her.

Nonikwe and the Great One, Marimba

Zulu [122]

Little Nonikwe was waiting. She was waiting with great impatience for something big and exciting to happen and she could hardly conceal the wild excitement she felt; it lighted her face like a midnight beacon. This was all because Nonikwe knew something the other girls in her village did not know as yet. She knew that the Great One, Marimba, was on her way to spend the night in the village—the very village in which Nonikwe's uncle, Mutengu, was headman.

Little Nonikwe was a pathetic creature. She was not only a hunchback, but she was also totally blind. But all this was amply compensated by the great and rare gift the gods gave her of seeing things clearly long before they happened.

This gift had saved the little hunchback child from being destroyed at the age of eight as all crippled and deformed children were normally destroyed according to the laws of the Wakambi. A child born with any defect was, however, allowed to live till the age of eight to see if it had any special gifts like seeing into the future or the past, reading minds or communicating thoughts to animals.

Little Nonikwe was allowed to live and she lived like a chieftainess in her uncle's village. She was the most well-hidden and well-guarded piece of property in the village, and this was because Mutengu had a bitter rival and enemy in another new village just beyond the river. This enemy was Lusu, the father of Nonikwe herself. When Nonikwe had been born, Lusu had been so disgusted with the child with which his wife had presented him that he had publicly declared that his wife had slept with a night-walking demon.

Nonikwe's mother had been disgracefully driven from Lusu's village and had sought refuge in the village of her brother Mutengu, where she died of a broken heart two moons later. Years had passed, the little girl had grown, and soon word had got around that she was a Blessed One, gifted with powers beyond human concept. When he heard this, Lusu the rascal tried to move the very stars and the mountains to get Nonikwe back. Mutengu had not only refused; he had seized Lusu and beaten him within a thumb's length of his fat and rascally life.

Mutengu and Lusu had since been deadly enemies and to get his own back, Lusu developed the habit of reporting directly to Marimba with all kinds of accusations against Mutengu—acts of corruption and many breaches of the laws of the Wakambi. These accusations were, of course, utterly false and unfounded.

Eventually Marimba decided to pay Mutengu a secret visit in order to find out for herself if he was really as corrupt and evil as Lusu had made him out to be.

But Marimba had forgotten about Nonikwe. The little hunchback had actually dreamt what the great princess intended to do and woke up early that morning to warn her uncle to expect a secret visit from his queen some time in the afternoon. Mutengu, though startled by this warning, had acted quickly upon it because the blind little hunchback had never before been wrong with her predictions. He had ordered scouts to be posted to give him early warning of the approach of the great queen and her retinue. He had made his wives prepare all manner of food to give the peerless Marimba a welcome feast fit for one of her high and queenly position.

Mutengu had nothing to fear from a visit by his chieftainess because he had no secrets to hide. And not only was he as loyal as the southern wind but he was also as honest as a worker bee. But he did not want to be caught unprepared in anything and he was a strong believer in giving each and every visitor to his village a welcome in accordance with his or her stature.

Mutengu was a very popular headman. Every man and woman in the village could vouch for his great kindness, courage and honesty, and they were all prepared to defend him with their lives against any scandal-mongering back-biter.

The huge clay pots were full of delicious buffalo meat. There were great basins full of well cooked yams and corn cakes. There were also wooden trays full of roast wild fowl, partridge and guinea fowl. There were baskets full of wild figs and stewed *marulas*,* and large cakes of fresh honey from his own beehives. Mutengu was the first man in the land of the tribes to keep bees. He kept them in hollow anthills, and handled them after drugging them with *dagga*° smoke. He had also discovered that bees were inclined to leave him in peace when he dressed himself in a hyaena skin *kaross*.†

Thus the great feast was prepared and brought in readiness for the unannounced arrival of the great queen Marimba. All the villagers settled down to await the arrival of someone who did not know she was already expected, whose surprise visit was a surprise no more. Visitors

---

* *Marula*, the fruit of the marula tree, which resembles plums.
° *Dagga*, either of two relatively nontoxic South African herbs, smoked like tobacco.
† *Kaross*, a simple garment or rug of animal skins.

from surrounding *kraals** and villages came as usual to have a free meal in this generous headman's village, and as usual they told him a lot of tales-that-are-not-true and departed with full bellies and oily smiles. It was also customary for angry men to bring their disputes to Mutengu's *kraal* and long arguments and trials took place under the Tree of Justice in the centre of the village. Fines were paid in ivory, ebony, and copper ore, and malefactors were taken outside and executed.

Life was taking its normal course in Mutengu's village. An old and very tired-looking man came into the teeming village at midday accompanied by his remarkably beautiful daughter and begged a guardsman at the gate to let him spend the night in their spare hut, as he was very tired and had come a long way. This was not unusual and the guards were all too happy to admit the old doddering traveller and his daughter. The shy, beautiful girl greatly interested the burly guards and many were the ravening glances cast in her direction.

The old man was given the whole haunch of a buffalo and asked to eat his fill; what was left he could take with him on his journey the following day.

The rest of the afternoon was taken up by ordinary activities, such as hauling yelling prisoners to the council tree for trial.

The sun was already setting beyond the western mountains and lengthy shadows were creeping eastwards when headman Mutengu completed his duties in administering tribal law. And still the queen of the Wakambi had not arrived. A small doubt began to gnaw at the back of the mind of the great *Induna*;° he began to wonder for the first time whether his little deformed niece was wrong in her prophecy. Eventually he strode into her hut and knelt down beside the blind child, holding her hand gently, reassuringly.

"Little one, for once the little spirits have played a trick upon my niece, for lo, the queen Marimba has not come yet."

"But she has, Oh honourable uncle, the queen of the Wakambi is here. I can feel the pulse of her thoughts."

Mutengu was aghast: "Child! What words are these? My scouts have brought no news of the coming of the queen. They have seen no warrior escort. And yet you say that the royal Marimba is already within this village!"

"She is, Oh uncle. I receive her thoughts quite clearly. At this moment she is pleased with the joke she has played on you, and she is convinced that my real father Lusu had accused you falsely."

---

* *Kraal*, a village or a single hut or group of huts.
° *Induna*, king.

"Where is she?" Mutengu demanded. "Has she made herself invisible?"

"No, uncle. Tell me, how many visitors are spending the night with us?"

"Well over a hundred, child, men and women, young and old."

"The Great One has come into the village as a common visitor, my uncle. You must command all visitors to report to your Great Hut and there I shall pick her out for you."

The one hundred and ten visitors were gathered at the Great Hut and a sumptuous supper was in progress. Already the *Induna* knew that one of these many women was Marimba and one thing remained—the identification parade!

Mutengu led his little blind niece, gently holding her hand, past all the guests. He noticed how most of the visitors shrank slightly with revulsion as the deformed child approached. He saw this and he smiled; if only these fools knew that the little deformed child was the equivalent of ten so-called normal human beings. Led by powers beyond human comprehension, the young girl made her way towards the old man and his daughter. The child knelt down beside the girl and gently removed the *kaross* of respect with which she had covered her head. Mutengu immediately recognised his chieftainess—in spite of her shaven head and the false scar she had improvised with a piece of fish bladder. Mutengu gently pulled off the scar and the great, mischievous eyes of Marimba smiled softly at him.

"My queen . . . living goddess of the Wakambi . . . what is the meaning of this cruel joke?"

"I heard that you were a corrupt and vicious man who broke every tribal law laid down. I wanted to see for myself, Oh *Induna*, and I am glad to say that I found all accusations against you false and groundless."

The assembled visitors fell on their faces in the presence of their great queen and a deep silence fell upon the gathering like a thick skin blanket. Then came Marimba's clear voice: "Arise, my people, and let us enjoy our meal. Then we shall perform a little dance to thank our host for his great kindness and generosity." And turning to Mutengu she spoke softly: "Tell me, Oh Mutengu, how did you know about my secret arrival?"

"This child, with her god-given sight, indicated you to me, your humble servant, Oh Marimba."

"I shall give the little one a gift to remember me by. And when we have unseated her evil father in the village across the river we shall appoint your niece as headwoman of that village for the rest of her life."

A roar of applause greeted the announcement. Men stood up and raised their right hands in salute to the little Nonikwe, Headwoman-for-life of a village and district. And then, into the hands of the little girl

Marimba pressed the newest instrument of music that she had invented. It was a "hand xylophone"—a mukimbe—made entirely of reeds.

A mukimbe is an instrument particularly suited for use by blind people or those left weak and convalescing after an attack of one of the numerous tropical diseases. Many a convalescent owed his recovery to the sweet, birdlike, soothing notes of the mukimbe. Thus this instrument soon acquired the nickname of "the sick one's comforter."

A good mukimbe is constructed as follows: The bulrush reeds must be cut in the middle of summer when fully grown but not yet hard or dry. They must be of equal thickness (a man's little finger) and of equal length (from the wrist to the elbow). Eight of these are cut and woven together with lengths of reed bark till the whole thing looks like a miniature raft. More strips of green reed are then attached to the raft, fixed both ends, and a strip of wood is then inserted to lift these strips away from the raft in the middle. The whole contraption is then left to dry in the sun for ten days. The woven knots tighten and the strips become taut while the spirit of music enters into them. The strips must all be of unequal breadth and arranged in order of thickness. For an additional rattle effect tiny pebbles can be inserted in the hollow reeds and the openings sealed with tree resin.

The blind child was overjoyed. Tears of pure gratitude welled from her sightless eyes and she clutched the instrument to her heart. She wept as if her soul would melt. "Thank you, Oh my queen. I honour you with all my heart, and may you grow as tall as the tallest of tall trees."

"Now, now, little Nonikwe, do not cry so. I am going to see to it that you are happy for the rest of your life and that you will never want for anything. Now come, all my people, let us dance before we go to sleep. I have a new dance for you, my lazy ones—the 'Three-Fire Dance'."

We are inundated by visual images of women who possess a certain type of beauty. We are so inundated that it is difficult to picture a heroine who doesn't conform to that image. How do you imagine Nonikwe? Is she bent almost double with her hunchback, or is it the kind of back with the big lump on one shoulder? Are her blind eyes the kind of milky white spaces of those blind with cataracts, or the uncomfortably half-open, vacant blind eyes? Or do you not see her physically at all but rather imagine her soul and her gentleness? For years I identified with Jane Eyre, a "plain" heroine, because I didn't consider myself pretty. Yet I never imagined Jane Eyre's plain, unremarkable face. In many films, television shows, books, and Cinderella tales, admiration for a woman is tied to an intimidating and limited image of beauty. We then internalize and reimpose this image on our own world where it continues to intimidate us. Heroines like Nonikwe can help break that mind set.

How the Milky Way Came to Be

South Africa[123]

Up there, in the sky, there are billions of stars. No one knows how many, because no one can count them. And to think that among them is a bright road which is made of wood ashes,—nothing else!

Long ago, the sky was pitch black at night, but people learned in time to make fires to light up the darkness.

One night, a young girl, who sat warming herself by a wood fire, played with the ashes. She took the ashes in her hands and threw them up to see how pretty they were when they floated in the air. And as they floated away, she put more wood on the fire and stirred it with a stick. Bright sparks flew everywhere and wafted high, high into the night. They hung in the air and made a bright road across the sky, looking like silver and diamonds.

And there the road is to this day. Some people call it the Milky Way; some call it the Stars' Road, but no matter what you call it, it is the path made by a young girl many, many years ago, who threw the bright sparks of her fire high up into the sky to make a road in the darkness.

The first time my daughter saw a big pile of autumn leaves, she plopped down in the middle and threw armful after armful of leaves into the air and laughed with joy as they fluttered down onto her head. Last New Year's Eve, she gasped with surprise at a sparkler's brilliant sparks bursting against the black night. Afraid of the fire, but entranced by the beauty, she traced patterns in the night. When the sparkler had burnt out, she raced up to me and exclaimed, "Oh, please, please, please let me have another one!" The little girl of this story creates the Milky Way with the same naive awe, the same playful and joyful connection to her creation. I was struck by the contrast between the playful appreciation of beauty and awe that lead to this little girl's act of creation and the powerful, ordered decisiveness of the biblical creation as depicted in the Sistine Chapel.

Nanabolele, Who Shines in the Night

Basotho People, Lesotho[124]

Long long ago, when the parents of our grandparents were still children, there were three orphans: two boy children and their sister, Thakáne. Their father had been a great chief when he was alive. But now he was dead, and it was Thakáne who had to take care of her two brothers.

She had to grind corn for them and make the porridge. She had to cook the meat that they brought back from the hunt. She had to fill the clay pots with water so that they did not have to drink from the spring like dogs.

She took care of them like a mother.

But when the time came that the two boys had to go to the tribal school, the school to which fathers take their sons so that they may become men, it was Thakáne who took them to the school. It was Thakáne who took them to the school, for they no longer had a father who could take them. According to the traditions of the tribe they stayed in the grass huts of the school for the required five months, and, when the time was spent, it was Thakáne who prepared their clothes and their skin shields and their weapons.

It was she who took the clothes to them to the huts in the mountains when all the fathers took clothes to their sons. It was she who took the clothes so that they could be loosened from those grass huts, the *mophato*. It was she.

But when her brothers saw the clothes they refused to accept them. They said that they would stay inside those grass huts until the day came that they each received a karos—a skin blanket—a cap, a skin to hang around the hips, and a skin shield made of the skin of the nanabolele, those horrible creatures who give off light in the dark, as the moon and the stars give off light in the dark. The nanabolele who lived beneath the waters.

"Why do you ask for the impossible?" asked the young woman. "Where shall I find the skin of the nanabolele? Where? *Ná?*"

But the two young men would not listen to her. They said if their father had still been alive it would have been the skins of those big monsters that would have loosened them from the huts of the school. It did not become them, the sons of a chief, to be loosened from the huts in the same way as all the others, with the same clothes. They, who were the boy children of a great chief who was dead, ought to have much finer loosening clothes.

Then word went out from Thakáne, and it was spread, spread, spread around until all the subjects of the chief had heard it. She called her people together.

When they who had been summoned sat together in the big gathering, the *pitso*, Thakáne opened her heart to them. She said: "You must choose among yourselves the bravest of all, so that they can walk with me when I go to find the nanabolele."

"*Yo wheh!*" they said. "How can you, who are only a woman, undertake such a dangerous task?"

But she answered, "If the father of my brothers had lived, his sons would have had clothes made from the skins of the nanabolele."

Chè, now they understood.

They gathered together a band of the bravest of them all. The women prepared food to take along, food for a very long journey. They took flesh of oxen, flesh of sheep, ground wheat, calabashes full of beer, and cooked corn balls that were made of ground sweet corn. Everything was loaded on the backs of pack oxen.

It was a very large company, with many pack oxen, that set off that day with Thakáne when she left her home to seek the dragons with the shiny skins, the dragons that lived beneath the waters.

When they came to the first stream, they saw that it was broad. Perhaps the nanabolele were beneath the waters of this stream . . . they did not know. They took the hindquarters of an ox and threw it in the water. Then Thakáne sang. She called with this song:

> Nanabolele, nanabolele!
> The sons of the chief, nanabolele!
> They want shields, nanabolele!
> Shoes from the skin of nanabolele!
> Blankets from the skin of nanabolele!
> And hats from the skin of nanabolele!

When she had finished singing, the waters began to move. They trembled. They churned. *Kattay, kattay, kattay!*

They were afraid, for they thought it was one of the monsters. But only a frog jumped out. He cried: "*Koo-rooo, koo-rooo, koo-rooo*, go farther. There where you can dip water with the husk of the poison plant, there you must cross."

They obeyed the frog, and, when they had crossed the stream, they walked farther until they reached the next stream. Here the water flowed broad and calm. Maybe it was deep also, they did not know. Maybe it was under those waters that the nanabolele lived. And again Thakáne sang and told of her search and what her mission was, as she had done by the first stream. Just so. *Yoalo.*

When she had finished singing, the waters began to tremble. They churned. *Kattay, kattay!* Again they thought it was the nanabolele, but as at the first stream only a frog leaped out, and he also cried: "*Koo-rooo, koo-rooo,* go farther. There where you can dip water with the husk of the poison plant, there you must cross." Just so. *Yoalo.*

At every stream the same thing happened, and they did not find the monsters with the shining skins. Then they came to the last river. The reeds grew high and thick on its banks, and the river was wider than all the others. Perhaps it was deeper also. They did not know, and maybe it would be beneath these waters that they would find the nanabolele.

They threw meat into the waters, but the river lay still. The waters did not tremble, they did not churn, they lay still.

Thakáne sang the song of the sons of the chief who had to have clothes made of the shining skins of the nanabolele, but the waters did not move. They threw meat into the water, but the waters lay still. They threw meat in again, but the waters lay still. Then they killed a pack ox and threw it in whole. Again Thakáne sang the song to the nanabolele, and as she sang the waters began to move. They trembled, they churned, they welled up over the banks, they boiled like water over a very big fire. It was surely the monsters, with their shining skins, they thought, and the men stood ready with their spears. But still it was not a monster, it was a very old woman who appeared. She leaned on a stick and invited them to follow her.

Then she went back into the waters, and the whole company dived in after her. Under the dark waters, under the thick reeds, they came to a big village. They were amazed, for it looked like the village of a mighty chief. Here were also huts with reed screens in front of them, and it was dry as it was dry above the ground. But still it was different, for the village was quite deserted. It was quiet. No people lived there. No children were playing there. The huts stood empty. There were no fires behind the screens. The clay pots were without water. The grinding stones lay idle.

"*Mè wheh!*" said Thakáne and her people. "Such a strange place we have never seen! Where then are the people, Grandmother?"

She replied: "They are all dead, the nanabolele ate them all, the adults and the children, the cattle and the sheep, the dogs and the chickens. Everything!"

"And you, Grandmother?" they asked.

"No, my children, I am too old. My flesh is too tough from much work through the years, and I am too thin. That is why these awful monsters have saved my life, so that I can work for them. I heard your song, young woman," said she. "You dare much!"

"*Yo wheh!* Now I see the danger is great," said Thakáne, because she suspected that the old one had lured them into a trap to supply food for her monsters, but the old woman reassured them and hid them in a deep, dark hole that she covered over with reeds and soil so that the nanabolele should not see them.

And just as they were well hidden they heard a roaring above their heads, a roaring like a huge herd of oxen passing over the ground . . . It was the nanabolele.

Dooma, dooma, dooma, they dived into the water and came to the deserted village beneath the dark waters that flowed among the reeds. They came to sleep, for they were weary from hunting.

Thakáne and her people peeped through the reeds. *Yo-ro-ro!* It was frightening! They saw a whole herd of dragons coming closer in the dark . . . *foo-foo-foo!* They shone! The skins gave off light as the moon and stars give off light at night. But they did not go to sleep, they walked around. They were looking for something. They put their noses to the ground and smelled. They sniffed: *foo-foo!*

Then they spoke. They said, "We smell the stink of people!" Then they searched through the empty huts, but they found nothing. And the old woman remained silent. *Tu-u-u* . . .

"*Sentho se nkha kae?*" they asked. "Where does that stink of human flesh come from?"

Then they searched, searched, searched, but they were so weary from hunting that they could stay awake no longer. They would sleep first, and the next day they would search again and find out where the stink came from.

As soon as they were asleep and snoring fearfully loudly, the old one came to fetch Thakáne and her people from their hiding place and told them that they must quickly choose one of the nanabolele and slaughter and skin it before the others woke up.

They did so. They chose the largest one and when they had skinned it they rewarded the grandmother with pack oxen laden with food. Then they had to leave.

But first the old one gave Thakáne a little ironstone pebble and said: "Tomorrow, when the nanabolele wake up and see that you have killed one of them, they will follow your spoor."

"*Yo wheh!*" groaned the people.

But she continued: "As soon as you see red dust clouds against the sky you will know that the nanabolele are following you. Then you must put that pebble down in the road. It will grow, it will grow until it is a high mountain. Then you must climb up on that mountain before it is too high. On top of that mountain there will be asylum for you."

So they took the skin of the nanabolele and left that village under the dark waters, the village asleep with all the monsters, the village where only one old woman lives, she who takes care of the nanabolele.

It was still dark when Thakáne and her company arrived above the ground again. They did not wait for the light, for they were in a great hurry to leave. Only when they had gone a long way toward their homes did the dark grow light. And it was still early in the day when they saw the red clouds rising against the sky behind them. And they knew it was the dust that the dragons were raising as they pursued Thakáne and her people.

They who were fleeing were afraid!

But when the dust clouds appeared around the last mountain peak, Thakáne quickly put the pebble down on the ground. And then it grew. They climbed up on it, and it grew, grew, grew. It became a mountain that touched the clouds. And on top of that mountain Thakáne and her company sat in safety. When the herd of nanabolele arrived at the mountain they tried to clamber up, but they could not climb up, for those mountainsides were of ironstone, and they were steep and they were slippery.

When the monsters were so tired from struggling that they could struggle no longer, they lay down on the ground at the foot of the mountain to rest. But they were so exhausted that they fell asleep immediately—and then that mountain of ironstone began to shrink. It grew smaller, smaller, smaller, until again it was only a pebble that could be carried in the hand of a human.

Thakáne took that pebble and she and her company fled, carrying the skin of the nanabolele with them.

The same thing happened the next day. *Yoalo. Yoalo.* Every day. And every day Thakáne came closer to home with that shining skin, every day. Behind them, following their footprints in the road, came the herd of nanabolele, and above them the red dust clouds also came nearer.

But the people stayed in the lead, and when they reached their own village Thakáne quickly called all the dogs so that they should come and wait with her. And when the monsters came to the ash heaps of the village, Thakáne set the dogs on them.

This they did not expect. The dogs rushed to the attack, and the nanabolele came no closer. They came no closer, but turned round and went back to their deserted village, taking their red dust clouds with them. Back to the old woman who cared for them under the dark waters of the deep river that flows among the reeds.

Thakáne was satisfied. She had done her duty toward the children of that father of hers who was no longer alive, she had found the skin that gave off light like the moon and the stars when the sun does not shine any more.

Now she summoned a man who was skilled in the making of skin clothes. And from the skin of the nanabolele he cut two shields, two blankets, two hats, two hip cloths, and two pairs of shoes. And when the clothes were ready, Thakáne herself took them to her brothers, there where they waited in the *mophato* for their initiation into manhood, waited to be loosened from those huts.

The two young men were glad when they saw the shining clothes that their sister had brought them. Not one of the other young men who had attended the school with them had such clothes. Nobody had ever had such clothes. Not only the people of their own region, but also the people of the whole country, told each other of the shining shields, the shining blankets, the shining hats, the shining hip cloths, and the shining shoes that the brothers wore.

And above all the honor that they received for their clothes, above the honor was a great gratitude for their sister. That was why they rewarded her out of their herds. They gave her a hundred head of cattle, and here the story finds its end.

Ke tsomo ka mathetho, which means: this is a true tale of the Basotho people.

Thakáne goes on a quest for the skin of the dragon, the nanabolele. She dares much. All her efforts are to give her brothers what their father would have given them had he been alive. Often women reflect society's assumptions about the inferiority of females even while they are contradicting them like Thakáne. For example, widows of merchants in medieval Europe enjoyed the extra freedom that owning and wielding capital gave them, yet they made no challenge to the laws or institutions that subordinated women and they left the fortunes they amassed to their sons.[125] When a working mother heard of this anthology, she said to me, "I've got a boy, he won't need that."

In most societies women, especially mothers, are the keepers of tradition. They teach the young children the basic structure and assumptions of the society. As transmitters of tradition, women can change society. Even boys need to hear the story of Thakáne, the dragon slayer. It will help them respect their mothers, their sisters, and their wives. It will help them respect women.

Jackal and Hen

Basotho People, Lesotho [126]

This is a story that the old people tell.

They say that Hen flew to the top of a stack of wheat one day to find food. From where she stood on the stack she could see far out over the fields. She could see far, and she saw Jackal coming from afar. She saw him coming toward her, she saw him out of the corner of her eye, but when he came closer she did not look up at all. She went on hunting for food.

"Good morning, mother of mine," Jackal greeted her.

"Yes, I greet you," she replied.

"Are you still living?" he asked, according to the correct way in which one person greets another.

"Yes, I am still living. And you? Are you still living also?"

"Yes, I too am still living, Mother," he replied. And then he asked, as the custom was, "Did you wake well this morning?"

And she answered, as it is proper, "Yes, I woke well."

And all the while he was talking, talking, talking, Jackal was looking closely at Hen, and he saw that she was young and that her flesh would be tender and that she would taste sweet if only he could get at her. But now she was standing on top of that stack of wheat, where he could not reach her. He could not get hold of her at all, not while she was on top of the stack of wheat, and he would have to think of a way to get her down.

Jackal had many plans. He was a man who was not just a little bit clever. No, he was very clever. Very clever. He asked her: "Mother, have you heard that there is peace among everybody on earth? One animal may not catch another animal any more, because of that peace."

"Peace?" she asked.

"Yes, Mother, peace. The chiefs called together a big meeting, and at that *pitso* they decided this business of peace on all the earth."

"Oh yes," said Hen. But she wondered about it. She wondered whether this Jackal could be telling the truth. He was a man with many clever stories, and many times those clever stories were nothing but lies.

"You say there is peace now?"

"Yes, Mother. The big peace. There has never been such a big peace. You can safely come down from that stack of wheat. Then we can talk about the matter nicely. We shall take snuff together. Come down, Mother! Remember the peace!"

But Hen was not quite as stupid as Jackal thought she was. She want-ed to make quite sure first that Jackal was telling the truth and that he was not telling her lies again. She turned around and looked far out over the fields behind her. Then she went to stand on the highest point of the stack and kept staring out over the fields until Jackal asked: "What is it that you see from up there that you stare so, Mè?"

"What do I see? Why do you want to know what I see? It does not matter what I see, for there is no danger any more for any animal on earth. Is it not peace among the animals? It is only a pack of dogs that are run-ning toward us."

"Dogs! A pack of dogs!" he cried. And his fear was very great. "Then I shall have to greet you, Mother. I am a man who has a lot of work wait-ing."

"*Kêkêkêkê!*" Hen laughed. "I thought it was peace among all animals on earth? Have you forgotten it? The dogs will do nothing to harm you! Why do you want to run away, Grandfather?"

"I don't think that this pack of dogs came to the meeting of the peace!" And Jackal ran so fast that the dust rose in great clouds from the road behind him.

"*Kêkêkêkê!*" laughed Hen, for then she knew that the story of the peace was just a big lie. And she knew that if she had taken snuff with that fel-low he would have caught her, so she made up a story herself and with it she had caught him beautifully.

"*Kêkêkêkê!*" she laughed. "I caught the storyteller with another story!" And this is the end of this story.

The jackal's propaganda can't fool this hen. When he tells her that there is peace between all the animals in the world, she takes note of the source and skepti-cally puts the jackal's news report to the test. In Backlash, Susan Faludi looks at pieces of "information" related to women, selected for propagation by mass-media and mass marketing. This "information" includes subjects like "infertility crises" and the "propensity of educated women to become spinsters." Faludi's historical analysis shows that these "crises" can be found in the media when women's attempts to gain more rights threaten the male-dominated status quo. For example, they were propagated after women got the vote in 1920, after WWII when many women had entered the high-er paying job force, and after the push for women's rights during the sixties. Faludi quotes many sources that document that these "crises" do not occur in the real world. It's not easy to differentiate propaganda from valid information, but both Faludi and this hen gives us a good starting point: take note of the source.[127]

Tales
from
North Africa and
the Middle East

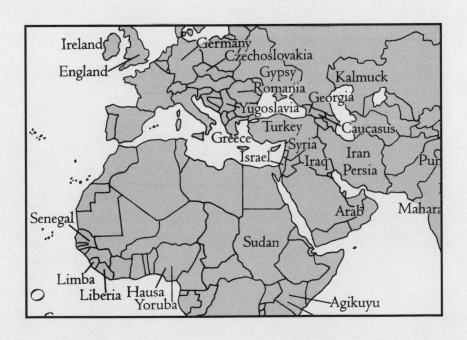

Women's Wiles

Syria[128]

There was a merchant, a very rich merchant—though no riches equal Allah's—who kept a store. Above it he had hung a sign which read, "Men's Wits Beat Women's Wiles." One day the master blacksmith's daughter passed through that part of the *suq*,* a beautiful girl who had drunk her fill of mother's milk. She saw the sign and it angered her. She was so determined to teach the shopkeeper a lesson that all night long she tossed and turned on her mattress, forming a plan.

In the morning she dressed herself in her finest gown, braided her hair and arranged herself with the greatest art, and went straight to the merchant's store. "Good morning, O my uncle," she greeted him. "A morning to bring happiness from Allah," replied the merchant. "God keep you happy," said the girl. Then suddenly she burst into tears. The merchant was astonished. "Tell me why! Speak!" But the girl only cried the harder. The merchant became alarmed. "Tell me what you need, only please stop crying," he said. "You are making my heart burn like fire! Whatever you want done, I'll do it." The girl sighed, "If only that were possible!" "Let me know what it is, at least," said the man.

Well, dear listener, at that the girl lifted her head and, looking the merchant full in the face with two eyes that shone like polished mirrors, asked, "Do you see any fault in my eyes?" When she put this question, staring up at him like a doe, the merchant began to feel a little faint. "Allah has not graced the gazelle with more beautiful eyes than yours," he said. And his mouth was dry. "Then what is wrong with my arms?" she asked pulling back her sleeves. When he saw her neatly turned arms, pale and smooth like peeled cucumbers, the merchant lost his senses. "Is crystal finer or marble whiter than this, O Lord?" he asked. With the tears still falling down her face, the girl lifted the hem of her gown. "What blemish do you see in my feet?" she asked. Now the poor man was quite overcome. "My eyes have seen nothing daintier. Only do not cry," he begged. Sobbing bitterly, the girl pulled off her headcloth, uncovering hair that hung down in thick ropes, black and shining. "Is anything amiss with my hair, then?" she asked. "It is perfect," said the merchant. "There is no silk in my store as fine."

---

* *Suq,* a market or bazaar.

Then at last the girl began to tell him this story. "I am the *qadi*'s*
daughter," she said, "and whenever a suitor comes to my father to ask for
my hand, my father tells him, 'My daughter is bald; my daughter is lame;
her eyes are crossed; her limbs are crippled.' Who would want to marry
such a person! Of course, they leave. A woman needs protection and marriage is her shelter. Now I don't know what to do." When he had heard
this tale, the merchant said, "Tomorrow I myself shall go to your father
and ask for you. Whatever he says, I shall reply, 'I am willing,' and 'I do
not complain.' Now there is no reason for you to be sad." So the girl left
him.

When the merchant closed his shop and went home that night, sleep
fled before him and thoughts of the girl's beauty filled his mind. When
the day dawned, he smoothed his whiskers and dressed with care, and as
soon as it was the proper hour for calling, he hastened to the *qadi*'s house.
When they had exchanged their greetings and were sitting face to face,
the merchant said, "I have come seeking kinship with your honor. I ask
for your daughter in marriage." The *qadi* put him off, saying, "Have I a
daughter?" But the merchant said, "I know for certain that you do." "But
she is squint-eyed," said the *qadi*. "I'll marry her!" cried the merchant.
"She is lame," said the *qadi*. "I have no objection!" answered the merchant.
"She is crippled," said the *qadi*. "I shall not complain," insisted the merchant. In the end the *qadi* said, "Can you pay her bride-money? It is ten
thousand dinars." The merchant paused, and remembering just how
beautiful the girl was, said, "It is less than she is worth." And so the *qadi*
finally agreed to the match.

Now began the preparations for the wedding. The paper was written
that "a well-born bride was bound in marriage to a groom of good family." All that remained was for the bride to be taken from her father's
house to the bridal chamber in her husband's house, for the night of the
entering and the unveiling. Pacing forward and backward, the merchant
awaited the wedding procession with impatience.

Who was that knocking at his door? It was a hired porter bent in two
under the weight of a huge covered basket. "This is from the *qadi*'s house,"
he announced. "This must be her linen," said the merchant, and told the
man to carry it up the stairs. To himself he thought, "Why not take a
look and see what she is bringing with her!" He raised the cover of the
basket, and what do you think he saw? A girl exactly like the squint-eyed
cripple that the *qadi* had described: not one deformity, not one blot wanting! "Who are you?" asked the merchant. "I am your bride, the *qadi*'s

---

* *Qadi*, the judge of an Islamic court of justice.

daughter." "How can you be? When you came to my store, you were like a full moon on the night of the fourteenth!" he cried. He left her in her basket and sat thinking. Then he lay on his bed and wondered, "What have I done, that that beautiful daughter of sin should want to play a trick like this on me!"

Next day he was back in his store. He sat with his head in his hands, and in a little while the master blacksmith's daughter came by. "May your day be glad!" she said. When he saw who it was, the merchant said, "May Allah not gladden yours! What have I done to you that you should make me fall so low?" The girl pointed to the sign above the store and said, "Whose wits, do you think, are sharper now?" "Is that what prompted your revenge?" asked the man. "Is that not enough? If you want me to help you out of this calamity, all you need to do is change your sign," she said, and went.

Wasting not a minute, the merchant took down his board and wrote in letters of gold, "Women's Wiles Beat Men's Wits." When the girl saw the new sign next day, she smiled. "Now I'll gladly help to save you from your present trouble," she said. "What you must do is this. Go to the Gypsy camp on the edge of the town and invite some twenty tinkers to bring their pipes and drums and come to your house in the evening. Tell them it is your wedding and that you want to celebrate with much noise and laughter. Let them wish you well and call you 'cousin.' You must also invite the *qadi* to be your guest at supper. When he asks, 'Who are these rough and noisy folk?' say, 'Honored uncle, he who denies his origins has none to boast of. These men are my cousins, for I am of Gypsy stock. But as you know, God has looked kindly on me, praise be to Him.' When he hears this news, he will surely demand a divorce."

The merchant did exactly what the blacksmith's daughter told him to. In the evening as he and the *qadi* sat together after their meal, a band of Gypsies suddenly burst into the house blowing their pipes, beating their drums, dancing and singing. They embraced the merchant and kissed his beard, shouting "God bless your match, O cousin!" Puzzled by all this movement, the *qadi* asked, "What does this mean, O my son?" The merchant said, "You have heard them, uncle, they are my cousins, coming to wish me well. He who disowns his ancestors has something to hide. I am what I am, and I have a *qadi* for a father-in-law, praise God!"

The *qadi* was enraged. "You never told me this before the marriage. I never would have given a daughter of mine to a tribe of Gypsies! You must divorce her—speak the words and I'll stand witness." "Had you asked me, I should have told you," said the merchant. "I value our kinship far too highly and I do not wish for divorce." "If I pay you back the bride-money, if I refund the expenses of the wedding?" said the *qadi*. But the merchant still refused. In fear and desperation the *qadi* finally said, "I shall pay you twice the sum you spent!" This time the merchant was persuaded. The *qadi* took his daughter home, and the merchant slept in peace the whole night through.

The first thing the merchant did when he woke up next morning was to go to the master blacksmith's shop. "I have come to ask for your daughter," he said. "I am willing to pay any sum you ask for her marriage settlement, but on this condition, that I see her first." "Has it ever happened that a man looked at his bride before the wedding?" the man objected. "I'll give you a thousand dinars above her price if you let me see her," said the merchant. Hearing this offer, one of the blacksmiths looked up from his work and said, "Why not, O uncle? Is your daughter lame or bald, that you are afraid?" So the master blacksmith took the merchant home with him. He called to his daughter to bring in coffee. When she saw who sat with her father, she laughed and asked him the purpose of his visit. He told her, "To be quite certain that I am not tricked a second time."

So the notables of the town were assembled and the wedding of the merchant and the master blacksmith's daughter was celebrated amid great feasting and rejoicing. And the bride and the groom lived in happiness as pure as gold of twenty-four carats.

The blacksmith's daughter wages a determined fight against a sign that publicly demeans women. In every culture there are possibilities for women to improve their status, but these possibilities are different from culture to culture. The question of women's rights is being examined all over the world, but goals and methods can differ. While most western women want equal pay for equal work, a Greek friend complained to me that she didn't want to have to go out and work. She wanted to stay at home, cook, clean, and take care of her children. A friend from Iran proudly pointed out all the folktale heroines her culture had to offer. I replied, "Yes, but they all dress up like men." She laughed and answered, "Well, they have to!" Women's needs, characters, and expectations depend on the culture and on the individual to such an extent that some women are trying to get out of the kitchen while other women are making heroic efforts to get into the kitchen.

The Feslihancı Girl

Turkey[129]

Once there was and once there was not a young man whose father was a *bey*.* This young man used to look out his window into the garden of a neighbor when a feslihancı girl watered her flowers. The girl wore a pair of golden sandals, and she poured water on the feslihan plants from a silver pitcher.

One day the son of the *bey* decided to tease the feslihancı girl. He said, "Every day you water your feslihan flowers. How many leaves does a feslihan plant have?"

"Son of the *bey*, you are a man who reads and writes, and therefore you must have great knowledge. Tell me how many stars there are in the sky."

Upset by the realization that he had been outwitted, the young man said no more and closed the window. On the following day, however, when the girl came again into the garden wearing her golden sandals and carrying her silver pitcher, he called down, "Feslihancı girl, feslihancı girl, you water your flowers every day. How many leaves are there on a feslihan plant?"

And the girl gave the same response she had given the day before: "Son of the *bey*, son of the *bey*, you are a man who reads and writes, and therefore you must have great knowledge. Tell me how many stars there are in the sky."

Angry at being bested again in this way, the son of the *bey* decided to find some trick to play on the girl in order to get his revenge. He did not have to search long for an opportunity to do this, for an illness that befell the girl's mother shortly after this suggested a suitable trick. The sick woman craved fish to eat, but fish were not available at that time of year. The son of the *bey* went to another village and bought some fish. Then he disguised himself as a fisherman and went up and down the streets shouting, "Fish for sale! Fish for sale! Here comes the fisherman!"

When the sick woman heard his cry, she said to her daughter, "Girl, go out and buy some fish for me."

Opening the door of their house, the feslihancı girl called out, "Fisherman, come here! I want to buy some of your fish!" When the fisherman came to the door, she asked, "How much do you want for your fish?"

* *Bey*, in earlier times bey meant "lord," today it means "sir" or "gentleman."

375

The fisherman responded, "I am not selling these fish for money. I am selling them for a kiss."

When the girl heard this, she shut the door and reported to her mother what the fisherman had said. Her mother said, "Well, why don't you give him a kiss? After all, he is only a peasant. Who will ever know that you allowed yourself to be kissed? Open the door just a crack and give him a kiss."

The girl wished to please her mother and serve her the fish that she wanted. She therefore went back to the door, opened it just a crack and allowed herself to be kissed by the fisherman. After kissing her, the fisherman handed her the string of fish and left.

On the following afternoon the girl again went into the garden to water the feslihan plants. The son of the *bey* began teasing her as he had done before. He said, "Feslihancı girl, feslihancı girl, you water your feslihan flowers every day. How many leaves does a feslihan plant have?"

"Son of the *bey*, son of the *bey*, you are a man who reads and writes and therefore you must have great knowledge. Tell me how many stars are in the sky."

The son of the *bey* replied, "I may not be able to tell you that, but I can tell you that you bought fish from me for a kiss."

The girl was surprised to discover that he was the man from whom she had bought the fish with a kiss. She was so disturbed by this information that she decided not to appear in the garden again by daylight to tend the feslihan plants.

Shortly after that the son of the *bey* became ill. Doctors were called from many places to attempt a cure. Every day the house was filled with people coming and going. Late one evening the feslihancı girl entered the house when most others were leaving, and she went unnoticed to the patient's room. She was wearing a fur coat inside of which she had sewed many small bells. Going to the patient's bed, she shook her coat over him until the jingling of the bells awakened him. "Who is it?" he asked.

"I am Azrail,"* she said.

"You may do with me what you will, as long as you do not take my life."

"I am Azrail," she said again.

And he repeated, "You may do with me whatever you want, but do not take my life."

"Uncover your buttocks," said the girl. She had brought with her a pair of sheep lungs through which were stuck many long canvas needles. She

---

* *Azrail*, the angel of death who comes to collect the soul.

now struck the man's buttocks repeatedly with the pair of lungs, inflicting hundreds of deep cuts. Although he cried loudly in pain, no one else in the house heard him, and the girl slipped away unnoticed.

The son of the *bey* was confined to his bed six months longer as a result of being so seriously wounded in this way. When he finally began to recover, he asked his attendants to place him in his armchair before the window. Looking down upon the neighbor's garden below, he saw the feslihancı girl again watering her flowers. He decided to tease her: "Feslihancı girl, feslihancı girl, you are watering your flowers again. How many leaves are there on a feslihan plant?"

The girl responded as usual, "Son of the *bey*, you are a man who reads and writes, and therefore you must have great knowledge. Tell me how many stars there are in the sky."

"I do not know the answer to that question, but I know that you allowed yourself to be kissed for a string of fish."

"I may not know how many leaves there are on a feslihan plant, but I know that you have been kept in bed six months as a result of your being paddled with a pair of sheep lungs that cost only fifty kurus."

Although the son of the *bey* now wondered what he could do to take revenge, he also had a certain affection for this young woman. At the same time, the feslihancı girl was beginning to feel some affection for him too.

A few days later the son of the *bey* said to his mother, "My mother, can you arrange to have me married to the feslihancı girl?" A matchmaker was sent to the girl's home, and after this person had conferred with her parents, it was agreed that she would become the bride of the son of the *bey*. Before she went to live at his home, the girl put into her chest a hammer, a pair of pliers, an adze, and several other tools which she might use to take vengeance against her groom. Also moved by vengeful thoughts, the son of the *bey* had dug beneath his house an earth cellar in which to keep his bride.

After the wedding ceremonies had been completed, the girl, wearing a veil, was taken to the groom's house and immediately put into the cellar. She received food and drink there every day, but she was never permitted to leave her underground dwelling place. Some time later it became necessary for the son of the *bey* to go to Aleppo on business. Speaking through the cellar window, he said, "Feslihancı girl, feslihancı girl, I have to go to Aleppo on business, and I may be there for as long as a year. I shall leave you with provisions enough to last that long, and so you should not suffer by my absence."

"Of course, I shall not suffer as long as you are alive," the girl said flattering her husband. "What kind of horse will you ride, and what color suit will you wear?"

"I shall ride a black horse and wear a black suit," he said.

During the time that she had been living in the earth cellar, the girl had dug a tunnel from there to her mother's garden, the place where she had long tended the feslihan plants. She used this tunnel frequently, and now she took the money which her husband had left her to her mother's house and arranged to have bought for her a black horse and a black suit just like his.

Before the young man departed on his journey, he came to the cellar window again and said, "Feslihancı girl, feslihancı girl, I am leaving now."

She prayed and then said, "May Allah speed you on your way."

As soon as her husband had left, the girl went to her mother's house. There she dressed in her black suit, disguising herself as a man, mounted her black horse, and rode off to overtake him. She caught up with him in the outskirts of the city. When he saw her, he called, "Where are you going, young man?"

"Tell me first where you are going."

"I am going to Aleppo," he said.

"I am going there too," she said.

He said, "Our suits and our horses are alike, and we are both going to Aleppo. We can be friends during this trip."

They went to Aleppo, eating and drinking together, riding and sitting together at resting places. When they arrived at that city, they went to a coffeehouse, and there, in her conversation with other customers, the girl began to search for a witch.* In those days there were witches everywhere. She asked those at the coffeehouse to direct her to the home of an old woman. "There is the home of a witch over there," they said, pointing down the street.

When the feslihancı girl went to this house, she said to the old woman who opened the door, "O grandmother, here is some money for you. Let me come in to talk with you." After she had entered the house and changed her garments to those of a woman, she said, "I want you to sell me to a young man who has just arrived at the coffeehouse. Go there and sell me to him as a bride, and I shall give you even more money."

The witch went to the coffeehouse and asked the owner, "Where is the young man who just arrived here?"

The owner went to the son of the *bey* and said, "Young man, you are being asked for by someone."

---

* *Witch*, in Turkish folklore witch may refer to someone associated with the Kingdom of Evil, a ghoul, or a wily and corrupt old woman whose services can be bought.

The son of the *bey* went to the door, where the witch confronted him and asked, "Where are you from, young man? Are you married or single?"

"I am from such and such a place," he said, "and I am single."

"Well, I have a beautiful young daughter whom I do not dare to marry to anyone here. Would you like to buy her as your bride? How long will you remain here in Aleppo?"

"I shall be staying here for a year," he said. He then paid the old woman the bride price that she asked.

The feslihancı girl, who had rearranged her hair and changed her appearance, was married to the young man. She lived with him during the year that he was at Aleppo, and during that time she bore him a son. When the child was three days old, his father brought a sword and a belt for him and said to his wife, "My time here has ended. I must leave, but I cannot take you with me, for our son is still too young to survive the journey. I shall return later to get you and the child, but if I do not come back, he will find me wherever I am." He still did not know that the child's mother was the feslihancı girl, for he thought she was the daughter of a witch. Leaving enough money for the maintenance of his wife and child, the son of the *bey* mounted his horse and rode away toward home.

The girl also made preparations to leave. Because the baby was very young, she stretched him along a small board and wrapped him in swaddling clothes so that he would not be injured during the trip home. Taking the baby in one arm, she mounted her horse and followed her husband at a great enough distance so that she would not be detected. Whenever her husband stopped, the girl also stopped in order to keep the distance between them. When she arrived back home, she went first to her mother's house and left the baby there. Then, using her tunnel, she went alone to the cellar.

A short while after the son of the *bey* reached his home, he went to the cellar window and called, "Feslihancı girl!"

"Yes, sir?" she answered.

"How are you? Have you been bored during my absence?"

"No, sir. Thanks to you, I have not been bored. I have gotten along quite well."

"Did you have sufficient money?"

"Of course I did," she said.

The son of the *bey* went upstairs and did not see his wife again for some time. As before, however, he had sent her all the food and drink that she needed. After a few months, he found it necessary to leave again for business, this time to India. He went to the cellar window and said, "Feslihancı girl, feslihancı girl, I must go to India for a year."

"Go, then, sir. I wish you good luck. What kind of horse will you ride, and what color suit will you wear?"

"This time I shall ride a red horse and wear a red suit."

Before he bade her farewell, he left her with enough food and money to support her for a year. Hastily taking the food and the money to her mother's house, she said, "Go as quickly as possible and buy me a red horse and a red suit of clothes!" After these purchases had been made, the girl put on the red suit, disguised herself as a man, and rode off on her red horse. Again she overtook the son of the *bey* at the edge of the city.

When the son of the *bey* saw her, he thought, "This is strange. Twice now when I have reached this point in my travel I have met a person wearing clothes like mine and riding a horse of the same color."

"Where are you going?" the stranger asked him.

"To India."

"So am I," said the stranger. "Let us ride along together."

They traveled together, eating and drinking together. After a very long journey, they finally reached the city in India where the son of the *bey* had business to attend to. There the young man proceeded to a coffeehouse, and his companion went in search of a witch. After she had asked directions from several people, she was taken to the home of a witch. When an old woman came to the door, the girl said, "O grandmother, here is some money for you. Please let me in to talk with you." Once inside, the girl took off her red suit and put on a woman's clothes. Then she said, "Grandmother, a young gentleman just stopped at such and such a coffeehouse. Will you sell me to him as his bride? Tell him that I am your daughter and that my husband died. If you will do this, I shall reward you properly with gold."

When the old woman heard the word *gold*, she went at once to the coffeehouse and said to the owner, "There was a young man who arrived here just a very short while ago. Call him here to me." When he came to the door where she was waiting, she said to him, "Welcome! Where are you from?"

He answered, "I am from such and such a town in so and so country."

"How long will you stay here?"

"I shall be here for a year."

"Are you married or single?"

"I am single."

"Can anyone stay here for a whole year and remain single? I have a beautiful daughter whose husband died all of a sudden. I did not wish to give her to anyone here, but I shall give her to you, for you seem to be a good person."

"But I shall leave this country at the end of a year," said the son of the *bey*.

"That does not matter. If you wish, you can take my daughter with you. If not, then you can leave her here."

"Very well," said the young man. "I accept your offer. Come here with your daughter in the morning, and let me know what you would like me to give you for your kindness."

The witch returned to the feslihancı girl and told her that the young man had accepted the proposal. On the following morning the two women went to the son of the *bey*. The young man married the girl and paid the witch the price she named.

After the two young people were married, they lived together in that Indian city for a year. During that time the feslihancı girl bore another male child. When the child was only three days old and its mother was still in childbed, the son of the *bey* came and said, "My time here has been completed. We could not take a three-day-old child with us on a long journey, and so I shall leave you both here now and return for you later. But if I should not return, my son will find me wherever I am at the time." Then he gave her for the child the same kind of belt and the same kind of sword that he had had made for his first son.

"All right. You go now but come back later to get me," his wife said.

The son of the *bey* departed after having left a large sum of money and a great quantity of food for the support of the child and its mother. She took the food to the home of the witch but kept the money herself. After placing the baby on a board and wrapping it in swaddling clothes, she mounted her horse and followed the son of the *bey*. She kept him in sight ahead of her but remained far enough behind to be unnoticed by him. Whenever he stopped, she too stopped in order to preserve the distance between them. After they had arrived in their own country, she took a different course in order to reach their native city before he did. Once there, she went again to her mother's house and left the baby there. Then she proceeded through her tunnel and reached her cellar residence before her husband got there.

As soon as the son of the *bey* had ridden up to his home, he handed his horse's reins to a servant and went to the window of the earth cellar. "Feslihancı girl, feslihancı girl," he called. "What have you been doing during my absence? Are you well? Have you been bored?"

"Welcome home! No, I have not been bored, thanks to you. I have enjoyed myself."

"Well, I have returned."

"Welcome home!" she said again.

Although he had traveled a great distance to reach his home, he was not to remain there very long. After he had been there for only three months, it again became necessary for him to leave home and journey to a distant land to attend to business matters there. Going to the cellar window, he said, "Feslihancı girl, I shall be gone again for a year to attend to matters of business. This time I must go to Yemen."

She answered, "Well, if you must go, go happily and come back again happily. What kind of horse will you ride this time, and what color suit will you wear?"

"This time I shall ride a white horse and wear a white suit," he answered.

He left enough money and enough provisions to take care of her needs for a year or so longer. Taking the food and money to her mother's house, she ordered that a white horse and a suit of white clothes be purchased for her. She made preparations to leave on this third journey at about the same time that her husband did. She then returned to her cellar to await his departure. It was only an hour before he came to the cellar window and said, "Feslihancı girl, I am now leaving."

"Good luck to you!" she said, and she prayed aloud for his welfare.

Returning then immediately to her mother's house, the girl put on her new white suit of clothes, disguised herself as a man, and mounted her white horse. Riding swiftly after the son of the *bey*, she overtook him again just as he was leaving the city. "O friend, where are you going?" she asked him.

"I am on my way to Yemen."

"That is where I am going too. Shall we be traveling companions on this trip?"

To himself the son of the *bey* said, "This is strange. Every time I reach this point, a fellow comes along riding a horse like my own, wearing clothes of the same color, and going to the same place that I am going. It is indeed very strange!"

The two traveled along with each other, eating and drinking together, stopping and staying at resting places together. When they finally arrived at the chief city of Yemen, the young man entered a coffeehouse. Taking note of the location of that coffeehouse, the girl inquired of passersby where she could find the home of a witch in that city. When she had been told where such an old woman lived, she went to her house and knocked on the door. When the witch opened the door, she said, "O grandmother, here is some gold for you. Let me come in and talk with you about a certain matter." After entering the house and exchanging her white suit for female garments, she said, "Grandmother, I want to hire your service. At such and such a coffeehouse a young man wearing a white suit just stopped. I want you to pretend that I am your daughter and that you wish to sell me to that gentleman as his bride. Tell him that I was married recently but that my husband died unexpectedly." By promising her much more gold, she persuaded the old woman to accept this work.

Going to the coffeehouse that the girl had described, the old woman went to the door and signaled a waiter. "Please bring me the young man who arrived here a short while ago wearing a white suit," she said to the boy. The boy did this.

"Welcome to this city, my son!" she said. "Where have you come from?"

"I have come from such and such a country."

"Are you married or single?"

"I am single."

"I have at home a beautiful daughter whose newlywed husband died quite unexpectedly. I would not wish to marry her to anyone here, but I should be glad to offer her to a gentleman like you."

"But I expect to remain in this country for only a year."

"What difference does that make? When you leave, you could take her with you, if you wished. If you did not wish to do that, you could make arrangements to provide for her here. With a wife, you could eat and drink more pleasantly during your stay. You would also have someone to wash your clothes and attend to your other needs."

The son of the *bey* thought, "She is right! When I got married at the other places I visited, I lived very comfortably. Why should I not marry the daughter of this old woman? These girls seem to be all alike, even if their mothers are somewhat different." To the old woman he said, "All right, mother. Come back with your daughter tomorrow, and at that time tell me what gifts you would like from me."

The witch went home, and she and the girl decided what gifts the old woman should request. In the morning they went to the coffeehouse and told the son of the *bey* what gifts they wanted. He bought generously of the things they requested, and he sent them food and clothing too.

Still not knowing who she was, the son of the *bey* once again married the feslihancı girl. They lived in Yemen together for a year, during which time his wife bore a daughter. When the girl was only three days old, the father came to the mother's childbed and said, "Good health to you! My time in Yemen has been completed. I must go but we cannot possibly take a three-day-old child on a long journey. What shall we do?"

"In that case, you should go now and come back for us later," the mother said.

The son of the *bey* went out and bought a golden bowl for his daughter. Giving it to the girl's mother, he said, "Someday my daughter will find me wherever I am. As for now, I shall leave more than enough money and food to support you." He did as he said he would before he left.

The feslihancı girl also prepared to leave on the day that he departed. She strapped the baby to a board and then wrapped her in swaddling clothes, just as she had done with her two sons. After her husband had said good-bye and left, she set out behind him, following at a great enough distance to be unnoticed. Once in their country however, the girl again took a different route in order to arrive in their native city before her husband did. When she got there, she left the baby with her mother, crawled through the tunnel to her cellar quarters, and sat down.

When the son of the *bey* arrived and the servant had taken his horse, he went to his wife's cellar window and shouted, "Feslihancı girl!"

"Yes, sir?" she answered.

"Are you well? Have you been bored during my absence?"

"No, sir. Thanks to you, I have never been bored. I have had an excellent time."

"Well, I have now returned."

"Welcome!" she said.

As she had done when each of her sons had been infants, the feslihancı girl returned to her mother's house to give suck to her baby daughter. She always nursed the child as quickly as possible and then returned to the cellar at once in order to be there when her husband asked for her. She wanted to be there to say, "Here I am."

After two or three years at home, the son of the *bey* went to his mother and said, "Mother, will you make arrangements to have me married again? I shall keep the feslihancı girl locked in the cellar forever. I want to marry another girl."

A girl was found for him, and a marriage agreement was reached with her parents. When the wedding ceremonies began, he said, "I married a girl in Aleppo and left her there. I married another girl in India and left her there. I also married a girl in Yemen and left her in that country. I have a wife that I keep down in the cellar, and so this new bride will be the fifth girl I have married."

On the final day of the wedding, however, the son of the *bey* fell seriously ill and was put to bed. He was so sick that when it was necessary to turn him in his bed, they did so by lifting one side of his sheet and rolling him carefully. Lifting his body caused too much pain.

During the delay in the wedding ceremony, the feslihancı girl decided to send a message to the son of the *bey* by means of their children. She taught each one of them what to say when they went to visit him. The older boy was to say, "O man of Aleppo!" The younger son was to say, "What is the matter, Indian gentleman?" And the daughter was to say, "They caught us by the arm and threw us out of our father's house in Yemen!"

As the three children went to the sick man's house, the boys wore the belts and carried the swords that their father had given them, and the girl carried her golden bowl. When they knocked on the door, an attendant came and said, "Get out of here! There is a sick man here. This is no place for children!"

The oldest child said, "O man of Aleppo!"

The second child said, "What is the matter, Indian gentleman?"

The third child said, "They caught us by the arm and threw us out of our father's house in Yemen!"

In his bed the son of the *bey* heard the discussion at the door and asked about it. The attendant said, "There are some children here who are talking about Aleppo, India, and Yemen, but I cannot make any sense of what they are saying."

"Let the children come here," said the son of the *bey*.

When the children were permitted to enter the room, they went and stood before him in a row. He recognized the belts worn by the boys and the swords that they carried, for he himself had determined the design of these objects. He also recognized the golden bowl in the hands of the tiny girl. "What is the matter, children? Speak!" he said.

"O man of Aleppo!" said the older boy.

The son of the *bey* thought, "He must be my child born in Aleppo!"

"What is the matter, Indian gentleman?" said the younger boy.

The man thought, "He may be the one born in India!"

"They caught us by the arm and threw us out of our father's house in Yemen," said the little girl.

The son of the *bey* thought, "The child born in Yemen was a girl, and she would by now be the size of this child!"

The son of the *bey* then said to two attendants, "Lift me by my armpits to a sitting position." When they had done this, he ordered, "Now put my overcoat over my shoulders." Then addressing the children again he asked, "Where are your mothers?" He supposed that their mothers were three different people and that these women having heard about the wedding, had come there from Aleppo, India and Yemen.

All three children pointed toward the earth cellar and said, "Our mother is down there."

"Take me to your mother," he said. With his overcoat over his shoulders, he walked very slowly and painfully, holding one son by the hand on the right side and the other on the left. The little girl walked ahead.

When the four of them came before the earth cellar, the children said, "Our mother is here."

"Feslihancı girl, feslihancı girl!" cried the son of the *bey*.

"Yes, sir?" she answered.

"Whose children are these?"

"Half are yours and half are mine."

"Open the door, feslihancı girl!"

She opened the door for them, and then she related from beginning to end all that had happened: "I did this, and I did that, and these three children are ours."

The son of the *bey* was astonished by all that he now heard. When the feslihancı girl had finished her account, all he could say was, "Well done, feslihancı girl!"

The wedding ceremony that was only half finished remained that way. The rest of the wedding was canceled. To the girl who was to have become his bride he said, "From now on you will be my sister, and you may live in our home as my sister." Instead of marrying that new girl, he remarried the feslihancı girl. She then moved upstairs, and they lived very happily together.

There are two heroines in this story, the feslihancı girl and her mother. The intelligent feslihancı girl gains the position of a respected wife and assures that her children will be well provided for. She outflanks her husband each time he might be tempted to have a child by another woman.

The heroine in the background of this story is the grandmother who continually helps her daughter. The grandmother's house is a haven from the feslihancı girl's prison. The grandmother makes arrangements, runs errands, and gets the proper color horses and clothing for each of her daughter's trips. The grandmother takes care of her grandchildren for years while the feslihancı girl foils her husband's attempts to control her. The feslihancı girl is free to struggle for her position and her children's posterity because she can rest assured that her children are being cared for by someone who loves them. Good childcare gives many women the help they need to compete and to succeed in the world and still be good mothers.

The Story of the City of
Nothing-in-the-World

Persia [130]

> Once upon a time there was a time
> when there was no one but GOD.

In the town of Hīch ā Hīch, the city of Nothing-in-the-World, there was a girl who had fallen and scraped her shin very badly. After a few days, when the wound was a little better, she went to her aunt to get some cooling ointment for it. The old woman said: "I'm sorry I haven't any," but she gave her niece two eggs to take to the drug-seller in the bāzār,* to see if he would give her some cooling ointment in exchange.

When the girl came back from the bāzār this is what she told her aunt:

I went to the bāzār, and on the way I lost the two eggs. I was very much upset, but I put my hand in my pocket and there I found a jinnū.° I wanted to get my eggs back again, so I gave the jinnū to some people in the bāzār, who made me a minaret out of a needle. I climbed and climbed right up to the top of the minaret, and I looked in every direction all round the town and saw that one of my eggs had turned into a hen and was in an old woman's house, and the other had turned into a cock and was threshing corn far away in a village.

So I said to myself: "First, I'll go and get the cock," and I went out to the village and said to the peasants: "Give me back my cock, and his wages too, for he's been working for you." After a lot of bargaining we agreed that they should give me half a cow-load of their crop, which was rice. When they had weighed the crop my share was manns,† but I had no loading bags to put it in. So I killed a flea and skinned it and made myself a loading-bag out of the skin. Then I put my rice into it, and loaded it on my cock's back and started off, for I wanted to bring my rice to market.

We were very far away from town, and when we got to the second-last halting-place, two days' march out, the cock was sore-backed. I asked the

---

* *Bāzār*, streets with rows of raised, open-fronted shops.
° *Jinnū*, a coin of very small value.
† *Manns*, a measure of weight of variable value.

people there: "What's to be done? Is there any remedy for this?" They said, "Burn the kernel of a walnut and rub it on his back and it will get well." So I half-burnt a walnut and put it on.

When I woke in the morning a large walnut tree had shot up and was growing from the cock's back. The village children had gathered round the tree and were throwing stones and clods of earth at it. I climbed a branch and saw that the clods had accumulated and covered about 100 qasab.* I got a clod-breaker to come and make the ground level, and I saw that it would be a good soil to plant musk- and water-melons in, so I sowed both kinds of melons.

Next morning I saw that the earth had produced very large melons. I broke a big water-melon, but when I was cutting it my knife got lost. I put a bathing-cloth round my waist and went into the hollow of the half-melon to hunt for my knife.

I saw there was a town there, and it was very big and full of crowds and noise and traffic. I went to the door of a cook-shop and gave them a jinnū and bought a little halīm° for myself and began to eat it. It tasted so very good that when I had eaten it all up I licked the bottom of the bowl so hard that it nearly broke.

I saw a hair at the bottom of the bowl and tried to catch hold of it to throw it away, but at the end of the hair there appeared a camel's leading-rope, and behind the rope there came seven strings of seven camels, all in a row, one behind the other, and each complete with all its gear.

They came out one after the other, and my knife was tied on to the tail of the last camel.

> And now my story has come to an end,
> but the sparrow never got home.[131]

This heroine gets side-tracked, but never stuck. She finds an unlikely answer to every unlikely problem. She reminds me of my three-year-old reasoning out how Santa will get in since we have no chimney, or my husband, the astrophysicist, explaining that we can't ask what came before the Big Bang because time was created with the Big Bang. In this whimsical flight of fancy "the universe is not only queerer than we suppose, but queerer than we can suppose."[132]

---

* *Qasab*, roughly 25 square yards.
° *Halīm*, breakfast food, concentrated ragu made from wheat, rice, mutton, cinnamon, and sugar, usually eaten in winter.

The "Pink Pearl" Prince

Iran [133]

Once upon a time there lived a merchant in Persia. He had three daughters: Razia, Fawzia and Nazneen. The merchant loved them very much. One day he called them and told them: "Your love stops me from staying away from you even for a day, but the call of Allah beckons me that I must visit the holy land of Mecca. I seek your permission."

The girls, noticing their father's keen urge to make the holy pilgrimage, said: "Go, by all means, our beloved father. Have no fears about us." They asked him to bring them presents from the holy land. Razia asked for diamond ear-rings; Fawzia wanted a diamond pin to hold her head-scarf in place; Nazneen asked for a pink pearl which she said she needed badly. She added that if he failed to get it for her, she would not let him enter his home.

The merchant was somewhat dismayed to hear Nazneen press her demand so emphatically: Since she was the pampered youngster, he brushed aside the roughness of her demand.

The merchant set off on his journey. After travelling many days he reached the holy city of Mecca. Having done with the religious rituals he set about shopping for his daughters. He bought the diamond ear-rings for Razia, a diamond pin for Fawzia, but try as he may, he couldn't find the pink pearl for Nazneen.

Some pilgrims were to return by boat from Basrah to their various destinations. So the merchant also embarked on a ship to Persia. But somehow the ship would not sail, for the channels got blocked. The crew tried and tried but the ship wouldn't budge an inch. At last the captain announced to the passengers: "Brethren: whoever has made a promise, must fulfil it; otherwise we shall not be able to sail at all."

The merchant remembered that he hadn't bought the pink pearl for Nazneen. So he left the ship and began once again to search for it. While he was searching here and there frantically, he met a man who told him: "That which you want to buy is not a thing but son of the king."

The merchant made straight to the palace where the "Pink Pearl" dwelt. He sought the prince's audience and told him the whole story.

"I will not come myself to Persia, good merchant," the "Pink Pearl" told him, "but take these three boxes to your daughter."

The merchant took the boxes and embarked once again on the ship.

This time the ship started well and sailed majestically on the open seas. The merchant ultimately arrived at his home.

The three girls greeted their father warmly. The merchant gave Razia the diamond earrings, to Fawzia, the diamond pin, and held out the three boxes to Nazneen. The merchant hadn't forgotten the trouble that Nazneen's demand had put him to and he told her gruffly: "You were the cause of my misfortune. Take these boxes and be gone. I don't want to see your face again."

Nazneen was very upset. With tears in her eyes, she left home. She walked for miles together. At last she reached an open plain. She put down the boxes and sobbed: "Perhaps whatever is in the boxes has been the cause of my being driven away from home," she thought. So thinking she opened the first box. And, to her surprise, a palace arose in front of her in a split second. She opened the second box and a retinue of maid-servants came out of it and carried her into the palace. Everything was breathtakingly beautiful. She spent the whole day exploring the palace— wondering at the miracle that had happened to her. But to open the third box she took some time; she wanted to enjoy the good things first in a leisurely manner.

One fine morning, she thought to herself that she must open the third box and see what it would produce. When she did so, in front of her arose a beautiful bridge. Over the bridge came a handsome youth riding a splendid horse. He moved regally and gracefully towards the palace. The maid-servants rushed to open the gates of the palace. He greeted Nazneen and said: "Do not shut the lid of the box while I am on the bridge, for if you do so I shall die." Nazneen promised him that she would not do so. The two drank deeply of each others beauty—and love.

Meanwhile, Razia and Fawzia became restless about Nazneen, their younger sister. "We must seek her," they decided and set out to look for her. They walked one whole day and they were exhausted. When the sun set, they noticed a palace in the distance, none other than Nazneen's.

They thought they had better rest there for the night. When they knocked at the gate, the maid-servants allowed them in. Nazneen heard familiar voices and rushed down.

Who did she see but her own sisters? She hugged them, kissed them excitedly and took them upstairs. The two sisters were astonished to find their little sister grown so rich, living in a palace, attended by a retinue of maid-servants and possessing all the luxuries one could dream of.

"O Nazneen," they said, "looking for you, we are just dog-tired. Let us take a hot bath to refresh ourselves and have a good night's rest."

The bath-attendants prepared a lavish bath for them with scented waters. Maidens helped them to bathe. Delicious food was served to them at dinner. They slept the night on silken carpets. Fully refreshed, Fawzia went round the palace next morning, seeing every nook of it. And, when she reached the top floor, she saw the three boxes. Two were open and one was shut. She opened the closed one and finding nothing therein; shut it again. Razia also took a look around and was simply amazed to find how rich their sister had become. Loaded with presents, the two sisters took leave of their Nazneen and went home.

Nazneen did not see the "Pink Pearl" for days together. So she opened the box. This time the bridge did not appear, nor did her beau. She got panicky and remembered that she had let the box be shut. She ran out quite upset, hardly knowing that she had reached a far-off roadside. Quite exhausted, she sat under a tree. Two birds, perched on the tree, were twittering thus: "The oil of the hair of the demon who sits at the foot of this tree will be good for the 'Pink Pearl'." The other rejoined, "If you understand, then do what is needed."

Nazneen understood them since she knew bird-language. She at once killed the demon and took the oil from his hair. Then, posing to be a doctor, she began to loiter, crying aloud: "I am a healer of all troubles." Thus wandering, she reached a palace. It turned out to be the palace of "Pink Pearl." His mother, hearing the voice of the healer, rushed down and called the doctor in, and took her straight to where "Pink Pearl" was lying in a coma, almost dead to all appearances.

Nazneen rubbed the "Pink Pearl" with the oil. And, lo and behold: her beloved prince came back to life. The royal parents of "Pink Pearl" were happy beyond limit to see their son alive after all.

"What can we give you as a reward for saving our son?" they asked the girl.

"Nothing but the betrothal ring and a necklace," she replied, simply. Receiving these gifts from the grateful parents of "Pink Pearl," she sped fast to where she had come from. She opened the box and there was the palace, the "Pink Pearl" on his horse crossing the bridge and brandishing his sword. Then she took out the ring and put it on her finger, and wore the necklace round her neck.

"Where did you get these from?" the "Pink Pearl" asked her.

"From your royal father and mother," she replied and narrated the whole episode.

Nazneen and "Pink Pearl" were formally betrothed. Their marriage was an occasion for great pageantry and pomp. And, they lived happily ever after.

Nazneen is a complicated mixture of helpless compliance and bold, intelligent power. She knows what she wants, demands it, and has the power to detain the ship until her father complies. When Nazneen is thrown out of her house, she walks helplessly, aimlessly and cries. When her lover's life is on the line, Nazneen leaves the house in panic but then she speaks bird-language, kills a demon, and cures her lover. Both Nazneen's helplessness and her power are integral parts of her personality. She breaks out of her cage but is never free of it. Luckily this is a fairy tale and Nazneen does live happily ever after.

Who Is Blessed with the Realm, Riches, and Honor?

Israel[134]

In the heat of midday, a handsome and comely prince noticed two snakes twisted round each other. Suddenly one of them crawled toward the prince and said to him in a human voice "Save me from the hands of my enemy. I have no strength left in me."

The prince was astonished and said to the pleading snake, escaping from his pursuer, "Swear that you will do me no evil and that you will leave me immediately your enemy is out of sight."

"I swear," promised the snake, in an imploring voice.

Then the snake entered the prince's mouth and penetrated into his body. After the other snake had left in disappointment, the prince called to the snake whom he had delivered, "Now get out of my stomach." But his call was in vain. The snake refused to budge and said, "I will remain here all my life. I like this place and feel at home here."

From that time on the prince's flesh began to waste away, and his stomach became so swollen that he could not move his limbs. Little by little he became so very ugly that even his own father, the king, lost interest in him and left his son to his own fate. When the prince saw that he had become a burden in the palace, and no one was concerned about him, he left the town and began to roam from place to place, begging for alms.

One day he came to a place in which a sultan dwelt in a palace with his three beautiful daughters. In the morning the sultan would call out to his eldest daughter, "Who is blessed with the realm, riches, and honor, my daughter?"

"You, father," the eldest daughter would reply.

Then the sultan would call out to his second daughter and ask her, "Who is blessed with the realm, riches, and honor?" She would reply, "You, father."

Then he would ask his youngest daughter, "Who is blessed with the realm, riches, and honor?" and she would always reply, "The Lord alone, my father." Each time the youngest daughter was given violent blows, but she never took her words back.

From day to day the sultan's anger with his youngest daughter grew, until one day he swore, "Tomorrow I shall give my daughter to the first beggar who passes the palace."

Early the next morning, looking through the window, he saw an ugly beggar with a swollen stomach, dressed in torn clothes and lying prostrate by the palace walls. He called his youngest daughter and asked, "Who is blessed with the realm, riches, and honor, my daughter?"

"The Almighty alone, my father!" answered the daughter as usual.

Immediately he called the beggar and pointing to his daughter, commanded, "Take her for your wife!"

"Do not make a fool of me, my lord," implored the beggar in confusion, "I am in a difficult plight."

"I mean what I say!" exclaimed the sultan. "Take her and depart."

While the man stood in bewilderment, the princess took him by his hand and said, "You are my luck, and this is my fate." And together they left the palace.

They arrived at last at a field beyond the town. There the princess put up a hut, made a bed, and helped the sick man to lie down. Next day she went to the forest, chopped wood, piled it up, and made a log fire. What a wonderfully good smell, as fragrant as the Garden of Eden!

The princess realized that the wood was of a special kind, and its fragrance excelled the finest perfume. She chopped down more trees, and every day, in disguise, she went to the market of the nearby town to sell the logs. When the citizens discovered the amazing properties of the wood, they began to buy more and more of the logs, and the couple did not suffer from hunger.

One day the princess lay the sick man to rest on a stone in the shadow of a tree while she herself was chopping wood. Suddenly she heard a sound like the croaking of a frog. Looking at the sick man, now asleep, she realized that the croaking came from his stomach. Suddenly she heard another sound, the voice of a snake whispering from outside, "Are you not ashamed to croak from a man's stomach?"

The princess listened carefully because she wanted to hear the answer, and indeed, it came from the snake within the stomach. "I feel at home here and am living in comfort. But you are stupid and miserable, working all day long to find bread for your starving soul."

"Get out, you coward, shameful liar, who repays evil for good," angrily whispered the snake from outside.

The snake within answered, "You are no better than I am. I know your secret very well. Under the nearby stone your stolen treasure is hidden."

"I have enough besides this treasure," was the answer. "But you are a traitor. What have you done to the worthy prince who saved you from death? If the girl had been wise enough, she would have taken leaves from the tree above, ground them, brewed a drink, and routed you."

After he had finished speaking, the princess sighed with relief and gratitude. Immediately she plucked the leaves from the tree above, ground them, and brewed a drink. Then she handed it to the prince, who drank the draft without a word. Suddenly he felt a severe stomach-ache. The snake came out from his stomach, bit by bit.

All the time the prince suffered great pains, and at last he fainted. The girl tended him with care, and after several weeks the prince had regained his health and was hale and hearty. Then the girl dug under the stone, and lo! she found the snake's treasure underneath it. In the months that followed the couple set about planning their palace. Both of them showed great diligence and knowledge and soon the building was completed. It was indeed a beautiful palace and contained a special reception hall for beggars and passers-by.

When everything was ready, the couple moved in. One day, after many years had passed, two old men appeared amongst the beggars visiting the reception hall. The couple recognized them as their parents; it so happened that the two kings had become poor, and their heartless children had driven them away. Now they came, shabbily dressed, after having tramped from place to place with beggars they met on their way. The couple invited the two old men to change their clothes and to tell their life stories. When they had finished, the young couple revealed who they were. The fathers recognized their children and listened the night long to each other's adventures.

There was great rejoicing in the palace, and before morning the girl's father concluded, "You were right, my daughter. The realm, riches, and honor are the Almighty's alone."

The wise, youngest daughter refuses to oblige her father's vanity. Cast out by her father and married to a sick beggar, she immediately sets to work to ameliorate her situation. Her resourcefulness cures her husband and makes them both rich. Both of the exiled children return good for evil and are reconciled with their fathers. Reconciliation is admirable, but folklorist Maria Tatar traces a historical trend in folktales over the last two centuries to present fathers more favorably and to forgive them. At the same time, she maintains there has been a corresponding and unquieting trend to magnify the evil of the mother.[135]

The Story of the King, Hamed bin Bathara, and of the Fearless Girl

Arab [136]

It is said that once, in the Island of the Arabs, was a great king, named Hamed bin Bathara, who had a beloved wife whom he loved more than life itself. And it came about that Hamed returned to his palace from war, and he discovered that his wife, his queen, was faithless to him, for she had lain with a slave. And the king was filled with a great anger, and he said: There shall remain in this land no woman save she who gave me birth, for women are false and faithless and there is virtue only in man. Nor shall any woman enter this land on pain of instant death.

And every female, from the youngest child to the oldest hag was thrown out of the king's lands. And there remained only men and boys and the mother of the king. Nor did any woman or any girl dare to return to that kingdom, and they remained in far countries. And a girl, whose name was Sherifa, the daughter of a neighbouring king, was astonished at the situation in the kingdom of Hamed bin Bathara, and she said: I will visit his land and I shall enter his house, and I shall learn how man can live without woman. But they said to her: You cannot go, for Hamed bin Bathara will surely kill you. And she said: I am without fear.

So the Princess Sherifa bought for herself the clothes of a prince. And she prepared a ship, and sailors, and soldiers, and made ready to visit the king, Hamed bin Bathara, but in the guise of a man, not of a woman. And she sailed to the kingdom of Hamed bin Bathara, and sent messengers to inform him that the Prince Sherif would wait on him in his service and be his guest.

So the Prince Sherif, who was really the Princess Sherifa, landed at the town of Hamed bin Bathara and was received with great magnificence and splendour. And she was amazed to see that in that city there were only men and boys, and even the washing of the dirty vessels at the well was the work of men. And the king, Hamed bin Bathara, thought that the Prince Sherif was a beautiful youth, and he knew her not for a girl. And the Prince Sherif stayed for many days at the court of the king, and accompanied him wherever he went, whether for hunting or for hawking, for jesting or for drinking. And the king, Hamed bin Bathara, felt a great friendship and love for the Prince Sherif, and he was puzzled, and thought: Perchance he is a woman. So the king went to his mother, who was the only woman in all that country, and he said: O my mother. There is come amongst us a beautiful youth, whose face is as the moon, were the moon sweet-scented with attar of roses, who is as straight and supple as the date palm, were only its fruit jasmine flowers, yet on that lovely face there is not even a thin wisp thinner than the morning mist where the moustache of manhood should sprout. Can then such loveliness belong to man, or is a woman come amongst us, for such a one I have sworn to kill. And the king's mother replied: If the prince is youth or girl I do not know, but take her to the market, then if she gazes at the shops of silks and jewels, and if she turns aside from the shops selling daggers and saddles and swords, then she is a woman, and you may do with her as you wish. So the king, Hamed bin Bathara, rode out with his court to the market, and by his side rode the Prince Sherif. And the king said as they passed: Look at those shops selling gold bangles and ruby earrings. But the Prince Sherif said: Leave those things. They are not for a man. Let us see the swords.

And as they rode further into the market the king said: Look at those shops selling rare silks of Persia. But the Prince Sherif said: Leave those silks, they do not concern us. Where are the swords?

And when they came to the shops of the armourers the prince dismounted, and entered a shop, and seized swords in his hands, making the blades sing through the air, and plying the merchant with questions as to their worth. And the merchant replied to the words of the prince, who purchased the finest sword in all that shop and in all that street, paying its value with a bag of gold.

And the king, Hamed, returned to his mother, and he said: It was thus and thus, and he behaved as a man. But does a man have a voice like a sweet dove cooing to its mate? And Hamed's mother said: Know you that a girl eats hot food slowly and delicately. Prepare a meal as hot as fire and full of peppers and cloves. Then when she eats it you shall know whether she is man or woman.

So Hamed bin Bathara prepared a meal as hot as fire and full of filfil and spices, and he bade his court be seated to eat of the meal. And blisters came on the tongues of Hamed and of his courtiers, and had they spat out they would have set fire to the earth. But the Prince Sherif heaped the food into his mouth and ate heartily, calling on the king and on the courtiers: Eat! Eat! The food grows cold while you dally.

And the King Hamed went to his mother and said: He ate better than any man could eat, but, O my mother, does a man have lips soft as peach blossom? And Hamed's mother replied: If you would know whether she is man or woman test her heart, for men's hearts are as cannon balls, but women's hearts are as soft as the ball of wool with which a child plays, for women's hearts are men's playthings. Let a child crave mercy from her, that you may test her heart.

So Hamed sat in his court with the Prince Sherif beside him. And the servant who brought them coffee spilt some on the dress of the Prince Sherif. And the king became angry and said: You would ill-use my guest, but to your own death. And a small child who was in the gathering burst forward weeping, and clutched the cloak of the Prince Sherif, crying: O merciful prince. Please intercede with the king and save my father. And the Prince Sherif said: Call me not merciful, for mercy is for women and justice is for men. Let then the king's sentence be executed here and in the presence of all, that all may see justice. And the king was astonished, for he had not really meant to kill his servant, since it was but a ruse, but he could see no way of avoiding the man's death.

But when the executioner came the king ordered: Flog him only, but with a hundred lashes, since there are no merciful women in this land from whom he can beg his life. And the executioner started to flog the servant with a great lash, and the child screamed and clutched the cloak of the Prince Sherif and begged mercy. And the king looked at the face of the prince and saw it as cold as stone. And the courtiers winced when they saw the lash fall on the man's bloody back, and even the king turned his eyes away, but the Prince Sherif made not a sign of mercy. And finally the king and the courtiers cried out and begged the executioner to desist, for they could stand the sight no longer.

And the king went to his mother and said: The heart of the prince is as hard as a cannon ball, but, O my mother, do men have hands which are smooth and slim and small? Do men have ears like little sea-shells? Do men have hair softer than silken thread, which the hand seeks even as the dove seeks its nest? Do men have bodies for which men yearn even as the shepherd yearns for rain?

And the king's mother replied: If you would know her man or woman, you must see her body, for she is cleverer than you and there is no other way. Take her with you beside the sea, then say to her: The day is hot. Let us doff our clothes and swim in the sea. And should she hesitate, then pull off her clothes as in a playful jest, as you would with a reluctant friend. But shall you see her and then kill her? And the king, Hamed bin Bathara, replied: Kill her I must, for my oath is sworn.

So the king, Hamed bin Bathara, rode out from his palace with all his courtiers and with the Prince Sherif, and he took the road towards the sea. And the Prince Sherif halted his horse in the great gate of the town, and quickly with his dagger, he wrote a verse in Arabic on the wooden door, and when the king and the courtiers glanced back at him he urged his horse forward, saying: I do but test the keenness of my dagger point, for a blunt dagger does not become a man.

And when they got near to the sea, at a beach on a bay where lay at anchor the Prince Sherif's ship, the prince cried out in a loud voice: O king, it is hot. Why should we not swim? And the prince galloped his horse into the sea, and jumped in fully clothed, shouting: Only women worry about wet clothes. But the king commanded: Catch him and bring him back. And all the courtiers and even the king hurled themselves into the sea fully clothed, but the prince swam faster than a fish, and easily escaped them.

And the prince swam easily to his ship, and the sailors hoisted the sail and sailed away. And the king and his courtiers rode back to the town with their clothes ruined by the sea. And the heart of the king was heavy for he thought: Now I shall never know if he be man or woman. But when they came to the great door they saw a crowd collected, gazing at the door. And they made way for the king, and he saw what they saw and read what they read. And on that door was carved a verse in Arabic, as well written as if by pen, yet cut deeply into the wood. And the king read out the verse, which said:

> Woman I came, I went no other
> To your despite, Hamed bin Bathara.
> Dakhalit athara wa kharajit athara
> Wa raghman alek, ya Hamed bin Bathar.

And the king grew hot with rage and he called carpenters and bade them efface the verse. But they cut with chisels and blades without effect, saying: This wood is teak, harder than iron; no man's weak hand can cut it.

And the king was mad with fury, and he said: This woman has defied me and scorned me, and she must die. So he disguised himself as an old man with a white beard, and he took a ship and sailed after the Princess Sherifa.

And after months of seeking and enquiry he found her palace and he entered it at the dead of night. And he entered the room of the princess and he was astonished at what he saw, for a lamp burned in her room and she stood naked before him, without any clothes on her body. And Hamed was amazed, for her skin gleamed as silver in the lamplight, and her waist was shaped for the embrace of a man's arms. And the girl Sherifa said to the king: I have waited for you, Hamed bin Bathara, and now, if you look, your question is answered. But you shall answer my question before you kill me.

And Hamed said: What is this question? Then the girl Sherifa asked him: What is a dagger without a sheath? And the king replied: A dagger without a sheath cannot be, for the blade would rust and decay and the edge would blunt, how then can there be a dagger without a sheath? And the Princess Sherifa said: If there can be man without woman then there can be dagger without sheath, for man is a sword blade, and woman is the sheath which protects him, and cooks his food, and keeps his house, and fulfils his desires. And the king, Hamed bin Bathara, was filled with an exceeding love for the girl Sherifa, and he returned his dagger to its sheath. And Hamed bin Bathara married the Princess Sherifa, and he returned to his country and ordered that all the wives and girl children should return to the land. For he said: Man there must be, and woman there must be, even as the sun and the moon must be, and, if the day is for man, what is the night without the light of woman?

Women expend much energy having babies and feeding and caring for their young. Men, too, invest in their children, but unlike women, they can't be absolutely sure that the children are really theirs. Assuring their paternity is thus a major obsession with men. Claustration and chastity belts can be seen as attempts by men to regulate female sexuality and assure themselves of their paternity. In angry reaction to his inability to regulate his wife, this king decides to eliminate women entirely.

Sherifa's courage and wisdom cure the mad king and teach him that women and men are in this together. She wins the king's admiration and love by staying one step ahead of the traps he and his mother set for her. When the king condemns his servant to death, Sherifa helps him to recognize the importance of women and to regret a man's hard heart. The king himself revokes the death sentence "since there are no merciful women in this land from whom he [the servant] can beg his life." Sherifa predicts the king's plan to kill her as well as she has predicted all his other plans. Her womanly body answers his question, but Sherifa poses an edifying question of her own: "What is a dagger without a sheath?" The result of Sherifa's wisdom and daring is that the king renounces his bitter war against women and all the wives and girls return to the land. Sherifa saves the king and his kingdom.

The Sultan's Daughter

Sudan [137]

Once upon a time there was a great Sultan who had many servants, a great retinue, and a lot of money. His wife had the virtues of husbandry: she provided against a rainy day, and she managed her husband's financial affairs, and did it well. The Sultan loved her very much, and they had one daughter who was very beautiful, clever, and shrewd. She, like her mother, had the virtues of husbandry.

The days went by, and there came the parting of the ways which comes to all loved ones; the Sultan's wife died. Her daughter, the princess, was about twenty years old. The Sultan was in great sorrow; he mourned and was in deep despair, so he resorted to drinking alcohol in order to forget the memories of his wife.

As time passed, drinking and dissipation became a habit to which he could not put an end. He became a wastrel, squandering any money he could lay his hands on in drinking and pleasures. Now he had a very large strong-box full of ingots of gold. After spending all he had, he turned to this strong-box. But whenever a day came that her father opened the strong-box, the clever princess took an ingot, dug a hole in the ground, and buried it. As time passed, the strong-box was completely emptied; but the beautiful princess had stored a large quantity of the gold.

Now the wastrel Sultan tried every means of getting money, but he failed. His belly was racked with hunger, so he came to his daughter, the princess, and begged her to find money no matter how, to get the food he needed.

The princess went to her store, took one of the ingots, and went to the market. She went to the biggest merchant of the town, and asked him to weigh and value the gold, and pay her what it was worth. But the merchant was amazed by the princess's loveliness, and all his defences fell to the magic of her beauty, and he fell in love with her. "Hearken, beautiful princess," he said to her, "I am willing to give you back your forty ounce ingot, and give you another forty, if you will accept me as your husband." But the beautiful princess disdained him and refused to marry him, and the merchant formed a grudge against her. When she asked for the return of the ingot, he denied receiving anything, and refused to give anything.

The beautiful princess was very sad, and went to the next merchant, and told him her story. She asked him to intervene with the first merchant for the return of the ingot. But this merchant in turn fell to the magic of her beauty. "Hearken, enchanting princess," he said to her, "I am willing to give you double its price, if you will accept me as a husband for one day." The princess refused his offer, and left him sorrowfully. She went to a third merchant, and told him the story of herself and the previous two merchants; she encountered in him the same desire. She went to a fourth merchant, and the same thing happened with him.

Sorrowfully, the princess went to the shade of a nearby tree, and while she was sitting in thought, a wise old woman passed by, felt sorry for the princess, and asked the cause of her distress. She told the old woman the story of herself and the four merchants, and how they had replied to her. "I am ready to help you," the old woman said to her, "much loved princess, but you must give me half of the ingot." The princess replied with a promise to give her what she asked if she succeeded in bringing back the ingot. Then the cunning old woman wove her plan, and planned how the princess should proceed; she bade the princess farewell, until some day on her return the promised half-ingot could be claimed.

The beautiful princess went to one of the carpenters, and asked him to make her a big wardrobe with four doors, each one opposite another, each compartment being big enough for one person. After some days, the princess went back to the carpenter and found that he had finished the wardrobe. She hired porters, took the wardrobe home, and put it in her private room.

The next day, the princess made her way to the market and went to the first merchant. When she was with him in his shop, she said: "My lord, have you decided to give me back my ingot? I am a poor girl, and very much in need of it." The merchant's eyes glinted, and he whispered: "Indeed I am! Let the princess hearken, I am ready as I said to give you two ingots if you accept me as a husband—even for a single day." The princess smiled, winked at him, and said: "I am ready to accept you as a husband for one day." "When?" he said, "I beg you to make it soon." The princess replied: "Come tomorrow at noon precisely." And when she had sworn to wait for him in her room, the merchant gave her her ingot.

The princess left him dancing for joy, and went to the next merchant, who welcomed her, and recognized from the expression on her face that she had agreed to his offer, and would accept him as a husband. "Let the merchant hearken," she said to him, "I ask you to go to your friend, take my ingot from him, and bring it back to me. I am very much in need of it, for it is all I possess." He replied: "Take two ingots from me at once, if you agree to my offer, and accept me as a husband for one day. In addition, I will bring your ingot from the other merchant." The princess said:

"If you come to me tomorrow shortly after noon, you will find me in my room." The merchant was delighted, and he was on the point of embracing her, but she escaped his hands and ran out of the shop. The merchant hurried after her with two ingots in his hand. He gave them to her, and she went away.

Then the princess went to the third merchant, and the same events took place; at the end of the meeting, she had two ingots from him, and promised to marry him for one day. He was to come after noon on the following day, at a time she fixed so as to fall soon after the arrival of the second merchant. She left him and went to the fourth merchant, and her fortune with him was the same as with the others: at the end of the meeting, she had from him two ingots, and promised to marry him the following day, fixing a time sufficiently after the arrival of the third merchant.

When she left the market, the beautiful princess had eight ingots with her. She went to her father, and gave them to him, after he repented of his prodigality. The princess asked her father to hide himself the next day in a place near the door of the house, and keep quiet. When he saw someone enter the house, he was to knock on the door; this was to be done every time someone entered, until all four merchants had entered the house.

The next day at noon, the first merchant knocked on the door. The princess went up to him with a warm welcome, and took him to her simple but elegant room. The merchant sat down overjoyed. Was this a dream or was it reality? At that moment, there came a knock on the door, and the merchant was taken aback. He was afraid that someone might come in and find him in the princess's chamber. "Where shall I hide?" he said to her in alarm: "Please, princess, hide me in a place where no one will see me." The princess went quickly to one of the doors of the wardrobe, opened it, and asked him to get in. The merchant got in, and the princess locked the door. She put the key in her bag

The princess sat and waited for the second merchant to come, and shortly he arrived, and knocked on the door. When he was on the point of sitting down, he heard a loud knocking on the door, and said to the princess: "Hearken, beautiful princess! Where can I hide? Please hide me in a place where no one will see me." The princess opened the second door of the wardrobe for him, hid him inside, and locked the door. She put the key in her bag. Then she sat and waited for the third merchant to come. The same things happened to him as to the others. In turn, he was locked in the wardrobe; and again the princess sat and waited for the fourth merchant to come. He arrived, and it was his lot to be locked in the fourth compartment of the wardrobe.

After the princess had locked the four merchants in the wardrobe, she went to the market and hired porters to take it to the auction place in the market. While the wardrobe was in the market, the Sultan of a neighbouring kingdom then visiting the market of this kingdom, saw it, was taken with it, and offered a high price. The princess agreed to sell it, but she made a condition. "Hearken, great Sultan," she said, "if you promise not to regret what you find in the wardrobe, then I shall not regret selling it." The Sultan made this promise, and bought the wardrobe. Then the princess went home.

Curiosity took possession of the Sultan, and he decided to see what was inside it, while people were gathered around. He opened the first door, and to the people's amazement, they saw their grand merchant sweating and cramped up on himself. They let him out with laughter and mockery. He opened the second door and found the second merchant, and again the crowd laughed mockingly. He opened the third door, and there was the third merchant. He opened the fourth door, and out came the fourth merchant. The crowd laughed at their four merchants, but they wondered how the princess had managed to lock them in the wardrobe.

The Sultan sent someone for the princess and asked her how she managed to get the four merchants in the wardrobe. The beautiful princess told him her story, and he was taken by her intelligence, her honour, and her beauty. He went to her father and asked for her hand in marriage. Some days later there were universal festivities; the Sultan married the beautiful princess, and her father became rich and happy as he was before.

The four merchants create a hostile, dog-eat-dog world where the rights of the opportunist include theft and blackmail. This is not an uncommon way to view the world, but there are other ways to live. The two women provide a counter-example. The Sultan's daughter and the old woman don't operate on an impossibly idealistic plane, their world, too, involves buying and selling. In return for her help the old woman will receive half the gold nugget. The old woman's plan transforms the princess's seemingly debilitating beauty into a weapon. The princess puts the plan into action and uses her beauty to bait the trap, which humiliates the merchants and recovers the gold.

Because folktales have been told by the common people for thousands of years, the tales often show an apparently powerless person up against a ruler with great, arbitrary power. In this folktale, the seemingly powerless women cooperate, use their intelligence, and turn their apparent disadvantages into advantages.

Yousif Al-Saffani

Sudan[138]

Long ago, there was a tyrannical Sultan who had seven sons, and he had a poor brother with seven daughters. Every day the poor brother used to go to the Sultan, and say: "Peace be upon you, father of the seven blessings!" And the Sultan would reply: "And peace upon you, father of the seven turds!" This carried on for a long time.

One day, the poor brother failed to earn his livelihood, and sent one of his daughters to his brother the Sultan, asking her to say to him: "My father could not meet you today because of a slight illness," and to say: "He could not earn our livelihood today. Could you give us something for our dinner?"

So the girl went and found her uncle sitting in his palace. She told him what her father had said. And the Sultan replied: "Go and take millet from that store." But on the way to the store, the wind blew her thawb,* and the Sultan her uncle said: "Cover yourself with your thawb, my girl, and then take the millet." The girl was angry. She left the millet, returned to her father, and told him what had happened. "Father," she said, "have nothing to do with that man. Our Creator will provide for us, God willing."

The following day, the girls' father went to his brother the Sultan and greeted him in the usual way, and received the usual reply. The Sultan asked him to sit down, and he did so. "Listen," said the Sultan, "if you do not bring me water which is not that of a well, or a river, or of rain, I shall have your head cut off." Sad and weeping, the father returned to his daughters. But his youngest daughter came to him and asked why he was weeping. And he told her what the Sultan wanted. To soothe him, she said: "Father, do not be sad. This is the easiest thing in the world." He was to go to the market and bring soap. When he brought it, she told her sisters and mother to take a bath. Then she lit a fire in the house, and put them in one of the rooms of the house. Naturally, they all dripped with sweat, which she collected. She filled a water-skin with it. Then she told her father to take the skin and give it to his brother the Sultan.

The father went and gave his usual greeting, and the Sultan gave the

---

* *Thawb*, the traditional outer garment of Sudanese women, which consists of some nine meters of cloth wound round the body, with a fold covering the head (but not the face).

405

usual reply. After sitting down, he gave the Sultan the water-skin full of sweat, and the Sultan admitted that he was right, and that he had got out of it. But he went on: "Now go and bring me milk which is not created in an animal or anything animate." Again, the man returned to his daughters sad and weeping. And the youngest daughter came to him and asked why he was weeping. To soothe him, she said: "Father do not be sad. This is the easiest thing in the world." And she took her water-skin and went out with her sisters to the wood, looking for a sodom-apple tree. When she found one, she cut it, and collected the white liquid that flowed out in her water-skin, till it was full. She brought this to her father, and said: "Father, how long will your brother the Sultan torment you like this? Give him this water-skin, and say to those who are present there: 'Which is better: seven daughters, or seven sons?' They are sure to reply that seven daughters are not worth the finger-nail of one son. Then say to his Highness the Sultan: 'In that case, bring your eldest and bravest son, and I shall bring my youngest daughter. Give them both money, and if your son makes a greater fortune by trade than my daughter, you can cut off my head, and make my daughters slaves at the water wheel; but if my daughter makes a greater fortune than your son, then I shall do as I will with you.'"

The father agreed to his daughter's suggestion. He went to the Sultan and gave him the usual greeting, and the Sultan gave the familiar reply. After sitting down, he gave the Sultan the water-skin full of the white fluid. Again the Sultan admitted his brother's success. After a pause, the girl's father said to those who were present in the Sultan's council: "Gentlemen, which is better, seven daughters or seven sons?" The question surprised them, and they replied: "Obviously, seven daughters are not worth the finger-nail of one son." So he said to the Sultan: "Your highness, bring the eldest and bravest of your sons, and I shall bring my youngest daughter. Give money to both of them to trade with. If your son's trade is more profitable than my daughter's, then cut off my head, and send my daughters down to the water-wheel. But if my daughter's trade is more profitable than your son's, I shall do as I will with you."

The Sultan agreed. He brought his eldest son, and his brother brought his youngest daughter. The Sultan gave them equal amounts of money, gave them each a sword and a horse, and sent them off to trade.

At once, the Sultan's son and the daughter of the poor man left the area on their horses. As they set off, the Sultan's son called the poor man's daughter by her name, saying: "Hey, Fatma . . . " But she interrupted, and said: "Shut up. From now on, do not call me Fatma, otherwise I shall cut off your head with my sword." "What should I call you?" he asked. "Call me Hassan the Clever," she replied. They rode on together until they came to a fork in the road. One way was called "The Road of Safety" and the other "The Road of Danger." The girl said: "Which will you choose—the Road of Safety, or the Road of Danger?" "The Road of Safety," he replied. And he did choose it. Off he went. But she in her turn chose the Road of Danger, and went along it until she reached a far country. She went to the market there, and asked what was the most expensive item. And they told her that salt was the most expensive. So she started trading in salt. During her stay in this land, she was disguised in men's clothing, and she called herself Hassan the Clever, as we said before. And from the time of her arrival, she lived in a house of the Sultan,* which he had vacated so that she could live there with his son. Of course the Sultan thought that she was a young man. So she lived with the Sultan's son disguised in men's clothing.

But the Sultan's son was suspicious, and didn't know whether to believe that she was a man. So he went to his mother and said: "Yousif al-Saffani's cheek is the cheek of a girl, but I am not happy with it." "My son," she replied, "there is no girl who could do such things—who could overcome so many difficulties and arrive in our country. He is a man, my son." But he persisted: "Yousif al-Saffani's cheek is the cheek of a girl, but I am not happy with it." "Well," she said, "I have a test. If she fails, she is a girl, and if she passes, she is a man." "What is the test?" said her son. "I shall make you coffee," said the mother, "and give you dates with it. If she eats the dates and throws the stones under her feet, she is a girl, but if she breaks the dates and throws the stones far away, she is a man." So the son took the coffee, and the dates, and when they sat to drink coffee, the girl took a date, broke it with just two fingers, and threw the stone far away.

The Sultan's son went back to his mother, and she asked him what had happened. "By God, mother," he said, "she took the date, broke it with two fingers, and threw the stone away." And his mother said: "Then he is a man." But her son said: "Mother, Yousif al-Saffani's cheek is the cheek of a girl, but I am not happy with it." The mother said: "Ask him to go hunting. If he catches something, and brings it back alive, he is a man. If he fails, then she is a girl." The Sultan's son went back and said to Hassan the Clever: "Hassan, let's go hunting," and she replied: "Is there hunting in your country?" The Sultan's son said that there was, and they went out hunting together. The girl saw an animal from far off. She spurred on her horse, and chased the quarry until she caught it alive, and brought it back

---

* This is a second Sultan, the Sultan of the far country.

to him. But the Sultan's son failed even to bring something which he had killed. His mother said: "My son, this is a man, and the bravest of men." But he replied: "My mother, Yousif al-Saffani's cheek is the cheek of a girl, but I am not happy with it." His mother said: "If you are not satisfied, there is another thing. If he looks at the ground while eating, she is a girl, but if he talks to you and looks you in the eyes while eating, then he is a man." So the Sultan's son went to her taking their lunch.

She ate looking him in the eyes. And when he offered her a small piece of meat, she refused on the ground that it was her practice to eat meat on big bones. Now when he went back to his mother, and she asked him what had happened, he said: "My God, she was eating and talking and looking me in the eyes, and eating big pieces of meat." His mother said: "My son, he is a man and more than a man." But he replied: "Yousif al-Saffani's cheek is the cheek of a girl, but I am not happy with it." His mother said to him: "Then ask him to go with you to your father's garden. If he agrees, ask him to climb a high palm tree. If he climbs to the top, he is a man. But if she is a woman, she will not be able to: the menstrual period will start, and she will come down." The Sultan's son went back and asked Hassan the Clever to go to his father's garden for a stroll. Hassan the Clever asked: "What is there in the garden?" "There are high date palms," said the Sultan's son. "Will you be able to climb them, Hassan?" "Yes," said Hassan the Clever, "I'm the only one who climbs my own father's palm trees." So they agreed to go to the garden. But before they left, the girl took a small knife and concealed it under her clothes. When the two of them reached the garden, the Sultan's son turned to Hassan the Clever and pointed out a high palm tree and asked Hassan to climb it. Hassan the Clever agreed, and started climbing the tree. However, half-way up her menstrual period came on. So she quickly took the small knife, and cut her thigh. She shouted to the Sultan's son that some of the dried boughs on the trunk had scratched her, and so she could not climb up. So she came down. The Sultan's son was worried by the blood flowing from Hassan the Clever, and wanted to bandage the wound. But Hassan the Clever refused, saying that it was a very trivial wound, and that he could manage until they reached home. So the Sultan's son was taken in.

But when he returned to his mother, and she asked him, he told her that the girl climbed the tree, and when she had nearly got to the top, she had a big cut, and blood flowed from her which he had seen with his own eyes. His mother said: "My son he is a man." But the Sultan's son replied: "Mother, Yousif al-Saffani's cheek is the cheek of a girl, but I am not happy with it."

So his mother said: "Go with him to the market, and tell him that you want to buy some things. If he likes men's things, then he is a man; but if he likes women's things, then he is a woman." The Sultan's son went back to his friend Hassan the Clever, and expressed his wish to go to the market with him to buy some goods. Hassan the Clever agreed, and they both went to the market. When they arrived, the Sultan's son tried to trick his companion. He pointed out a beautiful thawb, and said (showing his admiration): "Would you like to buy this thawb?" But the girl said: "No, I should like to buy that sword," and she did buy it. Again the Sultan's son pointed out a woman's dress, and said: "Wouldn't you like to buy these dresses for your sisters?" But she replied that she wanted to buy a spear. And so every time that the Sultan's son pointed out any women's objects, the girl bought men's things, until their stroll in the market came to an end, and they went back home. When the Sultan's son came to his mother, he told her what had happened, and she said: "I hope, my son, that you are now convinced that he is a man." But the Sultan's son replied: "Mother, Yousif al-Saffani's cheek is the cheek of a girl, and I am not happy with it." So his mother said: "There is another test which may reveal him. Go to him and ask him to have a massage. If he exposes his body, the slave girl will see."

So the Sultan's son went back to Hassan the Clever, and pointed out that they were both very tired, and said that he had asked their slave girl to massage them. Hassan was to be the first. Hassan the Clever agreed to this suggestion, but first took a water jug and went to have a pee. She met someone, and said to him: "Look, my friend, I am a stranger to this country, and my host has offered to have me massaged. But I don't want to take off my clothes in a house which is not my house because it is indecent. However, I don't want to upset my host. Could you go inside this room and let the slave girl enter and massage you, without telling her anything? I would give you some money in return." The man agreed, and went into the room. After a while, the slave girl came in and massaged him, and then went away again. The man hurried out, and the girl came in his place just when the Sultan's son was coming in. So she pretended to be putting on her clothes, and sat down. The Sultan's son went to the slave girl and said: "If you lie, I shall cut off your head. Is that a man or a woman?" And she replied: "By God, whether you kill me or spare me, he is a man." The Sultan's son was surprised, and told his mother, who said: "Did I not tell you that he is a man?" But he persisted: "Mother, Yousif al-Saffani's cheek is the cheek of a girl, but I am not happy with it." Then his mother said: "If you are still not convinced, I shall give you the last test. This one is beyond doubt. You couldn't be left in two minds

whether it is a man or a woman. Tell him to go bathing in the river." So
the Sultan's son went back to Hassan the Clever, and told him that they
should go swimming in the river. She was upset, and shivered at this idea,
since her identity would be revealed if she bathed in the river. However,
she pulled herself together and agreed, since there was no choice but to
agree. Secretly, however, she was praying to God: "O God, You know how
I left my home because of oppression. I beg You to take care of me until
I return." God granted her prayer. For when they went out, they came
across a bridal procession with many women dancing and ululating, and
men jumping to the beat of the drum. The Sultan's son became absorbed
in the procession, and while he was watching it the girl went and bathed
in the river. When the Sultan's son arrived, he found that she had finished
and was putting on her last piece of clothing very happily. He asked her
to go and swim again, but she refused and said that if she bathed again
she might fall ill. So the Sultan's son went in and bathed, and then came
out again. When he returned, he told his mother what had happened,
emphasizing that although she bathed, he did not see her. His mother
said: "My son, he is a man, you must be convinced."

Now during these tests and all the days when the girl was a guest of
the Sultan's son, she was trading in salt, which was rather profitable. In
due course, she was the owner of considerable wealth, with which she
bought horses, slaves, swords and other things. She bade farewell to those
with whom she had lived, and set off for home. But before leaving the
Sultan's house, she left a piece of paper under her bed with these words
written on it:

> "As a girl I came,
> As a girl I went,
> No boy did I find
> To outwit my mind."

The Sultan's son happened to find this paper. He went to his mother,
and said to her: "Did I not tell you that she was a girl? She laughed at
me, and made a fool of me. I must follow her." But his mother said that
he should let her reach home, and then follow her.

These then were the adventures of the girl who played the part of
Hassan the Clever, and came back having made her fortune. As for the
Sultan's son who accompanied her with the same purpose of making his
fortune, and who chose the Road of Safety, as we said, he kept on along
this road until he reached a prosperous town, where he settled, and began
to gamble and lead a life of debauchery, frittering away his money until
he was penniless. Then he took work in an eating-house in the market.

Now his cousin passed through this town, and happened to go to eat in the very restaurant in which he worked. Still disguised as a man, she ate, and ordered food for her slaves who ate also. Afterwards she called the owner of the restaurant and asked him to call her cousin whom she had recognized. When he came, she asked him whether he recognized her, and he replied that he did not. Then she said to the owner of the restaurant: "This is my brother, and I should like to take him away." The owner of the restaurant said: "He owes me a large amount of money, and I shall not let him go unless he pays me." So the girl paid what was asked from the fortune which she had amassed, took her cousin, and set off with him for their home. On the way, the girl told her slaves to go with her cousin to the town, pretending to be with him, and to leave her by herself. But when she headed towards her home, the retinue was to go with her, and leave the Sultan's son by himself. The slaves said: "We hear and we obey."

When the retinue neared the town and the Sultan's son was seen at its head, while the Sultan's brother's daughter was alone and far away from it, some people rushed happily to the Sultan and informed him that his son had come back with a great fortune. The Sultan in his delight had the drum beaten to celebrate the occasion. As for his brother, the father of the girl and of the other girls, he was very sad about what had happened to his daughter, and began to weep, thinking that she had failed.

But when the retinue approached the Sultan's house, and the Sultan was laughing happily and his brother weeping bitterly, the girl diverted her horse towards her father, and the slaves and horses with all their wealth followed her, and the Sultan's son was left by himself walking in dejection towards his father. The girl went to her father and found him weeping. She took his hand and raised it, saying: "Good news, father, your daughter is as good as a man." And the Sultan died with surprise and chagrin.

With her fortune, the girl rebuilt her father's house, and erected palaces. She improved his condition, ordering slaves to attend him. After the death of the Sultan, the eldest son inherited his position. He came and explained to his uncle that all their hostility and antagonism was due to his father who had died. Now there was no need for enmity and antagonism. "We are seven boys," he said, "and you have seven girls. Each of us will marry one of your daughters, and we shall live in peace. I shall marry Fatma who travelled far away, and came back with a fortune."

His uncle agreed to this, but Fatma refused the proposal vehemently. She reminded her father of all that his brother used to do. "If I had lost the contest," she said, "he would not have forgiven either you or us. Why do you forgive him?" In this way, she persuaded her father and he refused the offer.

As for the Sultan's son who had been the companion of Hassan the Clever, he waited until he knew that she had reached home. Then he followed her tracks, asking about her town until they showed him where it was. When he arrived, he began asking people if they knew the house of Hassan the Clever. Now the people knew that this was the name of the famous Fatma, and that "Hassan the Clever" was a pseudonym. They told him where the high palaces in the town were, and he went there. When he was at the door, one of the slaves came, and the Sultan's son asked: "Is this the house of Hassan the Clever?" The slave said that it was. He entered, and they led him into a separate room. Meanwhile, Fatma had gone out of the house for a wedding in all her finery. But when they told her that the Sultan's son had come to ask about her, she hurried back home, took off her women's clothes, and replaced them with men's clothes. However, she forgot one ear-ring.

She went to meet him. He greeted her, and began talking to her. After a while, he asked her a subtle question: "Is it the custom of your men, Hassan the Clever, here in this country, to wear ear-rings?" The girl raised her hand to her ear and discovered her mistake. She left in embarrassment.

But the Sultan's son, having discovered her identity, went at once to her father and said: "I wish to be associated with you. I am the son of the Sultan who governs the land where Fatma was, and where she used to live with us." The father welcomed this suggestion and asked what he wanted. He replied that he wanted to marry Hassan the Clever. And the girl agreed to the marriage. So he married her, and lived with her people.

Odds are against Fatma. She has to earn lots of money to save her father's life. At the same time, she has to stay one step ahead of the suspicious sultan's son. The sultan's son suspects Fatma, alias Hassan the Clever, is a woman based on her physical appearance but he can't devise tests that differentiate a woman from a man in his culture. He must ask his mother. Fatma knows that pink is for girls and blue is for boys. Women drop the pits under their chairs, men throw pits far away; women can't hunt, men can; women eat daintily and cast their eyes demurely at the floor, men eat big pieces of meat and look you straight in the eye. Fatma knows the culture's stereotypes of both sexes so well that she even brings a knife when she has to climb the palm tree. She is so adept at imitating a man that she outwits one sultan's son and completely out-trades the other. She says, "Good news, father, your daughter is as good as a man." Obviously, she is much better.

The Miser Who Married

Iraq[139]

Once there was a man who was old in years. The old man used to marry, but no woman would stay more than a month with him before asking for a divorce.

There was a girl who asked the former wives, Why did you get a divorce? Your former husband is a merchant, and a rich man. Why didn't you stay with him?

They answered, He killed us with hunger. Every day he would give us only a piece of bread this big, with a piece of cheese on it. We almost died of hunger. May Allah curse him and curse his wealth! We don't want such a rich man. We can't live with him.

The girl went to her mother and said, Perhaps that rich merchant will come and ask my hand. If he does you must agree to take him for me.

Huh, said her mother. That man takes wives and divorces wives. No one can live with him because he is such a miser. Don't be fooled by his wealth.

Well, Mother, answered the girl, I want him. I'll take the heart out of him and get his money.

What are you saying! The mother went to the father and said. This is what your daughter is saying.

Let her marry him, he said. She's a clever girl.

Well, do you know, the old miser came and asked her hand and the parents gave her away.

The daughter said to her mother, Mother, you allowed me to marry, but don't take my marriage into account. Whatever clothes I want, give them to me just as if I were still your daughter living at home. Bring me food, too, until I see my way clear with the miser.

All right, agreed the mother.

The miser used to come to the house every day with a loaf of bread for himself and his wife and her servant, with sometimes a few greens or a little cheese to eat with it.

His wife said, O my Husband, why do you go to all this trouble? My people will bring lunch and supper from my house for me and my servant and for you, too.

Huh! he replied.

Every day they would bring a tray and knock at the door. Knock, knock. Who's there?

I, and here is your supper.

Every time they would bring stew and rice and fruit and drinks. The miser was pleased. He thought Allah was bestowing those blessings. He was happy as long as he didn't have to take money out of his pocket to pay for something.

One day the bride pretended to be a little under the weather and she slept all day. She was awake during the night and she saw the miser get up,— get up very quietly and go downstairs walking softly. When she got up and looked over the railing she saw that he had reached the top of the cellar steps. She went down after him barefooted. She saw him light a candle, take out a purse this big, full of gold and begin to drop them one by one into the drain hole in the floor. When he was about to finish she quickly went back upstairs and got into bed. Her husband came up and went to sleep.

The next day she went to the cellar and spread out a reed mat and got a long stick, put a little soft tar on the end of it and a lighted candle. She heated the tar over the candle and then thrust the stick into the drain. She pressed it down into the drain and drew out a golden coin. She worked all day long. Now she had plenty of money. She gave some to her family so that they could cook and bring her food. She would go to the bath and pay for a servant, and she would be sent an excellent lunch with all kinds of fruit to eat at the bath. All day long food would be sent to her from her own home on trays, one course after another for her and her callers and her guests.

Those other women who had been divorced said, I wonder what she did to him to make him spend so much on her. She has golden ornaments, dresses well, spends much. She sits all day or goes out visiting. It must be her good luck. They didn't know about her cleverness.

One day her husband came and told her that he had invited fifteen people to lunch the next day. What will you prepare?

His wife answered, Bring us a kilo of meat.

Fifteen people and only one kilo of meat?

We'll cook meat hash, and spinach stew, and meat with nut and pomegranate sauce. Bring us some walnuts, some spinach, and so forth. Bring a chicken also to go with the nut and pomegranate sauce.

But how can one chicken be enough for fifteen people? he asked.

Oh, I'll open the upstairs windows and spread some seeds and catch some sparrows and cook them also with the nut and pomegranate sauce.

However, he had some sense and said, No, I'd better bring three chickens as well.

As you like, she answered.

The miser returned at noon and saw, extending out into the street, the preparations for staging the lunch. Each saucepan was as big as this. The spinach was black with the amount of oil used in its preparation. The nut and pomegranate sauce was boiling and bubbling in oil with whole chickens lying in it. The meat was so deliciously seasoned with saffron and cardomon that the aroma wreathed out into the street. The pot of rice was covered with saffron, almonds and raisins so that I can't begin to describe it, but there was one half of a sparrow hanging in the doorway of the kitchen.

The miser came in with his walking stick and saw the sparrow, and suddenly came to his senses. Seven pots aboil, with half a sparrow to spare? Couldn't you find a place to put this one-half of a sparrow in a sauce-pan with the rest? He was standing there leaning on his walking stick and he began to understand what was going on and his beard began to tremble and he had a heart attack. His wife took him by the hand and pulled him into the nearest room where he took one deep breath, ha-a-a-a, and died.

His wife said to the servants, Silence. Don't anyone of you talk about this. She called her father and she called her mother and they took care of all the guests who had plenty to eat. The servants carried the food upstairs to the dining room. When the guests had finished eating, the wife began to cry, Boo hoo hoo!

The guests said, What is the matter? And why haven't we seen the haji, your husband?

She said, We didn't want to spoil your good time, but just now the haji passed away. You were eating and the haji was having a hard time of it. He was not at all well, and just as you finished eating, the haji gave up the ghost. He is dead.

What a shock! So the guests became the mourners for the haji and followed him to the grave. His wife had killed him by the shock he had sustained when he suddenly realized what was going on and that she had found a way of getting his money and spending it. He saw it all at the moment that he saw half of a sparrow hanging in the kitchen doorway. Half a sparrow. Half a sparrow. Hang it in the kitchen doorway and save it as something special for another time?

The old man was buried and his inheritance had to be settled. The wife agreed to accept the house as her share of the inheritance. She counted out the money, and, as much as they tell you she had, it was still more. Of course no one knew about what was in the cellar drain. She opened up the drain and found that the drain had been lined with tar and that it was almost full of gold pieces, each worth a pound

Later the clever woman married again. Her second husband was a man of very great importance. A very important man came along and married her and she began to have children. He was fortunate and she was fortunate and so they lived to the end of their lives in happiness.

> Wealth finds wealth,
> And lice find the saddle bag.

Love is not a prerequisite for marriage to this miser. The clever girl does her research well. She goes into the marriage with a plan and a purpose: "I'll take the heart out of him and get his money." With the help of her mother, the clever girl survives the miser's famine regime. Her acquired wealth enables her to remarry, securing a man of great importance. The modern western world reveres the idea of marrying for love, but when poverty and famine are everywhere, wealth is more important. Some women have even suggested that the idea of romantic love may be male propaganda, a sort of emotional chastity belt, a way for men to control women and ensure paternity.[140]

The Sign of the Tassel

Iraq [141]

Once there was a man who married and took a wife. Every few days he would return home in a temper, and she would feel badly about it.

She said, O my Husband, this will never do. You are often in a temper. You come home in a very bad temper.

Yes, he said. Things go on in the town that upset me and I come home in a temper.

But, she said, this will never do, because I also have a very bad temper, and if we are both in a bad temper on the same day, who knows what may happen? You must give me a sign so that I'll know that you are coming home in a temper, and so that I'll make allowances for you. Yes, he said, you are right. That's a good idea.

In those olden days the men used to wear on their heads a red fez with a long black tassel hanging down at the side. So he said, I'll put the tassel of my fez toward the front on the day that I am coming home in a temper, and when you see the tassel hanging at the front you'll know that I am in a temper and whatever I say, or whatever my words may be, you mustn't feel bad or take them to heart.

She said, That's a good idea. But, when I am in a temper, what about that? I'll also give you a sign. She did this purposely to help him get rid of his bad habit. She told him, I'll wear a white apron, and when you see me wearing a white apron you'll know I am in a temper and you must put up with me. He said, All right.

She began to wait for him every day about the time of his return and to watch for him from the window. She could look out and see, when he reached the top of the street, if he had put the tassel at the front of his fez. When she saw him come stamping along with the tassel swinging back and forth at the front of his fez like the tail on the rump of an elephant, she would quickly get out her white apron and put it on. When her husband came in and saw her wearing the white apron he moved the tassel to the side of his fez, for it wouldn't do for both of them to be in a temper at the same time, or they might beat one another. So he gave in. Time after time, once, twice, thrice, the same thing happened, until the husband said, O Wife, your fits of temper come at the same time as my fits of temper. They come together.

O my Husband, she said, give up your bad habit and I will give up mine. A temper does no good. Allah has given human beings wisdom, but temper drives out wisdom. If you are in a temper in the city, what excuse have you for coming home in a temper? So my temper goes with your temper. But I can control and put aside my temper. I beg you also to put aside your temper and not to bring it home with you.

He said, Indeed, you are quite right. So from that time onward he did not put his tassel at the front of his fez and he gave up his temper just as his wife had suggested that he should, and they lived happily ever after and neither he nor she gave way to their tempers.

One kind of heroism has been left out of history and sagas and tall tales. It is a heroism that has to do with the way we lead our lives every day. It is a soft-spoken heroism that wells under the surface, a quotidian heroism like this woman's wise and patient teaching of her husband.

From the outset, this woman realizes she cannot explain with words and have her husband understand. She doesn't reproach him. Instead, the wife pretends to accept this problem in their relationship and merely informs him that she has a temper too. Her "solution" sets up a situation that gives the husband apparent freedom to vent his anger as usual. However, it also gives the wife a way to keep him from venting his anger on her. Others might have tried to use this set-up as a permanent device to outwit their partner. This heroine uses it to teach her husband that giving way to his temper is harmful. Gently she brings her husband to understand that they are working together to make their relationship happy.

NOTES

1. Theodore S. Geisel, *One Fish Two Fish, Red Fish Blue Fish*; *Green Eggs and Ham*; *The Cat in the Hat*; *If I Ran the Zoo*; *And to Think That I Saw It on Mulberry Street*; *The 500 Hats of Bartholomew Cubbins*; *Horton Hatches the Egg*; *Horton Hears a Who* (New York: Random House).

2. The italics are mine.

3. Males and females in 37 out of Dr. Seuss's 52 books were counted. Since his last two were illustrated by others, they were not included in the statistics. If there was any doubt as to the gender, the character was not included in the count unless the gender was defined in the text.

4. From a random sampling of 300 books.

5. Ludwig Bemelmans, *Madeline* (England: Picture Puffins, 1981).

6. Kay F. Stone, "The Misuses of Enchantment: Controversies on the Significance of Fairy Tales," *In Women's Folklore, Women's Culture*, ed. Rosan A. Jordan and Susan J. Kalick (Philadelphia: University of Pennsylvania Press, 1985), pp. 125–145.

7. From a random sampling of more than 1,000 tales in about 50 books. If these figures seem exaggerated, please spend half an hour at your local library and count them yourself.

8. Ethel Johnston Phelps, *The Maid of the North* (New York: Henry Holt Co., 1981), pp. 35–45.

9. Ronald M. Berndt and Catherine H. Berndt, *The Speaking Land* (Australia: Penguin Books Australia, 1989), pp. 145–147.

10. *Webster's Third New International Dictionary of the English Language Unabridged*, ed. in chief, Philip Babcock Gove, Ph.D., (Springfield, Mass., USA: G. & C. Merriam Co., 1976). This dictionary was used throughout to define unusual words in the texts of the folktales.

11. Yei Theodora Ozaki, *The Japanese Fairy Book* (New York: E. P. Dutton & Co., 1903), p. 129.

TALES FROM EUROPE

12. *The Stolen Bairn and the Sìdh*: Sorche Nic Leodhas, *Thistle and Thyme, Tales and Legends from Scotland* (New York: Holt, Rinehart and Winston, 1962), pp. 46–61.

13. *The Three Sisters and Their Husbands, Three Brothers*: Jeremiah Curtin, *Tales of the Fairies and of the Ghost World* (London: David Nutt, 1895), pp. 80–101.

14. *The Corpse Watchers*: Patrick Kennedy, *Legendary Fictions of the Irish Celts* (London & New York: MacMillan and Co., 1891), pp. 48–51.

15. *The Crookened Back*: Thomas Crofton Crocker, "Fairy Legends of the South of Ireland," in *Legends and Tales of Ireland* (New York: Crescent Books, 1987), pp. 341–345.

16. Z. Pallo Jordan, *Tales from Southern Africa* (Berkeley, Calif.: University of California Press, 1973), pp. xvi–xx.

17. *Introduction:* Claire R. Farrer, in *Women and Folklore* (Austin, Texas & London: University of Texas Press, 1975).

18. *The Horned Women*: Lady Wilde, *Ancient Legends, Mystic Charms, and Superstitions of Ireland*, Vol.I (Boston: Ticknor and Co., Publishers, 1887), pp. 18–21.

19. Sarah Blaffer Hrdy. *The Woman That Never Evolved* (Cambridge, Mass. & London: Harvard University Press, 1981), p. 17.

20. Sarah Blaffer Hrdy. *The Woman That Never Evolved*, p. 189.

21. *Whuppity Stoorie*: Norah Montgomerie and William Montgomerie, *The Well at the World's End, Folk Tales of Scotland* (London: The Bodley Head, 1975), pp. 35–38.

22. *Molly Whuppie*: Joseph Jacobs, *English Fairy Tales* (New York: G. P. Putnam's Sons, 1895), pp. 125–130.

23. *The Treasure of Downhouse*: Katharine M. Briggs, *British Folk Tales* (New York: Pantheon Books, 1970), pp. 195–196. Briggs refers to: J. R. W. Coxhead, *Devon Traditions and Fairy Tales*, pp. 39–41 and *The Borders of the Tamar and the Tavy*. Narrated: 8 January 1833 by Mrs. Bray.

24. *The Hand of Glory*: Katharine M. Briggs, *British Folk Tales*. Briggs refers to: Norton Collection III p. 21 and to Henderson, *Folk-Lore of the Northern Countries*, 1861, p. 241–242. Told by Bella Parkin, an old woman who was the daughter of the servant-maid.

25. *Tamlane*: Joseph Jacobs, *English Fairy Tales* (New York: G. P. Putnam's Sons; London: D. Nutt, 1891), pp. 159–162. A Scottish friend insists that the language of this tale reveals that its origin is Scotland not England.

26. *The Night-Troll*: Jacqueline Simpson, *Icelandic Folktales and Legends* (Berkeley: University of California Press, 1979), pp. 81–83.
    This story comes from an old woman in Rángárping. "Night trolls" are often associated with particular rocks, either from having been turned into them, or from living in them, or from being buried under them. Some night trolls are said to be malevolent, others are harmless.

27. *The Grateful Elfwoman*: Claire Booss, *Scandinavian Folk and Fairy Tales* (New York: Avenel Books, 1984), p. 600.

28. *"My Jon's Soul"*: Jacqueline Simpson, *Icelandic Folktales and Legends*, pp. 196–199.
    This tale is from the Rev. Matthías Jochumsson (d.1920).

29. *The Ghost at Fjelkinge*: Claire Booss, *Scandinavian Folk and Fairy Tales*, pp. 244–246.

30. *Little Red Cap*: Jakob und Wilhelm Grimm, *Die Kinder- und Hausmärchen der Brüder Grimm* (Wiesbaden, Germany: Emil Vollmer Verlag) pp. 125–128, trans. Kathleen Ragan.

31. For an excellent overview of the material written on *Little Red Riding Hood*, see: Alan Dundes, ed., *Little Red Riding Hood, A Casebook* (Madison: The University of

Wisconsin Press, 1989), and Jack Zipes, ed., *The Trials and Tribulations of Little Red Riding Hood* (New York & London: Routledge, 1993).

32. *The Wood Maiden*: Parker Fillmore, *Czechoslovak Fairy Tales* (New York: Harcourt, Brace & Co., 1919), pp. 165–175.

Fillmore notes that he used Czech, Slovakian, and Moravian sources.

33. *The Child Who Was Poor and Good*: Georgios A. Megas, *Folktales of Greece*, trans. Helen Colaclides. Folktales of the World Series, Richard Dorson ed. (Chicago: University of Chicago Press, 1970), pp. 138–140.

34. *The Pigeon's Bride*: Parker Fillmore, *The Laughing Prince, Jugoslav Folk and Fairy Tales* (New York: Harcourt, Brace and World, Inc., 1921), pp. 53–72.

35. For example: Maria Tatar, *Off With Their Heads, Fairy Tales and the Culture of Childhood* (Princeton, N. J.: Princeton University Press, 1992), pp. 140–162.

36. *How the King Chose a Daughter-in-Law*: Jean Ure, *Rumanian Folk Tales* (New York: Franklin Watts, Inc., 1960), pp. 19–21.

Ure notes that this story was told by a man from the village of Frătăuţi Vechi, in northern Moldavia, and gives the date September 1909.

37. *Marichka*: James Riordan, *Russian Gypsy Tales* (New York: Interlink Books, 1992), pp. 107–108.

38. *Davit*: George Papshvily and Helen Papshvily, *Yes and No Stories, A Book of Georgian Folktales* (New York & London: Harper and Bros., 1946), pp. 49–57.

39. *Anait*: Avril Pyman, trans., *The Golden Fleece: Tales from the Caucasus* (Moscow: Progress Publishers, 1971), pp. 146–165.

40. For example: Maria Tatar, *Off With Their Heads, Fairy Tales and the Culture of Childhood* (Princeton, N. J.: Princeton University Press, 1992), pp. 140–162.

41. *The Fortune-Teller: The Three Kingdoms, Russian Folk Tales from Alexander Afanasiev's Collection*, Vol. II (Moscow: Raduga Publishers, 1985), pp. 142–145.

42. For example: Jack Zipes, *Breaking the Magic Spell, Radical Theories of Folk and Fairy Tales* (New York: Routledge, 1992), pp. 129–160.

43. *The Tsarítsa Harpist*: Leonard A. Magnus, LL.B., trans., *Russian Folk-Tales* (New York: E. P. Dutton and Co., 1916), pp. 75–77.

TALES FROM NORTH AND SOUTH AMERICA

NATIVE AMERICANS

44. *The Vampire Skeleton*: Joseph Bruchac, *Iroquois Stories: Heroes and Heroines, Monsters and Magic* (Trumansburg, N.Y.: The Crossing Press, 1985), pp. 129–133.

The Iroquois were a confederation of five nations, originally the Mohawk, Oneida, Onondaga, Cayuga, and Seneca, and in 1717 the Tuscarora joined as well. At the height of their power, they controlled most of New York, Pennsylvania, and Ohio. The name "Iroquois" means "real adders" and was coined by their enemies, the Algonquins. The Iroquois referred to themselves as "We Who Are of the Extended Lodge."

With the arrival of European colonists, the coastal Native American nations were forced to move west where they ran into the Iroquois, which provoked constant warfare. The European powers took advantage of this situation and fought their wars in North America using Native American allies. As early as 1608, Champlain interfered on behalf of the Hurons against the Iroquois. This was to have long-reaching consequences, for as a result, the Iroquois aligned themselves with the English.

45. *The Flying Head*: Richard Erdoes and Alfonso Ortiz, *American Indian Myths and Legends* (New York: Pantheon Books, 1984), pp. 227–228.

This is retold from a 1902 tale.

46. *Where the Girl Saved Her Brother*: Richard Erdoes and Alfonso Ortiz, *American Indian Myths and Legends*, pp. 264–267.

The Cheyenne were especially known for their storytelling ability.

47. *Chief Joseph's Story of Wallowa Lake*: Ella E. Clark, *Indian Legends of the Pacific Northwest* (Berkeley: University of California Press, 1953), pp. 75–78.

The Nez Percé were semi-nomads in Idaho and eastern Oregon and Washington. They were famous for breeding the Appaloosa horse.

48. Ella E. Clark, *Indian Legends of the Pacific Northwest*, p. 75.

49. *The Origin of the Potlatch*: Ella E. Clark, *Indian Legends of the Pacific Northwest*, pp. 184–185.

50. *The Princess and Mountain Dweller*: Christie Harris, *The Trouble with Princesses* (New York: Atheneum, 1980), pp. 9–26.

Harris lists her sources as:

1899. *Tales from the Totems of the Hidery*, collected by James Deans for the Archives of the International Folk-lore Association.

1905. *Haida Texts*, collected by John Reed Swanton for the Jessup North Pacific Expedition Publications, Memoirs of the American Museum of Natural History.

1908. *The Koryak*, collected by Waldemar Jochelson for the Jessup North Pacific.

1909–1910 *Tsimshian Myths*, collected by Franz Boas for the Thirty-First Annual Report of the Bureau of American Ethnology to the Secretary of the Smithsonian Institution.

1953. *Haida Myths*, Illustrated in Argillite Carvings, by Marius Barbeau, Bulletin No. 127, Anthropological Series No. 32, National Museum of Canada.

51. See Maria Tatar, *The Hard Facts of the Grimms' Fairy Tales* (Princeton, N.J.: Princeton University Press, 1987), pp. 156–179.

52. *The Princess and the Magical Hat*: Christie Harris, *Mouse Woman and the Vanished Princesses* (New York: Atheneum, 1976), pp. 134–155.

Mouse Woman has no story of her own but appears in the tales of many other characters.

The apron given to Mouse Woman at the end of the story was a special style of fringed blanket made by the Chilkat, a Tlingit people. Cedar bark was used for the warp and the weft was of pre-dyed mountain goat hair. Every space of the blanket was filled with blue, black, yellow, and white designs, which were woven separately and put together at the end.

53. *The Lytton Girls Who Were Stolen by Giants*: ed. Franz Boas, *Folk-tales of Salishan and Sahaptin Tribes, Memoirs of the American Folk-Lore Society*, Vol. XI (New York: G. E. Stechert & Co., 1917), pp. 38–39.

For years, there was no traceable connection between many Amerindian languages. However, in 1987, Joseph Greenberg presented a new classification system with a broad-based overview of all the languages of the world. In this classification system all the American Indian languages are grouped into three large groups. In the Greenberg classification system the Eskimo-Aleut group has only about ten languages and ranges along the northern perimeter of North America from Alaska to Canada to Greenland. The Na-Dene has speakers living in Alaska central and the panhandle as well as the western part of Canada. The final and largest group is the Amerind, which stretches from northern Canada to the tip of South America and includes everything from Salish and Sahaptin to Iroquoian to Aztecan. See: *The Origin of Language*, Merrit Ruhlen (New York: John Wiley & Sons, 1994).

54. *The Legend of the Coppermine River*: Maurice Metayer, *Tales from the Igloo* (New York: St. Martin's Press, 1977), pp. 79–81.

55. *The Huntress*: Maurice Metayer, *Tales from the Igloo*, pp. 99–107.

56. *Story of a Female Shaman*: Howard Norman, *Northern Tales: Traditional Stories of Eskimo and Indian Peoples* (New York: Schocken, 1980), pp. 180–182.

Although the Reindeer Chukchee live in northeastern Siberia, I have included their tale in this section because culturally it belongs with tales from the other peoples of the subarctic regions.

57. *The Magic Eagle*: Genevieve Barlow, *Latin American Tales* (New York: Rand McNally & Co., 1966), pp. 89–96. Among the many gods of the now-extinct Timotean Indians, Ches was supreme.

NEW WORLD NEWCOMERS

58. *"I'm Tipingee, She's Tipingee, We're Tipingee, Too"*: Diane Wolkstein, *The Magic Orange Tree and Other Haitian Folktales* (New York: Alfred A. Knopf, 1978), pp. 132–134.

The island that Haiti and the Dominican Republic share was also known as Hispaniola, one of the islands visited by Columbus on his first voyage in 1492.

59. *The Innkeeper's Wise Daughter*: Peninnah Schram, *Jewish Stories One Generation Tells Another* (Northvale, N.J./London: Jason Aronson Inc., 1987), pp. 112–116.

60. *Molly Cotton-tail Steals Mr. Fox's Butter*: Anne Virginia Culbertson, *At the Big House* (Indianapolis, Ind.: The Bobbs-Merrill Company Publishers, 1904), pp. 245–252.

In Culbertson's book there are several more Molly Cotton-tail stories as well as some other female trickster tales. Culbertson notes that this story was collected in southeastern Virginia. She created the character of Aunt Nancy, the storyteller.

TALES FROM ASIA

61. *A Rani's Revenge*: P. C. Roy Chaudhury, *Best Loved Folk-Tales of India* (New York: Facet Books International, 1986), pp. 223–226.

Orissa is a state in eastern India, southwest of the border with Bangladesh. Before India acquired independence from British dominance, the subcontinent was divided into about 500 princely states and large semi-connected territories under British rule. India became an independent country in 1947 with Hindi as the proposed national language. Due to the demands of many groups, India's state boundaries were realigned along linguistic lines and official provincial languages were endorsed. The official provincial language of Orissa is Oriya, which belongs to the Indic branch of the Indo-European language family. Many of the modern languages of northern India are Indo-European languages because they are descended from Sanskrit, the language of the Aryan people who arrived in India from northern Iran c. 1550 BC.

62. G. K. Chesterton, "The Household Gods and the Goblins," reprinted in *The Coloured Lands*, 1938.

63. *How Parvatibai Outwitted the Dacoits*: P. C. Roy Chaudhury, *Best Loved Folk-Tales of India*, pp. 167–169.

   Maharashtra is a state in western India. Bombay is its largest city. The provincial language is Marathi, an Indo-European language descended from Sanskrit.

64. *The Close Alliance: A Tale of Woe*: Flora Annie Steel, *Tales of the Punjab, Told by the People* (London: Macmillan and Co., 1894), pp. 123–128.

   When the Indian subcontinent acquired independence in 1947, two states were formed—India, a Hindi state and Pakistan, a Muslim state. Much of the Punjab now lies in Pakistan.

65. *The Barber's Clever Wife*: Flora Annie Steel, *Tales of the Punjab*, pp. 220–229.

66. *A Wonderful Story*: Maive Stokes, *Indian Fairy Tales* (London: Ellis & White, 1880), pp. 108–113. Collected January 13, 1877.

67. *The Importance of Lighting*: P. C. Roy Chaudhury, *Best Loved Folk-Tales of India*, pp. 270–273.

   This tale was collected in Tamil Nadu, in southern India, where the major language, Tamil, is a Dravidian, not an Indo-European language. The Dravidian group contains over twenty languages with speakers mostly in southern India. It is likely that Dravidian languages had been spoken over much of central and perhaps northern India but then were driven south by the influx of the Indo-Europeans in about 1550 BC.

68. *The Child of Death*: Ruth Q. Sun, *Land of Seagull and Fox* (Tokyo: John Weatherhill, Inc., 1966), pp. 117–119.

   Having been under Chinese domination for about 1,000 years beginning in about 100 AD, Vietnam developed essentially a Chinese culture, a mixture of Confucianism, Taoism, Buddhism, and animism. Vietnamese is a tonal language about half of whose vocabulary is from Chinese.

69. *The Story of Princess Amaradevi*: Muriel Paskin Carrison, *Cambodian Folk Stories from the Gatiloke*, trans. Kong Chhean (Rutland, Vt.: Charles E. Tuttle Co., 1987), pp. 23–30.

   In the late nineteenth century, the Cambodian government commissioned a Buddhist monk, Oknha Sotann Preychea Ind, to collect popular folktales. This story comes from that collection, the "Gatiloke." In his introduction to the 112 tales, Oknha Sotann Preychea Ind said that he wrote this Gatiloke for children interested in studying tradition and morality. He also composed questions and answers for the tales, for example, " . . . if the student asks the teacher, 'Venerable, what does the word *Gatiloke* mean?' the teacher may answer, '*Gatiloke* means all the things that are going on in the world . . . *Loke* means "the world," and . . . *gati* should mean "the path," "the way of morality"." "

Carrison notes that a Chinese traveler to Cambodia in the thirteenth century was surprised to find highly educated and respected women, some of whom even held political posts at court.

70. Joni Seager and Ann Olson, *Women in the World, An International Atlas* (New York: Simon & Schuster/Touchstone, 1986), maps 10 and 22.

71. *The Tale of the Oki Islands*: Eric Protter and Nancy Protter, *Folk and Fairy Tales of Far-Off Lands*, Trans. Robert Egan, (New York: Duell, Sloan and Pearce, 1965), pp. 53–59.

The Oki Islands lie between Japan and Korea in the Sea of Japan, off the coast of the largest Japanese island, Honshu.

72. *The Monkey Bridegroom*: Keigo Seki, *Folktales of Japan*, trans. Robert J. Adams, Folktales of the World Series, Richard Dorson ed. (Chicago: University of Chicago Press, 1963), pp. 167–170.

Collected in Kuro-kawa-mura, Aso-gun, Kumamoto-ken by Sanji Yagi.

The opening scene in the Chinese film, *Field of Red Sorghum* presents a powerful picture of arranged marriages.

73. Keigo Seki, *Folktales of Japan*, p. 167.

74. For example: Maria Tatar, *Off with Their Heads, Fairy Tales and the Culture of Childhood* (Princeton, N.J.: Princeton University Press, 1992), pp. 140–162.

75. *The Mirror of Matsuyama: A Story of Old Japan*: Yei Theodora Ozaki, *The Japanese Fairy Book* (New York: E. P. Dutton & Co., 1903), pp. 119–139.

The Japanese language resembles Korean in grammatical structure. Japanese has three major alphabets. Kanji, Chinese pictographs, are used for major nouns, verbs, and adjectives. The kanji are supplemented by hiragana and katagana, two alphabets representing an identical group of about 55 syllables. Hiragana with flowing characters is used mostly for suffixes, particles, and conjunctions while katagana with its more angular characters is used mostly for foreign words.

76. *The Tiger and the Coal Peddler's Wife*: Suzanne Crowder Han, *Korean Folk and Fairy Tales* (New Jersey: Hollym International Corp., 1991), pp. 199–200.

The grammatical structure of Korean is most similar to Japanese. More than half the vocabulary is of Chinese origin, and Korean has used Chinese characters along with the Korean alphabet for centuries. As with Japanese, this is probably not only due to Chinese cultural influence but also because there are many Korean words that are homonyms, and the Chinese characters that represent concepts serve to clarify the meaning.

77. *The Plucky Maiden*: Im Bang and Yi Ryuk, *Korean Folk Tales, Imps, Ghosts and Fairies*, trans. James S. Gale (New York: E. P. Dutton & Co, 1913), pp. 83–89.

78. *The Phoenix and Her City*: Shujiang Li and Karl W. Luckert, *Mythology and Folklore of the Hui, a Muslim Chinese People*, Trans. Fenglan Yu, Zhilin Hou, and Ganhui Wang (Albany: State University of New York Press, 1994), pp. 132–137.

Recorded in Ningxia District by He Cun (Hui) in 1981.

Ningxia is located in north central China by the Great Wall. The Hui speak Mandarin Chinese, but unlike the Han Chinese, they are adherents of Islam.

79. Linda Peavy and Ursula Smith, *Women Who Changed Things* (New York: Charles Scribner's Sons, 1983).

80. *Sailimai's Four Precious Things*: Shujiang Li and Karl W. Luckert, *Mythology and Folklore of the Hui*, pp. 411–413.

This tale was narrated by Wang Yanyi (Hui) in Xiji, Ningxia, China, and recorded by Wang Zhengwei (Hui) in 1979. The wise Sailimai is the protagonist in several other stories in Li and Luckert's collection.

81. *A Woman's Love*: He Liyi, *The Spring of Butterflies and Other Chinese Folktales* (London: William Collins Sons & Co., Ltd., 1985), pp. 58–74.

The Uighur are Muslim and live a settled, agricultural life mostly in the Xinjiang province of northwestern China. The history of the Uighur can be traced back to the early Christian era. In about the middle of the eighth century, they established a large kingdom in eastern Turkestan. Uighur is a Turkic language.

82. *Maiden Liu, the Songster*: Louise Kuo and Yuan Hsi, *Chinese Folktales* (Milbrae, Calif.: Celestial Arts, 1976), pp. 127–133.

83. Louise Kuo and Yuan Hsi, *Chinese Folktales*, p. 127.

84. See: Jane Goodall, *In the Shadow of Man* (London: Collins, 1971).

Jane Goodall, *The Chimpanzees of Gombe* (Cambridge, Mass.: Belknap Press, Harvard University Press, 1986).

Dian Fossey, *Gorillas in the Mist* (Boston: Houghton Mifflin, 1983).

Biruté Galdikas, *Reflections of Eden, My Years with the Orangutans of Borneo* (New York, London: Little, Brown and Company, 1995).

85. *The Festival of Pouring Water*: Wolfram Eberhard, *Folktales of China*, trans. Desmond Parsons, Folktales of the World series, ed. Richard Dorson (Chicago: University of Chicago Press, 1965), pp. 82–83.

Along the canals of Bangkok, Thailand, the festival of Pouring Water is a smiling, laughing festival where adults and children splash each other with cool water. Notes to this story state that this text was collected in the Yunnan province, China, but the tale is much more typical of southern and western Asia with similar festivals in Iran and India. There are close resemblances to the "cold water festival," which was introduced from the Near East into China where it was popular during the Tang period. During the Tang Dynasty (618–907 AD) China was a strong, centralized empire whose armies had intervened in areas as far away as India, cental Asia, and Afghanistan. At this time, Chinese lyrical poetry reached its height and printing was invented.

86. *A Polite Idiosyncrasy*: Adele M. Fielde, *Chinese Nights' Entertainment* (New York, London: G. P. Putnam's Sons, 1893), pp. 159–161.

The collector, Fielde, notes that this tale was told in Swatow vernacular, a Chinese dialect, in the eastern corner of Kwangtung province in southern China. Chinese is spoken by more people than any other language in the world. It is spoken not only in China but also by over a million speakers in each of the following countries: Taiwan, Hong Kong, Thailand, Malaysia, Singapore, and Vietnam, and, in lesser numbers in other countries. It is, however, spoken by few people not of Chinese origin. Chinese is a tonal language, different tones or intonations distinguish words, which are otherwise pronounced identically. It is written with ideographs that represent objects as well as abstract concepts without relation to the sound of the word. This makes written communication possible between people speaking the many different languages and dialects in China. Words in different languages would be pronounced differently but written the same. One must learn about 5,000 characters to read a newspaper or novel.

87. *The Young Head of the Family*: Adele M. Fielde, *Chinese Nights' Entertainment*, pp. 60–68.

Told in Swatow vernacular, a Chinese dialect, in the eastern corner of Kwangtung province in southern China.

88. *Altyn-Aryg*: C. Fillingham Coxwell, *Siberian and Other Folk-Tales* (London: The C.W. Daniel Company, 1925), pp. 300–301.

This story was collected by Vierbitsky (d. 1890) who spent forty years as a missionary among the Altaians, shamanists who speak a Turkish language.

89. *Book of Black Heroes, Volume Two, Great Women in the Struggle*, Toyomi Igus, ed. (New Jersey: Just Us Books, Inc., 1991), p. 17.

90. *The Story of the Wife Who Stole a Heart*: C. Fillingham Coxwell, *Siberian and Other Folk-Tales*, pp. 212–214.

Coxwell notes that the Kalmucks, from whom this story was collected, are nomads who breed horses, cattle, and sheep. When eastern Turkestan was conquered by China in the seventeenth century, the Kalmucks moved to the Volga. Later they considered themselves oppressed by the Russians and although some remained, many returned to eastern Turkestan in 1771. Their language is closely related to modern Mongolian.

91. Sarah Blaffer Hrdy, *The Woman That Never Evolved* (Cambridge, Mass., & London: Harvard University Press, 1981).

TALES FROM THE PACIFIC

92. *Hiiaka Catching a Ghost:* W. D. Westervelt, *Hawaiian Legends of Volcanoes* (Boston, Mass./London: Constable & Co., 1916), pp. 111–116.

Close to 40 percent of the world's languages are spoken on islands in the Pacific and Indian oceans. Almost all of these languages belong to one of three families: Indo-Pacific (concentrated on New Guinea), the Australian family, and the Austronesian family. Austronesian (formerly Malayo-Polynesian) is the most widespread—its languages are spoken on practically every island from Madagascar to Easter Island and from Hawaii to New Zealand.

93. *Hiiaka and the Seacoast Kupuas*: W. D. Westervelt, *Hawaiian Legends of Volcanoes*, pp. 118–125.

94. *A Calabash of Poi*: Cora Wells Thorpe, *In the Path of the Trade Winds* (New York/London: G. P. Putnam's Sons, 1924), pp. 93–97.

95. *Rau-Whato*: A. W. Reed, *Treasury of Maori Folklore* (New Zealand: A. H. & A. W. Reed, 1963), pp. 457–458.

The Maori people were Polynesians who settled in New Zealand around 800 AD. They believed in a spiritual "essence" and their deities were rarely represented by images. They were remarkable craftsmen of elaborately carved dugout canoes, which when paddled at full speed could overtake European sailing ships.

96. *How Pulap Acquired the Art of Navigation*: William A. Lessa, *More Tales from Ulithi Atoll*,

A Content Analysis, Folklore and Mythology Studies: 32 (Berkeley: University of California Press, 1980), pp. 39–40.

Lessa notes that he collected his tales under interview circumstances, not in spontaneous social settings. This tale was narrated by Melchethal, male, age 58, whom Lessa describes as a member of the men's council, a canoe builder, navigator, and fish magician, endowed with superior intelligence, extraordinary memory, and a keen sense of humor.

97. *Rola and the Two Sisters:* William A. Lessa, *More Tales from Ulithi Atoll,* pp. 80–82.

Narrated by the woman, Taleguethep. She heard the story only once when she was young.

98. *The Old Woman and the Giant:* Laurence L. Wilson, *Tales from the Mountain Province* (Manila, Philippines: Philippine Education Co., 1958), pp. 137–138.

The Philippine archipelago of over 7,000 islands has been a crossroads of folk migration for centuries. It has been dominated or occupied by Malayans, Hindus, Chinese, Japanese, Spaniards, and Americans. In the fifteenth century, Islam spread to the southern Philippines from the Malaccan empire of Malaya, Sumatra, and Java. Islam's spread was halted in the sixteenth century by Spain, which methodically conquered and converted the island people to Christianity.

99. *The Magic Coin:* Exaltacion Mercado-Cinco, *A Compilation and a Study of Selected Fairy Tales of Eastern Leyte* (Thesis presented to Divine Word University of Tacloban, 1969) pp. 56–59.

Mercado-Cinco notes that most of her stories were collected from old residents of towns of eastern Leyte, Philippines.

100. *The Creation of Lake Asbold:* Laurens Hillhouse and Marie Mohr-Grandstaff, *Man in Essence* (1422 Meek Ave., Napa, Calif.: Hillhouse Publications, 1990), pp. 15–18.

The stories in this unique and exceptional book were collected by an ex-Peace Corps worker, Laurens Hillhouse, who lived with the Asmat people for a year and a half.

101. *Senan and Aping:* A. D. Galvin, *On the Banks of the Baram,* pp. 27–35.

The Kenyah cultivate dry rice in jungle clearings. Often their villages consist of a single communal house up to 400 yards long with a porch along the front that serves as a work area as well as a street. The Kenyah and other native tribes in Sarawak are now facing difficulties similar to those faced by the Native Americans during the last century. Large enterprises are chopping down the jungle, destroying the Kenyah's way of life, and threatening their survival.

102. *Ubong and the Head-Hunters:* A. D. Galvin, *On the Banks of the Baram,* pp. 67–71.

103. *Kumaku and the Giant:* A. W. Reed and Inez Hames, *Myths and Legends of Fiji and Rotuma* (Australia: A. H. & A. W. Reed, 1967), pp. 133–134.

Fiji consists of two main islands and over 800 smaller ones. Both the Melanesians and Polynesians of Fiji are outnumbered by the descendents of Asian Indian laborers brought to the islands to work the sugar plantations. Fiji became independent from the British in 1970 but remained in the British Commonwealth.

104. *Revival and Revenge:* John LeRoy, *Kewa Tales* (Vancouver: The University of British Columbia Press, 1985), pp. 210–212.

Narrated by Pipirainyu, a woman residing in Karapere.

This tale came from New Guinea where approximately 20 percent of the world total of languages are spoken. New Guinea has a great concentration and diversity of languages. Imagine if Britain, which is one-third the size, had two hundred languages separated by distances of only twenty miles. Along large portions of the coastline Austronesian (formerly Malayo-Polynesian) languages are spoken. The Indo-Pacific (Papuan) languages are relegated mostly to the interior. More than 700 distinct Indo-Pacific languages are spoken on New Guinea.

New Guinea has some tribes with cultures resembling those of the Stone Age and because of difficult terrain, isolated tribes have only recently been discovered. The first outside exploration of the Kewa was in 1935, but contact really began to develop in the 1950s and by the 1960s most areas were under colonial control. The Kewa are a people numbering about 40,000 who live in a portion of the Southern Highland Province of Papua New Guinea. The Kewa inhabit a plateau whose bedrock is sedimentary, mostly limestone or sandstone. The limestone areas are frequently pitted with depressions such as the "well" in this story. The Kewa language is rich in imitative words like the "Kilikili tatatata" of the girl falling into the well. Pigs are important gifts and are raised for cermonial exchange and periodic feasts. Although they nominally belong to men, women are usually consulted in the plans for the pigs. The staple of the Kewa diet is sweet potatoes. Feuding was a prevalent practice among the Kewa. Traditionally, women and children occupied dwellings scattered around one large house occupied by the men and their sons.

105. *Uzu, the White Dogai*: Margaret Lawrie, *Myths and Legends of Torres Straits* (New York: Taplinger Publishing Company, 1971), pp. 257–258.

Narrated by a woman, Asou Thaiday, July 6, 1966, on Yam Island.

The Torres Straits are a maze of reefs, rocks, and islands in the stretch of water separating the northernmost tip of Australia from New Guinea. The most populated is Badu Island with 650 people, the least, Stephens Island with 19. Yam Island where this story was told is about a mile in length and averages half a mile in width with a population of 300. The language of the islands in the western Torres Straits is Mabuiag, part of the Australian family. The language of the eastern Torres Straits is Meriam, an Indo-Pacific (Papuan) language.

The people of the Torres Straits own land, reefs, rocks, stones, stars, winds, tracts of sea, and even stories. (Lawrie, p. xxi). To the people of the Torres Straits, stories represent inherited knowledge. Therefore they are restricted to members of a specific group and territory and can be owned by groups or individuals. Usually there is one acknowledged teller, who knows the stories in their "authentic" detail. At some of the islands, before telling their stories, the men "called the blood" of their ancestors, back sometimes to six or seven generations, to prove their authority to speak. Rarely will someone tell another's story, therefore variants of stories are rare. Sometimes a story takes place on tracts of land that have changed ownership (e.g., through marriage). Since one may only speak for what is his, the teller might say, "There is another part too. You will have to ask so-and-so to tell it because it happened on his land."

106. *The Black Snake Man and His Wife, the Dove*: Ursula McConnel, *Myths of the Muŋkan* (Australia: Melbourne University Press, 1957), pp. 136–139.

Between 70,000 and 50,000 years ago, when low sea levels linked Tasmania, Australia, and New Guinea, humans came to Australia. Approximately 6,000 years ago, the water rose to its present level and made Australia an island. Thus the remains of original settlements, which had been concentrated on coasts and rivers, now lie offshore on the continental shelf. When the British claimed the continent in 1768, the Australian Aborigines were still leading a hunting and gathering way of life. European diseases, weapons, and desire for land destroyed the Aboriginal civilization. Only in the center and north did some Aboriginal institutions survive. The Australian language group consists of all the Aboriginal languages in Australia. Today there are about 250 Australian languages, but only five have more than 1,000 speakers.

107. *The Mogwoi's Baby*: Ronald M. Berndt and Catherine H. Berndt, *The Speaking Land* (Australia: Penguin Books Australia, 1989), pp. 145–147.

Told to C. Berndt in 1950 by the woman Danggoubwi in Djambarbingu dialect and refers to northeast Arnhem Land.

Catherine and Ronald Berndt have worked for fifty years among the Australian Aborigines. This and the following story were collected from women by C. Berndt and were essentially for adult listeners. Among the Aborigines there are no professional storytellers, everyone is a potential storyteller. Although a man steals a baby in this story, the focus is not on a moral judgment of his actions. The Berndts comment that the Aborigines as a rule seem to prefer their mythology not to be directly censorious and that the moral and immoral constitute a kind of continuum with unclear boundaries.

108. *Biriwilg (Told by Women)*: Berndt and Berndt, *The Speaking Land*, pp. 58–59.

Told to C. Berndt in 1950 by the woman Gararu in Gunwinggu language in the traditionally matrilineal area of northwest Arnhem Land.

For the Australian Aborigines the land is alive with signs that tell about how the land came to be, who was responsible for its becoming this way, who is now responsible for the land, and who owns the land. Myths are always connected to a specific place where the incidents were to have taken place. Australian Aborigines identify their destinies with the natural features of the land. The Berndts comment that the mythology of the Aborigines is not quasi-historical tales, it is alive. The people who tell the tales believe in them and use them to understand their lives.

For a highly edifying comparison of the difference between a heroine in a tale told by a woman and a heroine in a tale told by a man, compare "Biriwilg (Told by Men)," pp. 57–58 and "Biriwilg (Told by Women)," pp. 58–59 in the Berndts' *The Speaking Land*.

TALES FROM SUB-SAHARAN AFRICA

109. *The Woman, Her Husband, Their Children and the Dodo*: Frank Edgar, *Hausa Tales and Traditions*: An English Translation of *Tatsuniyoyi Na Housa*, Vol. II, trans. and ed. Neil Skinner (Madison: University of Wisconsin Press, 1977), pp. 85–92.

Hausa is spoken mainly in northern Nigeria and in Niger. The Hausa people are predominantly Muslim and their language contains many words of Arabic origin. With about 25 million speakers, Hausa is frequently used across West Africa as a language of commerce and as a means of communication between different tribes.

In similar stories from other cultures, the woman's husband is often killed by the ghoul.

110. *Ku-Chin-Da-Gayya and Her Elder Sister and the Dodos*: Frank Edgar, *Hausa Tales and Traditions*, pp. 100–104.

111. *Moremi and the Egunguns*: Harold Courlander, *Tales of Yoruba Gods and Heroes* (Greenwich, Conn.: Fawcett Publications, Inc., 1973), pp. 60–65.

The Yoruba inhabit southwest Nigeria in West Africa. Ife is best known for the naturalistic bronze heads made there in the thirteenth or fourteenth century. Yoruba is one of Nigeria's major languages. Tradition names Ife as the first of all Yoruba cities. Ife and other cities existed probably 400–500 years before European arrival in the fifteenth century. The Portuguese "discovered" West Africa in the fifteenth century and this area became one of the principal sources of slaves from 1500 to 1800. Slave wars launched by the neighboring Dahomey kingdom and slave wars between the Yorubas themselves resulted in the enslavement of thousands of Yoruba. Brazil, Cuba, Haiti, and Trinidad still retain some Yoruba religious rites, music, and myths.

112. *The Spider, Kayi, and the Bush Fowl*: Ruth Finnegan, *Limba Stories and Story-Telling* (Oxford: Oxford University Press, 1967), pp. 295–296.

Recorded in January 1964. Ruth Finnegan characterizes Fanka Konteh, the narrator, as a middle-aged man who told stories in a straightforward way, without many songs or elaborate imitations.

Sierra Leone is a country on the west African coast. The Limba are rice farmers who live in the hilly savannah country of northern Sierra Leone. Although stories are an important aspect of their artistic culture, the Limba consider drumming, singing, and dancing as equally, if not more, important.

113. *The Story of Two Women*: Ruth Finnegan, *Limba Stories and Story-Telling*, pp. 249–254.

Recorded in December 1961. Narrated by Suri Kamara, Finnegan's assistant in the field, a man partly Temne, who had been brought up in a Limba area. Finnegan comments that Kamara tended to focus on excitement or strength rather than subtle characterization or pathos.

114. *The Man Killed for a Spinach Leaf*: Ruth Finnegan, *Limba Stories and Story-Telling*, pp. 131–137.

Recorded in October 1961. Finnegan lists the narrator as Karanke Dema, a man who greatly enjoyed telling stories and vividly portrayed actions and emotions using mode of delivery and facial expressions, accompanying the narration with frequent introduction of songs. Finnegan included notes on style of delivery and audience reception, many of which I have included because they give a strong sense of being there. Karanke told the story under the name of Yaling and his friend Niaka "replied."

115. *The Leopard Woman*: Roger D. Abrahams, *African Folktales* (New York: Pantheon Books, 1983), pp. 150–151.

Liberia is a country in west Africa, which was established by former slaves from America in the 1820s.

116. Sarah Blaffer Hrdy. *The Woman That Never Evolved* (Cambridge, Mass. & London: Harvard University Press, 1981), p. 185.

117. *The Midwife of Dakar*: Charlotte Leslau and Wolf Leslau, *African Folk Tales* (New York: The Peter Pauper Press, 1963), pp. 58–60.

118. *A Woman for a Hundred Cattle*: Paul Radin, *African Folktales* (Princeton, N.J.: Princeton University Press, 1964), pp. 298–303.

Swahili is an important language of east Africa, serving as the official language of both Tanzania and Kenya and as a lingua franca for trade over much of east Africa and Zaire. Swahili was originally spoken in Zanzibar and the adjacent coast. It has many words of Arabic origin as this area used to be a part of the trade route to India from the eighth to the eleventh centuries. The name "Swahili" is derived from an Arabic word meaning "coastal."

119. *Wacu and the Eagle*: Ngumbu Njururi, *Agikuyu Folk Tales* (London: Oxford University Press, 1966), pp. 94–97.

The Kikuyu live in Kenya. The founding father of Kenya, Jomo Kenyatta was Kikuyu.

120. Toyomi Igus, ed. *Book of Black Heroes, Volume Two, Great Women in the Struggle* (New Jersey: Just Us Books, Inc., 1991), p. 16.

121. *Elephant and Hare*: Naomi Kipury, *Oral Literature of the Maasai* (Nairobi, Kenya: Heinemann Educational Books, Ltd, 1983), pp. 72–74.

The Maasai are nomadic herdsmen living in Kenya and Tanzania.

122. *Nonikwe and the Great One, Marimba*: Vusamazulu Credo Mutwa, *Indaba, My Children* (London: Kahn and Averill, Stanmore Press Ltd., 1966), pp. 37–41.

The author, a Zulu, describes himself as a "Guardian of the Umlando or Tribal History." Mutwa describes guardians as men and women with an ability to memorize well and with black birthmarks on either palm of the hands. When they learned the "history of the Tribes," they took an oath never to change a word or they would fall under a curse, which would last for three generations. The Zulu live in Natal, the easternmost part of the Republic of South Africa and Zulu is one of the most important Bantu languages in southern Africa.

123. *How the Milky Way Came to Be*: Charlotte Leslau and Wolf Leslau, *African Folk Tales* (New York: The Peter Pauper Press, 1963), p. 56.

124. *Nanabolele, Who Shines in the Night*: Minnie Postma, *Tales from the Basotho*, American Folklore Society Memoir Series, Vol. 59, trans. Susie McDermid (Austin and London: University of Texas Press, 1974), pp. 124–131.

The Basotho people live in Lesotho, a landlocked country inside the Republic of South Africa. Especially in the countryside, storytelling is still a prominent art form. Since the audience probably knows the outcome of the tale, the enjoyment comes from the manner in which the story is told and audience participation is limited to joining in a song if there is one. Although more and more disregarded, the taboo still exists that if one tells a story while the sun is still up, horns will grow from his head. Minnie Postma is a white woman who grew up speaking Sesotho, the language of the Basotho, as well as Afrikaans, the language of the white people in the Orange Free State near Lesotho. Even in childhood, Postma wrote down tales and their variants when she heard them. As she grew older she became a quite competent raconteur of Basotho tales, a very unusual feat for a white person according to the translator, Susie McDermid.

125. Bonnie S. Anderson and Judith P. Zinsser, *A History of Their Own, Women in Europe from Prehistory to the Present*, Vol. I (New York: Perennial Library, Harper & Row, Publishers, 1989), p. 426.

126. *Jackal and Hen*: Minnie Postma, *Tales from the Basotho*, pp. 115–117.

127. Susan Faludi, *Backlash* (London: Vintage, 1992).

TALES FROM NORTH AFRICA AND THE MIDDLE EAST

128. *Women's Wiles:* Inea Bushnaq, *Arab Folktales*, (New York: Pantheon Books, 1986), pp. 318–322.

129. *The Feslihancı Girl:* Warren S. Walker and Ahmet E. Uysal, *More Tales Alive in Turkey*, (Lubbock, Tex.: Texas Tech University Press, 1992), pp. 180–192.

Told by Gülsüm Yücel, housewife, age 83, in the kaza of Taşköprü, Kastamonu Province, Turkey, in August 1964.

Turkish belongs to the Altaic family of languages. This is a large family, which stretches from the Balkan peninsula to the northeast of Asia and contains about forty languages including Turkic, Mongolian, and possibly Korean and Japanese.

130. *The Story of the City of Nothing-in-the-World:* D. L. R. Lorimer and E. O. Lorimer, *Persian Tales* (London: MacMillan & Co. Ltd, 1919), pp. 6–8.

Persia is now Iran. The Persian language is one of the oldest in the world and at different times has been written in three different scripts: cuneiform, a script much used in the ancient world, Pahlavi, an alphabet created by the Persians, and Arabic script after the seventh century.

131. "And now my story has come to an end,/but the sparrow never got home."

This phrase at the end of the story is a typical closing like "and they lived happily ever after" in western fairy tales. An Iranian friend strongly expressed the opinion that the "sparrow" is in fact a crow. Crows are known for spying, and for getting and communicating information and new stories. When two crows are seen sitting together, it is said that they are telling each other stories. Since the crow is not home yet, this means that there are more stories. The crow is still out collecting them.

132. J. B. S. Haldane, *Possible Worlds and Other Essays* (London: Chatto & Windus, 1972).

133. *The "Pink Pearl" Prince:* Asha Dhar, *Folk Tales of Iran* (New Delhi, India: Sterling Publishers Pvt. Ltd., 1978), pp. 9–13

134. *Who Is Blessed with the Realm, Riches, and Honor?:* Dov Noy, asst. Dan Ben-Amos, trans. Gene Baharav, *Folktales of Israel*, Folktales of the World Series, Richard Dorson ed. (Chicago: University of Chicago Press, 1963), pp. 157–161.

135. Maria Tatar, *Off with Their Heads, Fairy Tales and the Culture of Childhood* (Princeton, N.J.: Princeton University Press, 1992), pp. 120–139.

136. *The Story of the King, Hamed bin Bathara, and of the Fearless Girl:* C. G. Campbell, *From Town and Tribe* (London: Enest Benn Ltd., 1952), pp. 16–23.

Campbell notes that the material in this book comes mostly from southern

Iraq and the Sultanate of Muscat and Oman. Arabic, the language spoken in this region, is a major world language spoken across northern Africa and in most of the Middle East. Although spoken Arabic varies from country to country, classical Arabic, the language of the Koran, the holy book of the Muslim religion, has remained largely unchanged since the seventh century and serves as a basis for communication between educated individuals of this region.

137. *The Sultan's Daughter*: Ahmed Al-Shahi and F. C. T. Moore, *Wisdom of the Nile: A Collection of Folk-Stories from Northern and Central Sudan* (Oxford: Clarendon Press, 1978), pp. 208–213.

Al-Shahi and Moore note that students collected these stories in Arabic from the riverain societies in the northern province of the Sudan. This province forms part of the Nubian and Libyan deserts, but on either side of the Nile River, there is a strip of cultivated land, rarely over two kilometers wide. These strips are inhabited by sedentary farmers and some nomads. Rainfall is very low. Land and even trees are owned by individuals.

138. *Yousif Al-Saffani*: Ahmed Al-Shahi and F. C. T. Moore, *Wisdom of the Nile*, pp. 134–143.

139. *The Miser Who Married*: Sarah Powell Jamali, *Folktales from the City of the Golden Domes*, (Beirut: Khayats Booksellers and Publishers, 1965), pp. 13–17.

Jamali, who went to Baghdad in 1932 as an English teacher, notes that her source for most of the tales was her husband's stepmother, Bahiya Jamali.

140. Sarah Blaffer Hrdy. *The Woman That Never Evolved* (Cambridge, Mass., & London: Harvard University Press, 1981), p. 178.

141. *The Sign of the Tassel*: Sarah Powell Jamali, *Folktales from the City of Golden Domes*, pp. 31–32.

FOR FURTHER READING

The following are not complete lists. They are lists of books with heroines, which my children and I have enjoyed.

PICTURE BOOKS

Aardema, Verna. *Rabbit Makes a Monkey of Lion.* Illus. Jerry Pinkney. New York: Puffin Pied Piper Books, 1989.

Berger, Barbara Helen. *When the Sun Rose.* New York: Philomel Books, 1986.

Brett, Jan. *Annie and the Wild Animals.* Boston: Houghton Mifflin Company, 1985.

Brett, Jan. *Beauty and the Beast.* New York: Clarion Books, 1989.

Cannon, Janell. *Stellaluna.* New York: Scholastic Inc., 1993.

Epstein, Vivian Sheldon. *History of Women for Children.* 212 South Dexter St., Denver, Col.: VSE Publisher, 1990.

Holabird, Katharine. *Angelina's Baby Sister.* Illus. Helen Craig. New York: Clarkson N. Potter, Inc., 1991. (There is a whole series of Angelina books.)

Holmes, Efner Tudor. *Amy's Goose.* Illus. Tasha Tudor. New York: Harper Trophy, 1977.

Hooks, William H. *The Ballad of Belle Dorcas.* Illus. Brian Pinkney. New York: Dragonfly Books, Alfred A. Knopf, 1990.

Huck, Charlotte. *Princess Furball.* Illus. Anita Lobel. New York: Greenwillow Books, 1989.

Johnson, Paul Brett. *The Cow Who Wouldn't Come Down.* New York: The Trumpet Club, Inc., 1993.

Kellogg, Steven. *Sally Ann Thunder Ann Whirlwind Crockett.* New York: Morrow Jr. Books, 1995.

Martin, Claire. *The Race of the Golden Apples.* Illus. Leo and Diane Dillon. New York: Dial Books for Young Readers, 1991.

Mayer, Marianna. *Baba Yaga and Vasilisa the Brave.* Illus. K. Y. Craft. New York: Morrow Jr. Books, 1994.

McCully, Emily Arnold, *Mirette on the Highwire.* New York: Putnam, 1992.

Munsch, Robert. *Purple, Green and Yellow.* Illus. Hélène Desputeaux. Toronto, Canada: Annick Press, Ltd., 1992.

Munsch, Robert. *The Paper Bag Princess.* Illus. Michael Martchenko. Toronto, Canada: Annick Press, Ltd., 1994.

Ringold, Faith. *Aunt Harriet's Underground Railroad in the Sky.* New York: Crown Publishers, 1992.

Samuels, Barbara. *Duncan & Dolores.* New York: Bradbury Press, 1986.

Schroeder, Alan. *Ragtime Tumpie.* Illus. Bernie Fuchs. New York: Little Brown and Company, 1989.

Uchida, Yoshiko. *The Wise Old Woman.* Illus. Springett. Canada: McElderry Books, 1994.

Waddell, Martin. *Mimi and the Dream House.* Illus. Leo Hartas. Massachusetts: Candlewick Press, 1995.

Williams, Jay. *The Practical Princess.* New York: Parent's Magazine Press, 1969.

Wood, Audrey. *Heckedy Peg.* Illus. Don Wood. New York: Harcourt Brace & Co., 1987.

Wood, Audrey. *Rude Giants.* New York: The Trumpet Club, Inc., 1993.

YOUNG ADULTS

The following list contains monographs and collections of fairy and folk tales most comparable to *Heroines in Folktales from Around the World.* The collections are shorter and less culturally diverse than this anthology. In some of these collections, the vision of a heroine is different from mine. I have listed them with my favorite ones first.

MacDonald, George. *The Princess and the Goblin.* New York: Macmillan, 1970.
 A fairy tale novel with an active heroine. I love this book.

Riordan, James. *The Woman in the Moon.* New York: Dial Books for Young Readers, 1985.
 A collection of world folktales with heroines where the definition of a heroine strongly coincides with mine.

Harris, Christie. *Mouse Woman and the Muddleheads.* New York: Atheneum, 1979.
 This and the following two books are collections from the Native Americans of the Northwest Coast. Mouse Woman is a mythological heroine who deserves more attention.

Harris, Christie. *Mouse Woman and the Vanished Princesses.* New York: Atheneum, 1976.

Harris, Christie. *The Trouble with Princesses.* New York: Atheneum, 1980.

Frank Baum. *The Wizard of Oz.* (series)
 A classic young adult novel with an active heroine.

San Souci, Robert D. *Cut from the Same Cloth, American Women of Myth, Legend and Tall Tale.* New York: Philomel Books, 1993.
 A collection of American folktales with a strong multi-cultural selection.

Minard, Rosemary. *Womenfolk and Fairy Tales.* Boston: Houghton Mifflin Co., 1975.
 A nice collection of folktales with heroines from around the world.

Zipes, Jack. *Don't Bet on the Prince: Contemporary Feminist Fairy Tales in North America and England.* England: Scholar Press, 1993.
 This and the following book are collections of modern literary tales by various authors.

Zipes, Jack. *The Outspoken Princess and the Gentle Knight: A Treasury of Modern Fairy Tales.* Illus. Stéphane Poulin. New York: Bantam Books, 1994.

Strachey, Majorie. *Savitri and Other Women.* New York: G. P. Putnam's Sons, London: The Knickerbocker Press, 1921.

 An interesting older collection of world folktales with heroines.

Phelps, Ethel Johnston. *Tatterhood and Other Tales.* New York: The Feminist Press, 1978.

 This and the following book are collections of world folktales with heroines.

Phelps, Ethel Johnston. *The Maid of the North.* New York: Henry Holt Co., 1981.

Barchers, Suzanne I. *Wise Women.* Colorado: Libraries Unlimited, Inc., 1990.

 A collection of folktales from around the world, retold by the author.

Carter, Angela. *The Virago Book of Fairy Tales.* London: Virago Press Ltd., 1990.

 A view of women in folktales that includes sexual exploits and victims as well as heroines.

See also: National Women's History Project, 7738 Bell Rd., Windsor, CA 95492-8518 for a wide variety of books, posters, and teaching aids on the subject of women in the U.S.

BIBLIOGRAPHY OF SECONDARY LITERATURE

Anderson, Bonnie S. and Judith P. Zinsser. *A History of Their Own: Women in Europe from Prehistory to the Present,* Volume I. New York: Harper & Row, 1988.

Bettleheim, Bruno. *The Uses of Enchantment: The Meaning and Importance of Fairy Tales.* New York: Random House, Vintage Books, 1977.

Bottigheimer, Ruth, ed. *Fairy Tales and Society: Illusion, Allusion, and Paradigm.* Philadelphia: University of Pennsylvania Press, 1986.

Bottigheimer, Ruth B. *Grimms' Bad Girls and Bold Boys: The Moral and Social Vision of the Tales.* New Haven/London: Yale University Press, 1987.

Dundes, Alan. *Little Red Riding Hood: A Casebook.* Madison: University of Wisconsin Press, 1989.

Faludi, Susan. *Backlash: The Undeclared War Against Women.* London: Vintage, 1992.

Galdikas, Biruté M. F. *Reflections of Eden: My Years with the Orangutans of Borneo.* New York: Little, Brown and Company, 1995.

Goodall, Jane. *In the Shadow of Man.* London: Collins, 1971.

Goodall, Jane. *The Chimpanzees of Gombe.* Cambridge, Mass.: Belknap Press, Harvard University Press, 1986.

Gunew, Sneja. *A Reader in Feminist Knowledge.* London/New York: Routledge, 1991.

Hrdy, Sarah Blaffer. *The Woman That Never Evolved.* Cambridge, Mass.: Harvard University Press, 1981.

Igus, Toyomi. *Book of Black Heroes, Volume Two: Great Women in the Struggle.* New Jersey: Just Us Books, Inc., 1991.

Larrington, Carolyne. *The Woman's Companion to Mythology.* London: Pandora/Harper-Collins Publishers, 1992.

Lieberman, Marcia R. "'Some Day My Prince Will Come': Female Acculturation Through the Fairy Tale." In *College English,* vol. 34, issue 3, 1972, pp 383–395.

Monaghan, Patricia. *The Book of Goddesses and Heroines.* New York: E. P. Dutton, 1981.

Peavy, Linda and Ursula Smith. *Women Who Changed Things.* New York: Charles Scribner's Sons, 1983.

Seager, Joni and Ann Olson. *Women in the World: An International Atlas.* New York: Touchstone/Simon & Schuster, Inc., 1986.

Stone, Kay. "Fairy Tales for Adults: Walt Disney's Americanization of the Marchen." In *Folklore on Two Continents.* Ed. Burlakoff and Lindahl. Indiana: University of Indiana Press, 1980.

Stone, Kay. "The Misuses of Enchantment: Controversies on the Significance of Fairy Tales." In *Women's Folklore, Women's Culture.* Ed. Rosan A. Jordan and Susan J. Kalicik. Philadelphia: University of Pennsylvania Press, 1985.

Stone, Kay. "Things Walt Disney Never Told Us." In *Women and Folklore.* Ed. Claire R. Farrer. Austin: University of Texas Press, 1975.

Tatar, Maria. *The Hard Facts of the Grimms' Fairy Tales.* Princeton, N.J.: Princeton University Press, 1987.

Tatar, Maria. *Off with Their Heads!.* Princeton, N.J.: Princeton University Press, 1992.

Weigle, Marta. *Spiders and Spinsters: Women and Mythology.* Albuquerque: University of New Mexico Press, 1982.

Zipes, Jack. *Breaking the Magic Spell: Radical Theories of Folk and Fairy Tales.* New York: Routledge, 1979.

Zipes, Jack. *Fairy Tale as Myth, Myth as Fairy Tale.* Kentucky: University Press of Kentucky, 1994.

Zipes, Jack. *Fairy Tales and the Art of Subversion.* New York: Routledge, Chapman and Hall, Inc., 1991.

Zipes, Jack. *The Trials and Tribulations of Little Red Riding Hood.* New York & London: Routledge, Inc., 1993.

INDEX